Richard Ford sits on
RSPCA and is a Senio
lives in an old and re
with his wife, son, an
of *Quest for the Faraa*
Tolkien and *Watershir*

By the same author

Quest for the Faradawn

MELVAIG'S VISION

Richard Ford

GRAFTON BOOKS

A Division of the Collins Publishing Group

LONDON GLASGOW
TORONTO SYDNEY AUCKLAND

Grafton Books
A Division of the Collins Publishing Group
8 Grafton Street, London W1X 3LA

Published by Grafton Books 1985
Reprinted 1986

First published in Great Britain by
Granada Publishing 1984

ISBN 0-586-05885-0

Printed and bound in Great Britain by
Collins, Glasgow

Set in Plantin

MELVAIG'S VISION

CHAPTER I

High up on a hill, behind the twisted trunk of an ancient oak, stood Melvaig. The tree protected him from the full heat of the sun and he was grateful for the cool shadows it threw upon the ground. Around him the purple heather and the rough mountain grasses baked in the merciless glare and he could smell the bare peaty earth as it roasted and cracked in the heat. He stretched out his hand to lean against the sheer rock face at his side, spreading his fingers so that they gripped the little crevices reassuringly, but after a few seconds it became too hot and he snatched it away.

Suddenly a joyful shout shattered the intense stillness. He looked down through the shimmering haze into the valley beneath him and saw Morven, her long hair tumbling about her shoulders as she chased Bracca along the banks of a stream. It had been his little boy who had shouted and now Morven looked up anxiously to where Melvaig stood. He raised his hand to signal that everything was clear and as she waved back he could imagine her sigh of relief. They should not really have been this far from the village, but unlike the others they yearned for privacy and the joys of their own company. Melvaig watched as Morven wrestled with Bracca in the heather and imagined the scene in the village; the men in the longhut, smoking and talking endlessly about methods of cultivation, food storage, animal yields and women, and the women in the children's hut gossiping about children, food preparation, each other and men. The elders forbade permanent attachments between men and women and the children were brought up by all the village in the large children's hut.

Morven and Melvaig had fallen in love and after Bracca had been born they had tried to spend as much time alone with him as they could. They knew the dangers of emotional ties – the grief when a loved one died, the responsibility of bringing up a child with the Sickness, the need for people to bear children as often as possible to make up the losses caused by illness or raids. But the love they had found for each other was too strong to ignore. Normally such an open breach of the rules would have been punished severely, but Melvaig was the village's most skilful warrior and the elders were reluctant to anger him. Then again, there was something in their love and devotion to each other and their son which struck distant chords of long forgotten feelings amongst the other villagers so that their attachment was tolerated as long as they both continued to have children by other mates. Recently, however, there had been signs that other young people had begun to be influenced by their example and the elders had warned Morven and Melvaig that unless they stopped being so open in their love, they would be kept forcibly apart. So now they were unable to live together in the little hut Melvaig had built and had to live with the rest in the large communal huts. Their times together were few and sacred and had to be stolen on afternoons like this.

'What if Morven were to be killed? Would not the loss be unbearable?' the elders had asked Melvaig.

'Yes. But the joys of our love now are worth the risk of that loss. Besides there is no good without a bad and no bad without a good.'

At this, Jarrah, the chief elder, had looked quizzically at Melvaig. Truly this is my son, he had thought to himself with amusement. For despite all the rules, he knew he had fathered this young man and as he had watched him grow he had experienced all those emotions which he knew were so unhealthy such as pride, affection and love.

'And if you both were to die, what then of Bracca? How would he survive without the village?'

'He would not,' replied Melvaig. 'But I would never want to stop my child being a part of the village. Still it is equally important for him to have the love that we alone can give him.'

'Love! You speak of love yet are willing to risk putting your child through all the pain which your loss would cause him; pain which he would not suffer if he did not know and love you as his parents.'

'Again, I feel the joys of that love are worth the risk of loss,' replied Melvaig looking into Jarrah's old eyes so knowingly that the old man looked down in embarrassment. Jarrah had spent more time than he needed to alone with Melvaig, teaching him the skills of weapon making, animal rearing and all the other arts of life. They had had long talks together in which Jarrah told him stories and legends about the old world Before the War; tales so amazing that even Jarrah doubted their truth – of men who flew through the air, of self-propelled transport, of areas where more people lived than could be counted. It was a world so complex that Melvaig would sit listening in rapt fascination until his mind could take no more. Then, lulled by the old man's gentle voice, he would drift off into daydreams about a life without constant fear of the Sickness, where there was always food and water; about a world where he would wander hand in hand with Morven through green woods thick with tall trees and by the side of clear rivers sparkling in sunshine. It was during one such talk, on a hot night last year, that Jarrah had told Melvaig of the existence of a Book which, if it was known to be present in the village, would lead to great danger for them all. Only the Chief Elder knew of it, and he passed that knowledge on to the person chosen as his successor. Jarrah felt that Melvaig would be chosen but even if he were not he still wanted the young man to know. It was then that Melvaig had become convinced that the old man was his father and he had felt a surge of affection which he only just managed to suppress for fear of embarrassing him. The Book was buried between the exposed roots of an old hawthorn tree by the Black Rock that stood at the back of the village. What the Book contained no one knew for the art of reading had long been lost to them, but it had been in the possession of the village from as far back as anyone could remember, handed down from generation to generation, its secret jealously guarded. The tales surrounding its origins were shrouded in mystery. Jarrah believed it had been written Before the War and its writer had been one of the few who had survived. He had gathered their present village together before he died and the Book had been in Ruann ever since.

'Some say it contains a story,' Jarrah had said, 'which if it is understood and followed could alter all our lives. This is why it is so desperately wanted by those who know of it. Guard it with your life and breathe not a word to anyone, for one day when the time is right then will it be called upon to unveil its secrets.'

Melvaig had bristled with anticipation and curiosity but Jarrah had silenced his questions.

'I have told you more than I should already,' he had said. 'Have patience.'

The scorching heat of the afternoon forced its way into Melvaig's thoughts and his mind came back to the present as a bead of sweat dripped from his chin and trickled down between his shirt and his chest. As the sun beat down out of the sky, Melvaig tried to imagine what blue skies must have been like instead of the vast expanse of grey which spread out above him, broken only by occasional streaks of black. White clouds in a blue sky – how often had Melvaig listened to Jarrah describe them as they used to be. Morven and Bracca were lying down now by the little stream and Melvaig looked beyond them to where the mountains fell away into the brown arid expanse of lowland that stretched into the distance. No one from Ruann had ever been further than the beginning of the foothills; it was said that nothing grew beyond there and anyone curious enough to want to see for himself was deterred by fear of the Sickness which was said to be stronger there than anywhere else, and by rumours of other terrible illnesses that dwelt in the plains.

The village of Ruann lay out of sight behind him on a plateau under the shelter of the mountain that gave the village its name. Two high rocky arms stretched out from Mount Ruann so that the village was enclosed on three sides leaving only the front vulnerable to attack along the track that led up to it through a narrow pass. This natural protection was so good that the village was only rarely raided and the inhabitants had grown out of the way of fighting, preferring instead to concentrate on tending their crops and finding new ways of healing the sick. Even so, whenever he and Morven went out from the village, Melvaig still kept lookout for any of the bands of raiders who roamed the mountains.

Now, in the heavy stillness of the afternoon, Melvaig found his attention caught by faint noises which seemed to come from beyond the range of hills that enclosed the valley where Morven and Bracca were playing. The sounds hung in the air with no breeze to blow them away so that they gradually accumulated into a long unbroken symphony of noise which Melvaig recognized as the clatter of horses' hooves and the drumming of wheels on hard earth. His heart began to quicken as he saw a distant cloud of dust rise

11

from the direction of the track that led up through the encircling hills to the village.

Melvaig raised the huge carved goat horn that hung from his belt and blew a long high mournful note. He saw Morven sit up suddenly, pulling Bracca with her, and he waved to her to run up the hill and join him, pointing down the track. She understood, took Bracca's hand and began racing up the rocky slope. As the sound of the horn had echoed out over the valley so the approaching noise had died away so that now all that disturbed the uneasy silence was the scrabbling of Morven and Bracca as they made their way painfully slowly up the hill. Then a little shout pierced the stillness and Melvaig saw Bracca trip and fall over a loose stone. Immediately he began to run down towards the boy and his mother. Morven tried to lift Bracca on to her back, but the boy was too heavy and Melvaig had reached her before she could manage it. He picked up Bracca, cradling him in his arms. Morven spoke urgently.

'It's his ankle. I felt it and it's swollen. What's wrong? I couldn't hear anything.'

Melvaig began to run up the slope.

'Raiders, I think. You wouldn't have heard them in the valley. I heard them coming up the track but they stopped when I blew the horn. Probably wondering whether to carry on or not. I would have come down to pick him up sooner but I wanted to keep an eye on them from the oak tree.'

Suddenly Bracca, who had been quiet until then, wrapped up in all that had been going on, began to cry as his ankle started throbbing and the tension in his parents' voices made him nervous. Melvaig looked into his face and smiled.

'Hush, little man. Hush. It's all right. We'll soon have you sitting down.'

'Where are we going?' said Morven.

'I want to get as far up the hill as we can,' Melvaig

12

replied, but his last words were drowned in a huge welter of noise. Desperately, without looking round, he turned and ran through the heather to the shelter of a large rock.

'Quickly, get in behind here,' he said to Morven.

Melvaig gently laid Bracca down on a large clump of heather and the boy's tears began to subside.

'Leg hurts,' he said in between sniffs.

'Come on, let me have a good look at it,' said Morven. 'We'll rub it a bit and you'll soon be better.'

Melvaig shuffled along on his hands and knees, keeping well down behind the rock so as not to be seen from the valley, and looked out at the scene below him. The raiders were already almost out of sight around a bend in the track that led up to Ruann.

'They're making for the village,' he said, looking at the last few riders lashing their panting ponies up the steep path, and already the awful noise of the battle cries of their companions had begun to fade into the distance. Some way behind there followed a large covered wooden wagon drawn by four great horses. It lurched and swayed over the rough road, its two drivers hunched forward on their seats furiously whipping the exhausted horses which heaved and strained in their frantic efforts to escape the stinging lash. The heavy rumbling of the wheels now almost drowned the distant shouts of the rest of the party.

Melvaig started as he suddenly felt Morven's shoulder against his. He put his arm around her without taking his eyes off the wagon which fascinated and repelled him at the same time, frightening him far more than the open aggression of the raiders. The closed part of the wagon was full of unseen menace and a gnawing fear clutched at Melvaig's heart.

'I'm frightened,' Morven said holding on to Melvaig tightly. 'Where are they from? And what's the big wagon for?'

'I don't know. I don't know,' he replied, almost to

himself. 'I've never seen raiders dressed like that before. The colours of their clothes. And their helmets: bright and shiny. And that wagon.'

While they watched, the wagon lurched as a wheel struck a large rock. Then it disappeared round the corner. They both stared vacantly after it until the rumbling and cracking was out of earshot and then Melvaig sprang violently to his feet shaking his head in an attempt to rid himself of the paralyzing fear that had enveloped him. Quickly he moved across to where Bracca was sitting on his seat of heather and knelt down on the hard earth in front of him.

'How are you, little man?' he said, looking up into the boy's face, streaked with tears. 'Here! Let's kiss it better.' Melvaig bent down and kissed the swollen ankle and the little boy put his arms round his father's neck. 'Better now, Melvaig,' he said.

'Good. Now listen.' He paused and waited for Morven to join them. 'You must look after Morven while I go up the hill to see where those men have gone. I shan't be long. All right?'

'Must you go?' said Morven. 'They may see you.'

'I'm only going to the top of the hill. I've got to see what's happening in the village. I may be able to help if I'm not too late.'

Morven's eyes were filled with fear.

'You're not going to fight them!' she said, her voice raised in alarm.

Melvaig looked at her sharply.

'Well – would you rather I just stood and watched while they're all slaughtered? Would you?'

She looked at him for a second before burying her face in her hands and turning her back to him; her shoulders shook with sobs.

Bracca called out, 'Morven, Morven. No cry,' and getting up tried to run across to her but fell over and sat looking from his father to his mother in anguished confusion.

'I'm sorry,' said Melvaig putting his hands on her shoulders and turning her around to face him. 'I didn't mean to shout. We're both worried. I won't take any risks – I promise – but I must go and see if I can do anything. Please, don't cry.'

She took her hands away from her face and Melvaig put his hands under her chin, lifting it so he was looking into her eyes. She forced a smile and he clutched her to him.

'I won't be long,' he said. 'Take care.' He kissed her quickly and pushed her gently from him, then, pausing only to say goodbye to Bracca, he ran off up the hill.

CHAPTER II

Never once did he look back as he forced his sweating body relentlessly up the steep slope, otherwise, he knew he would have been unable to leave them. Soon he passed the ledge from which, so little time ago, he had been lazily watching the happy picture in the valley. It seemed a different world. Now thoughts chased each other through his head so quickly that he felt as if he were spinning – who were the raiders, what was happening in the village, was he right to leave Morven and Bracca, was Jarrah safe?

Suddenly the top of the hill was just in front. He stopped and listened. Through the still air he heard the unmistakable sounds of fighting – the thud of club against shield, the ugly guttural shouts of men as they fought for their lives, and the screaming of the women and children. Quickly he covered the last few steps and threw himself down behind a clump of heather on the summit. He could see the village of Ruann spread out beneath him. It was as if it had been cut open as it lay there like a wound, exposed and vulnerable – the huts smashed and their precious contents littering the ground, the villagers running frantically and blindly in their desperate attempts to escape, while the raiders ripped their violent way through it all. They drove their ponies over the pockets of ground that had been so painstakingly cultivated, churning up the soil and mashing the vegetables that had begun to grow. The paths between the huts, which Melvaig had known since boyhood, were now simply spaces between piles of rubble. He could no longer even recognize the Long Hut or the Children's Hut.

Melvaig watched, numb with horror, as the raiders effortlessly flung aside the villagers' resistance. He saw Jelmo and Sarg and Marl all try to unseat the riders and saw all of them brutally smashed down by a swift blow from a club. The village had been unprepared: its young men unused to fighting and its old men unable to organize any sort of resistance. In contrast, the raid had taken on the pattern of a carefully prepared scheme. Melvaig noticed for the first time, sitting motionless astride their ponies, three riders. Their clothes were different from the rest of the band; angular, garishly coloured helmets covered their heads while their cloaks were similarly colourful, emblazoned with strange symbols whose patterns Melvaig did not recognize but which nevertheless distressed him. Their ponies seemed larger than those of their comrades, and the flanks of two of these had been brightly painted while large metallic spikes were attached to their foreheads. The third, though plain and unadorned, made the most impact of all, for it was pure snow white and the sun shone off it like silver. All three stamped their hooves restlessly, unable to control their tempers in the midst of the surrounding mayhem, while their riders observed the unequal skirmish before them, occasionally raising an arm in a gesture of control to which a section of raiders would respond by adopting a different tactic. And over all the screaming of the villagers came the shouts of these savage fighters: 'Xtlan. Xtlan. Slaves for Xtlan. Food for Xtlan.' Over and over the name rang out and reverberated through the hot still air to bounce against the mountains until Melvaig's head rang with it.

Now as he watched, he saw the rider of the silver pony raise his arm and immediately the raiders began herding the survivors together against the rock face at the back of the village. The young women and the children were in one group along with those of the young men who had not been slaughtered in the battle and who were still able to walk while the old people were gathered in another. The raiders reined in their horses and suddenly a strange quiet, broken only by the snorting and panting of the horses and the muffled whimpering of the villagers, descended on the village. Then, unable to comprehend what was going on, those Melvaig knew as the Entob, the Sick Ones, started to dance about in their ungainly way. Soon they had broken out of their groups and were scuttling around the remains of the village chuckling to themselves. The spectacle reduced the raiders to laughter, and a group of them rode forward and began prodding and poking at the Entob with their spears and clubs. To his horror, Melvaig then saw one of the raiders dismount, grab a mutant boy by the hair and start swinging him round over his head. When he let go the boy flew through the air, still cackling quietly to himself, until his head smashed open against the rock face, at which the raiders' laughter rose to an obscene roar. Others then began to leave their ponies and started tormenting the mutants, each raider attempting to outdo his companion in brutality. When one of their victims tried to escape, they would give chase, urged on by the others until the poor creature was recaptured, only to be rewarded for its sport by being deprived of its legs. When it was judged that no more amusement could be afforded by it, then the rider on the white pony would give the signal for it to be put out of its misery and a fresh victim would be singled out. Meanwhile, the other villagers could only weep bitterly.

Cold reason told Melvaig he could do nothing yet he felt unable simply to lie there on his bed of heather. Slowly he lifted himself up, moved back down the hill a few paces and then started to run gently along a small track that followed the line of the hill but would keep him out of sight. The sounds from the village now seemed distant and the only reality became the padding of his moccasins on the dry earth and the clouds of dust they threw up. He looked distractedly at the criss-cross pattern which the dry, prickly heather had cut on his chest where his jerkin was open and the little red lumps, already beginning to itch, on his stomach where some insect had bitten him. His senses were still reeling from everything that he had seen and he forced himself to concentrate on the steady rhythm of his breathing as he ran.

Suddenly a great surge of noise brought Melvaig to a halt. The path had led him out from behind the shelter of the hill and he was now standing in a gap from which he was fully exposed to the village beneath him. For one awful moment he imagined that the roar of noise had been directed at him and he froze with fear but when he steeled himself to look closely at the scene below him he saw that someone, an old man of the village, was running over in his direction to where one of the Entob was being savaged by a raider. As the old man ran, the raiders, most of whom had dismounted, were picking up stones and throwing them at him so that he kept stumbling and jerking as he was hit. As the old man got nearer and his face became clear, an awful realization swept over Melvaig. It was Jarrah. The old man's desperate tear-stained face was twisted with sorrow and pain yet he kept coming on and on, much to the delight of the raiders. Directly beneath him the Entob was being used to torment Jarrah, each bestial act against it seeming to spur the old man on until finally he reached his destination and began pitifully trying to wrestle with the raider in a vain attempt to stop the torture. Each feeble effort was greeted with roars of approval by the raiders and savage retribution by Jarrah's opponent.

Melvaig's stomach churned in horror as he saw the old man's arm wrenched fiercely up behind his back until he screamed with pain. His heart thumped so fast and so loudly that his ears became deafened and his mind seemed to cloud over in a red mist of anger so that he was no longer conscious of what he was doing. It was as if he was watching someone else taking the club from his belt and running down the steep track to where Jarrah was crawling pathetically towards the jeering raider, his broken arm flopping loosely over the ground. Melvaig's conscious mind watched with interest as this 'other body' then launched itself upon the old man's tormentor and brought the club down on his head with all the anger and hatred that had been simmering inside him. Taken by surprise, the raider was unable to retaliate and the sharp stone head of the club smashed his skull. He staggered back a few paces with an odd puzzled look on his face and then dropped to the ground where he lay twitching convulsively while his comrades fell silent and the villagers waited with hushed expectancy. It was then that Melvaig's conscious mind joined the rest of him and he realized where he was and what he had done. The parched earth was sticky and black with blood and suddenly the intense heat seemed unbearable. He looked down at the club that he still held in his hand and was sickened by the vivid red liquid that dripped off it.

The Entob that Jarrah had been trying to save lay still in a crumpled heap against the rock wall.

'Melvaig, Melvaig, come here.' The old man's urgent whisper broke into Melvaig's semi-trance and he turned and walked over to where he lay. Kneeling down, he lifted the old man until he was sitting up with his back supported on Melvaig's arm and then Jarrah spoke again.

'You shouldn't have come,' he said. 'They will kill you.' He stopped. The effort of talking was almost too much and the pain in his arm drew all his concentration.

'You know . . .' he went on. 'You know that you're my son. We shouldn't . . . but you, I think, understand. I have . . . loved you.'

Melvaig looked deep into the man's watery grey eyes and felt a love such as he had never known before well up from deep within him.

'Yes,' he said. 'Yes, I know. I've known for a long time.'

Jarrah's eyes became tranquil and a smile came to his lips.

'You've known. Good. That's good.' Then his faltering voice became urgent again and his eyes became agitated.

'The Book,' he said. 'The Book. You must look after it. Follow it. It's yours now. Promise . . .' and his voice tailed off as his head fell sideways on to Melvaig's shoulder and the breath rattled in his throat.

Melvaig sat heavy with grief, lost in the timelessness of the moment of death. He was oblivious to the thunder of hooves until they were almost upon him and then he looked up to see a savage snarling face and just a glimpse of the huge club as it swung down towards him. Then suddenly, for an instant, his head was filled with piercing silver flashes of light before he was swallowed up in an engulfing wave of pitch black nothingness.

The raiders took it in turn to satisfy themselves on the young women while their comrades either loaded up the wagon with food from the central store or gathered in the village goats from the surrounding hills and tethered them one after the other behind the wagon. The bleating of the goats as they were roughly lashed together became intermingled with the screams of the women so that the hills rang with a bizarre chorus. Finally, when Xtlan's raiders had had their fill, the young women were herded into the wagon along with the children and those of the young men who were not too badly injured to be of use. Then the heavy wooden back plate was slammed shut and at a signal from the leader on the white horse, the raiders

21

started to ride off, trotting contentedly back down the same path by which they had arrived so short a time before.

After them came the wagon creaking and jolting over the ruts and stones of the track. With each bump the weeping inside seemed to grow so that by the time it turned the corner and was out of sight of Ruann, it gave forth a terrible wailing sound which caused the drivers to stop the wagon and bang with their clubs on the sides. Then the wailing gradually subsided until all that could be heard was the whimpering of the children and the muffled sobs of the women.

CHAPTER III

It was dark when Melvaig's eyes finally opened. All he was aware of at first was an overwhelming sickness that seemed to grip every part of his body. Gradually he realized that he was shaking all over and the sickness became concentrated in his head which throbbed with a pain so severe that he believed his skull must have been split half open. His mind was so full of confused images and nightmarish visions that he closed his eyes again in the hope that they would go away, but there was no escape. They swirled around in a dreadful collage; pictures of severed limbs and smashed skulls were mixed up alongside silver horses and wooden wagons. And then the face of Jarrah would appear, at first twisted and desperate, but gradually changing to an image in which he seemed to radiate peace over all the scenes of horror and Melvaig would start to feel relaxed and calmed. But the image would suddenly shatter as it burst into a shimmering kaleidoscope of dazzling lights and he would be gripped by a violent nausea again.

During one of these bouts of nausea he became dimly aware of a face looking down at him through the whirling of his brain and thought at first it was one of the pictures in his head but then he perceived a voice calling his name, 'Melvaig, Melvaig.' Far off it sounded, and muffled, but with a huge effort he forced his whole being to focus on to that voice. It was either calling him on to death or back to life, he did not mind which, but he had to cling on to it and follow it wherever it might lead.

So, he followed the voice and after what seemed an age in which all his courage and endurance were tested in a way they had never been before, he opened his eyes apprehensively and saw the blurred outline of a face. As he concentrated, it gradually came into focus until with enormous relief he recognized the kind old face of Shennsah, one of the women elders.

'Melvaig,' she said querulously, and this time the voice was clear and so marvellously close that elation swept over him.

'Yes,' he answered in a whisper. 'Yes.'

He saw her smile and reach down to lift him up into a sitting position. He felt her arms go under him and round his back and then she began pulling, but he was heavy and she was old and she was finding it difficult. He tried to put his left arm out to help to push himself up but a searing pain shot through it and he collapsed. Turning his head, he could see his shoulder was covered in blood and when he attempted to move his arm, nothing happened except for the pain.

'Try your other arm,' said Shennsah. He pushed up from the ground and she pulled until eventually he was sitting upright but then his head started spinning furiously and a wave of nausea hit him again so suddenly that he retched violently where he sat. His stomach churned and heaved until there was no more and he was left feeling exhausted but much better. The giddiness at least seemed to have gone although the pain was still intense in his head and shoulder. Then he saw that he had been sick over himself and worse, over Shennsah.

'Shennsah,' he stammered out. 'I'm sorry. Your clothes. Forgive me – I'm sorry.'

The disgust he felt with himself triggered off an overwhelming sense of grief from deep within and he was unable to prevent himself from suddenly bursting into tears. His mind was as yet unwilling to accept the horrors it would soon have to face: the loss of Jarrah, the carnage in the village, the scenes he had witnessed. So he wept until he could weep no more while Shennsah nestled his wounded head on her shoulder and rocked him gently to and fro as if he were a little boy.

'It's all right,' she repeated over and over. 'It's all right,' and losing herself in the sound of her own voice, she lulled herself into a state of forgetfulness in which yesterday had not happened.

Gradually Melvaig's tears subsided and he pulled himself gently away from the old lady.

'Jarrah?' he asked, sniffing and wiping his wet face with his good arm. He looked around and saw that the old man was lying where Melvaig had dropped him after he had been hit. Jarrah's face still wore the expression of peace that he had died with and which had prevented Melvaig from succumbing under the weight of the visions in his nightmare. The young man leaned forward and gently ran his hand down over his father's forehead, shutting the lids over his eyes. Then he looked at the village.

The light from the moon threw the wreckage of Ruann into ghostly silhouette, the smashed huts sharp and jagged in the white light and the villagers' scattered possessions strewn on the ground like entrails. Through it all wandered those who had been left behind, the old ones, numb with confusion and lost in the aimless meanderings of their befuddled minds. An eerie babble of voices rose into the night as they picked their way through the remains of their home, isolated on islands of grief. Like spirits they walked, set adrift in a world that had no meaning for them any more. Melvaig looked at Shennsah questioningly.

'Where are they?' he said. 'The children, the others?'

'They took them in the wagon. Did you see it? A big wagon pulled by four horses.' She paused and then remembered. 'I'm sorry. Morven and Bracca must be with them. I'd forgotten. Oh Melvaig, I'm so sorry.'

'No!' he turned sharply to her. 'No! We were out when they came. All three of us. I left them up in the hills. They're there now.' There was silence while he tried to absorb all that had happened.

'All gone except for you and the other old people,' he said half to himself and half to her. 'They've taken everyone else. Or killed them. Why? Why have they taken them, Shennsah? Do you know? And where were they from?'

The old woman spoke slowly and sadly.

'I don't know,' she said. 'I don't know. I didn't recognize their clothing or their language. The last attack we had – they just took food and a few horses and goats. Nothing like this. Nothing . . .' and her voice trailed off as a misty faraway look came into her eyes.

'I'm going to fetch Morven and Bracca,' said Melvaig. 'Then we'll see about organizing ourselves again. We must bury the dead and then see what they've left us. We'll be all right. Don't worry.'

She looked at him but the strength she had found within herself to search around the village for the wounded now deserted her. She could not tell Melvaig that apart from the very old he was the only survivor; the others were either dead or so badly wounded that death would be a relief. The hope that had flared briefly when she had seen Melvaig's eyes open and realized that he was going to live, now ebbed away leaving her drained and empty.

'Don't worry,' she heard him say again as she helped him to his feet. Then he kissed her gently on the forehead and she watched him make his way slowly off across the rocky ground.

CHAPTER IV

Melvaig picked his way through the wreckage painfully. His head still throbbed relentlessly and the wound in his shoulder burnt with a constant fire. As he walked he kept seeing the faces of the people he had known illuminated in the moonlight as they lay dead on the ground, their limbs contorted so that he had to resist the desire to make them comfortable. The white light coloured their faces with a sickly ashen pallor and accentuated their expressions so that their lips and noses seemed to protrude more than he remembered. Often he came close to one of the old people, mumbling quietly to themselves, but he said nothing for fear of shattering the fragile shell of their privacy.

Sarg lay by the store tent, his axe still resting in his open hand and his shield still on his arm. This time last night – as on every night since they were both children – they had been snoring next to each other. Sarg, the friend with whom he had shared his innermost thoughts and feelings as they had got the goats in every evening. Such good long talks they had had, recounting the stories of Before the War which the elders had told them, picturing every detail in their imagination so that as they talked the world around them changed. The brown rocky landscape became lush and green and rich with high banks of trees. All around them, as far as the eye could see, stretched verdant pastures on which the tall grasses waved and rippled gently in a breeze fragrant with delicate scents. They saw themselves walking between corridors of tall hedgerows laden with white blossom in which hundreds of brightly coloured birds fluttered and sang, busily building their nests while above them a golden sun shone down from a deep blue sky studded with clean white clouds. The little muddy stream in front of them would change and become a majestic river, glistening with silver jewels from the reflections of the sun as it wound its way regally through green banks covered with flowers; reds, yellows, oranges and blues, and under cascades of overhanging branches which dipped and trailed their outermost boughs into the crystal waters.

Melvaig looked at his friend with sorrow. And yet the expression on his face appeared so peaceful that to his consternation Melvaig found himself almost envying Sarg and wondering whether the world he had entered when the gates of death were opened to him, was anything like the world they had so often visited in their imaginations. He leaned forward quickly and closed his friend's eyelids and then carried on past the children's hut, round behind the back of the men's huts and then out to where the ponies were kept. The raiders had knocked the enclosure wall down and taken most of the ponies but to Melvaig's relief there were still a few left. They had got out and he could see them grazing on the coarse mountain grass on the lower slopes of Mount Ruann. If his pony, Bendro, was there, he would respond to his voice. He called out and his voice sounded small and futile in the desolate silence. It bounced against the mountain and echoed out into the night. Almost immediately he was struck by the stupidity of what he had done; if the raiders were anywhere near they would hear the call and might send someone back. On and on the echo rolled around the mountains as Melvaig tried to control his pounding heart. Why wouldn't it stop? At last it died away in some distant valley and silence once again blanketed the night. For a few seconds, while Melvaig held his breath, there was no reply and then came an answering whinny and the drumming of hooves over the stony ground. His heart filled with joy and relief. The thought of walking back in his present condition to where he had left Morven and Bracca had been almost more than he could contemplate.

Bendro whinnied again as he trotted up to his master. Melvaig put out his hand and the pony began licking the palm. The last time he had seen him, yesterday morning, before he, Morven and Bracca had left for their work, the world had been so very different. It seemed an age away to Melvaig now and he was immensely grateful that some part of his old world remained, unspoiled and unchanged, with Bendro. His warm, musky smell was reassuring and he felt his love for the pony well up inside himself.

'Good boy,' he said, putting his mouth close to his ear. 'Good boy.'

Bendro stood still while Melvaig reached over his neck with his right arm and got hold of the reins which were always left on.

'Now,' he said. 'Let's see if I can get up.'

The pony moved his ears back and then forward again as if in answer. Melvaig tensed himself and then jumped, swinging his right leg over Bendro's back and pulling on the reins in his right hand. For an agonising second he seemed to hang halfway but then he felt his right leg slide over and he was on. He lay quietly for a short time, letting his head rest on Bendro's neck amongst the soft hairs of his mane and then slowly raised himself up. The sudden exertion had started his head spinning again and the jarring of his left shoulder as he had jumped up on to the pony had made the throbbing worse. A mist of pain drifted before his eyes. He fought to control himself and then, as he succeeded in driving the mist away, he tapped his feet lightly on

Bendro's flanks and the pony began to walk. With both reins in his right hand Melvaig guided the pony back through the village towards the track up which the raiders had come. As he rode, some of the old people were shaken from their dreams by the sight of the pony gently trotting by and looking up, would see Melvaig and call out to him happily as if everything was normal.

'Hello, Melvaig. Off down the valley, are you?' called out one old lady. Melvaig forced himself to reply with as much cheer in his voice as he was able to muster and she wandered happily away, walking through the Ruann of yesterday which existed still in her mind. There was something so grotesque in seeing her go through the motions of her life as if nothing had happened, opening imaginary doors, talking to imaginary people and carrying imaginary food, that despite himself Melvaig was gripped with a violent disgust for her and indeed for all of them, a disgust born of intense envy. Their minds, unable to cope with what had happened and what they had seen, had simply turned away and refused to accept it. He, however, was less fortunate. His mind was still intact. He was forced to face up to everything and to live in the world as it now was.

As he was almost out of the village, he spotted Shennsah near the place where he had left her. She was walking very slowly with her head in the air, quietly calling 'Jarrah, Jarrah.' When no reply came, she moved on again, repeating Jarrah's name as if it was some form of religious chant. On the ground Melvaig could see the dead body of the man she was calling, his father. He wondered whether or not he should stop and bury him now but decided that Morven and Bracca would be worried the longer he was away. In any case he would be back soon. Shennsah did not turn round as the horse walked slowly down the track and Melvaig did not call her; there would be time enough to see what state she was in when he returned. In a way it would be better, more merciful, if she had gone like the others.

Melvaig was pleased to turn the corner of the track and be out of sight of Ruann. On either side the high mountain pass towered up into the night blotting out any sound from the village. The air was soft and warm. It caressed his skin like the velvet touch of a lover as Bendro carried him slowly and gently over the rough track. Everywhere was deathly quiet and still. Only the muffled sound of the hooves on the track and the occasional snort from the pony disturbed the silence. Melvaig felt suspended in emptiness, an unreal state in which nothing existed except himself, and for a moment he thought perhaps he had died and that it was his spirit riding through the mountains. His shoulder and head were still painful but he had grown used to it and it had become such a constant accompaniment to everything he did that it was almost comforting. He existed in relation to and because of the pain, and without it he would have felt almost as if he had lost a friend.

Suddenly Bendro stumbled on a pebble and the movement sent a sharp pain shooting through Melvaig's shoulder so that he cried out and a rash of sweat broke out on his forehead. He looked down at the ground and saw his shadow outlined sharply by the light of the moon: a slumped figure hunched over a pony, riding with one hand holding the reins because the other arm was shattered and useless. This was no spirit. Would that it were! It was he, Melvaig, crippled with pain, whose life had just been mutilated. His home was gone, his people had been savagely murdered, captured or left to die and he was even now riding to take the woman he loved and their son back to a life which before the events of yesterday had been hard and brutal but which now, without an effective village, would be virtually impossible.

He became aware now of the sound of the stream on his left, and saw ahead of him the familiar valley as it widened out from the pass through which he had come. Just a little way further on was the spot where Morven and Bracca had been playing yesterday afternoon. Suddenly, for no obvious reason, a tiny prickle of anxiety began to play around the nape of his neck. The thought came to him that he, Melvaig, had been gone so long that Morven would surely by now have left her hiding place and gone back to the village; she must have seen the raiders ride back down the valley. He quickly banished the thought. He had told her to stay where she was. Besides, she was not to know that all the raiders had left Ruann – the logical belief would be that they had left some behind and gone to fetch the others. Then he remembered Bracca's injured ankle – she could not have taken him back to the village and she would not leave him. A flood of relief swept over him and, as if for reassurance, he leaned forward slightly and patted Bendro's neck with his right hand. The pony whinnied and tossed its head in reply.

It was then that Melvaig spotted something on the track just ahead. It could have been a large stone but somehow he knew it was not. Bendro took what seemed for ever to cover the few paces to where it lay. Melvaig's heart beat wildly and his mouth went dry. He pulled on the reins and the pony stopped. It was Morven's moccasin. It lay there, innocent and silent, yet telling its story with terrible clarity. Panic seized him and whipped his mind into a whirlwind of confused images – Morven, struggling, screaming as she was assaulted, losing her moccasin as they dragged her across the path before pushing her roughly into the cart with the others. Bracca, watching the violation of his mother and hearing the laughter of the men as the tears swept down her face: his little boy's heart breaking as the sobs shook him until he could cry no more. Then when they had finished throwing him into the cart with Morven.

Melvaig half slipped, half fell off Bendro, and picked up the moccasin, handling it delicately as if it might otherwise

32

shatter. He turned it over and over in his hands, looking at it with such intensity that it seemed incredible to him that she did not respond by coming back. The visions in his mind blurred together in a red mist of anger that gripped his whole body, and filled it with a strength born of pure energy. So huge was this strength that Melvaig felt his body unable to contain it: his hands shook, his knees were like water, his stomach churned over wildly. He was afraid he would burst and the energy pour out into the air in a flaming ball of hatred to pursue the ones who had done this. Over and over he repeated the names of Morven and Bracca as if they were some magic incantation that would bring them back, but they did not answer – the night was silent and unyielding. Eventually his sustaining anger dissipated into despair and to his shame he felt tears begin to well up inside him. The air felt heavy and oppressive, weighing him down and smothering him under a dark impenetrable blanket; waves of pain from his head and shoulder swept over him until he collapsed to the ground in oblivion.

It was Bendro's rough wet tongue against his face that brought Melvaig back from the dark world of forgetfulness where he had wanted to stay for ever. He opened his eyes to see the pony's nose pressed up against his cheek, the familiar warmth of his breath urging him to respond. As he stirred, Bendro whinnied and he sensed an urgency that forced him to clear his mind of the despair that had engulfed it. Bendro's ears were forward, twitching slightly as if straining to catch some sound. He pushed himself up from the ground and listened. Utter stillness.

'What is it, Bendro? What have you heard?'

The pony looked at him impatiently. Then he heard it. The sound of a child crying coming from the rocks above. It was very faint, as if the child had been crying for a long time, and there were long gaps in between so that Melvaig was on the point of believing he had imagined it when it came again: unmistakable now. His heart leaped. Bracca was all right. He scrambled to his feet and called out in joy, 'Bracca. I'm coming.' Melvaig's call rang out in the night and the crying stopped abruptly for a few seconds before resuming with increased intensity.

As Melvaig made his way slowly and painfully up the hill, his mind raced. Perhaps Morven was all right; up there with Bracca; injured or maybe passed out in the heat. Little arrows of hope began to pierce the walls of loss that had built themselves up around him. He hardly dared to let them in for fear that they would be misplaced and he tried to erect defences – Morven's moccasin on the path below – yet still they came, powerless as he was to resist their seductive flight.

He forgot about his injured arm and he forgot about the ache in his head. All he could think of was Morven and Bracca. He was certain now she would be there with the boy. The raiders had found her, dragged her down the hill but in her struggles they had injured her and left her for dead, as with him, or else having had their way with her, found there was no room in the cart and decided not to take her. She had then made her way back up the hill to Bracca before fainting.

The hill seemed endless and he kept stumbling and slipping on the stones and shale of the rocky slope. Every time he fell, a bolt of pain would shoot through his body and he would frantically reach out with his right hand to grab a rock or the twisted root of a clump of heather to pull himself up. And all the time the crying continued. There were no breaks now; the sobbing was constant and rhythmic, neither increasing nor decreasing in volume. Then suddenly Melvaig was there, standing where he had left them last night. He could see the two indentations in the heather where they had lain side by side watching the cart lumbering slowly over the rocks on the path. 'I'm frightened,' she had said, and she had held him close. But she was not there now. Only Bracca, sitting with his back against a large rock, staring blankly out at nothing with his eyes red-rimmed and puffy – his face awash with tears, his body shaking convulsively as he sobbed. He hardly turned his face as Melvaig called his name, just carried on weeping. Melvaig walked over to him, his heart aching with grief – the more cruel now for having allowed his hopes to blossom, only to see them crushed again.

He knelt down in front of the little boy, put his good right hand behind Bracca's head and pulled it into the cradle of his shoulder.

'All right,' he said. 'All right. I'm here now,' and gently rocked him to and fro. Questions about Morven burned in his brain but they would have to wait until Bracca had quietened down. For a long time the two of them held each other while the moon watched, impassive and unmoved, throwing their shadow on to the heather behind. Eventually the warmth of Melvaig's love broke through the horrors in the little boy's head and the sobbing began to subside. Then Bracca sighed heavily and the story began to unfold.

'Morven gone,' he said. 'With those men. Morven not want go.' He stopped as if trying to comprehend and accept what he was saying while all the time, Melvaig held his fragile little body, comforting him, soothing him, giving him something to hang on to in the chaos, so that he was able to reach back into the nightmare without losing himself in it.

'Melvaig long time,' he said. 'Long time. Morven go find. Worried. Nasty men fight Morven. Fighting. Morven not want to go. Not want go.' He suddenly pushed himself away and looked directly at Melvaig as if full realization had finally come. 'Melvaig. Morven gone. Morven gone,' and he burst into tears again. Melvaig's heart ached with pain yet he found consolation in sharing his loss. The flame of Morven would be kept alive in both their hearts and as he said to Bracca, 'We'll find Morven,' a quiet sense of confidence spread over him. Gone was the raging, burning anger he had felt at first – an anger that would soon have burned itself out – to be replaced by a feeling of purpose and destiny. He would search the wide world until he found her. And he would find her – of that he was certain. But there was something else, a stirring within him which he was unable to explain or describe but which somehow elevated him so that he knew from now on he was not alone. Never before had he had feelings or ideas of anything outside or beyond the reality in which he lived. Now as he looked up at the moon and round him at the rocks and heather he was aware for the first time of something watching, guiding, waiting, as if all that had happened and all that would happen was somehow planned. What the future held he did not know but he knew that he was a part of it.

CHAPTER V

The climb back down the hill was slow and painful. Bracca's ankle was still sore and Melvaig had to carry the boy in his one good arm, taking great care not to fall. Now that all the tensions and expectations of seeing Morven again had gone, the injury to his shoulder seemed more painful than ever. When they finally got to the floor of the valley again, Melvaig put Bracca down and led him, limping, to where Bendro was waiting. Morven's moccasin lay upside down where Melvaig had dropped it in his excitement when he had heard Bracca crying. So the story that it had told had been the right one after all, thought Melvaig bitterly, as he picked it up and placed it carefully under his goatskin jerkin. 'Morven's,' said Bracca, as he saw it.

'Yes. We'll have to give it back to her when we see her again, won't we?'

'Give it back to Morven,' the little boy repeated, and the look of happiness on his tear-stained face lightened the gloom of the night.

Bendro gave a whinny of recognition when he saw Bracca and stood still while Melvaig lifted him, with some difficulty, up on to the pony, before mounting himself. His first impulse had been to set out immediately after Morven but as the first fires of anger had begun to ebb, he had decided that it would be better to go back to the village first and see if the raiders had left any supplies which he could take to help sustain them on the journey, at least for a while. Then he had remembered Jarrah's last request to him, to find and look after the Book, and his mind had been made up. Besides, Xtlan's raiders should not have too much of a start on them. They would travel no faster than the cart and would not be expecting pursuit so, in all probability, they were indulging themselves on the women at every opportunity. At the thought that now Morven was among them, Melvaig had to use all his resolve to control his emotions and he forced his mind to race over the picture which flashed into his head. But the more he tried to push it away the more it returned, with renewed clarity and detail, so that he was immensely glad when they came in sight of Ruann and Bracca started to ask questions which required all his concentration.

Their first task was to see if there was any food left in what remained of the central store hut. No one noticed them as they rode quietly through the wreckage of the village. Once or twice Bracca saw an old man or old woman he recognized and he called out to them but there was no reply.

'Not many,' said the little boy.

'The others went with Morven.'

'Why?'

'Those men took them. The ones who took Morven.'

'Why not say hello?'

'Because they can't hear you.'

'Why?'

'Because they've had a shock.'

'Why?'

'Because lots of people, all their friends, have been taken. All your friends – they went as well.'

Bracca fell silent, trying to absorb what Melvaig had told him and looking around in disbelief at the destruction of his world. Very soon they were outside what had been the store hut.

'Stay here,' said Melvaig as he dismounted and tied Bendro to a post outside. The door and parts of the walls were still standing so that it was still recognizable. He went inside and picked his way over the mess until he came to where the food was kept. The doors to all the stone larders were either hanging open or broken off and he knelt down and looked apprehensively inside the one nearest to him. It was hard to see in the moonlight but it appeared empty and when he put his arm inside to feel, his fears were confirmed. He moved further along to the next and again it was empty, but when he came to the third he found a few skins of yoghurt hidden in the darkness at the back. He took them out and put them on the hard earth floor of the hut before going to the next. Here he found some more yoghurt along with some cheese and bread. With his spirits rising he went to the next and again found more. This was a relief – not only would he be able to take all that he could carry but there would be plenty left for the survivors so he would not feel guilty. Obviously the raiders had taken only what they had needed for the journey back. This meant that their homeland could not be far away unless they planned to raid other villages as they travelled. Their main purpose must have been been the capture of the women and children. Why? There was no time to think of these things now; he must get packed up and go.

Quickly he crossed over to the far wall where, hanging from wooden pegs knocked into the crevices between the stones, were a number of double panniers. He got two of them down and carried them back to the larders before going outside again.

'Come on, little man. You're going to help me,' he said lifting Bracca down. They walked together back to the panniers.

'Now,' he said, 'we're going to go and find Morven, aren't we? But she may be a long way away so we shall need lots of food. I'm going to go and fetch another pony for you and while I'm doing that I want you to fill up these baskets with the food that's in here. We want the same amount of everything so do it like this. Look. Bread, cheese, yoghurt, milk.' Melvaig packed them carefully round the bottom of one of the panniers and then did it once more in the same order.

'Now you show me that you can do it and I'll go. Say what they are as you put them in and then you'll know you haven't gone wrong. Can you do it?'

'Yes,' said Bracca, nodding his head.

Melvaig watched while the little boy packed the loaves of flat round bread, the pieces of cheese wrapped in butterbur leaves from the stream and then the skins of yoghurt and milk. Although the milk would go off after a day or two, Melvaig felt it would still be a drinkable liquid for them afterwards and so was worth taking. When he felt that Bracca had got into the rhythm of his task, he fetched a halter from the wall where the panniers hung. Then he went outside, untied Bendro, and rode over to the slopes where the ponies were grazing. There was one particular pony that he knew had been good with the children and he looked for it now, riding Bendro slowly and quietly through the herd. It was a smoky, dapple-grey colour and they had called it Sky. It did not take long to find it, standing a little apart from the others, its head up, staring away into the distance. Melvaig dismounted and, leaving Bendro, walked slowly towards the pony, talking quietly so as to avoid suddenly alarming her. Sky turned her head and watched suspiciously as the man approached but she did not run off and Melvaig was able to put the halter round her neck easily. Remounting Bendro, he led the pony up the slopes of Mount Ruann towards the huge standing stone known as Black Rock. Soon he reached the spot where it grew out of the earth. At the base it was sharp and rectangular but as it got taller the edges became rounded and it tapered gradually until it finished in a gently curving point. It was called Black Rock for it was the colour of the night, a deep, dark blackness that seemed to shine with an almost luminous intensity, as if it were constantly damp. Round the bottom were a number of strange markings which could have been natural but which some of the villagers had said were made by a people who had lived Before the War. It had always exerted a strange and compulsive fascination over Melvaig. As he looked at it now, he felt again as if he were being watched and guided by an unseen presence, only now it was stronger than it had been before. The Black Rock seemed to be a symbolic proof of what he felt.

The old hawthorn stood by the side of the rock on the same small flat piece of rocky ground. Behind it Mount Ruann soared up steeply while below, the heather-covered slopes fell away gently to the village. It was almost as if this little area had been designed as a resting place on the way up to the top of the mountain. The tree provided the traveller with shade, its twisted old branches stretching out and casting cool shadows on the earth. Now the moonlight threw the tree's silhouette on to the Black Rock so that it looked as if some forgotten mason, long ago, had set to work to cover it with the most intricate and delicate pattern he could fashion.

Melvaig dismounted and, tying the two ponies to a low branch, walked under the overhanging boughs into the darkness under the canopy of leaves. He had to walk with his back stooped slightly and he moved forward slowly in the gloom until he came to the huge trunk at the centre. There he could make out the two protruding roots which Jarrah had described. They looked like the two first fingers of an old man's hand, embedded deep into the ground for support. Other roots also spread out from the trunk, like the spokes of a wheel, but there was no doubt in Melvaig's mind that it was in the apex of these two that he would find the Book. He looked round for something to dig with and found, leaning against the furrowed bark of the tree, a large flat stone one edge of which was quite sharp. By its side rested a long thin stone which, used in conjunction with the other, would make the task of digging relatively easy. They had obviously been left there for just this purpose and Melvaig wondered if it was Jarrah who had last used them.

He set to work loosening the hard earth by jabbing at it with the stone spike and then shovelling it out with the flat one. Even though he was unable to use his left hand he still made quite good progress and became engrossed in the job.

Soon however, as the work went on and the hole got deeper and deeper with still no sign of the Book, Melvaig began to feel uneasy. The situation struck him as faintly ludicrous. Here he was digging a hole while Morven was being taken further away with every passing second and down the hill lay the ruins of the only life he had ever known. Was he digging in the right place? He looked again at two more roots a little to his right which initially he had discounted as being too small. Perhaps the ground had changed since Jarrah had last seen it or perhaps Jarrah had put more earth back when he had last dug the Book up so that now the roots protruded less. He moved across and began digging between these other two roots but then he saw more pairs of roots all the way round the tree. It could be buried between any of them. He could be here for days trying to find the Book. It was a hopeless and ridiculous task. What could be so important about a book anyway? Neither he nor any of the villagers was able to read, the art had long ago been lost, so any words of wisdom it might contain would remain unknown. Bracca would have finished packing by now and would be growing anxious. He might begin to wander about looking for Melvaig, get lost, anything.

Melvaig decided he had to stop this futile search.

Bracca's safety and the pursuit of Morven were of far more importance. He was just about to put his digging tools down and leave when something made him stop. What it was he could not be sure, but it seemed as if a dark shadow had passed over the tree and momentarily changed the pattern of moonlight on the ground. Then a vision of the dying Jarrah flashed before his eyes. 'Promise me . . .' he had said. The Book had been important enough for the old man to die with it as the last thought in his mind. Melvaig owed it to him to try a little longer. Calmer now, he went back to his original spot and once again began jabbing and scooping at the hard, stony earth. It was not long before he came across what he took to be a particularly large stone which seemed determined to stay where it was, so that he had to dig a much wider hole to be able to lever it out. When the spike hit the stone it made a strange sound, not like stone on stone at all, more a hollow knock. Perhaps this was it. Melvaig's spirits began to lift as he scrabbled away to clear the soil from round the corners and edges. It was too regular a shape to be natural and as the object revealed itself Melvaig saw that it was a rectangular casket. It should come out easily now. He put the sharp end of the stone spike under an edge of the casket and pushed against it with all his weight. Nothing gave. He cleared away some more earth and tried again. This time, to his delight, he felt it lift slightly so that the spike would go further under. Once more he pushed down on it and now the casket came up easily. Excitedly, Melvaig put his hands under it and lifted it out on to the ground in front of him. He decided to look at it quickly before he went back down to Bracca because he did not want the little boy to know of its existence yet. That, he felt, could be a mistake if the warnings of Jarrah were to be heeded. 'Guard its presence with your life and breathe not a word to anyone.' Melvaig still remembered the words and the thrill of excitement and curiosity they had aroused in him.

The box was encrusted with hard earth, and Melvaig used the sharp edge of the flat digging stone to scrape it away. It was of a metal he had not seen before. It shone in the moonlight with the same kind of light that the sun makes when it strikes water, and Melvaig could make out delicate and intricate patterns either embossed or inlaid into the surface. Even though much of this craftsmanship was obscured by the earth that had got caught in it, he still marvelled at the skill of the work. The gently curved top of the casket was the most beautiful. It had a central piece which appeared to be a kind of symbol so striking and direct was it in its simplicity. It consisted of a new crescent moon, a single blade of grass and a craggy mountain peak. Around this central symbol a number of scenes were depicted in which Melvaig could make out two human figures, a boy and a girl they looked like, with various animals, some of which, like the hare that appeared in a number of pictures, he recognized from occasional sightings round Ruann. He remembered also having once seen an owl when he had been returning to the village late one night with Morven, and he thought he could make out that distinctive shape in some of the scenes. The other animals he recognized only from the descriptions Jarrah had given him during their long talks about the way the world had been Before the War. These descriptions had themselves been handed down to Jarrah and indeed from generation to generation since their original source in one of the Survivors. He could see a badger with the long nose and broad black stripes on his head just the way Melvaig had pictured it from Jarrah's words. The only other animal that appeared was, he thought, a dog; one of the creatures which had had a particularly close relationship with man in the same way, he imagined, as they now had with goats and horses.

A thrill of excitement went through Melvaig as it now became clear to him that the scenes were of a time Before the War and that the casket and Book were themselves also of that time. There had of course been no books since and those that had initially survived had mostly crumbled into dust long ago. Melvaig had never seen one. As he looked in wonder at the casket he thought of the craftsman who had fashioned those beautiful scenes. For Melvaig the hundreds of years between were suddenly bridged; and now, looking at these pictures, he was transported back into the world Jarrah had woven for him – a world of tumbling rivers, of trees as tall as the sky, of streams and springtime and a deep blue sky. It must have been from these scenes, and the stories that had been told in turn to him, that Jarrah had had his inspiration. Had the world ever been like that? What then had happened to make them destroy it – and would it live on only in the artistry of long forgotten craftsmen and the inspired imaginings of old men?

The whinnying of Bendro broke suddenly into his trance-like ramblings. He must get back quickly. How long he had been here he did not know, but Bracca must have finished long ago. Hurriedly, and without really knowing why, he kicked the soil back in the hole where the casket had been and stamped it down hard until it looked undisturbed and then he replaced the two stones he had used to dig with. Picking up the casket in his good right hand he made his way back out of the hawthorn, bending low to avoid the huge sweep of overhanging branches. Bendro and Sky were stamping and tossing their heads restlessly. With difficulty Melvaig cradled the casket in his left hand while he hauled himself up on to Bendro's back. Untying Sky, he began the descent to the village. Halfway down the slope, a faint sound of crying came drifting up through the warm heavy air and Melvaig banged his heels against Bendro urging him to go faster, but the ground was too rough and littered with rocks for any speed.

Soon, however, he was in sight of the village and he made quickly for the store tent. He dismounted and ran inside.

All was quiet. No Bracca. He dashed up to the far end and inspected the panniers. They were full. Everything was as he had asked. Hurriedly, he buried the Book under some of the food and went outside. The crying seemed to be coming from the other side of the village. Why had Bracca moved? Why was he crying? Stupid child – if he had just stayed where he had been told to stay instead of wandering off! As if there wasn't enough to worry about without chasing after Bracca. Melvaig followed the noise and it was not long before he saw the little boy. He was sitting on Shennsah's knee as she rocked him gently to and fro, trying to calm him down and muttering soft soothing words in his ear. Melvaig's anger evaporated instantly in the relief he felt at seeing him.

'Look. I told you. Bracca, I told you Melvaig would come back. You're all right now. Look, here he is!'

The little boy, still snuggled in the arms of Shennsah, slowly turned his head and saw his father. He could hardly speak for crying.

'Long time,' he said, in between tears. 'Long time. Melvaig gone. Bracca no find . . .'

'Come here. I won't go away again, I promise.'

Shennsah handed the little boy to Melvaig who held him very tightly for a long time until the tears stopped.

'He's asleep,' said Shennsah. Melvaig, though he did not say so, was surprised at the change in the old woman from the pathetic broken figure he had last seen wandering aimlessly through the village, back to the lively, alert spirit he remembered. Perhaps the urgency of the need to look after the little boy had broken through her trance and forced her to get to grips with herself. He felt himself filled with a sense of love and sadness so poignant that he forcibly, almost angrily, dismissed it for fear that he would find it too much too cope with.

'He was wandering through the village looking for you. Crying,' she said. 'He knows me well and came to me. I must have been far away, dreaming or something. First thing I remember he was tugging at my hand. He's a lovely little boy. I didn't know where you were but I kept saying you'd be back.' She paused. 'There was no sign of Morven then,' she went on. 'I gathered that from what Bracca was saying. I'm sorry.'

'No,' he said. 'I found her moccasin. They must have taken her with them. That's where I'm going now – to follow them and try and find her. Thank you for looking after Bracca. I owe you a lot.'

'You owe me nothing,' she smiled and Melvaig knew that she really meant it. 'Helping you has helped me.'

'Come with us. You could help look after Bracca.' Melvaig said the words without thinking, so full of love and gratitude was he for her, and was filled with guilt at the relief he felt when she refused.

'What will you do?' he said.

'I've told you before. Don't worry about us. We'll be all right. If you want to do something for us, find Morven and make a new life for yourselves. That way, Ruann will live on.'

'There is some food left,' Melvaig blurted out. 'I've packed some for our journey but I think there's plenty left.' Even as he spoke, his words seemed ridiculous and inadequate. He was leaving Shennsah and the villagers to die. He knew it and she knew it, yet each had to pretend they did not.

'It's time you were going. Come on. I'll walk over with you.'

They walked in silence, both lost in their own private thoughts. Melvaig was tempted to tell her about the Book but reluctantly decided that its existence must be kept secret. Knowledge of it, and of its implications was too heavy a responsibility, particularly if, as was only too possible, the village was attacked again. When they reached the store hut Melvaig handed Bracca, still asleep, to the old woman and she sat down with him while Melvaig brought out the panniers and fastened them to Bendro and Sky. Then he went inside again and crossed over to the wall where the weapons used to hang. Most of them had been taken by the raiders but one or two had been left lying on the ground. He picked up a rather fine spear with a shaft of polished wood and a stone point that looked like flint lashed into the wood with thonging. A wooden blackthorn knife lay next to it and he stuck that in his belt next to the club he always carried. Finally he found, hanging on the wall where the panniers had been, a goatskin bag that appeared to be just the right size for the Book. He intended to wear the bag, with the Book in it, under his clothes, but that would have to wait until he got an opportunity to put it in when Bracca was asleep; the little boy must not know of it. For a second he stood, looking round him through the gloom at the chaos and remembering how it had been – so organized and carefully ordered. It all seemed so futile now – in the space of a night, everything had collapsed. Did he need anything else? On the floor to his right he spotted a heap of moccasins. He picked up a pair for himself and then, after a little searching he found a pair that looked to be Bracca's size. He put them in the goatskin bag, and then turned abruptly and went outside.

Shennsah looked at him and smiled. Bracca's head was slumped against her shoulder and his eyes were tightly shut while his little arms were wrapped as far as they would go around her waist. Melvaig checked that Sky was still tethered to Bendro. Then he tied the spear to his horse, slung the bag around his neck and mounted. Shennsah, sadly, wearily, stood up, walked across and, after kissing the little boy gently on his cheek, handed him carefully to Melvaig who held him in front with his injured arm while gripping the reins with his good hand.

'Still asleep. Poor little thing,' said the old woman and

then, looking up at Melvaig, 'Look after yourselves.' He leaned down and kissed her on the forehead. 'Goodbye,' he said. His throat ached with sadness and his eyes stung with the effort of holding back tears.

She walked slowly round the front of Bendro, who whinnied quietly as she stroked him on the nose, and untied him. Then Melvaig gently tapped the horse's flanks with his feet and Bendro started to walk away.

'Goodbye,' she said, and as she raised her hand to wave, the tears started streaming down her cheeks. Melvaig dared to look back only once. Shennsah was still waving aimlessly at them as if bidding farewell to her life. Behind her in the moonlight lay the jagged silhouette of the ruined village while, towering above everything, Mount Ruann looked down impassively, unchanged and unchanging. Unaccountably Melvaig had the distinct impression that it disapproved of his leaving and he had to shut his mind to the growing feelings of guilt and selfishness that threatened to tear him apart unless he turned back. Only when he had turned the corner of the track leading out of the village and the mountain was out of sight, did its massive brooding presence subside, and it was with a curious feeling of elation that he rode down the track away from his home towards a future where nothing was certain except his love for the sleeping figure in front of him, his determination to find Morven, and his strange conviction that somehow, in some way, all their futures were bound up in the Book.

CHAPTER VI

Dawn was breaking as Melvaig passed the spot where Morven's shoe had been lying. Ahead of him the sky was illuminated with vivid orange gashes and broad, flaming-red streaks; it was as if there was an enormous fire just beyond the edge of the world. The darkness seemed to run away in shame and hide before the onslaught of this army of colour, and for a brief magical time the earth was bathed in a strange yellow light. Melvaig felt suspended and isolated in a time and place that was far, far away from anything he had ever known – a time and place that would always exist and yet, which had never been. He did not hear the sound of the horses' hooves as they trotted along the stony path; he did not feel the pain in his arm, nor even the head of Bracca as it rested against his stomach. He was in another world and for a few blessed moments all memory and pain and worry were as nothing, for all that mattered was existence itself.

Thus it was that, for a few precious moments at dawn and dusk, Melvaig touched the very essence of life and received a glimpse of something far beyond the world he knew. It filled him with hope and gave him the energy to go on, whatever might befall him, for he felt in pursuit of something. What it was he was unable to explain, but there was no doubt in his mind that some small fragment of this vision had begun to reveal itself from the first moment he had set eyes on the Book.

Suddenly dawn was gone and once again the sky was filled with gently shifting patterns of greys and browns behind which the sun struggled to break through. It never succeeded. Instead there was a constant silver-grey aura which sometimes seemed to Melvaig to be almost solid. It was at this moment, when the dawn had just departed and the day was beginning, that he had always felt at his lowest ebb, but this morning, the euphoria that had gripped him lingered on and it was with a joyful heart that he made his way down the long valley that led away from Ruann. By midday, the heat was at its most merciless and Melvaig decided to stop and rest for the afternoon. He rode on until he saw a large outcrop of rocks a little way up the slope at the side of the path. When he got there he carefully dismounted so as not to wake Bracca and then with the little boy still in his arms he walked around the rocks until he found a cool spot and there he laid him down. For a second or two Bracca tossed his head to and fro and muttered little private words to himself, and then to Melvaig's relief he was still and the world of sleep claimed him again.

After Melvaig had taken the panniers from the horses, he set them free to graze on the sparse tufts of grass and the occasional bush which was all the vegetation he could see. It had never occurred to him that food for the horses would be a problem, but as they descended the valley Melvaig had become increasingly aware that even the landscape of Ruann, which to him had always seemed harsh and forbidding, was as a land of green and plenty in comparison with the world they were now entering.

He went over to where he had left the panniers and, removing some cheeses from on top, he found the Book and put it in the goatskin bag, having put the spare moccasins where the Book had been. Then he took off his jerkin, put Morven's shoe next to the Book and hung the bag round his neck next to his skin before replacing his clothes.

Then he settled down under the shade of the rock next to Bracca and, as he was about to close his eyes, the sight of the little boy's face so close to his suddenly made him realize that this was the first time he had ever slept next to his son.

Melvaig woke up to the sound of the little boy crying. It was dark. He had no idea how long they had slept. One thing though was certain; he felt terrible. His head was muzzy and ached terribly just above his eyes, all his limbs felt heavy and unwilling to respond to his wishes and his wounded shoulder was numb and lifeless. His sleep had been deep and mercifully dreamless yet to wake up from peaceful oblivion into a situation which reminded him instantly of all the terrible events of the past days was such a shock to his system that if it had not been for Bracca's cries he would have succumbed immediately to temptation and retreated back to the sanctity of sleep. With an enormous effort of will he pushed himself up with his right arm.

'Bracca,' he said. 'Bracca. It's all right. I'm here. What's wrong?'

The little boy had only just woken up and, like Melvaig, had forgotten where he was. He should have been in the children's hut with his friends, and instead it was dark, he was outside and, forgetting that his father was with him, he had thought himself alone and had been seized by panic. Now he remembered. He was with Melvaig and they were looking for Morven. They would see her soon and then they would go back home, back to the village. But there was something funny about that. He remembered seeing it in the moonlight but all the huts had been broken down and there had not been many people about. Only Shennsah.

She had been nice. She had held him and comforted him. Where was she? Why wasn't she with them?

'Bracca want Shennsah,' he said and Melvaig felt a shock of guilt and pity. Perhaps he ought to have insisted that she came with them after all. He thought quickly.

'Shennsah didn't want to come,' he said. Bracca refused to listen.

'Bracca want Shennsah,' he repeated between his tears.

'She's not here. She stayed at home. She wanted to stay at home. We'll see her when we come back with Morven.' At the sound of this lie he went inwardly cold and blanked his mind out so that as soon as it was said, he forgot it. Bracca jumped on it.

'See her soon. All go home with Morven,' he said and his tears started to subside.

'Yes, yes,' Melvaig said hurriedly and moved across to the little boy. He was just about to give him a comforting hug when Bracca said, almost suspiciously:

'Why Shennsah not come with Melvaig and Bracca? Find Morven.'

The raw wound of guilt that Melvaig felt about leaving the old woman behind, now screamed out with pain as Bracca once again prodded at it, and Melvaig lost his temper.

'She didn't want to come,' he shouted. 'That's it! Don't say it again. She did not want to come.' He said these last words very slowly and deliberately as if he could force them into the little boy's head. There was silence.

'All right now?' said Melvaig. Bracca looked at him and said nothing, but his crying had stopped.

'Good! Now, let's have something to eat. Come on.'

They got up and walked round the rock until they came to the panniers. Anxiously Melvaig looked around for the horses and to his relief he saw them grazing just a little way back up the valley. Melvaig opened the pannier lid and was immediately consumed with revulsion. Everything had turned black. At first he was not aware of the reason for this but then, as the blackness seemed to shimmer and move, he realized with horror that the panniers had been invaded by ants. He looked more closely and could see them, millions of them, swarming all over their carefully packed food in a mindless, relentless mass. He cursed himself for his stupidity. The panniers should have been left on the horses. Why hadn't he thought? Perhaps they could save some of the food if they shook off the ants. Yes – but he would need somewhere to put the food then, somewhere off the ground. He called Bendro. The horse looked up, put his ears forward, whinnied and carried on eating. He would have to go and fetch him. Suddenly Bracca spoke.

'Ants,' he said.

'Yes, ants. Lots of them.'

'Lots of ants,' repeated the little boy, almost to himself, as he stared in fascination at the thousands of little creatures each seemingly going their own, deliberate scurrying way.

There was something so extreme between Melvaig's panic-stricken horror and Bracca's awed fascination that the incongruity suddenly struck him as being funny and, almost despite himself, he found to his amazement that a bubble of laughter was rising up in his chest and although he tried to contain it, he burst out laughing. Bracca looked up with a broad smile on his face.

'Lots of ants,' he said and his eyes sparkled with pleasure at seeing Melvaig laugh.

'Yes, lots of ants,'said Melvaig. 'Now, come on. We've got to get the "lots of ants" off so we can eat our food before they do.'

Their laughter had lifted the tight band of anxiety from around his head.

'I'll go and fetch Bendro. You stay here.'

'Lots of ants,' said Bracca again.

'I'll "lots of ants" you, you rascal,' Melvaig said and he suddenly darted forward and tickled the little boy on his waist at which Bracca collapsed in a fit of giggling.

Bendro watched Melvaig as he walked towards him up the slope but he did not move away and Melvaig led him back down to where Bracca was waiting with the panniers. Sky followed out of curiosity and stood watching as Melvaig turned the panniers upside down and emptied all the food out on to the ground. Then he shook them vigorously until most of the ants were out before he carried them a little way down the hill, put them down, and began picking out the few ants that were still clinging stubbornly to the sides and the bottom. He placed the panniers on Bendro and Sky and then began the laborious task of sorting though all their food, salvaging what he could and throwing the rest away. The milk they would have to leave until they came to drink it, and the same with the yoghurt, but the bread and cheese they could deal with now. It was a heartbreaking task, seeing their precious food alive with the little black insects and having to decide whether or not to keep it. If a loaf or cheese was worth saving, this meant a long time spent trying to catch them and brush them off but the ants were quick, darting this way and that in their attempts to hang on to the prize they had found.

Bracca had got bored early on and had wandered across the track towards the stream where he was busily occupied in throwing pebbles into the water. Once or twice he had come back. 'Off now. Go,' he had said and when Melvaig had replied, 'No. Not yet – soon,' he had pulled a face and started to produce tears at which Melvaig had lost his temper and shouted.

'We will go when there are no ants left on our food,' he had said in that slow, clear, loud, distinct way which Bracca recognized as the last wall holding back the anger that would burst through if it was breached. So, not wishing to run the risk of that happening, he would turn round and go back to his stone throwing.

Once, he had come back and asked for milk.

'Well. I'm hungry as well. Let's see what we can find,' Melvaig replied and had got bread and some cheese from Bendro's pannier. Then he picked up a bag of milk from the pile of unsorted food and led Bracca back to the spot where they had spent the night. After knocking the ants off the goatskin bag he untied the thonging round the neck and looked inside. Luckily, only a few had managed to find their way into the milk and they floated on top; their black spindly bodies contrasted strongly with the expanse of white. One must have just fallen in because it was still moving its legs frantically in a futile attempt to rescue itself and escape from the thick white liquid in which it was slowly being engulfed. There was something so pathetic about the sight that Melvaig felt oddly moved and rather than kill it, as had been his initial impulse, he put his finger in gently, close to it, so that it desperately, gratefully, clung on to the solid skin while Melvaig lifted it out. Then, without really knowing why, he walked back to the pile of discarded food, watching it cleaning itself on his finger all the time as he did so, and placed it carefully on to a large piece of cheese. He watched it for a few seconds. At first it did not move, as if it could not believe its luck, and then it began to break a piece of cheese off with its pincers and devour it greedily.

As Melvaig turned away reluctantly and walked back he wondered why he had acted in such a way. He had provided a miracle. The ability to do that, and the power of life and death, had made him feel good – particularly when he had exercised it in favour of life. Perhaps he saw himself as the ant, struggling bravely against insuperable odds. As the ant had found a miracle, so perhaps would he when he was in just such a hopeless situation – at least he could now believe in them. Perhaps he was in some strange way afraid

56

of the ants and hoped that by his good deed, he would be ensuring a safe place in some future where they would be the rulers; or maybe he felt guilty about his slaughter of so many – the brown stain of their little bodies was engrained in the same finger with which he had conducted his miracle. Whatever the reason, as he walked back he felt buoyant and peculiarly fulfilled and he sat down to his bread, cheese and milk with a healthy appetite.

When he had picked out the dead ants that were still floating in the milk, Melvaig handed the bag to Bracca, who formed the mouth of it into a funnel, put it to his lips and then lifted his head back, holding the bag carefully so that it did not collapse. The little boy gulped thirstily as the cool white liquid went down his throat and a tiny trickle oozed its way out of the corner of his mouth.

'Bracca enjoyed that,' he said when he had finished. 'Now want bread and cheese.'

Melvaig broke off a chunk of the dark brown bread and handed it to him.

'Want cheese as well,' said the little boy impatiently.

'I know, I know,' replied Melvaig. 'I can't do everything at once. Wait a while.'

He put his hand inside the pannier and took out a cheese. It was white and crumbly and as Melvaig carefully broke some off, a scatter of little crumbs fell on to the ground.

They ate in silence, chewing each mouthful carefully, savouring it and then finally, when every essence of taste had been extracted, swallowing it. The sour taste of the yoghurt, which they scooped up with their fingers, contrasted well with the rich heavy cheese and the cheese in turn complemented the bread, helping to make it less dry and giving it a sharp edge.

When they had finished eating Bracca returned to his stone-throwing and Melvaig, after putting the remains of their meal back, continued with the depressing job of deciding what food was worth trying to salvage. It was nearly dawn when he finished. Of the four full panniers of food they had started with, only two now had anything in them and even they were not full. How far they could go with what was left, Melvaig did not know but they would have to be very strict with themselves from now on. Perhaps they would come to a village and could beg or steal some. Maybe he would catch up with the raiders soon. At this thought, a cold shiver went through him. He had not thought of what would happen then – all his energies had been focused on pursuit. What he would actually do when he found Morven he did not know. Desperately he forced the thought out of his mind. It was too unsettling. There would be time enough to worry about that when it happened. For now they must simply try and catch up. He looked across at Bracca, messing about in the trickle of water that meandered over the pebbles of the river bed, and tried to envisage what it would once have been like: a raging torrent, cascading crystal clear down the mountain. Then, the whole width of the river bed would have been filled from bank to bank with sparkling water; now the murky rivulet wandered aimlessly down the very centre of the water-course, leaving great expanses either side where the mud from the old river had been baked and cracked by the sun, the fissures gaping like open wounds in the skin of the river bottom.

'Bracca,' he shouted. 'Come on. Time to be off.'

The little boy looked up and, pausing only to throw a last pebble, ran across to the horses.

'Off now?' he said.

'Yes. Come on, I'll help you up.'

Melvaig lifted the slight figure of Bracca up on to the back of Sky, using his one good arm, and then with some difficulty hauled himself up on to Bendro. As they rode out they passed the pile of food which Melvaig had discarded. It seemed to vibrate with life as the ants swarmed all over it, shimmering with movement in the magical light of the dawn. It somehow represented defeat and Melvaig shook his head to rid himself of the impression of doom which had begun to close in on him.

CHAPTER VII

For three more days they travelled down the rocky path from Ruann. Instead of coming to a greener landscape, as Melvaig had hoped they would, the terrain grew worse. The water in the river bed had now virtually disappeared and grazing for the ponies had become an acute problem. While Bracca slept in the afternoons, Melvaig would travel back up the path with Bendro and Sky to find something for them to eat. There he would stay, dozing fitfully in the intense heat as the ponies ate and then, as night fell, he would travel back down with them, pick up the sleeping Bracca, and ride on, often carrying the little boy in his arms until he awoke.

Their progress was slow for the ponies were listless and Melvaig was tired. Often he would find his eyes closing as he rode and it would take an enormous effort of will to keep them open. His body grew heavy and every movement assumed huge significance, so that his mind became isolated and enclosed in the private battle it was waging against his limbs in its attempt to make them obey its commands. The pain in his left arm had almost gone though it still tingled occasionally when the numbness subsided. When he tried to move it, it seemed separate from his body so that he would watch dispassionately as his hand reached waist level and then, despite all the strength he could muster, refuse to go any further. Then he would allow it to flop down and hang by his side like some useless appendage, his mind exhausted and drained by the effort.

His constant tiredness meant that he became irritable and sharp with Bracca, so that their relationship lost much of the humour and fun which it had previously possessed. He snapped at the little boy and then was filled with remorse, vowing to himself that it would never happen again. Melvaig grew to dread their mealtimes. There always seemed to be less food in the panniers than he had imagined. He would get as much out as he dared but it never seemed to go anywhere; they would finish it almost as soon as they had begun and Bracca would ask for more.

'I'm hungry,' he would say. Then Melvaig would go over to the panniers once more and bring back an extra piece of cheese or a chunk of bread for both of them. That would go and then Bracca would start again in a plaintive whining voice.

'I want more cheese.'

'There is no more now. You can have some more later.'

'I want more now.'

Then Melvaig would shout, 'There is no more. No more!' and the little boy would start crying. Each tear would claw at Melvaig's heart until it ached and he would go over and try to comfort Bracca, putting his arms around him and trying to explain as clearly as he could that if they had more now there would be none later on, but the logic of this was lost to the little boy and he would push Melvaig off and shout again, in between little choking sobs, 'I'm hungry. Want more to eat.' In the end, because Melvaig was unable to bear the sound of Bracca's cries, he would give in, go back to the ponies and get more food until the little boy was full. But to balance this, Melvaig ate less, which left him confused, faint, lethargic and drained of any kind of energy or resolution. Often this emptiness in his spirit would attack him physically; his knees would become shaky and his whole body would begin to shiver uncontrollably in such a way that he would no longer feel solid. Even the air seemed heavy and he felt as if he were dissolving into it, being drawn gradually away to become lost in the dust and the rocks. It was insidiously tempting during these times to let himself be carried away on this sea of oblivion. Had it not been for Bracca he would probably have done so, but the sight of his little boy seemed to provide him with an anchor and he would call out to him, 'Bracca. Wait!' His voice sounded muffled and distant as if it belonged to someone else. Then he would slowly get down from Bendro and rummage blindly about in the panniers until he found some cheese. Once he had eaten it, the quivering would gradually stop and he would begin to come together again. Then he would remount and they would travel on.

On the morning of the fourth day after the incident with the ants they saw the desert of Molobb. For some time now the path had been widening; the valley down which they had ridden, after starting out as a narrow cleft in between high cliffs of rock, had flattened out into a broad rounded basin. The river bed had also become far wider, though the water in it had completely dried up leaving only a slightly damp, dark streak running down the centre.

Melvaig pulled Bendro to a halt and Bracca stopped next to him. They both looked out over the shimmering desert in silence. It was vast. Far into the distance there was nothing, only sand and the odd tuft of grass. Melvaig was too mesmerized by the awe-inspiring harshness of the place to do anything but stare. Emptiness, as far as the eye could see. The only movement was the dancing of the air over the baking sands as it bobbed and weaved in the intense heat. Melvaig even thought that he could hear the sounds it made in the silence – a jangling rhythm in the stillness. So this was Molobb! Stories and legends of the place had come to Ruann from the occasional traveller who had ventured down the path. Mentioned rarely, it had somehow always seemed to loom over their lives; the edge of their existence – the unspoken boundary of their world. No one, to Melvaig's knowledge, had ever crossed it. Its size was unknown – it could go on for ever. The legend was that at one time, Before the War, this had been an area thick with lush green vegetation and tall trees with animals teeming amidst the dense foliage. Multi-coloured animals of such strange shapes that they could not even be dreamed of – some of them vast lumbering creatures like walking mountains with noses that swept to the ground, others that wore armour-plating and possessed great horns on their noses and still others with vast necks that reached way up into the sky. And some there had been, so the stories went, that looked similar to Man: that walked on two legs with eyes, noses and mouths very much like their human relations. But they ate no meat and were covered in hair and could not do the things that man could do and they had vanished from the face of the earth, along with the rest of the fantastic creatures that dwelt in this dense green world, even Before the War, because their homes had been destroyed or because they had been killed for man's use or pleasure.

Melvaig stared out over the desolate parched place that stretched away before him for as far as the eye could see and tried to imagine it as Jarrah had described it so often in their long talks together. He tried to visualize mighty trees waving in the wind with uncountable numbers of birds singing and flying in amongst the branches – their bright plumage, crimsons, blues, greens and every other colour that existed, flashing and glinting in the sunlight. Then, in his imagination, he looked down below the tops of the trees to the world beneath – a world that hummed with the vibrancy of life, that buzzed with the energy of all the creatures that lived within; but try as he might the picture that came into his head was one which, he felt deep within him, fell far short of the reality of what the place had been like. When all he could hear was silence, how impossible to think of the air alive with the songs of birds; and when all he could see before him was an empty, parched, arid wasteland, how could he visualize the jungle?

So Melvaig's mind returned to the present and his eyes took in what they actually perceived and then his heart began to thump wildly, for there, on the very far horizon, he could just make out a little cloud of sand. At first he thought his eyes were playing tricks on him, for the shimmering air above the desert made it difficult to focus properly, but he blinked and looked again and it was still there, moving very slowly in the distance. Was it possible that they had caught up with Morven and the raiders? He looked again and tried to see the shape of the wagon amidst the shifting puff of dust, narrowing his eyes in an attempt to keep out the glare. It was impossible to be certain; sometimes he was sure it was there and then, when he looked again, it was gone. His mind raced. If it was them, they could not be more than two days' ride away at the most. If he and Bracca moved fast they could make up that time in, maybe, one day. But what if it was not them? They would be in the middle of that terrible baking arena, low on food and liquid and with little or no grazing for the ponies. Melvaig looked down at Bendro and across at Sky. Their ribs were already showing through their skin and their heads appeared gaunt and narrow, hanging listlessly down from their shoulder blades, the bony extremities of which protruded sharply upwards. They were barely more than skin and bone now. How far would they be able to make it over the desert?

But what choice was there? Even if it was not the raiders he could see, he was almost certain that they must have gone that way. Coming down the pass there had been sheer cliffs on either side, nowhere that a wagon could have gone.

Had they got to this point and gone round the desert? Melvaig looked at either side. For as far as the eye could see the shimmering expanse of sand stretched away. No. Instinct told him that they had crossed it. He looked again at the moving cloud on the horizon and felt certain that Morven was there. They would have to try and go across. But not just yet. To have any chance at all, they would need to travel in the cool of the night. There was no way they could enter Molobb in this heat and hope to survive long.

Just then Bracca, who had been silent and thoughtful, turned to Melvaig.

'Are we going over there?' he said.

'Yes. Tonight, after you've had a rest.'

'Long way,' he said. 'Long way over there.'

'It is a long way.' Melvaig wondered whether or not he ought to tell Bracca about the possibility that Morven could be out there but decided against it. It would do no good to raise the boy's hopes. It was difficult enough controlling his own.

'Come on,' he said. 'Let's go back a little way and find somewhere in the shade for you to sleep.'

They went a little way back until they found a shallow cave in a cliff. When Bracca was settled, Melvaig, as usual, took the horses to find some grazing. Luckily he found a little area of scrub quite nearby which was thick enough to provide Bendro and Sky with their best feed since they had left Ruann. The horses started eating hungrily and Melvaig walked around the little flat plateau gathering as much of the foliage from the squat, prickly bushes as he thought might fit into the spare panniers. When he had collected enough he rearranged the panniers so that all their food was together. This filled one pannier and then he pushed the feed for the horses well down into the other three. Finally, he lay down in the shade of one of the shrubs and tried to sleep but his terrible lethargy and tiredness had been swept away in a wave of energy which had come from the renewed hopes of catching up with Morven. His head was filled with pictures of her, of meeting her again, of the joy that would fill Bracca's face when he saw her. At these thoughts he would be buoyed up on a bubble of elation which would suddenly burst when the reality of the situation forced its way into his mind. How was he going to rescue her? And where were they going to go afterwards? Despair and fear then dragged his hopes down into a trough of despondency but somehow they would rise again and the conviction that they would be together reasserted itself and rose above the problems and difficulties that threatened to swamp him. He put his hands into the goatskin bag under his jerkin and found her moccasin. In some strange way he felt it linked her to him. He took it out and ran his fingers inside the shoe where the leather bore the imprint of her toes. The contact was strangely sensual and despite himself he felt his pulse quickening at the thought of her body. He smiled ironically to himself at the insatiability of man's desire, and the ridiculousness of the fact that, even at a time like this, he should find his mind turning to such things. He allowed himself the luxury of letting his mind dwell on the memories of her nakedness, before the crushing thought of her probable violation by the raiders sent a quiver of sickness through him and sent him once again reeling in anger and depression. Finally exhaustion pulled him under and he sank gratefully into an embracing cushion of sleep.

He awoke in the magical light of dusk, those few moments when, as with the dawn, the sky was filled with streaks of brilliant colour. That he should wake precisely at this devotional time was perhaps, he felt, a portent – a sign – of that higher purpose which he felt was guiding him: as was the good fortune in finding this plentiful grazing for the ponies so near Molobb. He called them over and they trotted across looking refreshed and considerably more rounded than before.

'Come on,' he said. 'Let's put the panniers back on you and go and see if the little man is awake yet.'

Bracca was still fast asleep when they reached the tiny cave where Melvaig had left him. Melvaig looked at him for a moment, the little mouth slightly open, the face blank and serene with sleep, the nose snuffling and snorting with the conscious effort of breathing. He was overtaken by a love for the boy so strong that it seemed to set his entire body on fire, tingling with the flames of a protective urge so powerful that if he had not fought against it, would have threatened to overcome him. Even so, he felt a hot tingling sensation behind his eyes and a tear trickled down his cheek. He knelt down and gave the boy a kiss on the ear. Bracca suddenly tossed and turned so violently that Melvaig could have been hit by a flailing arm. When he calmed down again, Melvaig gave him another kiss and this time Bracca opened his eyes and forced a sleepy smile while his body still seemed to struggle in a vain attempt to hang on to the blissful deliverance of sleep.

'Hello,' said Bracca. 'Is it time to go?'

'I'm afraid it is, little man. Did you have a nice sleep?'

'Yes, I did have a nice sleep.'

Melvaig helped the boy up on to Sky and they set off back down the trail. Soon they were looking out once again at the awesome emptiness of Molobb. Somehow though, in the silvery white light thrown down by the moon, it did not look as terrifying as it had earlier when they had seen it in the full force of the sun's rays and Melvaig's heart lifted a little. The ponies paused involuntarily at the edge of the desert and then, with slow reluctant steps, they began to make their way over the sand.

They made good progress that first night, walking at a slow steady pace over the loose sand. Although it was still considerable, the heat was a lot less than it had been during the day. Sometimes they would ride into a pocket of air that was almost stifling, so intense was its enveloping warmth, and the sand seemed to throw back all the rays that had beaten down upon it during the day; but at other times the air was almost cool and they would become refreshed and revitalized as they passed through.

When Melvaig judged that they had covered a good distance they stopped and ate. Now that there was at least a hope that they were within a day or so of catching up with the raiders, he relented on his strict rationing of their food and he ate until the empty pangs, that had gnawed away inside his stomach for what seemed for ever, were assuaged. The milk had now turned sour but this and the yoghurt satisfied their thirst and helped to dissipate the dryness in their mouths. However, liquid for the horses was a problem, as there was no hope of finding any water in the immediate area and already they were beginning to appear edgy and irritable. Melvaig gave them some of the scrub he had collected, in the hope that the stems and leaves would contain some moisture, but it appeared to make them worse. He dared not give them any of their milk and yoghurt, even if they would have taken it, and so the only hope was that they would be across Molobb before Bendro and Sky suffered any really serious effects.

Soon they were on their way again and the ponies seemed to settle down and forget their thirst, so that when the first streaks of dawn appeared in the sky, Melvaig was well pleased with the distance he believed they must have covered. He peered into the distance and to his immense joy he saw the little cloud of sand appear not as a speck on the horizon but as a moving line halfway between the horizon and himself. He was catching up. One more good night's ride and he could well be close enough to see whether or not they were in fact the raiders of Xtlan and, if they were, to begin to plan his rescue bid. He thought for a moment about riding on during the day but as the sun rose and started to throw its heat through the grey murk of the sky, the idea was quickly discarded. Besides, he might well be spotted now, just as he had spotted them. As he watched, the plume of sand stopped moving and very soon subsided so there was now nothing to be seen but a dark smudge which could easily be mistaken for imagination.

'I'm hot,' said Bracca. 'I want to sleep.'

'Yes,' said Melvaig. 'Yes, it is hot. We must find some shelter.'

He looked around at the flat expanse that stretched out in all directions. There was nothing, not a bluff or a crag or a rock. It had not occurred to him that there would be nowhere for them to get out of those piercing rays and suddenly a terrible panic spread up from the pit of his stomach. They could surely not survive a day in this heat with no shade. He looked again but it was hopeless. There was only one thing to do. He dismounted and helped Bracca down and then tried to make Sky sit down. The pony was tired and responded easily to Melvaig's pushing and shoving, as did Bendro when Melvaig made him lie down parallel to Sky, a few paces away. Now there was at least somewhere for Bracca and himself to get some respite from the heat, particularly when he placed the panniers at each end so as to form a long low rectangle. As long as Bendro and Sky stayed where they were and did not try and get up, they should be sheltered from most of the sun, except when it was directly overhead.

'Over you go,' said Melvaig, lifting Bracca over Sky. Then he himself got over and settled the boy down in the shadow thrown by the pony's stomach. Sky whinnied and Melvaig leant over and gently stroked her head.

'Good girl. You just lie there quietly. You'll be all right.'

He hoped the ponies would be able to withstand the heat. Already Sky's nostrils were flared and her mouth was open, panting heavily as the sun scorched down on her back and head. Bendro, the other side, was not yet in the direct rays of the sun and so seemed more settled. He might have to change them over to lessen the burden on each if either showed signs of succumbing. Then he had an idea. He went over to the panniers, took the lids off and, leaning over the pony again, placed three of them along her back and the fourth against her head. They might just take some of the worst of the heat off. Now there was no more he could do. He looked at Bracca. The boy had already fallen asleep but he was tossing and turning restlessly, shaking his head from side to side, puckering his eyebrows together into a frown and muttering under his breath. Melvaig lay down next to him, closed his eyes and went to sleep.

He awoke suddenly to the sound of Bracca crying.

'I'm hot,' he was sobbing frantically. 'I'm hot.'

Some time must have passed for the sun was now directly overhead. The ponies were still lying down but they seemed in a terrible state; their tongues were flopping out of their mouths dripping saliva on to the sand and their eyes were wild and staring. Melvaig watched in horror as their bodies heaved up and down in a desperate attempt to draw breath into their lungs. He felt utterly useless. There was no help he could give them: nothing to relieve the relentless pressure of this searing heat. He ignored Bracca's cries and got some goatsmilk from the panniers. Then he poured some out into the palm of his hand and held it under Bendro's mouth. In between pants the pony licked at the milk though his eyes failed to show any recognition or response. Then Melvaig did the same for Sky. Whether it was any help to them he could not know but he had to try and do something.

'I'm hot, I'm hot,' cried Bracca again in a plaintive whine which dragged at Melvaig's spirit and threatened to push him over the precarious line he was holding on to which separated him from the chasm of despair.

'I know,' he said. 'I know. But it'll be all right soon. When night time comes it will be cooler again.'

He moved over to where the little boy was sitting up and, despite the heat, he put his arms around him to comfort him. They clung together, their hot sticky bodies wrapped around each other, and the love that flowed from each to the other gave them strength. Bracca's cries stopped and Melvaig began telling him stories – the stories that Jarrah had told him: of how the world was Before the War, of the legends and fables of those times and of the beginnings of Ruann as they had been passed down by word of mouth from generation to generation until now, when those generations had stopped and Bracca was the last and youngest of them. The little boy listened and as the stories unfolded before him and Melvaig's storytelling grew in its lyrical power, he forgot the terrible heat that burned away at him as he became lost in other worlds and times. Melvaig threw himself into his task with such energy that he also forgot their desperate situation and became immersed in the web he was weaving.

When the storytelling stopped the sky was darkening into dusk and the air had lost its cutting intensity. Melvaig looked at the ponies. They were calmer now, their breathing more regular and their eyes full of the depth and warmth that had vanished in the terror of the afternoon. They were clambering to their feet of their own accord and Melvaig gave them some more of their food from the panniers as well as another palmful of goatsmilk each. Then he and Bracca ate and drank sparingly before mounting the ponies and setting off once again in the direction of the cloud of sand.

CHAPTER VIII

They rode easily and gently through the night, the light from the moon casting their shadows on the ground. However, the relief Melvaig felt at having survived the day was marred by the thought of tomorrow. If, as seemed likely, they would be unable to find shelter, they would have to face another ordeal in the heat and Melvaig doubted whether the horses could come through it alive.

Dawn broke upon them suddenly and they dismounted. There was no sign of the dust cloud in the distance and Melvaig struggled against a feeling of panic within himself. Had he lost them? Had it been imagination after all? No. They must have stopped travelling before dawn. Perhaps they had found some shelter in the night and decided to stay there. That must be what had happened. As Melvaig had expected there was, once again, nothing around them but a bare expanse of flat sand. He gave Bendro and Sky some more of the scrub from the panniers and then set about forming a shelter with them as he had done the previous day. They seemed too exhausted to protest and responded to Melvaig's wishes with an air of mournful resignation as if they knew what was to come. When the shelter was complete, Melvaig got some food and drink out for himself and Bracca and, as they began to eat, the sun started its inexorable rise into the murky sky and the familiar prickle of sweat began to break out on Melvaig's forehead and the small of his back. They had only five skins of goatsmilk left now; enough, if they were careful, for another four or five days. But if the ponies were to have any as well, which was essential unless they found water, this would reduce that expectation to two or three days at the most. Melvaig passed a skin across to Bracca.

'Be careful,' he said. 'Don't drink too much; there's only a little left.'

Bracca nodded his head impatiently.

'Not much,' he said. 'Not much.' And raising the skin to his lips started to pour the sour milk down his parched throat. Melvaig watched in anguish. How much could he let Bracca have? The little boy seemed to have been drinking for ever when Melvaig shouted, 'Enough now. Stop!' but Bracca ignored him. All the little boy was conscious of was the cool, gentle liquid trickling down his parched throat and invigorating his entire body with its refreshing fragrance.

Melvaig could watch no longer. 'Stop,' he shouted again and suddenly leaned over and tried to snatch the milk out of Bracca's hands. It came free of his fingers but Melvaig's, uncertain and hesitant, had not got a good grip on the bag and it fell, spilling its precious liquid on to the sand where it formed a large dark patch. By the time Melvaig had gathered his shattered wits together and picked the bag up, it was nearly empty. He turned savagely to Bracca who had not moved and whose face wore a blank, mask-like expression.

'I told you to stop. Didn't you hear me? Stop, I said. Stop, but you carried on.'

The mask dissolved into a flood of tears and Melvaig's anger gave way to remorse.

'All right, all right. I'm sorry,' he said, putting his arm round the boy and holding him close. 'I didn't mean to shout. It's just . . . there's not much milk left, you see, and I didn't want you to drink it all and leave none for later. I'm sorry.'

The tears subsided gradually and Melvaig laid him down to sleep under the shade of Sky's stomach. Already the sun was becoming unbearable out of the shade and, after Bracca had settled down, Melvaig lay on the hot sand and fell asleep.

He awoke inexplicably some while later and was enormously relieved to see that the sun had passed its highest point and had begun to descend so that it was now shining on Bendro. He and Bracca were now in its full glare. He moved the little boy, who was still sleeping soundly, across to Bendro's side and laid him down there in the shade. The ponies seemed to be in difficulties once again and he gave them some of the precious milk, but now that they had got over the worst there was a good chance that they would be all right and tomorrow he should catch up with the raiders. Surely then they would begin to come to the end of this terrible place.

It was while he was leaning over Bendro, rearranging the pannier tops against his back and head and holding a palmful of milk under the pony's mouth, that he became aware of a barely perceptible change in the feel of the air around him. It seemed even more still and heavy than usual, so that his own heartbeat seemed to be a noisy intrusion into the intense silence. His senses were stifled by the atmosphere and he had to fight to keep his mind from succumbing to the oppressive weight of the air and wandering off into flights of fantasy from which it might never return. Waves of shimmering lights began to pass before his eyes, their incandescence fluctuating in a monotonous and mesmerizing ebb and flow. Then through these hypnotic rhythms of light he saw on the horizon a long low bank of darkness. He struggled with his concentration and forced himself to focus. At first it did not seem to be moving but as he watched it grew in height and length and he realized that it was coming towards him. Suddenly he felt a rush of wind blow against his face, lifting his hair and playing against his skin. Welcome in any other circumstances it now seemed ominous, a portent of danger, advance guard for the mysterious black cloud that was sweeping onwards, growing steadily larger until it rose halfway into the sky. Only then did Melvaig shake himself free from his lethargic trance. The ponies were now struggling frantically to get up on to their feet and Bracca was thrashing around trying desperately to cling on to his nest of sleep. The wind had increased in intensity so that it was becoming almost difficult to stand. It pushed him back as he forced his way through it to Bracca who had by now woken up and was starting to cry.

'Stay there,' yelled Melvaig, but the roaring of the wind blew his words away and they were lost. He put his head down and burrowed against the gale, almost hurling himself through it until he had reached the boy.

'Stay behind the horses,' Melvaig shouted into Bracca's ear, before going to rescue the panniers, which had been blown over but luckily had lodged against Sky's back. Quickly he grabbed the spilt contents and threw them back in. The tops had blown away so he turned them upside down and pulled them across to Bracca. 'Hold these,' he said, giving him a pair for each hand and showing him how to hold them by the connecting piece in the middle.

Bendro and Sky were still fighting to get to their feet but the wind was too strong and they were too exhausted. No sooner had they managed to get their front hooves on the ground than, in their attempt to raise themselves up, they would get blown back and collapse whinnying in a tangle of legs. Melvaig threw himself first upon Bendro and then Sky, calming and soothing them and forcing them to stay lying down.

Now suddenly the dark cloud rose above them and the

sun was blotted out. At the same time the air was full of a fine choking dust which flew at them from all directions, stinging their cheeks and arms and legs and filling their nostrils. Even Melvaig's eyelids seemed to be full of the terrible dust, making them smart and water with pain. He lay down behind Bendro and holding the panniers down allowed Bracca to snuggle against his body as best he could, but the sand was everywhere and it was impossible to escape. Melvaig put his mouth to Bracca's ear.

'Are you all right?' he shouted, but the little boy only sobbed where he lay nestled against Bendro. 'Put your hand over your eyes. To stop the sand getting in.'

As Melvaig spoke his mouth was filled, in between his teeth, under his tongue and in the back of his throat. When he breathed through his nose, he drew in more of it so that he dreaded having to take a breath. Under him he could hear Bracca gasping between strangled sobs as the little boy fought for air. Even the warm wind seemed sickly and cloying so that every breath was nauseous and stuck in the throat until the lungs, in their desperate search for air, were forced to take it down. The ponies bucked and tossed with fear but were unable to move as the wind held them clamped to the ground. Melvaig turned his head and looked up, shielding his nose and mouth with his arm. Thick swirling clouds of dust blew all around so that it was impossible to see very far. He watched fascinated as the eddies of sand shifted in columns and circles, restlessly, frantically, constantly moving in their efforts to find a place to settle. He raised a hand to his head and felt a layer on his hair making it thick and dry and coarse. The back of his neck was itching with the sand that had found its way down in between his skin and his jerkin, scratching every time he moved. He felt smothered and, as he saw the sand building up in the relatively calm space between his body and Bendro's back, he had visions of being buried underneath mountains of the stuff.

He was just about to bury his head once again behind the pony when he caught a glimpse of something, a darker, more constant shape, just a few paces away. He looked again, peering frantically through the dust clouds and trying to ignore the mist of tears that flooded from his red raw eyes. Then he saw another shape just to the side of the first and suddenly a third also appeared, looming through the darkness, their outlines blurred and hazy but nonetheless their solid forms now unmistakable. Melvaig stared, stunned by disbelief, as the three figures edged their way towards him bent almost double against the wind. Now he could see them, three men, just the other side of Sky and then, without having the will or the ability to even try and stop them, he saw them climb over the ponies. In an instant they had thrown themselves upon Melvaig's inert, stupefied body and dragged him off Bracca. One of the three then pounced upon the boy and pulled him to his knees. He kicked and bit frantically. At the sight of Bracca, Melvaig was galvanized by anger and he managed to wrench himself free of the hands that were holding him. In a frenzy of desperate rage he smashed his fist into the face of one of his attackers and then looked around for the other. Now he felt himself grabbed from behind, both arms pinioned high up his back, and a burst of pain exploded in his injured shoulder, sending a sickening lurch through his stomach and turning his head giddy. He struggled fiercely but everything had dissolved into a haze of semi-consciousness. Every time he moved, the pain from his shoulder seared through his body. So much sand had got into his eyes that he could hardly open them but still he jerked himself this way and that in a frantic attempt to break away. Then, for an instant, he felt his attacker off balance and he flung himself backwards. Both men fell heavily to the ground but the attacker had been temporarily winded and for that moment the grip on Melvaig's arms was relaxed. He pulled himself away and turning around saw his opponent lying only a pace away from himself. Quickly he put a hand into his jerkin belt and pulled out his club, scrambling clumsily on his knees in the sand to get into a good position from which to swing. He raised the club high and was about to bring it down savagely on to the head of his adversary when a movement just ahead caught his eye and looking up into the swirling sand he saw Bracca held down by one man while the other, whom Melvaig had hit in the face, held a club in the air above the little boy. They were both looking at Melvaig and there was no doubt as to their message. Through the rushing whining wind he could hear Bracca's cries.

'No,' shouted Melvaig. 'No.'

He threw the club on to the ground and knelt with his arms outstretched in a gesture of defeat, his heart sinking in despair and his whole body trembling. Still Bracca was held down with the threatening club poised above him while the storm blew the sand in shifting clouds between them. The man Melvaig had winded had now recovered and was getting up. He moved over and, grabbing Melvaig's arms, forced them once again up his back and snatched the blackthorn knife from his belt.

How long they remained like that, with no one moving, Melvaig could not know but the time seemed to drag out interminably. Sometimes when the storm was particularly strong and the outlines of Bracca and his assailants were so blurred that they appeared as little more than a dark smudge, then Melvaig would start to imagine that it was all a dream, a vision, brought on by the heat and his lack of food but when the man holding his arm felt the need to remind Melvaig of his presence by pushing it further up his back, then the dream would shatter as pain dragged him back to the dreadful reality of the situation. Then he would begin to wonder about the attackers. Who were they? Why had they attacked him? What did they plan to do? Why, if their intentions were unfriendly, had they not killed him and Bracca? Then, when these questions met with no answer, he would think desperately about escape, and his pursuit of Morven and the raiders. Elaborate plans would form in his mind but they all collapsed before the fact that they held Bracca. Until he knew their intentions, he could take no chance. For the moment at least, Melvaig believed that they meant to keep Bracca alive if only to ensure that he, Melvaig, did as they wanted.

Finally, after what seemed an age, the wind dropped suddenly, the dust stopped blowing and a strange eerie atmosphere of calm returned. For a short time nothing happened, no one moved, as if they were unable to accept that the storm had really stopped. Now Melvaig saw the two who had Bracca. They were dressed in garments such as he had never seen before, in strange colours and of strange materials. On their feet they wore a sort of moccasin but it was of a smooth shiny substance. To Melvaig, who had only ever seen humans dressed in goatskin, they seemed peculiarly attired. Their faces, too, looked odd. They wore no beards, only a thick heavy stubble, and their hair was incredibly short so that their heads appeared almost naked and their features protruded with startling clarity from their faces. The lips, thick and bulbous and the nose, heavy and hooked. The eyes, too, seemed to stick out from under puffy eyebrows and possessed an unreal, penetrating light so that when Melvaig looked at them and his eyes met theirs, it was like staring into the blackest night, so little response was there from them and so empty did they seem. It was the eyes that frightened Melvaig for in them he could see no feelings or compassion, no trace of warmth or understanding. All these had been obliterated in the merciless struggle for survival, in the face of which every trace of emotion had been driven out. They would do with him and Bracca precisely what was in their best interests, and their lives and suffering were worth no more than a grain of sand to them.

Now one of them moved, the one whom Melvaig had hit in the face. He lowered the club with which he had been threatening Bracca and came over to where Melvaig was being held and as he walked Melvaig was startled to see that the man's stomach was fat and rounded as if he had had too much to eat. He stood just in front and then without warning swung his fist hard against Melvaig's cheek and then in a flash brought it back the other way so that his head snapped to left and right. The man leaned forward putting his face close and a stream of harsh, guttural sounds that Melvaig did not understand poured out of his mouth. Then he spat into Melvaig's eye while the man holding him from behind laughed and jerked his arm even higher up his back. Melvaig's face stung and throbbed where the fist had smashed into his cheekbones and he felt the foul glob of spittle slide down the side of his nose. He had closed his eyes involuntarily when the man lashed out and spat on him and now, as he tried to open them, he could feel the eyelids stuck together. His stomach heaved at the thought of it and he looked up at his attacker with a hatred so strong and powerful that he felt himself about to burst. The man was leaning back now with a sneer of satisfaction on his face, well-pleased with his revenge. Melvaig looked at Bracca. The little boy was staring, wide-eyed with terror, unable to comprehend anything of what was happening. His tears were all spent, his heart numb with anguish and terrified confusion.

Now that Melvaig had suffered retribution he and Bracca were hauled to their feet and held fast while Melvaig's adversary moved towards Bendro and Sky. While the storm had blown they had lain quietly, too weak to panic, but now it was over they were restless. The man took hold of both of them by the halters round their necks and pulled them up. Then he tied Sky to Bendro so that he could lead them easily together. As the man handled them, Melvaig watched their behaviour. They were still frightened and nervy from the heat and the storm and were only barely controlling themselves. Bendro kept tossing his head in an attempt to break free and Sky too stamped and whinnied and pulled on the rope tying her to Bendro.

Melvaig then felt his arms being released and he was pulled round roughly to face the man who had been holding him. He pointed to the panniers and once again Melvaig heard the sounds of this ugly language he did not understand. Melvaig did not move, partly because he was relishing the blessed relief of having his arms free and partly because he was too dazed to be bothered to try and understand what was wanted from him. The man shouted again and slapped his face, gesticulating excitedly. Melvaig guessed that he must want the panniers collected and put on the ponies.

When this had been done, two of the men mounted the ponies. Bracca was then handed to the one riding Sky and they set off with Melvaig walking and the third man, the one who had held his arms, walking behind. They moved slowly, for although the sun was now low in the sky, it was still hot and the sweat broke out all over Melvaig before they had gone many paces. He walked in a cloud of bewilderment, his injured shoulder, which before had been stiff but not painful, now throbbing again with a regular ache. His face where it had been hit, burned with a stinging fire which the sun's heat seemed to feed upon, and his head felt as if it had swollen to many times its normal size. His mind was raging with the indignity of having to accept all the beatings and abuse without retaliating and he struggled with himself to control the fury that threatened to break out in some action or gesture that could only jeopardize Bracca's life and any possibility of escape that might occur later. Patience in himself and cringing humility towards the attackers would have to dominate his thoughts and actions if they were to have any chance of surviving this nightmare.

They had not gone far when Melvaig saw a collection of

brightly coloured shelters and as they got nearer he was able to make out four horses tethered to stakes in the sand. He assumed that this was the men's camp. It did not take long to reach it. The man holding Bracca passed him down to the one who had walked behind Melvaig and then both the riders dismounted. They seemed very organized. The shelters were large and round, made out of a substance he did not recognize and Melvaig could see a large stock of supplies inside one of them. Their horses were sleek and well fed, and they whinnied energetically at Bendro and Sky who stood listlessly with their heads hanging down while the panniers were taken off their backs. When these had been taken into the store shelter and the ponies had been tethered, Melvaig and Bracca were led into the largest of the shelters. Inside it was relatively cool. Melvaig looked anxiously at the boy who still seemed unable to grasp anything of what was happening. His face was dirty and streaked with tears and as he looked at Melvaig his eyes bore so deep an expression of sadness and pain that Melvaig felt his heart aching with such intensity that he started to run across to him. No sooner had he started than he felt a hand clamped fiercely on his shoulder to stop him and he was forced across to the far side and pushed roughly down on to the sand. Bracca was also brought across but was held at a safe distance away, for the attackers were taking no chances of Melvaig grabbing the boy. The third man now went out and when he returned he had with him, to Melvaig's astonishment, an old man. He was totally unlike the other three; long white hair and a white beard that hung down to his waist gave the immediate impression of an old billy goat and he was clad in a motley collection of ragged and oddly-shaped garments. His wizened, wrinkled face had been burnt a deep dark brown by the sun which contrasted strongly with the white frame of hair around it.

The three men talked with him for some time in the strange language which Melvaig could not understand, and at times the conversation became animated. The old man mostly listened, his head nodding occasionally as one of the three addressed their remarks to him. Melvaig felt as if none of this was actually happening to him. The delicious cool inside and the patterns of shade thrown on to the sand by the colour of the shelter, clashed with the jerky staccato rhythms of the unknown language of the conversation which was obviously about himself and Bracca. One sound though, amidst the jumble of other noises, he did recognize and it kindled the flame of hope which had been almost extinguished: Xtlan.

The conversation continued and as it did so Melvaig realized that the old man, whom he had first assumed to be the leader of the three men because of the dignity which exuded from him, was in fact a prisoner like himself. Eventually the talking stopped and the old man turned towards him. His eyes were bright and sparkling and twinkled with a humour which lifted Melvaig's spirits so that he immediately felt a warmth towards him. The old man smiled and the confidence which Melvaig had lost returned in a flood of strength.

'My name is Arkron,' he said and Melvaig was startled to hear his own language. 'I am a Hebbdril, a Reader. Some call us wise men but that is not what we would call ourselves. Would that I were able to greet you in happier circumstances for I am, like yourself, a captive of these three. They are Mengoy: scavengers. They live by their wits on what they can find and take. They are based in the land of Xtlan to which they are returning with us, for there will be rich rewards for them for my capture. We of the Hebbdril are few, for the art of reading has been lost to all but a handful and it is with us that the only remaining books are to be found. Thus we are of great value to those who wish to build again in the ashes of the old. These three, Gebb, Nekdog and Shuinn, set out to find me in my cave in the mountains of Hemmsorr knowing the prizes that would be theirs if they were successful, for Xtlan is thirsty for knowledge and he has no Hebbdril.'

The old man paused and looked quizzically at Melvaig, whose mind was racing with excitement. They were being taken to Xtlan. There was still hope of finding Morven even if he were unable to escape and rescue her from the raiders. No longer need he worry about how to trace this land or how to get in once he had arrived if he did not find her beforehand. Now all he needed was patience. And here was someone who could read the Book to him, the Book which even now he could feel in the goatskin bag under his jerkin. Then Arkron spoke again.

'I tell you all this by way of introduction. But who are you? And the boy? I have been told to find out what you were doing in the middle of Molobb. Only a fool attempts to cross it the way you have tried. It is a strange turn of fate that you were seen by them for you would not have survived. It is at least three more days to reach the far side. Your dust was seen some two days ago and they slowed down to let you catch up, waiting until the sand storm before capturing you. They are pleased with their find, for you will be useful in the mines and the boy should grow up strong and healthy, so together you will be of quite some value. They have told me to tell you that provided you do not try to escape they will keep you fed and provide you with liquid. To ensure your obedience they will keep close guard on the boy and they will not hesitate to kill you if you do not co-operate with them. Gebb, in particular, is waiting for a chance to take his revenge for the broken nose you gave him. He argued that you were not worth the risk but the others dissuaded him. Still, you are vulnerable and they will dispose of you and keep the boy. He is easy to control and of more value to Xtlan for he will grow up to the life of slavery you will have to lead and thus accept it. You, who have known freedom, are potentially dangerous.

Do not give anyone the excuse to destroy you. Now tell me of yourself.'

Melvaig paused, trying to absorb what he had been told. The immense disappointment he felt at realizing that the dust cloud he had seen on the horizon had not been Morven and the raiders but his three captors, was relieved by the knowledge that he would at least be taken to Xtlan. Once there he could make plans to find her. But he understood nothing of what Arkron had said to him about slavery. Still he would have time to ask him on the journey. Now he must think carefully and decide what to tell Arkron. He decided to relate everything – the complete truth. The old man could decide what the three captors should be told.

'I am Melvaig, from the land of Ruann,' he began, 'and this is my son Bracca.'

Arkron listened quietly and attentively while Gebb, Nekdog and Shuinn watched them, their senses strained to catch any word they recognized or any inflection in Melvaig's voice that would indicate something to them. Knowing this, Melvaig omitted any mention of the Book, deciding that he would tell Arkron later when there might be a chance for them to be on their own. His tale took a long time as Melvaig, trusting the old man, recounted the thoughts and emotions and feelings he had experienced on the journey. As he talked he relived all that had happened since he and Morven had first heard the raiders. He was so relieved to find someone to pour out his soul to that he forgot where he was and got carried away in the tragic drama of his story until suddenly Gebb broke in and said something angrily to Arkron.

'He says to be quick,' said the old man.

Melvaig hurriedly finished his story and then Arkron looked up at him.

'We will talk later,' he said. 'I will tell the Mengoy

nothing about Morven. Otherwise I will inform them of everything they want to know.'

Arkron then turned to the three men and began telling them the relevant parts of Melvaig's history. At one point, to Melvaig's startled surprise, they burst out laughing, looking first at Bracca and then himself.

'They are amused that you should know your son,' said Arkron. 'As in Ruann, though perhaps for different reasons, familial ties are unknown in Xtlan.'

When he had finished, Arkron waited while the three talked amongst themselves. They questioned him on one or two matters, particularly Melvaig's decision to cross Molobb which, having omitted any mention of Morven, Arkron had explained by saying he was following his people. They seemed to find this difficult to believe but Melvaig's attachment to Bracca, his son, was equally strange so they accepted the story. Eventually, after some deliberation, Shuinn, who was holding Bracca, spoke briefly to Arkron who then looked at Melvaig.

'Xtlan is some distance ahead. They were not expecting to have to feed anyone else so you will have to kill one of the horses when the food is near to running out.'

Melvaig felt sickened by the idea for he had grown to love both Bendro and Sky on their journey together.

'There is no other way?' he said. 'Perhaps if Bracca and I ate less . . .'

'No. You would starve. Either you kill one or the Mengoy will. I am sure you would prefer it to be yourself. In any case it is doubtful whether you will be able to keep the surviving horse in Xtlan. Slaves are allowed no possessions.'

Melvaig's heart felt as if icy tentacles were spreading themselves around it. Fear of Xtlan began to fill his mind with black shadows and he forced himself to quell them. Thoughts of the life he was being taken into were full of unknown terrors but for the sake of Bracca and Morven he had to submit. If it were not for them he would have taken the first opportunity to escape. He looked again at the little boy, sitting by Shuinn with the man's huge hand gripping his wrist tightly. Fortunately Shuinn, who was the biggest of the three, seemed also to be the least vicious and Melvaig nursed a hope that perhaps some sort of relationship would spring up between them. Sometimes the man would look at Bracca and Melvaig would think he could see the flicker of a smile flash across his face, but then when he looked again all trace of it would be gone and the mouth and eyes would once more be set into a hard cruel pattern, devoid of any trace of warmth.

Now the sun outside had almost vanished beyond the horizon and it was time to go. The three men told Arkron to pack up the shelters with Melvaig and load up the ponies. They would eat as they travelled. Soon they were ready to leave, Gebb in front followed by Shuinn who carried Bracca in front of him on his horse. Then came Arkron and Melvaig while Nekdog came last. Before they left, Nekdog, the smallest of the three and the one whom Melvaig judged to be the weakest, came round while they were mounted and handed them scraps of dried meat to chew on. The horses had been fed and watered from the supplies of the Mengoy but Bendro and Sky were still listless and lethargic, hardly even whinnying a recognition when they saw Melvaig and Bracca. Melvaig rode Bendro who was, he thought, perhaps slightly stronger. There was no rider for Sky and she had been loaded up with supplies and attached to Bendro by a rope. As Melvaig had tied it to her nose band, Sky had looked directly into his eyes as if she knew that her fate had been decided. She tried to nibble Melvaig's fingers and rub her forehead against his shoulder as if she were trying to establish some contact with him and Melvaig had responded by stroking her gently on the nose.

'It's all right,' he whispered in her ear. 'It's all right,' but his heart bled with the thought of what he would have to do. He looked towards Bracca and saw that the boy had turned his head round and was staring at him. Melvaig forced a wide smile and lifted his hand in a gesture of reassurance. Shuinn saw it and laughed uproariously, wrapping his arms around Bracca in a mock gesture of protection. The boy's face puckered with the beginnings of tears but Melvaig shook his head and frowned and he held them back. At least, Melvaig thought, there was some humour in the man. Perhaps by playing on the paternal affection he had for Bracca and making a joke of it, he could try to win some spark of consideration from Shuinn. He bowed low in a parody of thanks and again the man laughed. Melvaig felt relieved and pleased; this was something he must nurture carefully. Then he saw to his joy that Shuinn's laughter had penetrated Bracca's wall of isolation and he was smiling. Then Gebb turned round, glowering at this levity, and barked an order at which the strange little column set off into the night.

CHAPTER IX

They rode in silence for a long time, the only sound being the swish of the horses' hooves in the sand. Melvaig cursed the pain in his shoulder but his spirits were high. Though captives, he and Bracca were going to the place they would have been travelling to if they had still been on their own, and in some ways it was fortunate that they had been taken by the Mengoy. As Arkron had said, it would otherwise have been difficult if not impossible to have crossed Molobb. If he controlled his temper and obeyed orders he and Bracca would be fed and sheltered until they reached their destination. Once there he would be in no worse position than if he had arrived without the company of his captors.

He was pleased also to have met Arkron for he no longer felt quite so alone. Ever since that dreadful afternoon in Ruann he had had no one to share his thoughts and problems. No one to talk to about possibilities, plans, alternatives and choices. At times Bracca had been the only thing that had kept him going but Melvaig had longed for some adult company as well. Now the responsibility for survival was not all on his shoulders. He could relax for a time at least behind the wisdom and knowledge of the old man and hopefully they would be able to talk. Thus he could gather his wits and energies for their arrival in Xtlan.

Melvaig had been longing to speak with Arkron since they set out but he did not want to break the silence. Now, after they had ridden for a while, Shuinn moved up alongside Gebb and began talking to him. Melvaig saw the opportunity and very gradually edged Bendro alongside the old man's horse. As he did so Arkron turned to him and smiled.

'You were thinking what I was thinking,' he said quietly. 'I think it will be all right to talk but we must keep our voices low.'

Immediately Gebb and Shuinn turned round but did not say anything. Arkron smiled at them and they turned back.

'You are from Ruann,' continued Arkron. 'I knew of Jarrah. A good man and a brave one. Tell me, are you his son?'

'Yes,' said Melvaig surprised.

'It was just a guess,' he said. 'I did not know. I never met him and he did not know of me, but word of him and Ruann had spread to Hemmsorr and beyond. It was probably that very fame that led to the attack by the raiders for Xtlan must have heard of it and known there would be rich pickings there. It was by all accounts a well run village and it is indeed a tragedy that it should be no more. Tell me of it.'

So Melvaig told Arkron of his life at Ruann and as he talked it lived again and the people he had known once more walked over the mountains or tended the goats or reared the children or told stories in the cool of the night in the big hut. He described Jarrah and Shennsah and the others and in his words they were brought back to life: their happiness, their tears, their foolishness and their wisdom, their arrogance and their humility. He spoke of their fears and of their struggles, the constant fight for food and the ever-present fear of illness and when he had finished he was drained of all emotion for he had poured it all out in his re-creation of their world: the life he had lived for so long and which he had thought could never come to an end.

Arkron said nothing for some time. He could remember little of the time before he became a Hebbdril and though he knew of the life others lived, never before had it been described to him so vividly and with such depth and he felt strangely humbled by the bravery and courage of these people. Simple people, living a life where their greatest aspiration was survival, yet creating out of it something of such fragile delicacy and beauty that he was stunned by it. What was it, he wondered, which held that world together and gave it its special quality. Though they had banished the word and the idea to make their lives easier, Arkron believed that it was love.

Melvaig looked anxiously ahead to see how Bracca was and was relieved to see that the little boy was asleep, slumped back against the large body of Shuinn.

'Tell me about yourself,' he said to Arkron.

'If you wish,' the old man replied, 'though there is not much to tell. I can remember little of my childhood. I was born and brought up in a village much like your own, away to the west of Ruann in the land of Hemmsorr, but unlike yourself I was never aware of either of my parents. I remember being restless when I was a child with a strange, powerful yearning that ate away at me so that I took to wandering alone in an effort to appease this hunger. At first I would go just a short distance but as my confidence grew and I got older I began to travel further and further from the village. I remember those days with pleasure; the excitement as I discovered new mountains and sometimes a little copse of trees or a valley with a river running along the bottom of it. I tried to imagine them as they had been Before the War for we, too, had men in our village like Jarrah who told us tales which had been told to them about the old world and the way things used to be. Sometimes I would stay out all night, so lost was I in the joys of discovery, and when I returned to the village, I would be scolded publicly for I was a bad example to the others. I can see now the reasons for their concern but at the time it made me angry and I felt alienated and different.

'One day, by chance, I found that I had stayed out after dusk again and I found that I did not wish to go back. On my walks I had spent a lot of time thinking; my mind would wander in the strangest of ways into worlds and places which came into my head from somewhere above and beyond the life I knew. Now, when the chance presented itself on this particular night, I realized that there would never be any contentment for me in the village and so there was no point in my returning. So I wandered over the mountains for three or four days until lack of food and water drove me into oblivion and I passed out. When I came to, I was in a cave being tended by an old man. He nursed me back to health and then told me of himself. His name was Derrionn and he was a Hebbdril. Like you, Melvaig, I had never heard of these people before so he explained to me what they were.

'In the War, he said, countless numbers of books had been destroyed and in the aftermath the survivors were too concerned with staying alive in the horror that they found themselves in to bother about such things as reading or writing. So as the years went by and the generations passed, these arts were lost. Some there were though, as there have always been and will always be, who were concerned that the heritage of man as written down and passed on throughout the ages, was being lost. These men withdrew then, with as many books as they could salvage, to places where the pressures of survival were not so great, to remote and inaccessible places in the high mountains. There, in their caves and shelters, they scratched a living from the hard earth with their goats and with their donkeys, and they nursed and nurtured their minds on the few books that they had. It was a hard life but they learned to do without, to eat little and to survive on almost nothing. They gave up human company for it was there, with the thin veneer of civilization now stripped away, that mankind once more became lower than the savage and there was no place there for men of gentleness and thought.

'These were the original Hebbdril. Many perished on their journeys; others lived but a little time in their chosen place. All were men of vision driven by a desire to save something of the past, of the world Before the War. Some of them survived and became legend so that men of similar nature came to them. Occasionally a village would form around them and such a place would be a just, good and fair society, though as the years passed the villagers too would neglect their studies as the demands of community living made themselves felt. Nevertheless the Hebbdril would be well pleased for something at least had come from his work. A living testament that hopefully would last and from which perhaps something great would one day emerge. Ruann was just such a village, founded by Emmkor many generations ago.

'Others of the Hebbdril would continue to lead their solitary lives, some dying with their knowledge locked away and lost for ever while still more, by fate or chance, would meet with one to whom he could pass on his knowledge: a disciple. Just such a one was I to Derrionn as he in turn had been to Aeksor and so on back to the first survivor.

'I myself had a disciple Pekkmar who, knowing of me, had sought me out to learn from me all that I could teach. The Mengoy slew him. He fought them but was unskilled and though filled with courage his nature was not suited. So they killed him.

'So that is my story, Melvaig, and the story of the Hebbdril. Now I am being taken to Xtlan for the profit of the Mengoy. There, Xtlan will attempt to use my learning for his own ends. He will try to make me teach his own people to read and write that they may learn from the books he has amassed by pillage and looting so that his people will grow ever more strong and powerful. He will have me with him as his counsellor to advise and instruct him on matters of science and logic and art. But he will fail with me as he has failed with the other Hebbdril he has captured or who have been taken to him for I would never use my knowledge to help the evil that is Xtlan. I will go and use my position as best I can to mitigate the harshness and cruelty of his rule for it would be foolish and arrogant not to try, but it will not be long before I am found out – though the cleverer I am the longer I shall survive – and then I shall be destroyed as the others were.

'And now I will tell you of Xtlan—for you must be prepared when you arrive. His is a world where all the foullest parts of man's nature have been encouraged to blossom and flourish. It is a world based on evil and cruelty – where everything good is ruthlessly driven out so that there may be no aspect of light in the darkness. Degradation, humiliation and cruelty are worshipped as the highest aspirations of those who rule. There is no order, but a perpetual and unchanging anarchy, for the governors are very nearly as vile to each other as they are to the governed so that there are constant shifts in the pattern of rule: unending denouncements, purges and vilification of those who were once in power to make way for their accusers. There is no trust, no love, no friendship between people. Neither is there nobility, forgiveness or mercy. All the most worthy and sacred human emotions have been banished so that the flower in the soul of man has been crushed, its petals ripped apart and stamped upon, its stem left bleeding so that never may it take root again. Man is thus left as an instrument of evil with nothing to redeem his unbridled savagery: no tenderness to curb his passions, no gentleness to temper his lusts. Thus a great dark cloud of evil hangs over the place and it grows daily as the cancer within spreads and thickens over the land.

'And over all this chaos stands Xtlan, immutable and secure – the only stability in the maelstrom of unceasing change. Alone he reigns, the power of his evil towering above that of those he rules as a mountain over a valley. The nature of his cruelty is such that your mind could not accept it and the gratification of his desires so foul that your body would retch in disbelief were I to describe them to you, and your mind reel into insanity were you to witness them. In him, all evil is gathered and magnified a thousand times. All fear him and none may challenge his unbridled authority, for he governs with a rod of fire and those who fall foul of his unsure temper suffer so horribly in their death that their wailing may be heard in one's soul for ever, tormenting the mind and warning all who think of treachery to banish their thoughts instantly lest he perceives them. Yet the aspect of his rule that is most fearful is the insecurity he nurtures around him. Thus one who has served the Lord Xtlan well and faithfully, obeying every whim and order, for many years, may suddenly find himself suffering the same terrible fate as one who has committed an act of disobedience. Nothing is safe, nothing is constant, save terror and fear.

'Where he came from is not known. He travelled unnoticed for many years round the land, gathering together a band of followers and trapping them in the web of his power. The ones he collected were those in whom he could perceive the greatest potential for evil, whose souls were ripe for corruption to his ways and who willingly abandoned the last remaining vestiges of their humanity. These were the arrogant, the proud and the cruel, the mean and the greedy, the selfish and the sadistic. Small men, whose gross desires and dreams he fed and nurtured till they grew into all-consuming needs which he allowed them full licence to indulge. Thus where they had been insignificant, of no consequence, now they felt themselves to be powerful.

'As these men left their villages, so those remaining were glad and relieved to be rid of them. They were gone and forgotten as was the dark fear the villagers had felt when they first saw the evil stranger who had come uninvited into their midst – talking in corners and lurking behind walls. He had not stayed long enough for them to take action against him and when they looked for him, he was gone.

'The years passed and Xtlan's evil band grew until one day those same villagers who had been glad to forget him, whose minds had blotted out his evil memory, saw him again. Now, though, he came at the head of a vast army which attacked with such ruthless and vicious cruelty that nothing could withstand its terrible onslaught. The very old and very young he killed or left to die. The others, those who had not perished in the brief and tragic fight, he took back to the place he had founded as the centre of his world: Eggron. There he set his captives to work as slaves, working on the land, building roads and shelters, constructing wagons. Those with whom he was especially displeased, he sent to work in the dreaded mines of Gurrtslagg, deep within the earth, where the strongest man weeps even as he claws away at the rock, and the metals and ores that are mined are sent up stained with blood. A man who is sent to the mines may not expect to live to see daylight again for he will be kept down there till he dies.

'Of the women, those fortunate enough to be displeasing in the face or body are sent to work on the land in the goat farms or making garments and weapons. The others, those who are cursed with the possession of that which men desire, these are herded together into groups and these groups are kept under female guard in various shelters which are called Gravenndra throughout the land. Their lives are dedicated to feeding the base and loathsome appetites of Xtlan's warrior raiders. There they are forced to perform the vilest acts until these men, who nurse the darkest desires ever conceived by mankind, are fully satisfied. The Elimsorr they are called, these most piteous and tragic of creatures. When their minds and bodies are shattered then they are released to be used by the men amongst the slaves, and only when they are no longer of any attraction are they discarded to be finally free of their repugnant obligation. Many of them will then take their own lives, if they have not done so earlier, but those who survive are too weak to be of any use so they are banished into the Hinterland known as the Lemgorrst, there to dwell amongst the human wreckage of Xtlan's world. In the Lemgorrst live the ill, the infirm, the mentally and physically crippled and all who have fallen foul of Xtlan or his men. It is a living death. They are kept alive solely for the sake of amusement, fed on handouts at the whim of those who guard them. Many die of starvation or disease and those who manage to find the will to live, bitterly regret that choice when they are picked to take part in the sports for which they have been preserved. It is at these sports that Xtlan's warriors indulge their blood lusts, killing, torturing and maiming until even their gross needs are satisfied. They vie with each other for ever more cruel and painful ways of killing, deriving satisfaction from the suffering of their victims. Sometimes they will compete for the greatest number killed in the shortest time, bringing their victims together in large enclosures and chasing them with mace and club till all are dead or dying, when a fresh batch will be brought in. The task for these is made more difficult as the bodies of their predecessors obstruct them, but this all adds to the enjoyment and the challenge for those who pursue them.

'At other times it is the thrill of the chase that Xtlan's men will seek, releasing one or more on foot and then taking after them on their horses.

'It is said that these sports are crucial to Xtlan's world for it is here that the young men learn the art of killing and cruelty, acquiring a taste for it and a need to indulge it. The sports are used by Xtlan as a reward, so that he will hold them after a successful raid. At other times they may be used in between raids if the men are bored and need a distraction to amuse themselves. I do not believe the sports to be so crucial. The sports are a symptom, not a cause, Melvaig. These men are not made more cruel by them; it is as a result or consequence of their cruelty that the sports are held.'

The old man stopped speaking, and once again silence resumed its reign over them. Melvaig's head reeled in a confused blur, recoiling from each horrific vision only to find another one in its place. He dared not let himself dwell on thoughts of Morven and he clung desperately to the hope that the raiders had not yet arrived, looking ahead of him into the sky as the dawn broke and trying to let the power of this magic time break into his mind and fortify it against the mists of darkness which threatened to overcome him. Waves of sickness and repulsion broke over him as each part of the terrible mosaic that Arkron had created impressed itself into his consciousness.

CHAPTER X

When the sun began its ascent, Gebb halted and gave orders to Arkron and Melvaig that the shelters be erected. Bracca still seemed in a daze as he was handed down by Shuinn to Nekdog who took him around with him as he fed and tethered the horses. Occasionally the little boy would look across at Melvaig and their eyes would meet for a brief moment before he was dragged off again. When the jobs were done they all gathered in the big shelter where they ate and drank before Nekdog came across and tied the wrists and ankles of Melvaig and Arkron. Then he attached some rope from them to his own wrist before indicating that they were all to sleep. On the other side of the shelter Melvaig could see that although Bracca had not been tied up, nevertheless there was a rope from his ankle to Shuinn's. The possibility of escape that Melvaig had once contemplated seemed to be receding as the time went on, and never once did the Mengoy allow an opportunity to present itself. And even if he did manage to escape, how would he survive in the desert and how would he find his way into Xtlan?

Melvaig turned on his side and closed his eyes. Before he realized it, the mental and physical exhaustion which had been building up within him dragged him down into the blessed oblivion of sleep. Even there the world of Xtlan refused to let him be and he was constantly tormented by nightmare fragments that pulled and tugged at his mind and would not allow him any peace.

He awoke to the familiar sound of a child crying. For some time the noise had haunted him in his sleep but now that he was awake, he realized that it was Bracca. He sat up quickly and felt the rope round his wrists tighten as he did so, as they pulled on Arkron's wrists in turn. Bracca was sitting upright, his face raised into the light and the tears streaming down his cheeks. The dazed shock that had protected him until now seemed suddenly to have cracked and all the fears and terrors and confusions of his world were gushing out in a flood of anguish. Great sobs escaped from his mouth and his body threw itself into huge convulsions. Gebb barked an order out at him but Bracca ignored it, neither knowing nor caring what the man said. Again Gebb shouted his command and again the little boy refused even to acknowledge the man's presence. Then Gebb got to his feet, raised his arm and brought the palm of his hand down with all the force he could muster against Bracca's face. For a tiny moment there was a stunned silence as Bracca, momentarily shocked out of his hysteria by the pain, turned his head and looked wide-eyed with terror at the brute, ugly face of Gebb. Then he burst out crying again with renewed strength.

Melvaig felt his stomach churning over with a terrible apprehension at what the man would do. Gebb yelled with fury and bending quickly down grabbed Bracca by both shoulders and lifting him up began shaking him violently backwards and forwards so that the little boy's head seemed loose upon his neck, bobbing to and fro like a puppet. Melvaig tried to get up on his feet but, although he succeeded in getting his bound ankles under his body, when he attempted to lift himself up, he toppled over. As his wounded shoulder hit the sand with a jarring thud a wave of nauseous pain lanced through him. For a second he involuntarily shut his eyes and when he opened them again it was to see the great shambling bulk of Shuinn grabbing Gebb's right arm to hold it still and in the same instant wrenching Bracca away. Gebb stood still, staring at Shuinn, and his eyes were blazing with a dark fury so intense that Melvaig could feel its presence almost as a living thing filling up the tent, stifling and oppressive. Then in an instant Gebb had gone, turning his back and storming out through the entrance. As he went Melvaig felt his tension evaporate, and Bracca's tears slowly began to subside until they became little more than an occasional sob. Shuinn still had not put the boy down and he stood with Bracca in the same position as when he had snatched him off Gebb, the little boy's back against his chest with his left arm cradled around Bracca's stomach. It was a bizarre sight; this giant of a man clutching the little body of a boy to himself like a shield and staring out through the entrance after Gebb, hardly able to believe what he had done – what strange and long-forgotten chord had been struck within him to make him act the way he had. Slowly he turned around and, as if in a daze, he laid Bracca down gently on the sand before sitting down himself.

'Gebb will not kill the giant now,' Arkron whispered quietly into Melvaig's ear. 'He needs him too much. He will wait until we are in Xtlan but then, at the first opportunity, Bracca's big friend will be dead.'

'Why are you so sure it is Shuinn who will die?' whispered Melvaig.

'Because Gebb is one of those who always wins. It is the way of things. Some men are like that. Besides, in the ways of Xtlan, where there is compassion or kindness or gentility then there is weakness. See – look at Shuinn now. He has lost all confidence in himself. He is shaken, defeated already.'

At that moment the flap at the entrance to the tent

opened and Gebb walked in. Melvaig watched in amazement as he moved across to Shuinn, smiling broadly with his arms extended in a gesture of the warmest friendship. Shuinn also was surprised by this unexpected change and at first he was so taken aback that he was unable to move but then a look of relief spread over his face and he stood up hurriedly lest the moment should pass. Gebb clapped him heartily on the shoulders and said something to Shuinn in a warm friendly tone.

'What did he say?' said Melvaig.

'Forgive and forget. He says they must stick together. Now, Melvaig, he is at his most dangerous. Shuinn has not only lost his confidence; he is also off his guard.'

Gebb lay down again and Shuinn followed. Once more, quiet returned to the tent, broken only by snores and heavy breathing. Melvaig, seeing that Bracca had gone to sleep, drifted off into a state of semi-wakefulness which lasted until, some indeterminate time later, he felt a sharp tug on his ankle and, opening his eyes, saw that Nekdog was on his feet as were Arkron and Gebb. Nekdog then shook Shuinn who was still snoring loudly and then Bracca woke up.

The sun had gone down and when the tents were packed and the horses tended, they rode out again in the same order as before, chewing on their pieces of dried meat. Once more Gebb and Shuinn began talking though there was now a different feeling to their conversation. Shuinn seemed garrulous and effusive, anxious and over-eager, while Gebb's voice was as cold and passionless as stone – betraying nothing.

For a little while Arkron and Melvaig did not speak but then Arkron started talking of the world Before the War. He spoke of the birth of that world when the land was ruled by giant beasts. He told of the end of their reign and of the influx and the growth of man from his humble beginnings to his final position of dominance, when the numbers of his kind were impossible to count and he had used up all his space. He described the destruction of the natural world: the great areas of forest cut down to provide energy, fuel and materials for the ever-increasing glory of the power of man. He talked of the savagery and ignorance with which animals and plants, precious creations of life itself, were destroyed or killed. He spoke of cities and of houses, of roads and of cars, of railways and of planes. He talked of travel to the moon and stars, of journeys to the bottom of the sea. He told Melvaig of medicine, that most worthy of man's creation, and its use in the relief of suffering.

He spoke of philosophy, science and of art; great thinkers and writers and sculptors and painters. He told of good men and of evil men, of those who had loved and those who had hated. He described the world of woods and trees, of rivers, streams and mountains, of animals and birds and he spoke of the way in which man treated that world.

And lastly he told what he knew of the Last Great War and Melvaig reeled in horror and disbelief at the enormity of man's crime.

When he had finished, Melvaig's mind was spinning. It was impossible for him to absorb all that Arkron had said but the magic of the old man's words lingered with him for ever, so that he found he was able to recall them and muse upon them at his will and work out for himself their full and proper meaning, dwelling upon each word and line until it became a part of him.

Now he felt it was the time to tell Arkron of the Book which he could, even at this moment, feel weighing heavily in its bag around his neck.

'I have something,' he said, a little apprehensively, 'which I would like to show you. A Book,' and he went on to tell Arkron of Jarrah's words and of how he, Melvaig, had dug it up. He went on to describe the casket and, as he spoke, Arkron's eyes lit up with a sparkle of excitement and he could hear the tension in the old man's voice.

'Keep it well hidden,' he whispered. 'Don't bring it out now. I have an idea of what it may be and if I am right then I am indeed blessed to have this chance of seeing it. But Jarrah was wise; guard it safely and secretly for none must know of it. Wait until daylight when the others are asleep. Then pass it to me. I will read it and tell you of it as we ride tomorrow night. Say no more now. Look, the sun is nearly risen. Soon we shall be camped.'

He broke off and almost as soon as he had done so, Gebb and Shuinn came to a halt and the routine of the previous night was repeated; the horses were tethered and tended to, the tents erected, something to eat and drink and then sleep. Melvaig closed his eyes but listened intently until he could hear three sets of snores. Then he cautiously got up on one elbow and looked around him. All were asleep, even Bracca, who lay with his eyes tight shut and his mouth open. A pang of emotion pulled at Melvaig's heart as he looked at the little boy and then, so slowly that he hardly seemed to be moving, he put his bound hand under his jerkin until he found the goatskin bag. Putting one hand inside he felt first Morven's moccasin and then the hard case of the Book. He took it out and looked across at Arkron who was lying dead still with his head turned towards Nekdog, ready to move his ankles and warn Melvaig if the Mengoy should show signs of waking up.

Melvaig handed the Book across to the old man, gently pushing him in the shoulder with it. Arkron turned and very slowly grasped it in his tied hands, ensuring that there was always plenty of slack in the rope between himself and Nekdog. At one point the Mengoy gave a great sigh and shook his head to and fro, muttering something under his breath. Arkron and Melvaig froze, their hearts beating furiously, but Nekdog quickly settled down again and resumed the regular pattern of his snores.

As Arkron took the Book and looked at the symbol and

the carvings on the casket, his face broke into a smile so broad and so warm that Melvaig was almost afraid he would jump into the air and shout for joy. He studied the scenes carefully, running his fingers delicately over them as if he was afraid to believe the truth of what his eyes told him. When he had immersed himself in each picture, he opened the casket and took out the Book. Then, when he saw the title, he looked up at Melvaig, nodded his head in affirmation of the fact that this was indeed what he had hoped and expected it to be, and with the blood pounding in his ears opened the first page and began reading.

'It was still snowing in Silver Wood. All night large flakes had been falling relentlessly . . .' The words rang in his head with a great triumphant clarion call from that other world, the world he had read so much about, which he had envisaged day after day sitting in his remote cave in the mountains of Hemmsorr, as he read all the books bequeathed him by Derrionn. But the world he read about now was not a world with which he was familiar from those books. Never before had he come across this hidden realm of the animals and the elves and as he read, his viewpoint of the world Before the War became disoriented as he perceived that world through the eyes of the animals.

He read all day, the words drawing him into magical and secret places, summoning up within him feelings, emotions and powers which had lain dormant and unknown. He finished the tale just as the sun was sinking. On the far side of the tent Gebb was stirring and with very slow, even movements Arkron put the Book back in its case and leaned over to Melvaig who was already awake and looking at him with anxious, expectant eyes. The power of the story and the truths revealed by it had left Arkron feeling exhausted and it took an enormous effort to wrench himself away from the world he had been reading about back to the present. He looked at Melvaig and smiled with a gesture of satisfaction. What, he wondered, would the effect of it be on this strange young man? Melvaig put the Book carefully back in the bag round his neck and he had just taken his hands back out from his jerkin when Gebb suddenly woke. He sat bolt upright, staring hard at Melvaig whose heart thumped wildly in his chest, afraid that he had been seen. Then abruptly, and to Melvaig's intense relief, Gebb turned away, got to his feet and clapped his hands. Nekdog woke immediately but Shuinn had to be shaken for a while by Gebb before he came to. Melvaig looked at Bracca stretched out beside him. The little boy's eyes were open but he was just lying quietly, staring vacantly up at the roof of the tent. If Melvaig thought too much about what was happening to his little boy's mind he was unable to stand the pain so he turned away quickly and got up, stretching out a hand to Arkron to help him to his feet. As he did so, Gebb came across with a sly smile on his face and spoke to the old man. When he had finished Arkron turned grimly to Melvaig.

'He says their food is low. It is time for you to kill one of your horses.'

Grinning savagely, Gebb handed Melvaig a knife and then spoke again to Arkron who translated.

'That was a warning not to think of using the knife on anything else but the horse. He, Gebb, will have a knife at Bracca's throat until the job is finished.'

Even as Arkron was reciting Gebb's words, the Mengoy had walked over to Bracca, picked him up roughly by the arms and was brandishing a knife threateningly at the little boy.

Melvaig walked out through the entrance with a heavy heart. He had known that this moment had to come but now that it was here, his soul shrieked in protest at what he was about to do. Sky was tethered next to Bendro and they both whinnied a greeting as he approached. Melvaig unhitched the rope tethering Sky to the stake and as he did so the pony leaned forward and nuzzled his forehead. He looked up and blew into the pony's nostrils, smelling the distinctive richness of her breath. His heart wept as she pushed her soft nose against his mouth and he felt the tears welling up behind his eyes.

'Come on,' he said. 'It'll soon be over. Better perhaps for you dead, than for us left. Don't be afraid.'

He led her away round behind the tent out of sight of the other horses. Bendro stood and watched, his ears pricked forward, his eyes wide and alert until they were gone. Melvaig gently pulled Sky down on to the sand until she was lying on her side.

'Goodbye, Sky,' he said, kissing her behind the ear, and then quickly he pulled the knife from under his jerkin and drew it down with all the strength he could muster across her throat. But the knife was blunt and the cut not deep enough. Sky began threshing around neighing furiously, her eyes dilated with fear, her legs kicking frantically in desperate attempts to get to her feet. Horrified, Melvaig watched as she rocked grotesquely to and fro and then he ducked under the flailing hooves and slashed again. This time the knife went in and he felt the warm blood gush all over his arms. Again he plunged the knife into the wound in an attempt to hasten her death, his mind reeling in a welter of sickness and horror. It seemed to last for an age, the awful dying tremors, the twitching, and the final pitiful whinnies as she sank into oblivion at last.

When it was over Melvaig flung himself on to her, the tears pouring down his cheeks, guilt and remorse dragging at his heart.

'I'm sorry,' he wailed. 'I'm sorry,' and then through the fog of grief that surrounded him he grew aware of the sound of laughter. It pierced his isolation and froze around his heart. Loud, mocking laughter, rising in a crescendo as Gebb and the other Mengoy enjoyed the sight of his torment. Then like a jewel set in a sea of filth he heard, above and beyond their obscene laughter, the sound of tears, and they hurt him far more than the laughter ever could. It was Bracca. He opened his eyes and saw Gebb holding the little boy's head with one hand under his chin, forcing him to look. The blood set in Melvaig's veins and he swallowed back his tears. Slowly he lifted his head from Sky's body, seething with anger and hatred, his soul burning with the desire for revenge, yet to his amazement his mind remained icily calm. Every fibre of his body screamed out to him to lunge into these people with the knife which he held, still dripping with Sky's blood, in his hand, but his mind called out to him to conquer his pride, to save his energies and strength for later when it would be needed, to think of Bracca and to have faith in the corner of his soul which had seen above and beyond everything that was happening to him, that part of him which had been touched and awakened by the magic of the dawn.

So Melvaig banished the laughter from his ears and began the grisly task of cutting Sky into pieces small enough to pack away in the panniers. Soon the Mengoy grew bored and turned away to resume their other tasks, leaving Melvaig to continue his revolting work alone.

'Sky is dead,' he kept saying over and over to himself. 'Her suffering is over,' and it helped a little as the familiar shape of the horse vanished into a pile of shining red slabs.

Melvaig had finished by the time the Mengoy were ready to move. Gebb came over and took the knife back while Arkron helped him to carry the panniers, heavy now with Sky's meat, back to the horses and load them up. Bracca refused to look at him. The little boy's eyes, red and raw-rimmed with weeping, were fixed on the ground at his feet and his back was turned against Melvaig.

'Don't worry,' said Arkron, as he and Melvaig were fixing the last pannier on to Bendro. 'Some day you will be able to explain and some day he will understand.'

'Why, Arkron? Why did they do it?'

'It is the kind of thing they enjoy. It amuses them. You

will have to get used to it in Xtlan; the important thing is staying alive. Only then can you fight. Have courage.'

'I do not lack courage,' snapped Melvaig. 'I lack the strength to endure seeing my little boy suffer and to have him turned against me. I cannot bear it.'

Melvaig's hands began to shake and he felt the tears flood up within him once again.

'I know,' Arkron said gently, putting his hand on Melvaig's shoulder. 'I know. I'm sorry.'

Suddenly the harsh voice of Gebb barked out an order and they mounted. As they rode out, Melvaig turned back and looked at the pool of blood on the sand, a dark patch glinting in the light from the moon. For a moment Melvaig imagined that he could see Sky standing there, whinnying gently in the way that he knew so well, but then the pony vanished and soon the stain was out of sight.

For some time they rode without speaking, all thoughts of the Book forgotten behind the terrible memories of Sky. Melvaig concentrated on trying to get all the blood from his wrists and arms, scraping it off with his nails where it had dried on. After a while the gentle rhythm of Bendro beneath him as they walked quietly over the sand soothed Melvaig's turbulent mind and his thoughts turned to the Book.

'Tell me what you read,' he said to Arkron.

The old man began to speak, his words slow and deliberate, and as he spoke they grew in stature so that none of the power of the Book was lost. Slowly the story was revealed. Melvaig learned of Nab, left as a baby in Silver Wood to be found and brought up by Brock and the other animals of the wood. He learned of the owl, Warrigal the Wise, and the hare Perryfoot, whom they called The Fleet, of Sam the dog who befriended the animals and accompanied them on their epic journey in the quest for the Faradawn. And Arkron told him of Beth, who loved Nab and travelled with him and the animals and learned from

Nab the ways of the wild creatures and of the world about which Melvaig himself had dreamed. The green world, the world of trees and rivers and streams, of woods and meadows basking in fragrant springtime sunshine with the songs of blackbirds and thrushes echoing through the air, or frozen in the grip of winter under a blanket of crisp white snow. And Melvaig saw it as Arkron spoke the words: the flowers, the grasses, the bracken and the bluebells, the majestic beech and the mighty oak. He saw the blue sky with little white clouds floating through it, and he felt the rain as it washed the earth. He knew the changing of the seasons, from the melancholy golden mists of autumn to the awesome might of winter, from the fragile promise of spring, bursting with hope, to the sleepy haze of summer. And Melvaig's heart ached with yearning for that world, so that his spirit sang with the strength of his longing.

Arkron spoke of the mighty Elflords, Wychnor, Saurélon and Malcoff and he told Melvaig of Wychnor's words even as they had been spoken by Wychnor to Nab. He learned of the Efflinch: Ashgaroth, Lord of Good, and Dréagg, Ruler of Evil, who have struggled against each other since time began. He learned of that race of man known as the Urkku or Great Enemy and of the destruction and pain they inflicted on the world, and he learned of the Eldron, the Friends, those men who have rejected the power of Dréagg and to whom all cruelty, pain and suffering is abhorrent. To these men Ashgaroth granted a view of the world as the animals and the elves see it so that they might be blessed. And as Melvaig heard these words the pattern of life as he saw it in the world he knew became clear and he perceived that surely Dréagg was victorious. Even now he must be watching, well pleased, as the Earth, that jewel of Ashgaroth's creation, languished sick and obscene after man's great crime, wounded and dying, governed by the vilest of men, its colour, light and richness extinguished for ever. And he thought of Xtlan and it seemed to Melvaig as if in him Dréagg had come down to Earth, the better to savour his victory, to wallow in the revolting world which he had created through the agency of his pawns, the Urkku. On Earth he could manipulate man to the fullest extent for his amusement, indulge himself so as to extract the greatest satisfaction from the foul results of his labours and wallow in the horror and anarchy of man's floundering attempts at survival.

Where now was Ashgaroth? Where were the Elves and where were the companions from Silver Wood, granted the immortality of the Elves by Ashgaroth? Had they perished in the war and had their world died with them? Had Ashgaroth deserted the world he had created, to leave it finally to the mercy of Dréagg? These questions rang through Melvaig's mind as he heard of the struggles of Nab, Beth and the animals. Nab, whose coming had been foretold by legend, born of the Eldron yet imbued with the spirit of Ashgaroth so that he would have the powers to fulfil the task destiny had chosen for him; Saviour of those who look to Ashgaroth for the essence of their souls.

The tales of their heroism and courage, and the great and eternal cause for which they fought, gripped Melvaig so fiercely that when Arkron came to the end of the story he, Melvaig, felt totally drained yet also elated, filled with a power and strength he had not known before, inspired by the force of what he had heard. For the first time he perceived a meaning in the stirrings he had felt all his life, deep within his soul. It was Ashgaroth who was guiding him and protecting him, directing the framework of his life for reasons which Melvaig did not even try to think about. But, in the Book, he had seen the world about which he had dreamed for so long. It had been real; it had existed and now he was set in the conviction that it could not have died. Somewhere it lived still, and he must find it. There was no doubt in his mind as to what he had to do and he would pursue his goal with absolute faith. Ahead of him now there beckoned a halcyon vision. All was becoming clearer: the struggles, the pain, the suffering, all now seemed endurable in the certainty that they were not aimless but part of a wider purpose. What he would find when he got there and what he would do, were not questions that concerned him. He simply knew that this was the reality of his life with Morven and Bracca.

Melvaig looked at Arkron. The old man's head was bent, his shoulders hunched and his wizened face seemed somehow drawn in and sunken. His years now sat heavily upon him; the upheaval, the journey, the uncertainty, all these bore down with a force that suddenly, now, seemed to have taken their toll.

'Arkron,' called Melvaig quietly.

There was no reply.

'Arkron,' and he moved Bendro closer to the old man so that he could shake him by the shoulder. Now Melvaig could see that the old man's eyes were shut. He shook him again and the eyes slowly prised themselves open.

'Was I asleep?' he said, and the words were heavy and thick, coming not of their own accord but being forced out by a huge effort of will.

'No sleep yesterday,' he said. 'I must have dozed off. I can't seem to keep my eyes open.'

'You must try. You'll fall off your horse.'

'Yes. Yes, I'll be all right. It must be nearly dawn.'

Ahead of them, a thin golden line on the horizon heralded in another day but it was a different skyline that greeted them this morning. No longer was it flat and uniform, an unbroken vista portraying nothing but desert. Now there were shapes silhouetted against the golden line of dawn, sharp angular shapes, unfamiliar to Melvaig, breaking up the sky ahead of them into an unsettling, half-finished mosaic. Arkron spoke.

112

'We have crossed Molobb,' he said. 'Soon we shall enter Lemgorrst, the Hinterland.'

Just then Gebb pulled his horse to a halt, gave the familiar orders and once again the shelters were erected and, having eaten, they fell asleep as the cool shadows of the tent played over them. To Melvaig's relief, they were still eating the old supplies and so the panniers containing Sky remained unopened. Arkron had gone to sleep immediately, exhaustion claiming him with a welcoming hand, but Melvaig lay awake for a while, his mind wandering back through the story Arkron had told him, dwelling on each part and letting it stay until it became fixed in his heart, so that one day he could tell Bracca. Then he too fell asleep, his spirit still roaming through the world of Nab and Brock, Warrigal and the others.

CHAPTER XI

Melvaig was woken up by a vigorous shaking from Nekdog. It was still daylight when he and Arkron went outside and started packing up the tents. Now the way ahead of them was clear. The desert faded out gradually, the flat sands of Molobb giving way to a gently rising slope of hard earth where here and there tufts of grass had broken through the greyish brown crust. They were on a track which led upwards until it disappeared into a deep ravine that ran through a huge natural wall of rock stretching away at either side as far as the eye could see. The ravine formed the only way through this barrier of stone, and the land immediately behind it was hidden from view. But in the far distance, way beyond the wall of rock, Melvaig could see the jagged shapes he had noticed at dawn. They spread out like an ugly broken crown over the top of a tall flat-topped hill that rose high above the surrounding land. The setting sun behind bathed them in flaming reds and crimsons and to Melvaig it seemed as if the place was being washed with blood.

'That is where Xtlan lives, the Blaggvald or, in your tongue, the Black Palace,' said Arkron. 'It can be seen for many, many miles so that none who are within his rule may forget his presence. It rises up from a valley wherein the city of Eggron is found. Eggron, the centre of Xtlan's world, one of the few places not totally destroyed by the War.'

The sun had now almost vanished behind the hill and the houses stood out black against the red sky. Melvaig and Arkron stood and stared, unnerved and dreadfully fascinated by the power that emanated from its dominating presence. The cold fingers of fear crept into Melvaig's stomach. He was unable to tear himself away from the awesome sight, his eyes rooted to this pinnacle of evil as if by some strange compelling force. It was not until Arkron shook him violently by the shoulders that he broke free of its hold.

'There will be time enough later to look at it,' said the old man. 'Come. Let us get the horses packed.'

Soon they were on their way, riding slowly up the track. No longer were the horses' hooves silent in the sand; now they almost clattered on the parched earth and the sound seemed to echo against the rocky wall ahead. In vain Melvaig had tried to catch Bracca's eye as he had been loading up the horses but, although Melvaig had often seen the boy looking at him, as soon as he tried to meet his son's gaze, Bracca turned away quickly and Melvaig's heart was pierced with anguish.

As they climbed, the air began to grow noticeably cooler and, after the suffocating heat of Molobb, Melvaig felt almost refreshed. The night was dark, but here and there he could make out the shape of a bush or a small tree, and somewhere in the distance, the faint trickle of running water filtered through the air. They all rode in silence; even Gebb and Shuinn were quiet, subdued by the sight they had all had of the Blaggvald which even now could be dimly made out as an almost luminous glow in the barely perceptible white moonlight that was diffused through the ever-present blanket of cloud. Its presence weighed heavily upon them all, an omnipotent brooding cancer, gnawing away at their spirit and their will, until Melvaig had to fight to regain some awareness of his own identity.

On they walked until all at once the sky was blotted out and, looking up, Melvaig saw they were under the shadow of the wall. Out of sight now was the Blaggvald, hidden behind the towering barrier of stone that loomed high above them. It was pitch black and they walked slowly, the horses afraid of stumbling and their riders, even the Mengoy, reluctant to take themselves nearer the entry. Then suddenly they were enclosed by the steep walls of the ravine. It was almost like being in a tunnel; on either side the rock rose up sheer above their heads while ahead of them the dense blackness seemed to suck them in. Melvaig could see nothing; he just followed the sound of hooves in front and tried to control the furious pounding of his heart and the roaring of the blood in his ears. He seemed lost in a timeless vacuum and as they moved deeper and deeper into the black tunnel, he lost all idea of space and direction. He could have been riding upside down, or spinning round or backwards. Desperately he looked around for something to fix his eyes on to, something that would hold him down and stop the awful careering through this black void. The clatter of hooves echoed loudly around the walls, coming at him from all directions, circling round and round his head in a confusing nightmare of sound; the noise seemed to rise and fall, to ebb and flow in his head as it reverberated in his ears.

Then, through the air he heard a different noise and, at the same moment, a strange new smell stung his nostrils. He focused all his concentration on them and slowly, to his immense relief he felt himself regaining a sense of reality.

Looking ahead, he saw that the wall of black was broken by a little patch of grey – the end of the tunnel – but as they drew nearer the noise and the smell grew until they seemed to overwhelm everything else. It was a terrible noise, harsh and strident, and yet at the same time with a low mournful undercurrent that reached down into the depths of despair. It was the sound of ultimate suffering, the awful wailing and crying merged together into a sound that seemed to want to tear the ground apart and bury itself in the innermost furnaces of the earth, while behind and under it there throbbed the pulsating hum of human moaning. It was a sound stripped of every redeeming aspect of humanity, torn out were all traces of dignity, self-respect and modesty and in their place sat degradation, humiliation and total destruction of the soul. Melvaig felt himself being ripped apart as the noise dragged at his mind, tearing and pulling at him with its abject desolation. Then he felt a hand grip his arm and peering through the darkness he saw that Arkron was pointing ahead to where Gebb and Shuinn had stopped. As they rode to catch them up Melvaig shouted to the old man.

'That noise. What is it?'

'It is known as the Wailing of Lemgorrst,' he called back. 'I had heard of it but never imagined it to be so dreadful. It is the sound of the outcasts in the Hinterland.'

When they were together, Gebb ordered them to dismount and see to the feeding and watering of the horses. Once Melvaig and Arkron had finished they walked over to where the three Mengoy with Bracca were sitting down at the side of the track, leaning against the cliff wall, eating and drinking. The stench that came from the end of the tunnel was terrible, an acrid pungent odour that stuck in the nose and throat, heavy and sickly-sweet so that when Melvaig tried to eat a piece of dried goatsmeat with some cheese, his stomach refused to accept it and he was immediately sick. The Mengoy laughed and then to Melvaig's horror, Nekdog went over to the horses and, opening the pannier that was filled with the flesh from Sky, took a piece out and brought it back. Smiling, he handed it to Melvaig who took it. The blood oozed through his fingers and his heart curdled with revulsion. 'I must eat.'

The thought pounded inside his head. 'I must eat.' Closing his eyes and his mind he bit a piece of flesh off and began chewing it between his back teeth, shutting himself off from everything – the smell, the noise, what he was eating, the texture, the taste – he forced his jaws to move mechanically up and down until the thing in his mouth had lost all shape and substance and then he swallowed it. He carried on until he had finished, his stomach gurgling in revolt and his eyes aching with the effort, but finally it was over. Thankfully he drank down some yoghurt to clean the taste away but it lingered on – a thick fatty coating on his teeth and the smell of blood in his nostrils.

Now Gebb began to speak, shouting above the noise, and when he had finished Arkron turned to Melvaig.

'He says we are nearly there. We must ride with you and Gebb on one side, Nekdog and Shuinn on the other, while I ride with Bracca in the middle. The strongest and healthiest of the outcasts wait at the end of the ravine for travellers such as ourselves, to attack us and take what they can. I am the most valuable to the Mengoy and so I am to be protected. Bracca is also worth much. Gebb will give you a club and he will ride behind you should you think of trying to use it on any of the Mengoy. You must ride hard and as fast as you can, striking out with the club at any who try to pull you off. Don't stop until Gebb tells you.'

Melvaig looked at Arkron. 'Is there a chance of escape for us?' he said, trying to keep the excitement in his voice under control.

'I don't know,' said the old man. 'Maybe. But where would you go? You would soon be spotted as an outsider and survival in Lemgorrst would be almost impossible with Bracca. And Morven, how would you find her? She will be somewhere in Eggron now and you would have to enter Xtlan to reach her. And you have no Tang. All who dwell in Xtlan who are not slaves have a brand or mark on their chest. It is burned on with fire, a test for those who would give themselves to Xtlan and ride and fight for him. There is no way you can enter without being inspected.'

Melvaig's mind raced as he tried to think of solutions to the problems Arkron had foreseen. Just then Gebb spat out an order. Arkron spoke. 'It is time to go,' he said. Melvaig looked at him.

'I must try. There may be no other chance. Try and keep at my side while we are riding. When the time is right I will take Bracca off you; then we will see what happens. Do you think you can stay with us?'

'I'll try,' said the old man. 'But don't bother about me. Save yourselves. That is what's important. May the fates be with you.'

Again Gebb shouted. Shuinn rode over with Bracca and passed him to Arkron. The little boy smiled at the giant and Shuinn tousled Bracca's hair before he rode away. Melvaig watched and his heart ached, for never once did Bracca look at him.

Melvaig turned away and looked behind him. Gebb was there, his eyes as expressionless as stone. He leaned forward and handed back to Melvaig the club he had lost during their encounter in the desert. As he grasped the familiar handle, Gebb threw out his hand quickly and gripped Melvaig by the hair, twisting and pulling until Melvaig's face was tilted at such an angle that Gebb's eyes were looking directly into his. It was as if he was seeing straight into Melvaig's mind and into his ideas of escape. They bored a hole into his head so that he felt utterly vulnerable and exposed – every part of his spirit revealed to that awful searching gaze. Gebb said nothing. There was no need, for his eyes had said everything. Then abruptly Gebb let go of Melvaig's hair. His head dropped suddenly and stupidly as it was released from the grip and for an instant Melvaig remained motionless, stunned with fear and drained of energy. Then he looked up and at an order from Gebb at which Shuinn, who was riding opposite on the other side of Arkron, moved forward, he too started to ride towards the patch of grey light that beckoned them towards it at the end of the dark tunnel.

Soon they were riding at a gallop, faster and faster as the noise and the smell grew until suddenly they burst out into the light. Melvaig gagged at the foul stench whose acrid pungency seemed almost solid. It struck at his nose and throat and he ducked his head instinctively against it. At the same time he was aware of hands grasping at his legs and he felt Bendro slow down. Raising his head he saw, all around and in front of him, a mass of humanity, so united in their purpose and their pitiful squalid state that they seemed to be as one creature, a massive writhing animal, barely recognizable as man, whose only aim was survival. He did not look at the faces or the hands of those who were trying to drag him and Bendro down, nor did he think about what he was doing as he brought the club down with all the force he could gather. He felt the stone head connect and give slightly as it sank into the crowd. Through the bedlam he heard a sudden screaming more intense than before. His left leg was released, and lifting the club over his head he brought it down on the other side. Once again the hands that had gripped him slowly loosed their hold and slithered down over his ankle. Now he leaned forward and smashed the club down on either side of Bendro's head, kicking the pony fiercely in the ribs in an attempt to get him to move faster. Behind him he could hear Gebb's rasping shout and then to his relief he felt Bendro surge forward and he was off, forcing a way through this sea of human wreckage, panic driving the pony on so that his pounding hooves cleared a path over and across the bodies. Now he dared to look. Bendro's neck and head were covered in blood that had dripped from the club which he held in his left hand. Appalled, he gazed in horror at the head of the club. Tufts of hair and pieces of flesh sprouted from the stone or were stuck in the rope fastening it to the handle. Looking down he saw, for the first time, the faces of the people. So ugly were they that they were almost unrecognizable; their parchment-yellow skin, blotched and tightly drawn over the huge skulls, seemed about to split as the cheekbones threatened to break through their flimsy covering. The lips were drawn back from the gums leaving rows of protruding brown and blackened teeth. As he looked he felt the eyes of these piteous creatures pulling at him, large eyes empty of all emotion, blank and frightening in their vacuity. Nothing was left save the barest of instincts, the will to survive.

Now as Bendro galloped faster, so Melvaig looked beyond those who were near him to the others, the ones too old or ill or maimed to even try to attack him. Fleeting images of despair flashed before his eyes as he forced Bendro on; at first the sight of them filled him with horror, pity and guilt but as they kept appearing so he grew used to their misery. Some had no legs, others no arms. More were sightless, paralysed, crippled or malformed. Mothers nursed babies, pitifully urging milk from their empty withered breasts. The limbless crawled around on the hard-packed mud, the stumps of their arms or legs waggling frantically and uselessly in vain attempts to assist their owners. Mutants lurched, stumbling, through the mass of bodies, moaning and wailing in their private hell, kicking at the crippled and the dying in a careless and pitiful show of power. Packed together they were, these tragic vestiges of humanity, writhing and squirming together, their skin caked in excrement, as insects ravaged their bodies; ghastly putrefying wounds oozed with matter and seemed to move with a life of their own. Sometimes Melvaig spotted a child, its face drawn into the wrinkled visage of an old, old man while it tottered crazily to and and fro, its stomach gross and distended. Its mouth would be open, its eyes puckered together but no sound and no tears would come.

Melvaig's mind recoiled before this nightmare and,

unable to cope with it, his eyes glazed over, reducing the individuals to a blurred mass. Now, as Bendro bucked and tossed his way through them, Melvaig looked for Arkron. To his relief the old man was by his side. Turning round he saw that Gebb was some way behind and that Nekdog and Shuinn were also lost amidst the throng.

'Now,' yelled Melvaig, and Arkron nodded his head.

Melvaig guided Bendro towards Arkron, and when he was alongside he grabbed Bracca. Cradling him under his left arm, he spurred the horse on, at the same time wielding his club savagely on either side of the pony and shutting his mind off from the consequences of what he was doing.

They seemed to be in a kind of passage. On either side strange buildings, such as Melvaig had never seen before, lay in ruins. There were no roofs although in some of them, flat pieces of stone had been laid across the corners of the tumbledown walls to make shelters. Suddenly he came to a dead-end. In front of him a ruin blocked his way but there was a choice on either side. Which way to go? Now from the alley on one side there came a horde of people, their arms outstretched towards him as if in prayer. He swung Bendro's head round and made off away from them down the other alley, the sound of their yelling and shouting rising above the general wailing. On either side of him the jagged skeletons of old red brick walls rose up from the ground, the colour of ancient wounds, so that Melvaig felt enclosed and stifled by the atmosphere of decay. Behind him the shouting of the mob echoed around the walls burying him beneath its deafening roar. He did not hear Bracca crying but when he looked at the boy's face, he saw floods of tears running in torrents down his cheeks. He turned and saw the crowd pouring after him down the alley, their hands clawing frantically at the air as if they hoped to pull him back towards them. They careered down the alley, jammed between the walls, and those who slipped or stumbled were quickly lost beneath the relentless, charging feet of those who followed after. Melvaig glimpsed the faces of the leaders, ashen faces patterned with pulsing veins of red, strings of lank hair flopping around their heads as if in some crazy dance. Where the mouth should be, a black gaping hole and the eyes straining, bulging, mesmerizing in the intensity of the lust which poured out from them.

Melvaig quickly turned back, the image of their slavering faces burning in his mind, and desperately urged Bendro on, faster, but the horse was not used to running in such a narrow enclosed space and the walls threw shadows across his path so that he did not see the pile of scattered bricks until it was too late. His hoof struck them and he stumbled. Normally he would have recovered his balance but now, with the terrible noise and the strange surroundings and Melvaig's frantic urgency, he panicked. For a few awful seconds he teetered and then he fell to the hard earth. Melvaig was thrown against a wall and lay momentarily stunned and winded where he had fallen. Bracca too was shocked and had stopped crying. By the time Melvaig recovered from his daze, the crowd was almost upon them. Desperately he scrambled to his feet, swept Bracca up and ran through a gap in one of the walls. Once inside the ruined building he hurried along against the outer wall so that he could not be seen from the alley. He stopped by a spot where the wall was low and raised his head carefully to see over it.

To his horror, the mob had fallen upon Bendro. Melvaig had assumed that they were chasing him and not the horse, but he had been wrong. He could hardly see Bendro; the mob were swarming all over him shouting out in triumph. And then suddenly, over and above all the noise, the air was pierced by the most terrible squealing. It seemed to rise and then stop short at the height of its terror before starting once more. Again and again Bendro shrieked his agony and Melvaig clutched at his ears to try and shut out the awful sound. Bracca, wailing in a chorus of sympathy, nestled against Melvaig who had thrown himself on top of the little boy. They lay there, huddled together under the rotting brick wall, their senses battered into oblivion. Then the pony's screeching rose to a new pitch of torment and everything fell silent. In that sound Melvaig heard all the pain of the world. Embodied in it was all the grief and suffering, fear and horror, he had ever known or seen. It wrenched at his guts and dragged at his mind, threatening to pull him over the abyss into insanity, the only defence. But that release was not to be, even though he did not try, consciously, to resist it. Although the sound had now stopped, it still seemed to hang in the air. Even the crowd had fallen silent and in this strange lull, Melvaig slowly rose and looked out once again over the wall, and in that very moment he realized why they were quiet. They were eating. Bendro was buried under a mass of people and as one came away, clutching a dripping piece of red flesh, so another would take his place.

Suddenly a noise behind him made him turn. Even before his eyes had taken in the scene before him, he knew what he would see. There, in a gap in the wall where the bricks had collapsed, was Gebb, his eyes as cold and hard as rock, his mouth set in the mocking leer of victory. On one side stood Nekdog, pathetically imitating the stance of his leader, while on the other side the giant Shuinn held the horses, four of them. The old man, Arkron, was bound hand and foot and had been lashed across his horse's back.

Arkron spoke, his voice strained with pain and the effort of speech.

'They say they will kill me if you try to escape again. Do not believe them. I am too valuable. Run if you have a chance.'

Melvaig was unable to move. His feet were rooted to the ground, his mind crushed in disappointment, his spirit drained and weary. He had failed. The chance that had been given to him had been taken and lost. Gebb walked slowly towards him, his hand outstretched to take the club. Melvaig was mesmerized, neither afraid nor unafraid, neither frightened nor strong. He was almost relieved to surrender himself to capture once again, where he would not have to think. He did not move when Gebb grasped the club and pulled it out of his hands nor did he do anything when Nekdog gripped Bracca roughly round the waist and carried him away.

Gebb never stopped smiling. He moved one step closer to Melvaig and then with a sudden, savage thrust brought his knee up into his groin. Melvaig collapsed, retching in agony, to the floor. Waves of red mist passed before his eyes and time seemed to stand still. Then he heard a voice in his ear, Gebb's voice, harsh and evil, dripping with malice and hate. One word it uttered, 'Gurrtslagg,' over and over until it seeped through his pain and bore into his consciousness, enfolding his heart with terror.

He was jerked to his feet and thrown next to Arkron over the back of the horse. When his hands and feet were bound, a rope from his hands was passed under the horse's stomach and lashed to his feet, stretching him as if on a rack. As the horse began to move the pain in his groin caught fire again, fuelled by the jarring of the horse. Then a blaze of stars exploded in front of his eyes and mercifully he passed out.

CHAPTER XII

Melvaig recovered consciousness once on the journey. Through a haze of pain he became aware that the horse had stopped. With great effort he lifted his head to see an enormous gate hanging from a square black column of stone. In front of it Gebb was talking animatedly to a group of men dressed in strange garments which seemed to be covered in a number of shiny metal plates. They wore pointed helmets, and carried large maces and spears while the sound of their voices was loud and brash, an arrogant jangle which jarred and grated against Melvaig's battered senses. The Mengoy were holding their jerkins open to show the guards the Tangs on their chests. When the guards seemed to be satisfied, Gebb walked across to the horses and led one of them back. There he opened one of the panniers and began to take out the great slabs of flesh that had once been Sky. While they were standing there bargaining over the size of the bribe, Melvaig turned his attention to the wall that stretched in a straight line for as far as the eye could see. It was black, the same sort of stone as that which formed the gatepost, and was made up of large rectangular blocks. He tried to lift his head to see how high it was but found that he was unable to. From far away came the sounds of hammering and of metal against stone. It was only then that Melvaig realized with a shock of surprise that apart from that sound and the voices of the guards there was almost complete silence. He strained hard to hear the terrible wailing that had so tormented him and after a little while he fancied he could just catch it faintly on the air.

A movement at his side broke into his thoughts. It was Arkron. The old man's head was out of sight on the other side of the horse and Melvaig whispered fiercely two or three times before, to his relief, he got a reply.

'Are you all right?' he said.

'Yes. But you. How are you?' answered the old man.

'I'll be all right. Where are we? Do you know? Where are the outcasts?'

'They are on the other side of the wall. We are through into Eggron. I was conscious for longer than you. After we left there were no more attempts to stop us. They were too busy squabbling over what was left of your horse to see us go, and the further away we got the worse was their condition. They could hardly walk, let alone attack us. Gebb was right. The danger was from those who had not been there long, the newest and freshest of them. The nearer we got to the wall, the nearer to death they were. They did not even have the strength to cry, and the space about the wall was completely empty of them. I suppose it is fear that keeps them away.'

Melvaig's head began to swim again and he felt himself sinking back into oblivion. The last of Arkron's words seemed to come from a long way away and echoed in his head. He heard Arkron calling him but was unable to reply, and then he fell once more into unconsciousness.

When he came to again, it was to the jerking sensation of his hands and feet being untied. Then he was gripped by the hair and pulled off the horse so that he half slid and half fell down to lie in a crumpled heap on the ground. Dazed, he looked around him. His first impression was of a milling mass of people. From where he lay, all he could see were legs, either standing still or shuffling aimlessly around in circles. Their lack of purpose or direction puzzled him and he fought to regain his concentration. The atmosphere around him was smothering, the air filled with low murmurings and heavy with an almost tangible sense of lethargy which weighed upon his soul like a dark cloud. Suddenly he became aware of a disturbance in the crowd, a ripple of commotion spreading towards him. Then he saw a small band of riders making their way through the mass. As they came on, so those in the way parted to make a path for them, and silence fell as the riders passed by. Melvaig desperately scrambled to his feet and as he did so he saw Gebb, Nekdog and Shuinn standing close by. Shuinn held Bracca while Gebb had placed Arkron on a horse and was holding the reins. The riders kept stopping at various intervals and would hold a short discussion before moving on.

Gebb looked across and saw that Melvaig was on his feet. He gave the reins of the horse to Nekdog and, coming over, took Melvaig by his bound wrists and led him across to the others. Arkron looked down from the horse and their eyes met. The old man smiled and Melvaig marvelled to see a glitter of life in his eyes, a spark of hope. It was as if nothing they had been through or that they might endure in the future could ever extinguish that flame in his soul. Melvaig's heart lifted and he answered the smile bravely.

Then Melvaig turned to look at Bracca. The little boy was staring down at the ground, his shoulders hunched over, his face set in an expressionless mask, the lips tight together and his eyes blank. Melvaig stared hard at him as if by doing so he could wrench the boy out of his trance, but no matter how much he concentrated his will, Bracca remained motionless.

The riders were coming nearer. Melvaig saw that one of them had a short thick piece of wood in his hand while a number of large buckets hung at the side of his horse. When they stopped, he would dismount and having apparently come to a decision, he would then daub the faces of those who were in the crowd with green or red or black dye from one or other of the buckets. Always there were some in the crowd who addressed the riders and who appeared more at ease, better dressed and healthier. Now Melvaig began to realize that these were other Mengoy, or simply warrior leaders and that those who were being daubed were captives like himself.

Now the riders were standing in front of Gebb. Their faces alone were enough to put a chill of fear into Melvaig's heart. Two of them had dark glowering eyes sunk back deep on either side of a great hooked nose, their mouths little more than a cruel contemptuous gash. The other two were strikingly different. They were blond, their pink round faces shining and glowing. Their eyes were small and round and bright and seemed under constant threat of sinking into their fat cheeks. A smile played around the thick lips, a sardonic, mocking smile, unsettling and unnerving. Where the two dark ones were thin, these were fat. They sat on their horses, oozing sweat in the heat.

Melvaig was grimly fascinated by the contrast between them and found himself wondering which he was most afraid of. Gebb let go of him and walked up to them. He began to talk quietly and as he did so they looked first at Bracca, then at himself and finally at Arkron. They seemed very excited as they looked at the old man, smiling with satisfaction and apparently well pleased with Gebb. Doubtless Xtlan would reward them well for bringing this Hebbdril to him. One of the blond riders put his hand deep into a bag that was hanging from the back of his saddle and brought out a number of pieces of metal that Melvaig had not seen before. They were rounded and glinted in the light. Gebb received them with ecstasy, bowing low in a cringing gesture of supplication and gratitude. Then one of the dark riders rode across to Arkron and took the old man's horse by the reins. The two men looked at each other and Arkron's gaze was fixed and calm, betraying not a flicker of emotion, his eyes staring straight into those of the warrior until, seemingly unnerved by Arkron's resolute and gentle defiance, the man turned sharply away and returned to the other riders, pulling Arkron's horse along with the old man bobbing up and down on its back, unable to hold the saddle because his hands were tied behind him.

Now Gebb pointed to Melvaig and the eyes of the riders fell upon him. As the Mengoy talked Melvaig could see a look of triumph in his eyes, and around his mouth that same vicious smile that he had turned on him after he had been recaptured. It was the same smile that he had worn when Shuinn had defied him in the desert and now as then it froze the blood in Melvaig's veins. The riders listened attentively, nodding their heads in agreement, eager to please the man who had captured the Hebbdril. After a little time they seemed to shift their attention away from Melvaig and on to Shuinn. They looked at him in much the same way as they had examined Melvaig although the smile on Gebb's lips seemed larger while the coldness in his eyes was even more intense, flickering with the icy dance of revenge. Shuinn must at first have thought that Gebb had picked him out for praise and was perhaps telling these envoys of Xtlan about his bravery and courage and the part he had played in the taking of Arkron and the capture of Melvaig and the boy. He smiled back at Gebb and the riders with a ridiculous expression of self importance and pleasure at being discussed by them, and then as the message from Gebb's eyes bored into his consciousness, the smile seemed to freeze, turning his face into a pathetic mask, empty and dead. The blood drained away from his face and Melvaig saw his eyes mist over with fear. He stood rooted to the spot while the rider with the buckets dismounted and walked briskly over to him. The man dipped his daubing stick into one of the pots of colour and then savagely slapped it down one side of the big man's face leaving a wide band of some thick black substance across his cheek and neck. Shuinn immediately put his hand to his face, wiped it and then looked disbelievingly at the colour on his fingers.

'Gurrtslagg,' he said with a tremor of panic in his voice but quietly, as if speaking only to himself. Then he looked up slowly and fixed his gaze on Gebb, repeating the name of the mines as he did so, louder this time as if it was some magic spell.

All around, the other Mengoy and their captives turned to look at him with a mixture of expressions on their faces. Some were laughing, others smiled, while those few who had also been daubed with the black but did not know what it meant, stared at him with horror. Louder and louder Shuinn shouted the name and then suddenly he stopped and fixed Gebb with an imploring look. His voice changed now. He began whining, and begging with gestures of such abasement that Melvaig found himself growing angry with him. The giant fell to his knees, looking up at Gebb as a whipped dog will look at its master. Inside Melvaig the resolution grew that nothing would ever reduce him to such a state. Nothing was left of Shuinn – all dignity, grace and spirit had drained away in this awful display.

All the time, throughout Shuinn's anguished imploring degradation, Gebb laughed. A full-throated laugh, with his head thrown back and his hands on his hips. The riders too were chuckling in amusement at the spectacle, pointing to him and conferring with each other as if analysing every aspect of the man's grief. Melvaig looked at Nekdog. He was laughing also but his was a false nervous laugh, tremulous with anxiety lest he should be next, yet over-loud as if trying to boost his own confidence, suppress his inner fears and show

Gebb and the others how ridiculous it would be to even contemplate putting him in the same category as this stupid giant.

Shuinn stopped his whining now and began clawing desperately at the black substance on his face but it had dried into a hard crust and when he tried to pull it off, the skin of his cheek stuck to it. He sobbed, the tears glistening as they ran over the black crust and still he tried to scratch away at the stuff on his cheek.

The rider who had marked Shuinn then came over to Melvaig, and, as he had expected, stuck the stick in the pot and slapped the black liquid over his face, standing back then to watch the reaction. The sticky tar-like substance felt heavy and warm on his cheek but inside his emotions were drained. His spirit was numb and this curious lack of feeling left him in a state of invincibility. Nothing, he felt, could harm him and so, glorying in this new strength, he found to his surprise that a smile had unwittingly come to his lips. He looked at Gebb, and the riders and Nekdog, and at all those around who were staring, and he smiled. It was a genuine smile of happiness, not at them but for himself at this discovery.

This was not what Gebb had expected. The laughter froze on his face and an expression of frustrated anger twisted his mouth into a snarl. He strode across swiftly and brought his hand hard against Melvaig's face. Still he smiled and then the riders called to Gebb and started to move away taking Arkron with them. Melvaig, his face still burning from Gebb's blow, found the old man's eyes as Arkron turned in the saddle. There was a happiness in his face which seemed to fill Melvaig with warmth and to banish the hurt of separation. It was as if the old man had seen in Melvaig a sign of the qualities that the young man would need to survive and succeed, and that somehow amidst all the despair and the nightmare landscape of desolation that stretched away behind and ahead of them, there was hope. An indefinable, intangible glimmer it

132

might be, flickering precariously and sometimes seeming to be snuffed out, but nevertheless it would always be there.

Melvaig kept his eyes on Arkron's face as his horse carried him further and further away through the crowd. Frequently the riders would stop to examine and brand the captives and then they would ride on slowly again until finally, almost without realizing it, Arkron was gone. For a few frantic seconds Melvaig's eyes roamed desperately through the sea of heads and faces at the edge of the crowd but the riders had disappeared. He turned sadly away and tried to conquer the emptiness he felt inside.

The waiting was interminable. What they were waiting for, Melvaig could not know but because of the terrible uncertainty as to their fate, time seemed to drag. It was as if it were being held back by some evil force that was using it as a weapon with which to destroy any vestiges of energy or passion that might have been lurking in the souls of the captives. The heat bore down upon them like an enormous weight, crushing the spirit from them as the sweat poured out. In the near distance rose the hill upon which stood the citadel of the Blaggvald. In the hazy grey light the dark, broken shapes blurred together so that they seemed to be almost one solid mass, a massive brooding presence, watching them, revelling in their misery, wallowing in the pain that hung like a cloud above their heads. Melvaig's eyes were drawn to it as they had been the first time he had seen it, an evil web of fear encircling his soul.

Still time passed and nothing happened; nothing moved except for the feet of those who stood and waited. This way and that they shuffled, a pace here, a pace there, moving their feet slowly and deliberately over the brown packed earth as if to try and derive some comfort and reassurance from its stability under their toes. Shuinn was hunched forward on the ground, on his knees, his forehead resting on the earth. He was still, but Melvaig could hear quiet moans from him. Occasionally he would sit bolt upright, suddenly, and stare around him wildly for a few seconds as if woken from a nightmare before going limp once again and returning to his crouch.

Bracca was still in the awful trance from which nothing seemed to be able to shake him. Even Shuinn's display had failed to have any impact on him and the little boy had simply watched, wide-eyed, as the giant, to whom he had seemingly grown so attached, tore himself apart with fear. Then, apparently bored, he had turned away and begun staring once more at the ground. Melvaig wondered desperately whether he might be able to walk over and try to talk to him. Gebb was out of their immediate circle talking to another Mengoy and Nekdog was staring at Shuinn with a mixture of fascination and fear. Very slowly, he shuffled towards the little boy, and as he got nearer to Bracca his heart began to pound in fear of being stopped. Every part of his being ached and yearned to be near his son, to look into his eyes, hold his face in his hands and touch his hair. An all-consuming longing seemed to drag at his stomach and push his feet along faster so that he was sure he would be noticed. Finally, he was standing at Bracca's side. How would Bracca react to him now after the anger and resentment he must have been nurturing at the killing of Sky? During their escape bid together there had been no time to think or speak but now Bracca would be able to respond fully.

'How do you feel, Bracca?' Melvaig said quietly but there was no response.

'Bracca. Are you all right?' Still the little boy said nothing.

Then Melvaig gently placed his hand on Bracca's shoulder and squeezed. He felt the little boy shiver under his grip and then suddenly without raising his head Bracca swung round and threw his arms around Melvaig's legs, letting out a sob that seemed to come from the very depths of his soul, a heart-rending cry that burst out of him with such force that an awful vision flashed into Melvaig's mind of Bracca literally tearing himself apart. Now he was sorry he had tried to break the trance for the dam had burst, the precarious defence that Bracca's mind had erected against all the horrors he had witnessed had been destroyed and now all the pain and confusion was pouring out. Melvaig's heart wept and he felt a sickness well up inside his stomach – a sickness born of remorse and guilt at his selfishness in trying to make contact with Bracca again and the horror he felt at what Bracca was going through. He knelt down and slipped his bound hands behind the little boy's neck so that Bracca's head could rest on Melvaig's shoulder. Now Bracca clung fiercely to his father and all the while his body was convulsed with sobs.

'It's all right, it's all right. I'm here.' The words, repeated over and over like some mystical chant that by repetition would come true, sounded hollow and futile. Worse, they were a lie. Once again, Melvaig felt he had let his little boy down. He had unconsciously closed his eyes in the first rush of grief that had swept from Bracca, as if by not seeing him cry he could shut it out, but now he forced himself to open them and looking around he saw a sea of staring faces. The Mengoy were smiling and laughing in ugly, distorted amusement, while the other captives were unmoving, their expressions dull and defeated and, if anything could be read from their faces, pleased at this diversion that was distracting their minds from their own fate.

Melvaig shut his eyes again to close them out but no sooner had he done so than Nekdog, eager to please Gebb, came to them and wrenched Bracca away from his father. The little boy screamed. Melvaig scrambled to his feet and lunged blindly after him. Nekdog held Bracca out, almost offering him back but just as Melvaig's fingertips brushed his son's arm, the Mengoy scooped him up and threw him through the air to Gebb, standing a few feet away. Melvaig lurched forward in this new direction but once again, just as he came in reach, Gebb tossed Bracca to another Mengoy, a stranger. The little boy was screaming in a piercing high pitched squeal and his arms were outstretched in a pathetic attempt to make it easier for Melvaig to catch him. The awful ritual was repeated and the little boy was thrown to another stranger. The crowd divided to make a passage for Melvaig as he ran after him again, the sound of the mob's laughter stinging his ears and gnawing at his spirit, but still he ran after those little hands held out towards him in desperate supplication. Someone put his foot out and Melvaig fell over it, banging his head on the hard earth as he did so, but he got up again and ran on. Now the crowd were in uproar and their faces merged into a blurred bank of round open mouths. Still he ran, though his heart was breaking with pain and his legs could hardly carry him, until suddenly he came to a wall, the wall of the compound. It was tall and built of stone and he could not see over it but standing against it was a guard and, in his arms, Bracca hung limply. Melvaig stopped running and walked slowly towards them with his head held high and proud. The crowd grew hushed and silent as he approached, wondering what the guard would do. Then as Melvaig approached, the guard contemptuously hurled the little boy towards him. Melvaig caught him and turned back, making his way once more down the passage the crowd had made. Bracca was still, only the occasional long choking sob causing any movement in him. The crowd were silent, the hilarity of some few moments ago at the desperate and ridiculous pursuit by Melvaig had turned now into other, different emotions. The Mengoy were sullen and angry at the guard's action, feeling that it had let them down and that, in some way they could not quite define or understand, Melvaig had emerged with some kind of victory. The other captives were embarrassed and confused by this show of love, shameful at their own earlier conduct and yet at the same time touched with a feeling which buoyed up their hearts, and opened a tiny door at the end of the tunnel of darkness in their minds through which there now shone a faint shaft of golden light.

Melvaig held Bracca close against his chest with the little boy's head resting on his shoulder. Walking like this down the human corridor with all eyes upon him, witnessing his strange and unexpected reward for the humiliation he had endured during his pursuit of Bracca, he felt as if he were walking towards his destiny. He kept his eyes straight ahead, looking up towards the grey sky and suddenly to his amazement a small patch of grey began to break up and through it he saw, for the first time in his life, a vivid glimpse of blue. He would never forget that first sight of the blue sky – the colour was so deep and rich and pure that he could feel his veins singing and his heart lifting up to meet it. And then the sun found this gap in the blanket of grey that had defeated it for so long and it poured its golden rays through – great splintered columns and shafts of light which illuminated the sky and dazzled all who saw it. The crowd raised their heads in astonishment and seemed bewildered – the brilliant light dazzling them so that they had to shut their eyes and turn away. For Melvaig it was another sign of fate – confirmation again of his belief that he had been chosen to play a role in the pattern of history which he could not escape even if he wished to. The sun's rays bathed his face and body in their gentle warmth, playing around his eyelids and his cheeks and filling his head with light, lingering like a halo. He stopped walking and turned Bracca's face into the gold so that he too could feel its glory. The little boy sighed deeply and a smile came to his lips, bringing a look of such deep contentment that Melvaig felt his heart would overflow with relief and gratitude.

Then the light went out as suddenly as it had come. It could not have lasted for more than a few heartbeats yet even now, when the dirty grey-brown layer above their heads had closed over and sealed the gap, the golden aura seemed to remain, lightening the darkness and the misery and lifting his soul above all that was around him. He walked on to where Nekdog and Gebb stood watching over Shuinn, and as soon as he got back he grew aware of an undercurrent of movement in the crowd. Gebb looked at him with an evil leer and then pointed to him to move forward. The passage the crowd had left for him had now closed up but there was a space in front left by those who had walked forward.

Slowly, the crowd moved. The captives were silent and had a condemned air of resignation to their fate. They shuffled along with their heads down while the Mengoy watched over their charges with gleeful anticipation. Melvaig clung to Bracca, letting his love flow through to the little boy. His thoughts were confused but somehow the vision in the sky overwhelmed these so that he was able to see all that was happening now in a far wider context. Faith and confidence began to bolster him up against whatever might happen in the future.

Although it took a long time before they arrived at the gates, for Melvaig it could not be long enough, for every moment they were in the compound was another moment before his inevitable separation from Bracca. Eventually they were in sight of the gates with only three or four groups to go through before them. Some of the guards were sorting out the captives into different areas according to the colour on their faces while others were handing over small pieces of shiny metal to the Mengoy most of whom received them with obvious satisfaction, although some seemed to argue and the sound of voices raised in dissent drifted up into the still air. Melvaig recognized the metal as the same as that which Gebb had received for Arkron.

They moved still nearer to the gates and then Melvaig saw a dreaded and horribly familiar sight. Covered carts lined up outside, similar to the one that Morven had been taken away in, looking as ominous now as they had the first time he had seen them, as he lay with Morven on the slopes outside Ruann. Memories flooded back at the sight of them. So long ago. Painful memories – how he had left Morven crying as he had gone off up the hill to see what was happening in the village. The horror of losing her – of thinking he had found her again in the desert of Molobb and then his hopes being crushed.

Now suddenly they were at the gates. It was their turn. Before Melvaig knew it they were through them and out on the other side. A few paces and then, in a flash, Bracca had been torn from his arms and was being carried roughly away by a guard to a cart at the end from which he could hear women's voices. Bracca had begun to cry again, waving his arms about and lifting his head up so that he could still see his father. No point this time in running after him. Melvaig had tried to resign himself to this moment during their long walk towards the gates but still the pain in his heart swelled and the cries tore at his mind as he watched the little boy being taken further away and finally thrown into the cart. Melvaig raised his hand as if to wave goodbye but it was too late; Bracca had been swallowed up in the bowels of the wagon. Gone. For a second he stood still, stunned with shock, unable to accept that Bracca was no longer with him. Inside himself, a voice screamed 'No'. It rose and rose, getting louder all the time until it seemed as if it would burst forth from him but then he heard another voice – the voice of faith – and it fought to vanquish the other, to banish the horror of losing Bracca for ever under its steadfast message of hope. Have no fear, this other voice said. You will be together again. Only wait, with patience. The strength of your love for each other is too great to be broken in such a way.

And as he listened to the voices, first to one then to the other, across the short expanse of hard bare earth the wagon stood like an ugly black excrescence. From inside Melvaig could just hear the wailing of children while, rising above it, he heard the harsh, strident tones of a woman's voice as she attempted to control her charges. Then the unmistakable crack of leather against flesh rang out and there was silence except for one high-pitched yelp which soon dissolved into a terrible cacophony of cries.

Melvaig recognized Bracca's tone. His stomach heaved and his knees buckled. In a blind fit, his eyes stinging with tears and his head ringing with Bracca's cries, he made as if to lunge towards the wagon but he had hardly taken a step when he felt a sharp searing pain across his back and a harsh voice yelling at him. He turned and saw a guard, the whip in his right hand and a stick in his left with which he was gesticulating angrily towards one of the wagons at the other end of the line from Bracca's. Melvaig looked blankly for a moment at the snarling face of the guard, his back smarting fiercely and then he felt a hand on his arm. Turning, he saw the familiar face of Shuinn. The giant smiled at him. The terror that had been in his eyes when Melvaig had last seen him had given way to a quiet resignation. Melvaig remembered the warmth of the relationship which had grown between Bracca and Shuinn and realized with a shock that the loss of the little boy must have affected the giant as well. Shuinn looked towards Bracca's wagon as if to confirm Melvaig's thoughts and to emphasize their shared loss. The hand on his arm was firm and strong and Melvaig felt himself being led away gently towards their cart, grateful beyond words for the discovery of this friend who shared with him the terror of the Gurrtslagg as well as memories of Bracca.

They stopped and turned round just in time to see Bracca's cart lumbering away up towards the slopes of Eggron. Down by the gates of the compound, Melvaig saw Gebb and Nekdog surrounded by a horde of their fellow Mengoy. They were laughing, heads thrown back, not even looking at the carts. Bracca, Shuinn, Arkron and he were forgotten already, even by those who had delivered them to their fate, and this seemed to be the final indignity.

The sun had now begun to set. The grey sky had broken up into streaks of reds, crimsons and purples but what Melvaig would normally have considered beautiful, he now found obscene as the colours flooded the sky behind Eggron. Rivers of crimson blood appeared to run between the black silhouetted rows of the houses and the ground looked bruised and beaten as the purple light shone down upon it.

Once again he felt Shuinn's grip on his arm and turning away he walked slowly up the plank to vanish into the blackness of the cart.

CHAPTER XIII

The wheels rumbled as the wagon creaked along the road, jarring Melvaig where he lay on his back on the floor. Every time it came to a bump he braced himself for the moment it would crash down again, holding himself up on his elbows so that he would be spared the full impact. The wagon itself filled the air with groans as the horses dragged it along, the sound of its sufferings an expression of sympathy for the misery of those inside it.

The air was heavy with the pungent stench of sweating bodies and when Melvaig had first entered the cart with Shuinn and had scrambled over the arms and legs of those who were already inside, he had been assailed by a chorus of shouts and grumbles as he trod first on someone's hand, then a leg, then a chest until finally he had found a spot in one of the corners over a wheel, an unpopular place and so left by everyone else. Shuinn had forced a way next to him and had lain down alongside.

Now only the sounds of the wagon and the occasional neigh of one of the horses broke the silence. At first Melvaig had been unable to see anything in the darkness but now he guessed that the sun was coming up, as chinks of daylight began to shine upon a foot or part of a jerkin or sometimes a face. He could now make out two guards sitting slumped on seats at the rear end of the wagon, seemingly asleep. All around him in the gloomy half-light lay the inert bodies of his travelling companions. They appeared to have nothing in common with each other except the awful black mark on all their faces. Otherwise their style of dress differed, from the simple jerkin of Melvaig and one or two others through the embroidered colour of Shuinn's tunic to the finery and colour of three fat figures who lay across from Melvaig, who guessed that they must have been officials who had somehow incurred the wrath of Xtlan. These three lay, their eyes open and staring, utterly defeated. Their mouths twitched with nerves and the heavy jowls around their necks quivered with the shaking of the cart. The gilt and brocade on their clothing had become tattered, torn and dirty and the blood on their faces bore witness to the treatment they had already received.

Melvaig turned away just as the cart crashed over yet another bump. This time he had not been ready for it and the small of his back landed on the wooden floor with a crack that knocked him sick and winded him. Time to think now. Of Morven, of Bracca – but the pain of his memories was too strong and he banished them from his mind with a huge effort of will. He thought of Ruann and his life there, the security and happiness of those years which he had taken for granted. Pictures of Jarrah came before his eyes and then confusingly became jumbled up with the face of Arkron and then his fingers, resting on his chest, found the shape of the bag hanging around his neck under the jerkin. He had almost forgotten it was there and now he was flooded with a sudden feeling of elation as memories of the Book began to come back to him and he heard again Arkron's telling of the story.

How long he would have remained in his other world he would never know, for a pain in his bowels, that grew worse with every bump and jolt of the cart, forcibly dispelled the visions in his mind and reluctantly he let them slip away. There was no way of knowing when the cart would stop so he would have to shit now or risk the pain getting so bad that it would debilitate him. He had seen others doing it through what he presumed was a hole in the bottom of the cart near the opposite wall, so he got up and carefully made his way over the bodies of the others until he found a space in the human carpet in the centre of which was, as he had guessed, a hole in the floor. The wooden boards around it were running with filth and the stench stung his nostrils and made him want to heave. All eyes were on him as he trod carefully over and, after removing his lower garments and ripping a small piece of his jerkin sleeve off, proceeded to squat down over the hole as best he could. There were two wooden handles attached to the wall but even with the aid of these to hang on to it was incredibly difficult to ensure that he was above the hole at all times. He also found it unnerving to have this most private of activities watched by all these people. Even the guards were now looking on with amusement at his struggle to remain steady as the cart bumped and rolled relentlessly on. His head swam with nausea from the smell and from the effort, but he persevered until eventually he was rewarded with success but just at the crucial moment the wagon hit a huge bump and he was thrown over on to one of the watching captives. A horrified shout burst into the air as the man leapt up, frantically shaking his soiled hand. As the others saw and realized what had happened a ripple of laughter spread through them and gained momentum when the guards joined in, until the sound filled the cart. For the captives it was a release into which they channelled all their anxieties and fears so that many of them became convulsed with uncontrollable fits until the tears rolled down their cheeks. Even Melvaig, who had hurriedly wiped himself and got dressed again, found himself infected with the tide of laughter so that despite himself a smile started to play around his lips as he watched the unfortunate victim wiping his hand against the wall to try and clean it. Then the man turned and saw Melvaig's look of amusement and finding it too much for his pride to bear, he flung himself on to Melvaig who fell backwards heavily on to a cushion of flesh as the man's hand gripped his neck and shook it until his head started wobbling stupidly. The men he had fallen on scrambled quickly out from under him and Melvaig grew aware of a chorus of shouts as all the captives became involved in this unexpected diversion and started yelling encouragement and abuse to one or the other of the fighters. Melvaig now had his hands fastened tightly round his assailant's neck and was pressing his thumbs against the man's Adam's apple. He felt the hands slacken slightly and was just about to summon up the strength to try and throw him off when he saw one of the guards bring down a heavy wooden club on the back of the man's head with a loud crack. Immediately the hands came loose and he flopped forward heavily on to Melvaig, pinning him to the floor. Then the guard picked the unconscious man up and tossed him into a space where he landed with a thump and lay perfectly still in a heap of jumbled limbs.

The captives, so vociferous such a short time earlier, were now silent and wary, looking first at the guard who had stayed at the back and then at the other, the one who had stopped the fight. Melvaig got to his feet fast, his heart quickening in anticipation of what the guard might do to him. He felt the guard's narrow eyes looking at him carefully and saw his hand clench around the handle of the club but then to Melvaig's relief he turned and went back to join his companion. It was a strange atmosphere that emanated from the captives, partly relief and partly disappointment – their blood had been sent racing in turn by laughter, excitement and tension and now there was no release from it and it remained pent up and simmering inside them.

Melvaig felt the air crackle around him as he made his way carefully back in between bodies towards his spot against the wall. He looked at no one but was aware of their eyes boring into him until at last he saw Shuinn and lay down in his space next to the giant. Shuinn smiled, a warm welcoming smile and Melvaig once again was grateful for the man's presence. Finding his spot again, and having someone there to greet him, was almost like coming home and Melvaig was surprised to find himself suffused with a sense of security which had been unknown to him since he had left Ruann. He looked across at the body of his assailant and saw with relief that the man had begun to stir and was gingerly feeling his head where the club had caught it. He had a mane of thick black hair that hung down in greasy strands and clumps over his shoulders and the face was rounded and squashed. Melvaig guessed that the man was about his age but somehow this slightly babyish face made him look younger. As Melvaig was watching, he suddenly moved his head so that, to Melvaig's embarrassment, their eyes met. For an instant Melvaig assumed there was anger in them but then he perceived that instead they were swimming with pain, the pain of humiliation and defeat and he thought with shame of his part in the man's degradation – the laughter that must have stung his spirit and finally goaded him into attacking Melvaig. He tried to hold the man's eye and to transmit an apology to him but the man lowered his head quickly and turned away.

Melvaig turned on to his stomach and was surprised to see a thin shaft of light shining on to the floor by his side. It was coming through a small gap between two of the planks in the side of the cart and fortunately it was just at eye level. He shifted himself across slightly, nearer to Shuinn and tried to look through the hole by putting his right eye up against it. He could see out but the field of vision was too small to make any sense of what he saw. He would have to try and make the hole bigger. Slowly and carefully, so as not to alert the guards or any of the other prisoners he began pulling at the wood round the hole and Shuinn, realizing what Melvaig was doing, began to help. The wood was old, probably in use Before the War and salvaged from something else to make the cart, and it had begun to get worn and rotten along the joints, so that it was not long before they enlarged the hole enough to give a good view outside. Melvaig kept three of the longest and thickest splinters of wood and put them inside his jerkin. They were sharp and pointed and it occurred to him that they might be of use some time. Then, with a feeling of excitement, he put his eye to the hole and looked out.

They were travelling along a wide, flat road which looked as if it had been made out of one long continuous smooth piece of stone except for the numerous cracks and fissures that patterned it. Out of these cracks weeds grew – pushing up out of the ground and forcing their way towards the light, criss-crossing the grey road with lines of green.

At the side of the road, Melvaig saw nothing but buildings. All were in ruins but, even so, many were still tall and seemed to Melvaig to soar way above him so that he could not see the top of them. Sometimes he would see one that people had attempted to repair, and the contrast between the old and the new would strike him as bizarre. The buildings that were still reasonably intact or that had been repaired appeared to be occupied. Voices drifted up into the hot dry air and horses were tied up outside. Sometimes numbers of riders, all men, could be seen travelling along the street talking and laughing loudly, their voices echoing amongst the buildings and the clatter of hooves ringing out into the silence. Melvaig would hear them coming a long time before they passed in front of his vision. Many of them wore strange, colourful clothes and he wondered if any of these strange garments had come from the time Before the War.

Once he heard, in the distance, the steady tramp of many feet forced into the pace of a march rather than a walk. Mingled with it were hoofbeats, shouts and the cracks of a whip. The sound grew nearer and, as it passed, the rhythmic drumming of the feet reverberated up into the cart and Melvaig saw a column of prisoners trudging along the road, hardly able to pick up their feet, their heads sunk deep into their shoulders and their backs rounded with weariness. As they passed before his gaze, one fell down. A neighbour stopped and tried to pick him up but one of the guards rode up and brought a whip lashing down on them both. The one who had tried to help jumped back with a yelp of pain, clutching his hands, but the other lay inert as a streak of blood ran out of a gash on his forehead where the whip had caught him. Then his arms moved and he tried to raise himself but he had not the strength or the will. The guard shouted and brought the whip down again on to the man's back. Again and again it fell as his fellow prisoners, who had stopped, stared open-mouthed and vacant. The jerkin that had provided a little protection at first had now been cut to shreds, exposing his back. Melvaig watched, horrified, as the whip now started to take away the flesh, each lash sending a shudder through the man's body. Then, as the cart moved slowly on, the ghastly scene slid away out of his sight so that all he could hear was the merciless crack as the whip continued to fall relentlessly down on to its victim.

Inside the cart the atmosphere was charged with fear. Each man felt the whip on his own back as the sound rang out and was sick in his groin with the pain until eventually, thankfully, the noise receded into the distance and vanished.

Later they passed another group of captives, working on

some buildings and once when they came near to the wall, Melvaig saw numbers of captives as far as the eye could see breaking up stone, carrying it, fitting and shaping and laying it for the erection of this fortification round Eggron, the inner enclave of Xtlan.

Another time they passed a cart much like their own which had apparently just stopped, as the back was being opened and a number of girls and young women were being herded out and directed into one of the buildings at the side of the road. Many were crying, their clothes were ragged where they had been ripped apart, and they scrambled down clutching what remained of their garments around themselves in a pathetic attempt to conceal their nakedness from the probing eyes of the guards and the collection of finely dressed officials who had gathered for the arrival of this new batch of Elimsorr. They jeered and shouted as the girls were forced to parade past them and a roar of laughter burst out when one of the girls tripped and fell, exposing herself to them completely as she lay spreadeagled on the ground. It was too much for one of the officials, who tore his clothes off and jumped upon the girl forcing his way into her to the delight of the crowd who shouted their encouragement to the man.

Melvaig was stricken with guilt and shame to find excitement rising in him also. He looked away and then his mind reeled with shock as he spotted one of the girls climbing down from the cart. He only saw her face for an instant but it seemed to Melvaig as if she looked directly at him. Morven! He fought to hold her eyes but she turned away and was gone, lost among the other girls, leaving his body tingling, every nerve end raw as a storm of tangled emotions raged through him. Morven. He said the name quietly to himself as if to convince himself that it had not been a dream. Then as his cart trundled on, leaving the scene behind it, doubts began to chip away at his certainty. He tried to picture again the face he had seen but it blurred and refused to stand still. Was it his mind playing tricks on him? The more he tried to recall it the harder it became, yet when he stopped trying there was Morven's face looking at the wagon. She held her head tilted slightly to one side and her body was poised in the way he knew so instinctively. Relief, anger, crushing disappointment, joy and sickening worry fought each other for supremacy in his mind, each victorious in turn for a second before yielding to its successor. He buried his head in his hands and closed his eyes in an attempt to control his mind but the blackness inside his head made it worse so he raised his eyes again and tried to focus on the buildings; to concentrate on them and blot out all thoughts of her but it was impossible. Images of her kept flooding back, running over the hills near Ruann, lying in the heather, rolling over with Bracca, tickling him – the sounds of their laughter bringing music into his soul. He pictured them making love together – the soft white voluptuousness of her body, their joy with each other. Then the image fell apart as he remembered where he had seen her and what Arkron had told him of the Elimsorr and his mind recoiled in horror while his stomach churned over in sickness.

On and on went his tortured spirit, lurching from one emotion to another, endlessly, like a great wheel. Eventually, thankfully, the strain wore him out and he became so exhausted that he fell asleep, crushed beneath the weight of his mind, while the wheel continued to roll under him, disturbing his sleep and punctuating it with little nightmarish fragments.

He woke to the feel of a hand clamped over his mouth and instinctively he struggled, panic-stricken, to free himself from its grip. But another hand was also holding him by the shoulder and as he struggled under it, a stab of pain shot out and forced him to be still. Then he remembered where he was and through the gloom, for now it had gone dark, he saw Shuinn's face looking down at him. It was the giant who had been holding him to the floor. Melvaig's mind raced in confusion but then Shuinn took his hand off Melvaig's bad shoulder and, putting a finger to his lips in a gesture of silence, slowly removed the hand from his mouth. From the signs that Shuinn then began to make, Melvaig guessed that he must have been shouting in his sleep and he smiled at the giant and patted him on the shoulder, hoping that Shuinn would realize that this was an indication of thanks. Shuinn nodded his head, returned the smile and then lay down again. Melvaig wished that they spoke the same language. Up until they had taken Bracca, there had always been someone with whom he could communicate. With Arkron he had been able to share his worries and his fears but now there was no one. All his thoughts were private. He felt a terrible isolation, utter loneliness, and it somehow seemed pointless and futile even to think. He began to long for someone with whom he could talk. Perhaps there would be somebody from Ruann at the mines. Maybe, given time, he could learn Shuinn's language and Shuinn could learn his. In the darkness the cart had stopped and Melvaig lay awake, staring into the pitch blackness and thinking. He was calmer now. Why, he did not know, but the sense of destiny and guidance had returned so that he was able to look on all that had happened and was happening with a curious feeling of detachment. If only he could cultivate this feeling and be able to summon it at will, he would be so much stronger. He thought of the mines and of all the fear they engendered and yet he felt, at this moment, a confidence and certainty that he would live through them. He thought of Morven and Bracca and knew that they would all be together again at some time in the future. Yet also he knew that this certainty would vanish as easily and inexplicably as it had come, that the shield of near invincibility that he wore at these times would crumble before the onslaught of pain, suffering and deprivation, whether in himself or others.

He turned towards Shuinn and wondered how the giant's mind worked. How strange that he should feel such an affection for him now. He thought of the closeness which had arisen between the giant and Bracca and then he remembered the look on Shuinn's face when the black mark had been daubed on him and he had realized that he was being betrayed and was being sent to the Gurrtslagg. Now his eyes were shut and Melvaig could hear him snoring quietly. His crop of short straw-coloured hair protruded at odd angles from his head and the stubble on his face had grown so that it was almost like a short beard. Even his features seemed to Melvaig to have lost much of their harshness.

Eventually, morning came and the cart started to move again. Melvaig turned over to lean on his elbows and look out through the gap and was surprised to see that there were no more houses. Instead they seemed to be climbing a hill that was sparsely covered in grass and heather. He looked down the slope up which they had travelled and saw the collection of houses in a valley beneath them, while at the far end he could just make out the enclosure. On the opposite side of the valley rose the hill upon which stood the Blaggvald. It was higher than the slope the cart was on and Melvaig looked across and up to it where it lay, exuding an atmosphere of evil so oppressive and dominant that Melvaig once again felt its chill grip close around his heart. One tower rose above the rest, its black windows like the eyes of some terrible creature looking out over its domain and Melvaig was certain that he could feel Xtlan's gaze upon him.

Inside the cart, it was even more oppressive than usual; not the usual airless dry heat but a humid atmosphere that pressed relentlessly in upon them. Melvaig looked up through his gap in the side and saw to his surprise that a great bank of darkness had covered half the sky. As he watched, it moved slowly towards them, blotting out the pale rays from the sun and plunging them into gloom.

The guards opened the top part of the doors at the back of the cart and all eyes looked out as the gathering storm clouds loomed high above them. The silence was intense, only broken by a loud whinny from one of the horses. Then Melvaig heard a rush of wind outside. Looking out through the back he saw the branches of a large hawthorn blowing about and the dust from the cart being carried up into the air in a little cloud before being scattered.

The wind grew rapidly stronger and then, as suddenly as it had started, it stopped and a breathless hush descended again. Melvaig put his eye to the gap and looked out. There was an unearthly light everywhere, an ethereal yellow pallor which filled the air with a luminescent glow. Melvaig heard a sound on the road and looking down saw a small dark spot appear on the dusty surface. Then another sound and another spot appeared, another and another, until suddenly the rain was pouring down in torrents, covering the track with little rivers as the water lashed down on to the hard ground. Ferociously the sky emptied its load so that solid-seeming sheets of water landed on the track with such force that the splashes bounced back high up into the air.

The rain drummed deafeningly on to the roof of the cart and within seconds little drips had begun to fall through on to those unfortunate enough to be under any leaks. Soon the savage downpour had found a way through almost every part so that there was nowhere to escape. Water dripped almost continuously on Melvaig's head and another stream of rain fell down his back. Shuinn had moved closer to him, trying to avoid a particularly bad patch above his head. He tried to move backwards, further into the cart, but his foot came up against something soft and an angry shout and a sharp blow with a fist on to his ankle forced him to go back. His jerkin was now soaked and a cold wetness enveloped him, while the water dripped over his head and down his neck. On the floor water sloshed from one side to the other as the cart lurched along forcing him to lift himself up off the floor on his elbows and hands until the water ran away again to another part. He tried standing, holding on to the cracks and crevices in the wall of the cart but the bucking and tossing made this too precarious and he fell on to Shuinn. He tried squatting on his haunches but again this proved impossible so he returned again to lying down.

How much longer would the rain continue? He remembered these occasional rains in Ruann, greeted as they were with a mixture of huge relief yet apprehension at the damage that they might cause. Sometimes they had lasted for only half a day, at others much longer. Inside the cart, above the noise of the rain, he could hear angry shouts and involuntary cries as the captives tried to avoid the relentless drips and the water on the floor, banging into one another as they did so. Then suddenly there was a loud crash and the cart veered crazily over at a steep angle, Melvaig's end going down while the opposite end rose high into the air. In an instant he found himself buried in bodies as the prisoners slid and fell on top of him. An elbow scraped against his cheek and a knee came up in his stomach as the man on top tried to raise himself. He screamed in anger but the sound got no further than his lips, muffled and absorbed by the bodies. A wave of panic rose inside him, a terrible blind panic as he found himself unable to move, every limb pinned down, paralysed, not even capable of shielding his face. Light began to flash before his eyes, gold and silver bursts filled the darkness in his head, until it felt as if it would suddenly split open to let them escape. Then he felt his arm gripped by a hand and was aware of a violent surge of movement at his side. A body suddenly fell against him and he knew it was Shuinn. The giant put an arm around Melvaig's waist and then raised his knee so that his foot rested on the boards beneath it like a spring. Melvaig instinctively knew what Shuinn was about to do and braced himself as best he could. The giant then exploded forward, the thrust from his coiled leg giving him the impetus to burst through the bodies piled on top. Melvaig felt as if he was being torn limb from limb as Shuinn dragged him out. Angry voices rose on all sides as the giant found a foothold against a body and lunged forward again. How many times he hurled himself on in this way Melvaig did not know but each time they gained a little ground, squeezing, pushing, shoving and elbowing their way through the tangle of bodies and limbs. Melvaig's strength and energy soon faltered but Shuinn had the power of two and pulled him on until at last they felt air on their faces and were able to breathe freely again, the rain splashing down upon them seeming to Melvaig to be the most welcome sensation he had ever known. They scrambled forward with other prisoners up the sloping floor of the cart until they reached the open doors at the back. Then they jumped down into the teeming rain, landing amongst a small group of captives who were standing in a huddle looking lost and bemused as the muddy water flowed around their ankles.

Melvaig saw that the back wheel of the cart had fallen over a sharp drop at the edge of the road. The thought of escape flashed through his mind as he saw no sign of the guards and his blood quickened, but then they came into view from the other side of the cart. The two who had ridden inside with the captives had been joined by some others whom Melvaig assumed to be the drivers. They all walked purposefully across, their heads bent against the rain and then they began gesticulating and shouting to the prisoners. Those who understood the language then started to walk slowly and dejectedly over to the rear end of the cart, splashing and slipping in the mud as they did so. Melvaig glanced at Shuinn and they followed, scrambling down the little embankment over which the cart had fallen and finding a place from where they could push. Melvaig was so drenched with rain now that it no longer bothered him; but the thick squelching mud around his ankles frustrated him and made him angry for, every time he tried to push, his feet just slid backwards. As more prisoners got out of the cart, the area around Melvaig became thick with heaving bodies, each desperately trying to show the guards, who wandered round cracking their whips and shouting, that they were putting all their strength into the effort.

In front of him, Melvaig could see the two fat, finely clothed administrators. Their podgy faces were drawn and pale and their heavy jowls shook with the effort of pushing. The guards seemed to be particularly vindictive towards them, either kicking their legs from under them or else lashing out with a whip across their buttocks. Melvaig could sense the sweet revenge against all their sort, which the guards were extracting out of the changed fortunes of these two and he looked away. There was something so revoltingly flabby about them that he had begun to find himself laughing with the guards at their humiliation, revelling in their pain, and the experience of these feelings within himself shocked him.

Eventually, the wagon began to slide slowly forward. Bit by bit the bottom scraped along the ridge so that those who had been pushing from underneath had to get out and join those at the back. At last, only the two rear wheels were wedged against the embankment that led up to the road. Now the guards told them to lift the cart to avoid breaking the wheels. Gradually the heavy cart rose up so that, with the horses still pulling, it suddenly lurched forward on to the road.

Immediately the captives rushed forward, anxious to get out of the terrible rain. Shuinn grabbed Melvaig by the arm and they forced their way through the crush so that they were among the first to get back up into the cart. They made their way gingerly over the slippery floor until they reached their places at the far end. Melvaig was about to sit down when in the gloom he saw the dark shapes of two men lying bunched up together against the back wall. Quickly he moved across to them. They were dead, crushed or asphyxiated as he had almost been when the cart first tipped up. Shuinn came over and they pushed the two bodies along the floor towards the doors. More hands grabbed them, and then more until they were thrown out into the mud. Then the guards climbed up, shut the doors behind them and gave a loud shout, at which the cart started once more to lurch along the track.

The atmosphere inside the cart now was heavy with depression. It hung over the captives like a black shroud. They stood, squatted or lay in their attempts to avoid the wet though by now they were all soaked to the skin. Their legs were encased in mud from the track and many of them had their arms and faces spattered as well from where they had slipped and fallen. The pool of water on the floor rolled and sloshed from one side to the other as if it had a will and a mind of its own. The image of the two bodies lingered in their minds; the faces twisted in agony and the crushed and broken limbs flopping uselessly about as they were pushed up the cart and out on to the track. Without Shuinn, Melvaig knew that he would have been with them. Would that have been better? A blessed relief from everything. An escape. No more suffering, no more worry. Then he thought of Morven and Bracca and of the Book that still hung round his neck and the conviction returned to him that one day he would be with them again in the world of green that Arkron had described to him from its pages. Again, his spirits were lifted as he contemplated the visions that filled his head, seemingly so real to him that he felt it was impossible for them not to exist. And he would find this world; of that, suddenly, he was sure. With Morven and with Bracca. That was the destiny which he had felt driving his spirit ever since he was young. He recalled again the certainty he had felt when Arkron had finished reading to him that it was Ashgaroth who was watching over him, and his spine tingled with excitement. Now all thoughts of death, of escape, suddenly seemed to be ridiculous, impossible, while there was so much worth fighting for. He lifted his hand up to the bag round his neck and felt the solid weight of the Book, as if to reassure himself.

Melvaig's thoughts were interrupted by a feeling that the cart was slowing down. He heard shouts, muffled by the rain, and he heard the drivers call out. Suddenly the doors of the cart were opened with a loud crash and the damp chill of the rain swept in across the captives. The guards jumped out and began yelling at them to get down. At first the captives near the door remained still, gripped by an intense lethargy. The damp that had seeped through to their bones, the gnawing pains of hunger that made them feel dizzy and faint, and above all fear, had combined to paralyze them so that movement seemed not only an enormous effort but also one that was utterly pointless. Then a whip cracked viciously and a piercing scream split the air, penetrating the befuddled minds of the captives and galvanizing them into shoving past each other in their frantic attempts to get off the cart before the whip fell on them. Melvaig and Shuinn were among the last and as they jumped down they passed the unfortunate man who had been picked as an example. He was lying on his side, his knees hunched up to his chin, and he was clutching himself around the groin, whimpering like a baby. For an instant Melvaig hesitated and then he went over to him and tried to take his arm to help him. Shuinn took the other and together they lifted the man down. Then with a shoulder under each arm they made their way after the other captives but the man was in too much pain, crying out when his feet caught on the ground, so the giant lifted him up and carried him in his arms.

Melvaig looked around. Through gaps in the rain he could make out a large valley that swept away below them down a barren rocky slope. Looking up he saw other hills stretching out all around the valley encircling it like an enormous amphitheatre. The other captives were crossing a natural rock bridge that went over a steep ravine. On either side of the bridge the ravine plunged down further than he could see, its sides littered with jagged protruding rocks. Melvaig guessed that in the old world, a river would have cascaded along the bottom all the time and not just occasionally, as now, when torrents of rain had struck and the narrow ravine echoed to the sounds of the old river. As Melvaig crossed the bridge he could hear those sounds far below, a plunging, rushing, shout of water, hurtling headlong with a raw energy that was like life itself. It was so exuberant in its joy that those who heard it felt themselves touched by a power that never left them. In the old world such wonders were all around for those who could hear, but now they were few. Melvaig had heard the river that ran down from Mount Ruann on the rare occasions that the rains had come and had listened in awe then as he listened now to this majestic song, but never before had he heard it with the knowledge that he now possessed and it seemed as if it was the voice of Ashgaroth talking to him, giving him strength and hope and faith.

Slowly they made their way over the bridge, heads down under the pouring rain, and when they arrived on the far side they found they were, with the other captives, on a large man-made area of flat earth, cut into the side of the hill. At the far end, built against the sheer rock wall of the hill, was a large wooden hut and it was towards this that they now walked slowly, each man reluctant to meet the fate that awaited him. The guards shouted and cracked their whips in an attempt to hurry them on but still the ragged column refused to quicken its pace. As Melvaig looked at the guards it suddenly occurred to him that, had the prisoners all acted together in a concerted movement, they could easily have overrun the guards, so few were they. Again plans of escape flashed through his head. Somebody would have to make the first move and initiate a rush to escape. Would the others follow or would they leave him to be caught; and what fate then would await him? He could make the move with Shuinn but two alone would have no chance. He looked at the other prisoners, beaten and crushed, the flower of life withered inside them, each with his eyes fixed on the ground in front. No, he thought; they would turn their heads and look but it was impossible to conceive of them doing more. He felt angry with them and his anger grew worse the nearer they got to the doors of the hut and the more he saw the possibility of escape disappear. Now suddenly it was too late, for the double doors had been swung open and the head of the little column had vanished inside as if it had been devoured by the mountain. Melvaig watched as each man, just before he entered the hut, raised his head and lifted his eyes up to the sky as if he knew that this was the last time he would see daylight. The rain, which had seemed so cursed, now was like a blessing, baptizing their anguished faces with its drops of cool clear liquid and its unique light.

Melvaig too lifted his head when the doors were only paces away and let the rain and the light cast their spell upon him.

And the vision that appeared before him was Ashgaroth, coming before him for an instant in a shimmering cascade of light. Almost as soon as he appeared he was gone, yet the image that Melvaig saw never diminished in clarity nor in power, so awesome was its majesty. And through all the dark days ahead, the sound of the song of the river and the vision he had seen in that timeless moment, sustained and nourished him so that he never felt lost or abandoned or deserted for he had only to recall them and his spirit would lift and his soul would fly and the spark of hope would once again rekindle in his heart.

CHAPTER XIV

The doors of the shed banged shut and for a few moments Melvaig could see nothing. No one moved except the guards. The captives waited in silence; their breathing was harsh and heavy with fear. The weight of the injured man was starting to cause a twinge of pain in Shuinn's back and he tried to let the man take some weight on his own feet but as he did so, a cry of pain escaped from his throat, shattering the silence, and Shuinn painfully lifted him up again.

Melvaig's eyes were growing used to the gloom and he could see at one end of the shed, a large pile of rocks, all of a roughly uniform size, heaped up to the roof. Around the walls were some tallow candles throwing out a flickering yellow light and in this light the rocks seemed to glint with little shimmering specks which danced before his eyes. Ahead he could see, over the heads of the others, a grey wall of rock with a large fissure in it, just about the height of a man and as wide as a horse. The entrance to the Gurrtslagg. He could see nothing through the entrance except a deep, dark blackness and his heart started to beat a little faster.

Suddenly a loud noise rang out in the shed and seemed to travel down into the mine, echoing as it did so until finally it died away, lost in the body of the earth. It was the sound of a horn. Melvaig looked and saw one of the guards raise it to his lips and, standing in the entrance, give another long blast. Then silence fell once more; the captives gripped with a paralysing fear of the unknown and the guards standing still, their heads held at an angle as if they were listening for something. Only the rain, drumming on the wooden roof of the shed could be heard, and Melvaig found himself wishing he was back in the cart, in his corner. The sound of the rain took him back there and to his surprise, he remembered it with affection, the hole he had managed to make in the wall and the pattern and grain of the planks.

His thoughts were interrupted by the sound of another horn, answering the first, which came drifting out almost lazily, seeming to get louder as its low mournful tone floated up into the shed, passed over their heads and then vanished into the hills outside. Melvaig looked at the guards. They seemed relieved, chatting away excitedly to one another, joking and laughing. Soon the sound of footsteps could be heard from the entrance. Slow and heavy, the steady smacking of feet on stone came nearer until, standing in the stone archway, Melvaig saw a man. He walked forward and was followed by another and then another. They stood for a moment, looking at the captives, and the light from the candles bathed their ugly features in a yellow pallor, playing upon their lips, their flat squashed noses and their heavy jowls and accentuating the bulbous protruding eyes, heavy-lidded and rheumy, that cast around over the captives.

Their bodies were huge, all three of them dwarfing Shuinn, their great barrel chests seeming about to split the goathide tunics they wore. Their legs and arms, uncovered and thick with hair, revealed strands of sinew that flickered with every movement, wedges of muscle that rolled as they walked. At the sight of them, Melvaig felt overcome by sickening terror. Even the guards, laughing and talking only a few moments before, had fallen deathly silent, mesmerized by their presence. They smiled as they looked at the sea of frightened faces that gazed at them; a smile of the mouth only, while the eyes widened, the heavy lids drew back and an expression of the most terrible cold cruelty flooded out from them. These were the Hurll, the dreaded guards of the Gurrtslagg, hand-picked by Xtlan for their strength and their extreme viciousness, who wallowed in heartless savagery. They owed loyalty directly to Xtlan, answered solely to him, their job the creation of a place so terrible that its very existence would be enough to control the disparate subjects of his realm. The mention of its name was usually sufficient to quell any murmur of dissent that there might be. And these men, the Hurll, were the cruellest and most evil that Xtlan could find in all his terrible kingdom. They moved slowly over to the guards from the cart who, having exchanged words briefly with them, left as quickly as they were able, almost stumbling over themselves in their efforts to get out of the shed. As the doors opened, and the light from outside flooded in, a great bellow was let out by the Hurll who flung their hands over their eyes to shield them until the doors were shut. Melvaig, at the back, could hear the guards running away over the bridge and the neigh of the horses as they were whipped savagely to take them from the mines.

Now the captives were left, terrified, gripped with a sense of utter isolation, at the merciless whim of this terrible place. Melvaig's stomach fluttered and danced in the anguished sickness of fear. One of the Hurll gestured towards the entry and with his head down one of the captives at the front scuttled as fast as he could across the short stretch of beaten earth that separated him from the dark opening in the rock. The others followed, in single file, as the Hurll stood at one side and watched, inspecting each captive carefully as he walked past, implanting him in their memory, judging his strength from the body and his character from the face. They stopped some to examine them more carefully. The two officials, their once-fine garments now ripped and spattered in mud, were stopped and the Hurll, laughing cruelly, gripped their faces by the chin, spat in their eyes and then savagely kicked them through the entrance. Others, on an impulse, were given a lash across the back or the shoulders and their cries of pain echoed down into the mine, bouncing off the walls with a strange reverberating rhythm.

Eventually, after what seemed an interminable wait, Melvaig and Shuinn, having shuffled forward as the column moved, now found themselves passing in front of the Hurll. Shuinn, in front, was stopped. One of the Hurll, who was completely bald, grabbed the hair of the man Shuinn was carrying and pulled so that he fell out of Shuinn's arms and landed heavily on the floor. He let out a shriek of pain and Shuinn moved forward instinctively to help him up, but as he did so, another of the Hurll brought his whip down across Shuinn's chest and Melvaig saw his friend hunch forward, clutching himself. Then Shuinn looked up and met the eyes of his attacker. Melvaig's mind flashed back to the compound when Shuinn had learned of his betrayal by Gebb and for an instant he feared that his friend would crumble again but to his relief, whatever had happened in Shuinn's mind since that occasion remained constant now, and the look he gave the Hurll was steady and unflinching. Melvaig saw Shuinn's mouth clamped together in an expression of repressed rage, his eyes narrowed in anger as he took his arms from around his chest. The goatskin jerkin had split where the whip had cut into it and three lines of red oozed slowly out. All three of the Hurll were standing in front of him now, looking at him with smiles on their faces, confident of their superiority, waiting for him to challenge them further so that they could have some fun with him. Melvaig, anxious to prevent any further trouble, grabbed him by the arm and pulled him towards the opening. At the feel of his friend's hand, the giant seemed to shake himself out of the grip of his anger and with a look at the injured man on the floor, whose eyes were wide and staring with fear, he turned sharply round and moved off quickly towards the black entrance into the mine.

As soon as they had passed under the little stone archway they could hear cries of pain behind them from the man they had left. The Hurll were obviously enjoying themselves and at each cry Melvaig and Shuinn involuntarily flinched and a prick of guilt stabbed into their guts at leaving him. They were descending a very steep flight of stone steps, cut into the rock, which led them down a smoothly rounded tunnel, just large enough for a man to walk in with ease. The steps were worn into a groove in the middle, and an old wooden handrail ran along one wall. Melvaig guessed that the tunnel had been here since Before the War and as his foot trod on the steps and his hand ran over the smooth wood, he tried to look back to those times and imagine the people who had used these same steps and this rail to help them as they went down into the earth. He tried to conjure up in his mind a picture of the old world and the lives they had gone back up to, using Arkron's description as a guide, but he found it impossible, so dominant and powerful was the present, and he even began to wonder whether the whole idea of a world Before the War was a myth. But then he thought of the Book weighing reassuringly, even now, against his chest, and his momentary doubts were dispelled.

The other captives were out of sight further down the steps. All he could hear was the slapping of their feet on the stone, echoing up the tunnel, while ahead all he could see in the flickering yellow light cast by candles set at intervals in the wall, were more steps. They had not gone far when a sudden shout made them stop and turn round. They saw the three Hurll standing in the entrance and then, tumbling down the steps, they saw the injured man. He made no sound as he fell but as he came nearer to them they heard the crack as his limp body dropped on to each step. Melvaig, who had been following Shuinn down the tunnel, quickly started to climb back up to stop the man falling any more and as he did so he heard the sound of laughter from the entrance. It did not take long to reach the man and Melvaig grabbed him to prevent him rolling. The man's face was covered in weals and bruises from the beating the Hurll had given him and there were patches of blood in the long black hair that fell to his shoulders. He opened his eyes as Melvaig spoke to him and muttered something in a language Melvaig could not understand. Shuinn was with him now and they picked him up together and began slowly and laboriously to carry him down the steps. He seemed to be unconscious because several times Melvaig slipped and the man's body fell yet there was no cry of pain.

Further and further they went, deep into the bowels of the earth, until they felt as if it was devouring them. They began to sense the weight of the rock over their heads, bearing down upon them, and with each downward step the more they felt lost to the outside world above them. The steps would sometimes stop and they would find themselves on a long, gradually-sloping rock path before, abruptly, it would fall away and the steps would start again. And all the time the air got colder. Neither Melvaig nor Shuinn had ever experienced the cold before and they found their bodies reacting strangely to it. Little lumps came out on their arms and legs; their bodies seemed to want to contract and to shrink within themselves for warmth, and they began to shiver uncontrollably, their teeth chattering of their own accord and their shoulders quivering. Their garments, still wet from the rain, became almost unbearably uncomfortable.

Eventually the tunnel began to grow wider and ahead of them they saw a large circle of orange light. They could see no one in front but they could hear a low hum of conversation and they guessed that they had reached the end of their descent. Melvaig felt sick with apprehension at what they would find but he was relieved at the thought of being able to put the injured man down; he was a dead weight and Melvaig's back and shoulders were hurting badly.

Slowly they approached the orange circle and then suddenly they were walking through a high stone archway and entering an enormous cavern. They looked up but were unable to see the roof which was lost in darkness, though they could just about make out the opposite wall. Standing around on the floor of the cavern were the captives as well as other groups of men they had not seen before. The captives stood together in a large group against one of the sheer rock walls that soared up to the roof and a number of them were talking animatedly to each other. As Melvaig and Shuinn walked over to them they stopped talking and turned their heads to stare. None of them had seen the incident with the Hurll and Melvaig realized with a shock that they might be thinking that the man had been beaten up by him and Shuinn. And if not, why else were they so long after everyone else? Had they been talking to the Hurll, coming to some kind of agreement with them? Perhaps they were to report back on those captives who were lazy or too weak to work; to spy on them. Melvaig had already made his presence felt after the incident in the wagon so that they all knew him by sight. As these thoughts went through Melvaig's mind, he thought he saw his fears confirmed by their sullen angry looks and he cursed the language difference that made it impossible to explain to them. Nevertheless he decided that he must try, so as soon as they had laid the injured man down against one of the walls, Melvaig started to walk across to them. He was almost there when a stir of movement at the other side of the cavern caught his attention and he stopped short. Men were coming out of the earth, first one, then another and another and each one, as he saw the crowd of captives standing watching, seemed to react in the same way. Their faces, gaunt and haggard as they were, seemed to freeze in an expression of terror.

Every so often a man would emerge who appeared to have some authority. He would wait for those who came after him and then when his group appeared to be complete, he took them across to a long section of railing which stretched along one side of the cavern. There was a space between the railing and the wall but Melvaig could not see what was in it. The leader would line his men up against the old rusty railing facing this gap with their backs to the cavern and there they stood, until eventually the earth stopped disgorging its human entrails and the last miner had walked across and joined the end of the line of men who stood with their shoulders hunched and their heads down while their leaders went across to the Hurll.

Everything was quiet; the only sound, the slight slapping of footsteps on the stone floor of the cavern, echoed briefly up until it became lost in the vaulted stone heights above their heads. Melvaig, Shuinn and the other captives watched with terrified apprehension as the Hurll handed over a large stone-headed club to each of the leaders, who walked back to the line swinging the club sensuously to get the weight and feel of it, bringing it up to waist height and then letting it fall back of its own accord. The line of men against the railing seemed to shrink as each miner, hearing the footsteps, lowered his shoulders and bowed his head even more in dreaded anticipation of what was to come, as if by so doing they could somehow shield themselves from what they knew to be inevitable. The leaders then began to walk very slowly along behind the men of their group. When they reached the last man they would turn round and walk slowly back again, pausing sometimes behind one of them or else tapping him lightly on the shoulder, relishing the power they wielded and the fear they engendered. The Hurll watched in amusement, enjoying the irony that made the leaders, chosen from among the captives, even more savage to their own kind than they themselves could bother to be. In their joy at being chosen, and their desire to keep their position, their cruelty knew no limits and they revelled in domination.

Now suddenly, as Melvaig looked on in horror, it started. A club rose high in the air and came down with a terrible crack on the skull of a miner. A ghastly scream rose into the air as blood gushed from his head and then, as his legs folded under him, the scream died into a choking gargle. The leader then shouted an order and the two miners who had stood next to him bent down, picked him up and then threw him over the railings. Silence, for what seemed an age and then they heard the thud of the body as it landed at the bottom of the precipice.

Then it was the turn of the next group, then the next and the next, one from each group, until the dreadful rota came round to the first group again when a second miner would be executed. Those chosen to die were too old or too ill to work well; those the leaders had accused of slacking; those secretly denounced by a fellow captive as having spoken disparagingly of Xtlan or of having mentioned escape or rebellion. Others would be chosen for having displeased the leader in some way, for not submitting to his sexual appetites or else just on a whim – walking along behind the men, something about the back of a man's head, or the way his hair fell, would suddenly irritate him and he would bring down the club with a terrible satisfaction at the exercise of such total power. Others might be killed to complete a pattern of those left or else simply as an example to maintain the level of fear and uncertainty that kept the miners working.

On and on went the killing until the stone floor around the railings swam with blood and the walls rang with screams even in the silences. It was done slowly, individual by individual, so that the full horror of each death could send its icy grip into the other miners and the new captives looking on in terror. At each footstep behind them now the miners shivered uncontrollably with fear, their hands clasped over their heads and their shoulders weaving piteously in a futile attempt to dodge the blows. Often when the club fell on someone next to him the survivor would also scream, so certain was he that it had been his turn. And then at the leader's shout, he would quickly bend and pick up the twitching body of his comrade and throw him into the gorge, doing everything as fast and obediently as possible in a pitiable and obscene attempt to win favour with his leader.

Melvaig's mind was so numb with horror and fear after the first few killings that he became dispassionate, comparing the way the miners died; who died instantly and who suffered, which of the leaders had the strongest blow, trying to guess whose turn it would be next. And he looked at the faces of the leaders, the way their eyes shone with a terrible pleasure, gleaming as they looked unseeingly at their next victim, fired with the spirit of Xtlan as they immersed themselves in their dreadful task so that their souls were as one with Dréagg and it was his light that shone from their eyes. Melvaig watched the way they held their mouths, half-open, slavering with trickles of saliva dribbling down the chin, as blood dripped from their arms and the clubs glistened red in the dim candlelight.

Eventually it was over and now, before the new batch of captives were brought forward to replace those who had gone, the leaders walked up in a line and stood facing the Hurll. For an instant the two rows faced each other and then one of the Hurll, who appeared by his clothes and demeanour to be of a higher position than the others, pointed to one of the leaders. The other leaders then fell upon him and dragged him back to the railings where, after severing his feet to leave him helpless, they abandoned him to the mercy of the miners. At first the miners watched, still terrified by their ordeal, but soon their terror turned to a gloating fascination as they watched the man writhing and screaming on the floor, blood spurting from the ends of his legs. Then a terrible desire for revenge swept through them and they fell upon him as all their pain, their humiliation, their sufferings and the anguish in their souls rose up and extracted an awful vengeance upon this symbol of their oppression. Melvaig turned his head away in revulsion as he saw the man's limbs, torn from the body, lifted high in the air and waved triumphantly about in a grotesque representation of victory. Mercifully the screams did not last long, as he lost consciousness, and the only sounds in the cavern were the frenzied shouts and laughter that rose from the bloodied miners and bounced around the stone walls, the echoes merging together and blending to form a bizarre symphony as an accompaniment to the scenes of carnage on the floor of the cavern.

Eventually the leader was no more, his dismembered body thrown in pieces over the precipice, and the pack of miners, their eyes glassy with the frenzy of their revenge, looked desperately around for something else to vent themselves upon. But the Hurll, watching with amusement until now, stepped forward and the one Melvaig guessed to be the Captain brought his whip down on the floor with a crack that seemed to cut its way into their minds and immediately they fell silent; their shoulders moving up and down jerkily as they fought to control themselves. All that could be heard now was their panting excited breath, like the hissing of some large venomous creature.

Now the Hurll directed the leaders to walk forward and stand, spaced widely apart, against one of the walls. The surviving miners then broke up and went to join their leaders, standing alongside them with smug arrogance; they had survived and they would make sure they survived again if it meant pulling every one of the new captives to bits to do so. Their eyes ranged over Melvaig and his companions from the cart, with a terrible, unthinking viciousness, the viciousness of frightened, defeated men who have found something more vulnerable than themselves.

The Hurll then came towards the captives and divided them up into groups, sending each group to one of the leaders to make up the numbers of those who had been despatched. When Melvaig realized how they were being split up he looked around frantically for Shuinn in the hope that if they were standing together, they would be put in the same group. To his relief he found that the giant was by his side, with the injured man cradled in his arms. They were at the back of the captives and were among the last to be assigned. One of the Hurll, a large man whose black stubbly hair seemed to grow out of his head and face in all directions, approached them and when he saw the man Shuinn was carrying, he stopped. Then he came forward more slowly and started to say something to Shuinn. The giant understood, for the Hurll spoke in the language of Xtlan, and he replied. The Hurll spoke again, at some length this time and with a nasty little smile playing about his lips, and when he finished Shuinn turned to Melvaig. He put the man down and began moving his arms, gesturing as if hacking at the rock. Then he pointed to the man on the floor and to themselves and then he pointed to the railing and the precipice beyond. Melvaig understood. If they wanted to keep the man from being killed now, he and Shuinn would have to gather the amount of stone which he would have done were he able to work. Thus between them they would have to do the work of a third man and if they failed then they would meet the fate they had just witnessed. It was their choice.

Melvaig's instinctive reaction was to accept the risk and try to do the work. They could not let the man be killed. But then other thoughts started to come into his mind. Why should they put themselves to this effort, having to work almost twice as hard and running the risk of death much sooner than they would otherwise face it, for the sake of someone they did not even know? What was he doing even thinking that they should not be rid of him right now? This was the kind of thought that Jarrah, so long ago in Ruann, had warned him against. He must look after himself. Surely if there was some destiny that called him, it was up to him to make sure that he survived to fulfil that destiny. The man was badly injured. No great loss then if he met his fate earlier than he would anyway. He might even be spared suffering.

Melvaig looked at Shuinn, and the giant simply pointed to him as if indicating that it was Melvaig's decision and in some strange way Melvaig knew it was. Shuinn would do what he asked. What would Arkron do in this situation? What would Jarrah have done? Jarrah, who had warned him of the dangers of letting emotions and affections cloud his actions and blur his instincts and yet who had also been secretly warmed by the thought that Melvaig was aware of these feelings.

And so Melvaig agonized over the decision while the Hurll watched in amusement. He had just made up his mind and was about to indicate that the man should be killed when he heard a groan from the floor and looking down he saw that the man had opened his eyes. Melvaig looked at him and their eyes met and now, suddenly, he knew that it was impossible to have him destroyed for he could not ignore the life that he saw there. He thought of the incident on the path down from Ruann when he had refrained from killing the ant and he remembered the strange feeling of power over life and death which he had experienced then, and which he was experiencing now, and he found himself to be immensely relieved to have made the choice he had. Quickly Melvaig gestured to Shuinn that the man should not be killed and the giant told the Hurll who shrugged his shoulders and laughed. Then he pointed to the group at the end of the line and they walked across the hard stone floor of the cavern feeling awkwardly conspicuous. They could sense the eyes upon them; the Hurll, already mindful of the wilfulness of these two, the surviving miners wary and determined to watch them, and the new captives suspicious and mistrustful. Melvaig and Shuinn kept their heads down and their eyes averted as if unaware of the interest in them, frightened at the loss of their anonymity. And yet, as Melvaig now realized, the decision he had taken was bound to mark them out from the rest.

As soon as Melvaig and Shuinn had joined their group, their leader led them away from the wall and off to a corner of the cavern where the rock was indented to form a small antechamber. The other groups also found their places in the cavern and then all the leaders walked over to a little cave where some of the Hurll were waiting for them. Melvaig saw each of them being given something and then they returned to their groups carrying containers of water and a number of large slices of dried goatsmeat. Melvaig's group sat down and the food and water was placed on the floor. At the sight of the goatsmeat Melvaig's stomach began to rumble and his mouth watered. They had only been fed once in the cart and that must have been three days ago. None of the new arrivals made a move, instinctively aware of the hierarchy that gave the leader and the two surviving miners in their group the privilege of eating and drinking their fill first. So Melvaig and Shuinn watched as the food was consumed. The leader, who was known as Teggrogg, was large and fat and completely bald, his naked dome shining yellow in the light from the candles. He was small-featured with little black eyes set well back under his forehead. They glinted as he tore at the meat with his teeth and cast wary glances at the others. He had no eyebrows and the light from his eyes seemed to be intensified by the shiny pink flesh of the cavities around his eyes. The large fleshy mouth shone with saliva as it guzzled hungrily on the flesh.

At a signal from Teggrogg, the two surviving miners, called Schtell and Gebble, began on the meat. Similar in appearance, they had long hair, matted with dust and dirt, that appeared to be white or grey beneath its coating of filth and were thin to the point of emaciation, the faces sunken and angular, the skin stretched tight over their cheekbones before being pulled inwards and downwards to meet under the chin. Their eyes were sunk way back in dark cavernous sockets and flitted nervously around them as they ate, never resting, constantly vigilant for any warning signal, anything they could do or report to the Hurll which would earn them favour. They had survived two previous purges before this last one, something only very few managed to do, and so Teggrogg and the others were particularly wary of them, keeping out of their way as far as possible.

Schtell and Gebble ate slowly, enjoying the anguish of those frantically watching them. Soon there was little left, as much to share among the six remaining members of the group – the new captives from the cart – as Schtell and Gebble had each consumed. At last they finished, picked up the goatskin water bag and in turn gulped back huge mouthfuls of the precious liquid, letting it dribble out of their mouths and down their chins to spill on the stone floor. Then they luxuriously wiped their mouths on their sleeves and let out an enormous belch. Still those anxiously watching did nothing, just sat riveted in a rapt hypnotic trance until suddenly, at a gesture from them the new arrivals made a desperate grab for the few remaining pieces of meat. Melvaig had been too slow and his hands were left scrabbling at air but Shuinn had managed to get hold of the largest of what was left and immediately, selflessly, and to Melvaig's embarrassment, began to tear it in half for him to share. The other captives were too busy to see this but

Schtell, Gebble and Teggrogg had noticed and began laughing, a vicious throaty cackle that sent a ball of fear around Melvaig's guts even while he was pulling at the hard flesh.

Teggrogg had hold of the water container. For the sake of keeping the group alive and their quota of rock up it was important that they all get some water. Otherwise they would die and the others would have to make up the workload of the dead man. This was the delicate balancing act of the leader. To instil total fear and unquestioning obedience, utter subservience to his will, by using the most powerful weapon he had, control of their food, while at the same time keeping their strength up just enough to get the maximum amount of work from them. To make his task even more difficult there was the question of those who had gained favour, like Schtell and Gebble, to whom one could not be too harsh for fear they would report you, but who often deliberately tried to keep the quota down by starving those beneath them so that the leader would be deposed and they would take his place.

Melvaig soon finished his half of the meat Shuinn had given him and felt worse than he had before. His stomach, expecting more, began to rumble and he felt sick and faint. Now the water was being passed round, each man tipping up the bag and letting the spout pour the liquid down his throat, trying to fill the aching void inside himself until the leader judged that the man had had his share. When Melvaig's turn came he rejoiced in the feel of the water running down his throat and into his stomach, closing his eyes and putting all other thoughts out of his mind. But, too soon, Teggrogg snatched it away and passed it on to Shuinn. Before taking any himself, the giant bent over their injured friend and lifted the spout to his lips. They parted slightly and he gave a little groan as the water started to seep into his mouth. Teggrogg let Shuinn continue for a short spell before stopping him and telling him to have a drink himself but then no sooner had the giant taken a mouthful than the container was pulled out of his grasp and Teggrogg pointed to the injured man. So, Melvaig realized, they would have to provide food and drink for him out of their own rations but now he felt terribly guilty for, by his own selfishness in not thinking of the man, he had had the whole of his ration while Shuinn had only been allowed a small amount to drink. And after he had given Melvaig half of his food as well. Shamefully he looked at the giant expecting to see anger in his face but instead there was a smile and a shrug of the shoulders and once again Melvaig was touched to the heart by the warmth of his friend.

As the water was being passed round Melvaig studied the remainder of the group. He recognized two of them from their time in the cart. His adversary, the man he had had the fight with and whose name was Beddrang, kept casting quick angry glances at him, still smouldering from the humiliation he had suffered.

Next to him sat one of the officials, Krill, small, fat and pudgy, his mean eyes glazed over in empty desolation as all the thoughts of his once powerful and important past receded into disbelief that the man he looked back on in his mind was the creature he had now become. One day he had made the mistake of telling a friend that he thought Xtlan should grant more privileges to those who did the real work in the empire, those who organized the purges and those who really ran things – the officials. It was all very well for Xtlan to sit in his citadel, watching over them, but he had lost touch with what went on beneath him. His world could not exist without the administrators.

The next day they had come for him, dragged him from his bed and thrown him, crying bitterly, into the cart. The friend had supervised, smiling and laughing as Krill had protested his innocence and indignation.

Next to Krill sat the last two in the group, neither of

whom Melvaig had noticed before. First there was a small dark man with large melancholy eyes which he never once seemed to lift from the floor. It was his complexion that most caught Melvaig's attention, a sickly gangrenous yellow that seemed to exude a pallid light of its own – almost, Melvaig thought, the light of death. This was Gorpenn.

Finally, and in striking contrast to him, there was a young man with long golden hair and a fresh fair skin. The hair framed his face in a tumble of curls and wisps and peering out from under them were two blue eyes whose intensity startled Melvaig. Yet he was smiling, a pleasant open smile, fixed on whoever he was looking at at the time. Melvaig smiled back and felt the gimlet eyes boring into him with a concentration of emotion that was almost frightening: burning resentment, a furious raging anger, terrible hatred and crushing bitterness; Melvaig tried to read the message in the eyes and saw all these and much more seething behind the mask-like smile. His name, Melvaig learned, was Tamrett. A child captive brought up by the women of Xtlan to serve the tastes and pleasures of Xtlan's chief warriors, to cater for their every whim in servility and abject obedience, he had refused, when the time came, to deny his own inclinations and subject himself to the fate for which he had been reared and trained.

Time and again, when prevailed upon to succumb, he had fought back and rendered it impossible for those seeking to have their pleasure with him to succeed. All the years of training, the most lavish attentions, the best clothes and the finest foods – all these wasted. The fury of the women had been terrible, for they themselves were blamed for his recalcitrance, and they extracted terrible revenge upon his virility. In the end the warriors had their way by force while he was held down, again and again, in a nightmare which still haunted his every waking moment, screaming in his head and inflaming the very spirit within him so that he felt constantly as if his soul were being consumed by fire.

Melvaig looked and turned away, so terrible was the light in those eyes.

When Tamrett had finished the water, Teggrogg went over to a small aperture in the rock wall and drew out a number of objects. He brought them over and passed them round to all the group. A pick each, with a wooden handle and a sharp pointed metal head. These had been found when the mine had first been discovered, a large store of them, and there were so many that when one broke, the Hurll provided a replacement. Melvaig liked the feel of the smooth, wooden shaft, stained dark with the sweat of many hands before him, and when he picked it up the weight in his palm felt good. The metal had fascinated him, hard and heavy like stone and yet shaped. He guessed that it came from Before the War and he wondered about the hands that had held it, about the lives led by those who had swung its sharp point into the rock.

As well as the pick, Teggrogg gave each man a leather band and two candles. Melvaig and the others then copied Schtell and Gebble as they fastened the band round their heads and stuck one of the candles in a small leather ring attached to the band. Looking around the cavern, Melvaig saw that the other groups were all doing the same and then suddenly, at a shout from one of the Hurll, the leaders got up and, summoning their groups, started to walk towards the far end of the cavern.

Melvaig's group were one of the last to arrive while the other groups stood waiting in front. The cavern floor sloped down quite sharply in this corner and Melvaig could see over the heads of the others. They were being lowered down some kind of shaft into the ground. At one side of where they were all standing, there was a row of little carts on wheels while hanging on the walls were lengths of rope and buckets. He shivered involuntarily with the cold and was alarmed to find himself feeling shaky and weak. He was still ravenously hungry, his stomach churning over inside, gnawing at itself in its vain attempts to find something to work on. Now his legs started to ache as the cold air seeped into his bones and suddenly he began to feel very scared. Desperately he tried to summon up the vision of Ashgaroth he had glimpsed at the entrance to the Gurrtslagg, the silver cascade of light, the song of the river. His part in the paths of destiny, and his faith; these seemed somehow remote now and faintly ridiculous. Yet, the story from the Book and these stirrings were all he had. He must cling to them for he knew that without them he was lost. Still hungry, cold and weak, he nevertheless was sustained. The empty desolation of a few moments ago had disappeared and as he stood now, waiting his turn to descend into the earth, he felt once again that Ashgaroth was somehow near, guiding and watching.

All the other groups had gone down and now it was Schtell who stood on the edge of the narrow fissure in the rock floor, which had swallowed them up. On either side of this small aperture stood a tall wooden post, while across the top lay a beam with a rope wound round it. A handle on one of the posts turned the beam which in turn raised and lowered a thick length of wood attached to the end of the rope. Schtell took hold of the rope and placed first one foot and then the other on the wood that hung suspended over the hole. He swung slightly for a moment or two and then at a shout from him, the Hurll who stood by the handle, slowly began to turn it, lowering Schtell down into the blackness. Melvaig watched as he used one hand to manoeuvre himself away from the sharp edges of rock that protruded all around the hole. At one point he seemed to have to squeeze himself through a very tiny gap, using the swaying length of wood under his feet as his only protection from the drop below while he used both hands to climb around and under a large bulging outcrop in the rock. Then suddenly Melvaig could no longer see him, only the rope unwinding more and more until eventually it stopped, two jerks shook it and the Hurll started to wind it up again.

Gebble descended and then it was Melvaig's turn. His stomach had wound itself into a tight knot of fear and he felt sick as he grabbed the rope and gingerly placed a foot on the wooden support. Then he quickly took his other foot off the ground and tried to find the length of wood with it but the instant he took it off, all his weight went on to the foot that was already on the support causing it to drop down sharply so that his other foot could not find it. He was left swinging over the gaping black void with both hands clinging desperately to the rope while his feet thrashed around beneath him, seeking the support which seemed to slip away from him as soon as he rested a foot on it. He could hear the Hurll laughing at his side. Finally he lowered both feet gently on to it and with a surge of relief felt it take his weight.

The rope started to unwind slowly and looking down he saw the gap get narrower. Suddenly he felt as if the rock was closing in around him, relentlessly bearing in upon him. He let go of the rope with one of his hands to fend off the vicious splinters of rock that came at him from all around. Beneath his feet the wooden support swayed precariously and suddenly he felt a sharp pain in the back of his shoulder as he was gashed by the rock. Instinctively he threw his weight forward to avoid it but then both knees scraped against the rock in front. Down he went, bumping and grazing his way around the outcrop, further into the earth, until the darkness closed over his head and he could see nothing. At first he felt strangely elated at being by himself, as if, once again, he were free; but then he became aware of the presence of the rock, its inanimate mercilessness crushing him. He grew breathless and little lights started to dance in front of his eyes, slowly merging together into a blood-red haze. He was aware of himself screaming, he knew his mouth was open and sounds were coming from it even though he could not hear them. Desperately he fought with himself, trying to control the nausea that sent his head spinning and made his throat sting with bile. And then a sudden sharp jolt shook his body and he felt his legs on solid ground again. Looking around he saw that he was standing in a long narrow tunnel. Candles fixed at intervals along the walls threw out a dim yellow light and with a feeling of relative space around him the awful panic he had felt coming down on the rope began to subside. Schtell and Gebble were standing staring at him, their dark cadaverous faces mask-like and unsmiling. Schtell came forward and jerked twice on the rope, at which it began to slowly swing its way back up into the rock above Melvaig's head.

The tunnel stretched away in both directions for as far as Melvaig could see. Smaller tunnels led off from the main one and the distinctive hammering of picks as they clanged into the rock echoed around the walls in sporadic flurries and clusters of sound. While they waited for the rest of the group to descend, Melvaig watched as miners appeared from these side tunnels pulling carts like those he had seen in the main cavern, filled with lumps of rock. They took them up the tunnel to what appeared to be a central collecting spot where the rock was unloaded, put in buckets and hauled up on a rope through a shaft in the roof, presumably to be sorted somewhere on the surface.

Shuinn was next to come down, bleeding from a large cut on his leg, and soon all the others had joined them. Teggrogg was last and, as soon as he was down, he led the way up the main tunnel for a short while before turning down into a very small passage leading off it at right angles. A few paces down here there was another shaft, wider than the first, into which, once again, Schtell was the first to descend. This time, somewhat to Melvaig's relief, there was a ladder attached to the side but when he started to follow Gebble down he found that many of the rungs were missing and several times he was left holding on grimly to a rung while his feet groped about in the emptiness beneath him as they attempted to find something to stand on. But this shaft was wider and shorter than its predecessor and he was able to control the twinges of panic that he felt start to rise in him again. Or was he getting used to the feel of the stone? Already the world on the surface seemed far away, the sky, the grass, the trees, the space.

The shaft brought them out into another smaller tunnel where, once again, Teggrogg led them a small distance to yet another shaft which they descended by ladder.

As they went deeper and deeper into the earth Melvaig became aware of an almost dreamlike feeling that had begun to envelop him. Everything seemed to have an air of unreality about it. The air, musty, stale and cold, seemed to take on a tangible, almost visible thickness as it lay heavily upon them. There was total silence such as Melvaig had never before heard, a silence so complete that he found it had a sound of its own – a sort of high-pitched, whining buzz which sang in his ears. Above their heads, the unimaginable weight of the earth pressing down upon them formed a barrier between them and the world of the surface so devastatingly complete that life had already begun to mean something in a different dimension to that experienced before.

CHAPTER XV

At last Teggrogg's group arrived at their tunnel. The third and deepest of the seams, it was also the smallest. Where they were now standing at the bottom of the shaft, and for a few paces on each side, there was just room enough to stand although Shuinn and Beddrang both had to bend their heads slightly. Teggrogg had lit one of his candles with the aid of a flint and some tinder which he took from a crack in the rock and now the others came forward to light the candles in their hats from it. Melvaig could see the way the tunnel quickly narrowed, its roof dropping down so that beyond the space beneath the shaft, there was only room to move on hands and knees.

Teggrogg stood facing them for a few seconds and then, moving forward, divided them up into three groups. He grabbed Tamrett by the shoulder and pulled him roughly to one side for the boy was to be with Gorpenn and Beddrang. Krill, the official, would be with Schtell and Gebble and that left Melvaig and Shuinn on their own. That way it would be easy to see whether or not they had gathered as much rock as the groups of three and thus done the work of their injured friend. He then gave each group one of the small trucks and addressed them briefly for a few seconds in the language of Xtlan. When he had finished,

Schtell's group went in one direction while Teggrogg led all the others the opposite way. When they came to the point where the roof dipped they had to squeeze their way along, lying almost flat, for some time before eventually they were able to crawl. There was just room for the carts. Beddrang pulled one and Melvaig the other, holding on to lengths of rope attached to the front. The carts were heavy and ungainly and the wooden wheels irregularly shaped and loose on the axles so that they were very difficult to pull even now, when they were empty.

They crawled for a while, Melvaig's knees giving him considerable pain both from the cuts they had received on the way down the shaft and from the pressure on the rough stone floor, littered as it was with myriads of little chippings that kept cutting into him. When they got to a part that was wide enough, Shuinn went back past Melvaig and took over their cart, pulling it until they reached a spot where the tunnel divided into two. Here Teggrogg told Shuinn and Melvaig to go one way while he led Tamrett and Beddrang in the other.

Melvaig and Shuinn had not gone far when, at last, they arrived at the face. They stopped, doing nothing for a few seconds while they let their situation seep fully into their consciousness. Freed, if only for a while, from the constant eyes of an enemy, they felt elated and suddenly Shuinn began chuckling. Melvaig remembered the last time he had heard the giant's laugh, when he had been playing with Bracca way back in the desert of Molobb. A heavy, intensely poignant wave of longing to see his little boy again swept over him but then, forcibly banishing these painful yearnings he let the warmth of his friend's laughter wash over him, carrying him along in its infectious spirit so that he too started to laugh. What they were laughing at, Melvaig did not know, nor did it matter, for all that was important was that for a few short seconds all pain, loss and misery were vanquished. It was a crazed, almost mad laughter that gripped them, feeding itself so that it grew in intensity until their shoulders were shaking and tears came into their eyes.

Then as suddenly as he had started, Shuinn stopped and for a few seconds sat in silence, feeling empty and vaguely foolish now that the laughter had gone. And then, with no warning, the giant turned to the face and smashed his pick down hard against the rock. Melvaig crawled up alongside him on his hands and knees and similarly swung his pick into the rock face. Then Shuinn, then Melvaig again, on and on in a relentless rhythm that drove them along with its insistent pattern: neither wishing to let the other one down. Melvaig became almost hypnotized by the remorseless regularity of his movements until eventually the cart was filled and it was decided that Melvaig would take it back to unload while Shuinn continued at the face.

The journey back seemed to last for ever. The cart was so heavy that it took all his strength to drag it along and yet because he was only able to kneel, he could not get a proper leverage to pull. His knees were causing him a lot of pain and as it was these that were having to take all the pressure, he came to dread every drag on the cart. Next time, he swore, they would not fill it so full; it would be better and quicker to make more journeys and they would probably not lose any more time at the face. When he arrived at the narrow place where they had to crawl he decided to unload some of the rock and come back for it. Then he tore two lengths of goatskin off his jerkin and bound them round his knees in an attempt to gain some relief for them.

The rest of the journey, with a lighter load and the protection on his knees, was much less arduous. When he finally arrived at the bottom of the shaft he was surprised to find a Hurll sitting down against the tunnel wall. He looked at Melvaig with sardonic amusement and pointed to some buckets on the ground. Melvaig filled three of these with the stone in the cart and then fixed one of them to a hook on the end of a rope that hung down the shaft. The Hurll tugged sharply on the rope and the bucket began its ascent. When the rope came down again, the process was repeated, and again a third time at which point the Hurll scratched three lines on a flat piece of slate that he held in front of him. The cart had a mark on it and Melvaig saw that the three lines had been drawn alongside a similar mark on the slate. This then was the way in which their workloads were recorded.

Now that the cart was empty Melvaig started to make his way back and met Beddrang as he was emerging into the standing space around the shaft. He waited so as to let Beddrang past and was surprised to see a smile on his normally surly face. He looked straight at Melvaig and there was a strange glint in his eyes, almost, Melvaig thought, a look of triumph. He looked at Beddrang's cart which was full to overflowing. Was it his imagination or was it bigger than the one he and Shuinn had been given? Then he noticed the great thick leather patches strapped around Beddrang's knees and the heavy gauntlets on his hands. Teggrogg was obviously determined that his little trio would come out with a good record. Probably Schtell and Gebble were similarly favoured and thus, because they were allocated food according to their workloads, it would be he and Shuinn who would get least to eat and so be less able to work. So it would go on until, at the next purge to make way for new arrivals, Melvaig and Shuinn would be, justifiably, the ones to be got rid of first. Melvaig guessed that such was the case amongst all the groups.

When Beddrang had passed him, and the infuriating smirk on the man's face had burned itself into Melvaig's consciousness, he knelt down and started pulling his cart back up the tunnel. Soon he reached the spot where he had left the stone and, as he had suspected, it was not to be seen. He was consumed first by anger and then depression and then anger again. There must have been at least two more bucketfuls there. All that work – wasted, because he couldn't be bothered to make the extra effort to pull the heavy cart. He thought of Shuinn and decided not to tell him. Nor would he mention their smaller cart, or the knee pads or the gauntlets until the giant himself saw them. They must retain hope for as long as they could. If Shuinn was not aware of the conspiracy against them, then perhaps he could keep both their spirits up. That was crucial.

So it was that with a huge effort of will Melvaig drove out from himself the sickness he felt in his heart and when he got back to Shuinn, redoubled his efforts with a smile and a laugh. The giant in his turn, at seeing his friend in such a good mood, was encouraged and pleased and so once again they set up their rhythm, only this time it was at a faster pace than they had managed before. Melvaig found solace, even pleasure, in the oblivion of the work.

On they worked, with a momentum that powered itself, until the cart was filled with another load. Melvaig took it to the Hurll at the shaft and then returned to Shuinn who had not slackened his pace. But Melvaig now found, to his dismay, that when he tried to join in on the rhythm again, it took all his willpower. His shoulder, the injury which he had almost forgotten, so long had it been since it had hurt, now started to give him trouble. Every time the pick bit into the rock, the impact jarred all the nerves in his shoulder and set them throbbing so violently that he felt sick. His knees, despite the protection he had given them and which had afforded a temporary relief, had now become painful again. He felt he could have overcome the pain but he had also now been gripped by a wave of nausea which made his head swim and seemed to drain away all his strength and energy. His legs and arms turned to jelly and felt as if they were shaking uncontrollably and he broke out in a hot sweat so that his whole body seemed on fire, the warmth coming from somewhere inside himself and then breaking out through every pore in his skin.

It was hunger; it was also fear that there was no way in which he could cure himself. In his mind he saw his body falling into a vicious downward spiral that led from no work to no food which in its turn meant less ability to work to get food. The only way to break the spiral was to somehow conquer his body's weakness, achieve a good quota and then with extra food inside, produce an even better quota. But he and Shuinn were still having to do the work of three men and share out their food with the injured man who was lying back in the cavern. And they were working against Teggrogg who, as Melvaig had realized, intended to ensure they had low quotas so they could be sacrificed for the survival of the others.

He tried to banish the feeling of hopelessness that threatened to swamp him with its bleak, cold truths. He attempted to use his mind to conquer the weakness in his limbs and he forced himself by sheer willpower to grasp the pick and swing it into the rock. Shuinn turned to him and smiled and Melvaig swung again, and again, blindly, unthinking, until the cart was full for the third time.

Once again to Melvaig's relief, Shuinn indicated to Melvaig that he should take the cart while the giant carried on at the face. This time though the journey back through the narrow tunnels seemed even worse than working with the pick. At last he came out into the small area under the shaft where he could stand. Thankfully he stood up, filled the buckets and rested against the wall while they were hauled up, wallowing in those few precious seconds of peace when he did not have to do anything. As the third bucket-load was disappearing up into the shaft, he glanced across at the Hurll and happened to see the tablet on which he was marking the quotas. He could see immediately the three columns for the gangs, theirs and the two others and to his horror he saw that the other two had many more strokes against them. So all that effort, that determination,

189

the pain he had endured, had been pointless, futile. For all Melvaig knew, the Hurll might be in collusion with Teggrogg – deliberately marking himself and Shuinn down. He felt utterly powerless: impotent and enraged, his heart pounded with anger even as his body languished exhausted, against the wall. He tried to think of Ashgaroth, to summon up his faith, the power of his visions so that they would lift him out of this abyss of despair but he did not have the strength. He felt betrayed and bitter. Better to let go of the rope on the way down the shaft and kill himself than carry on like this. For what? Some vague feeling of destiny, the ramblings of Arkron – an old man. The words of a Book he could not even read. Morven and Bracca both gone – to what fate he dared not even contemplate.

Suddenly the darkness in his spirit was shattered by the sound of a horn. It was the signal for the end of the session of work. Melvaig, not knowing what was expected, began to go back down the tunnel to join Shuinn but the Hurll shouted something and gestured to him to stay. Melvaig was almost grateful for the interruption in the black torpor that had seized him. He stood back and watched as the groups emerged from the tunnels. Teggrogg's group first with Beddrang and Tamrett, the boy wearing a scowl that looked odd and out of place on his fair and pleasant face. Then came Schtell, Gebble and Gorpenn from the other end, all of them walking slowly, their knees stiff and their backs unused to being upright. Finally Shuinn arrived and at the sight of the giant's face Melvaig's heart lifted and the depression of a few moments ago, the doubts and uncertainties, receded as the light in his friend's eyes sparkled and shone with a vibrancy that made all things possible. He felt himself caught up in that light, his spirits buoyed up by its strength and purity while tumbling into his mind came images that warmed and comforted his soul and soothed his jagged nerves. The face of Arkron as he rode off with the guards, Bracca and Morven playing by the river at Ruann – the sound of their laughter ringing in his head, Bendro whinnying, Jarrah and the love that emanated from him, he and Morven together, loving, walking. And then into his mind came the vision he had seen outside the Gurrtslagg, the dazzling silver light of Ashgaroth and the music of the river.

And so, as he made his way back up the shafts, he was lost in clouds of light. They seemed to be speaking to him softly, gently, but unmistakably. 'Believe,' they were saying. 'Only believe, and trust.'

CHAPTER XVI

They reached the cavern again and made their way back to their place. Then Teggrogg went over to where the Hurll were dispensing the food and came back with two buckets, one filled with water and the other with pieces of meat and chunks of black bread. He had with him the tablet on which the Hurll at the bottom of the shaft had marked their quotas. Teggrogg sat down, his thick lips drawn back into a smile while his little black eyes shone in the candlelight. How he enjoyed this time! This was real power. The dispensation of life or death. In a way it was even more satisfying than the purges; they were too quick and required too much effort and there was always the fear that it would be your turn to go at the end.

But feed times: they were different. Here there was the delicious feeling of knowing that in your hands you held everything they wanted. What they would not have given to get more, their bodies churning and their brains on fire as they watched you eat, slowly devouring every mouthful, as much as you wanted before sharing out the rest according to their work. The terrible look of longing in their eyes, the tension that crackled in the air as they waited: these Teggrogg relished.

Melvaig watched, knowing Teggrogg was enjoying his

suffering but unable to quell the yearning, the pulsating anxiety, that raged within him. He hated the fat little body, the evil shiny dome of his head. Gone now was despair, dissipated was the cushion of euphoric images that had come to rescue him. All he perceived were the pieces of food that Teggrogg was picking out of the bucket, playing with in his hands and then cramming into his mouth. Every fibre of his being was focused on them, concentrating on them as if by sheer willpower he could draw them through the air towards him.

At last Teggrogg finished. Leering at them, his mouth still packed with food, he started to dole it out to the others. With the tablet in front of him, he counted out so much and gave it to Schtell who immediately fell upon the pile and then began slowly, lingeringly to tear little pieces off and eat them.

Then after a similar amount for Gebble, it was the turn of the others. For Beddrang an amount nearly as great as that given to the two survivors and then, for Tamrett, Teggrogg ingratiatingly passed over some of his own food that he had kept on one side, along with the amount he was entitled to receive by his work, a much smaller lot than Beddrang's. The boy's mask-like face, fixed with a smile, turned to the leader and then suddenly his head shot forward and a glob of spittle flew out of his mouth to land in Teggrogg's eye before it began to slide slowly down his cheek.

Teggrogg's smile froze on his face and his eyes seemed to contract under the great jut of brow. Melvaig sat without breathing, mesmerized with intense anticipation, waiting for the reaction. Teggrogg, still looking at Tamrett, put his hand to the spittle and wiped it off his cheek. Then, slowly and deliberately he put out the hand with the spittle still on it and, leaning forward, stroked Tamrett's thigh as he sat cross-legged, rubbing the spittle into the skin. The boy looked down at the floor, unmoving and unblinking, rigid with hatred and fear. Teggrogg said something to him, to which Tamrett barked out in reply a short sharp retort and then Teggrogg got up suddenly and moved across the floor of the cavern to where a number of Hurll were standing.

They spoke together for a few seconds and then, pointing at Tamrett and laughing, they started to walk back with Teggrogg to where the group were sitting. All this time the boy sat, his face the colour of ash, his eyes fixed on a point directly in front of him and his face set into that eerie smile. The Hurll were almost upon him when he suddenly leapt to his feet and made a desperate frantic dash towards the steps that led up out of the cavern. Melvaig, his heart beating, watched as his feet sped crazily across the floor. He almost reached the first step before a prisoner from another group grabbed him round the legs and he fell sprawling in a heap. He struggled to get up but the Hurll, howling with amusement, were now upon him and they carried him kicking and struggling across the floor until they came to an outcrop of rock which shielded them from sight.

There was silence for a few moments. None of the prisoners moved – they seemed frozen, some of them with food raised to their mouths had simply stopped where they were, unable to continue. The atmosphere was filled with a sharp sense of terrified anticipation. The sounds of scuffling could now be heard and then suddenly the air was shattered by a scream, then another, and another, echoing around the stone walls, knifing their way into the ears of those who heard them. Melvaig's stomach heaved and he covered his ears with his hands but still the awful screams lacerated his brain.

How long it went on he did not know, for thankfully his mind became numb, blocking out the sound and locking itself away behind a wall of immunity, for to really listen to those screams would have driven him mad.

Finally they stopped and he looked across to the outcrop of rock. After a little while Teggrogg emerged and after him, kicked forward by the Hurll, the limp and broken body of Tamrett dragged itself across the floor. Every time the boy stopped, one of the Hurll would bring down a whip across his back and he would crawl a few more paces. He made no sound now as the lashes fell or a foot connected with his shattered body, for he could feel no more pain.

Melvaig watched, horrified, as Tamrett slowly approached. The smile was gone from his face. Instead there was a look of such blank and empty despair that it seemed as if his soul had been sucked out of him. He was naked and his fragile body shook uncontrollably. His back oozed rivulets of blood where the whip had bitten and his legs splayed awkwardly out behind him as if it hurt to bring them together. Slowly, agonizingly he pulled himself towards the group while Teggrogg, grinning broadly all over his face, swaggered ahead of him.

Eventually he reached the group, where he lay painfully on his stomach with his head cradled on his arms. The Hurll walked away, laughing, after one of them had given him a final vicious smack on his bare rump and then as if nothing had happened, Teggrogg carried on giving out the food rations. Only the sight of Tamrett where he lay whimpering, and the glint of triumph in Teggrogg's eyes remained of the incident.

Krill received his share gratefully, bowing his head to Teggrogg in thanks, and Melvaig felt a wave of disgust pass over him at this show of abject humility. Then Gorpenn, his thin predatory face untouched by any flicker of emotion as Teggrogg handed him the black bread and meat.

Now it was the turn of Shuinn and Melvaig. Teggrogg made a great show of studying the tablet, his face contorted into an expression of quizzical surprise. Melvaig could feel the eyes of the group upon them, sensing the decision that Teggrogg, relishing the situation, had made. Someone was worse off than they were. This fact seeped into their consciousness, lightening their outlook, putting them in a position where they could feel some flicker of achievement and dignity. Here were two people who would suffer more than they would and on whom they could look down. These two would go first and that gave them more chance so they were not, after all, at the bottom of the pile.

When Teggrogg finally pushed across their share, Shuinn's face fell into an expression of horrified disbelief. Even Melvaig, who had been expecting the worst, felt his heart plummet at the amount. Three little pieces of meat and about twice that amount in bread. It lay on the floor in front of them; irrefutable evidence of their helplessness, mocking and scorning them. Shuinn, his face aghast, said something to Teggrogg in a voice strangled with suppressed emotion at which the leader, smiling in mock sympathy, leaned forward and showed the giant the loads marked down on the tablet. They had simply not done the work; they would have to do better next session, then they would have more or less the same as the others. Food according to effort – surely that was fair. And then of course, pointing to their injured friend, they were having to do his work as well. He shrugged his shoulders; they had brought that upon themselves. They had a choice – he drew a finger across his neck and smiled.

Both Melvaig and Shuinn then turned and looked at the man they had saved. They had almost forgotten about him. He lay where they had left him, broken and bruised, his back propped against the wall, groaning constantly.

Melvaig looked for the man's eyes and met them. He found it impossible to consign him to death as he had hoped he would be able to do. In any case, surely the man was dying – they would soon be rid of him. Melvaig smiled at him and the man's lips parted in a pathetic attempt to return it. He knew what was in Melvaig's mind, that his life hung in the balance, and he was grateful for the respite. Melvaig picked up his share of the food and moved over to him as the others watched in amusement. Shuinn went the other side and then they took turns in trying to feed him. When it was their turn to have the water, he gulped back a number of mouthfuls, but then shook his head when Melvaig offered him some more food. Melvaig felt relieved and examined the amount he had left. Not much. He decided to have one more mouthful and keep the rest for the next session of work, so when he had broken off a piece of bread to eat now he put the rest carefully up under his jerkin. As he did so he felt the bag round his neck with the Book in it next to Morven's moccasin and a stab of yearning made his heart ache as he thought of her. A picture of her face, as clear and real as if she was beside him, flashed in front of his eyes but when he tried to hang on to it, to hold and keep it there, it moved away and the more he tried, the further away it went. Where was she? Was she even alive and if she was, what kind of state was she in? Had it really been her he had seen from the cart? Terrible images started to torment him; pictures of her naked with Xtlan's warriors, the things they were doing to her. He felt his pulse quicken and his nerves tingle with a huge yet impotent anger and hatred. And then the dreadful thought came into his mind that he would never see her again and with this his stomach seemed to collapse inward so that his legs felt unattached to the rest of his body. His hands began to shake and he started to go limp all over. At the same time the cold and the damp of the cavern penetrated right through to his marrow so that every joint and every bone ached with a pain so sharp and so intense that he let out an involuntary groan and hunched himself over, holding his arms tightly around his chest to try and give himself some warmth.

He looked in front of him and the faces of the others had

become blurred and exaggerated into gross, taunting caricatures. He started seeing pictures of Arkron, Jarrah, Shennsah, Sarg – his friend from Ruann; all of them whirling round, talking to him in little snatches of conversation none of which he could understand. And then, like a blessed soothing balm there came a light, a silver light, spreading over everything, filling his mind so that the images grew still and quietly disappeared, the cold in his body subsided and his disembodied limbs came back together again. Still the glorious silver brilliance grew within him and his spirit became calm. And he knew this was Ashgaroth coming to him again, giving him a sign, helping him. 'Have faith; only have faith'; he could almost hear the words.

He opened his eyes and saw Teggrogg, Beddrang and the others watching him curiously. As he looked at them they turned away, almost, thought Melvaig, with embarrassment, pretending they had not been looking. Then he saw Shuinn's anxious face and he smiled at him. The giant, who had been beside himself with worry as Melvaig had screamed and shaken uncontrollably, was now filled with relief that his friend seemed all right again. Shuinn had moved across and was sitting next to Melvaig, his warm brown eyes searching Melvaig's face for confirmation that he really had come round. When he was certain that his worst fears had not been realized, a great smile came to his face and lit it up, the eyes shining with pleasure and his mouth broadening into a grin. He laid a huge hand on Melvaig's shoulder, grasped it firmly but gently and shook him in little jerks, three or four times for sheer exuberant joy.

Looking around him now Melvaig saw that all the other groups were lying down sleeping and that Teggrogg and the others were making themselves as comfortable as they could on the hard stone floor. Shuinn mouthed something at him and Melvaig in return said what they used to say in

Ruann, 'May sleep be your friend.' If only, he thought angrily, they could speak the same tongue. And then, lying down and putting both arms curled together under his head for a pillow he closed his eyes and went to sleep.

It was the sleep of the innocent and the untroubled. Ashgaroth's silver light still lingered in his mind and though he dreamed, his dreams were tranquil and peaceful, of himself and Morven walking together through lush green woods that were filled with flowers and echoed with the songs of birds, of Bracca running and playing in the tall bracken, laughing as he hid from them.

Then suddenly the scene shifted and they were walking along a path over the mountains. The air was still and shimmered with a sparkling clarity while above them in the cathedral of the sky, a lark sang his heart out for the joy of life. Bracca was ahead of them, older now, almost a man, and he kept looking back at them as they walked together hand in hand. As he turned round he smiled and his face shone with care and love and happiness. He waved to them and ran off down the track until he disappeared in the steep cleft of a wooded valley and they could see him no more. Then they saw a hare bounding across their path, his great back legs pushing him forward in huge leaps. He stopped when he saw them, sat up with his ears erect and spoke to them. Melvaig answered him and then they all went off together across a wide expanse of purple heather littered with yellow gorse. It grew warm and so they sat for a while looking out over the hills. There they were joined by a badger, an owl and a dog and they all talked together of many things before moving on. Bracca rejoined them. He had someone with him, a girl, but when Melvaig tried, in his dream, to look at her he was unable to focus on her face and all he was left with was an impression of dazzling golden light. Soon they came to a deep river valley, cutting its way through the hills and suddenly the scene changed, a thick covering of white lay upon everything – a pure white such as he had never seen before. The trees towering up to the sky were thick with it, their branches heavily laden and bending under the weight. The river stood out black against it and there, standing along the bank, were a host of elves. Melvaig and the others walked up to them and then the river seemed to flow up all around and over them until they were submerged in a welcoming pool of oblivion.

When Melvaig woke to the feel of Shuinn's hand frantically shaking his shoulder, it took him some time to realize where he was and to come back from where his mind had taken him. For an instant he thought he was still there; but when realization dawned on him a feeling of sickness spread through his body and a cramp spread its fingers round his heart.

With shaking legs he got up and followed Teggrogg and the others as they made their way over the cavern floor to the shaft to begin another work session.

CHAPTER XVII

Time dragged on. With no night and no day, no light and no dark, Melvaig became suspended in a world that seemed so unreal that many times he wondered if he had died and this was where the spirits dwelt. At other times he believed it to be one long dream from which eventually he would wake up back in Ruann with Morven and Bracca, Jarrah and the others. His mind grew disoriented; the line between what went on inside his head and what went on outside ceased to exist; they merged into one awful tumbling vista of blackness out of which images emerged – whether from his head or in reality he never knew nor even cared. He followed the motions of what something somewhere dictated: down the shaft, hack at the stone, load the cart, back through the tunnel. At the end of the session, when the horn sounded, up the shaft, receive the meagre supply of food and the mouthfuls of water, try to empty his bowels if he could face the stench in the cavern area reserved for that purpose, and then sleep.

The food got less and less as both he and Shuinn grew weaker and their loads diminished and yet always Shuinn was there, a constant reality, supportive, warm, with a strength of mind and an endurance that constantly pulled Melvaig back from the brink of some black abyss which seemed to want to drag him into itself. The giant was all Melvaig saw. Teggrogg, Beddrang, Krill and the Hurll were all creatures; visions from a world that could no longer touch him. Tamrett was dead. They had been lowering him down the shaft some time after the incident with Teggrogg when he had fallen and split his skull on the rock. Whether he had been too weak to hang on to the rope or whether he had deliberately let go, was impossible to know. Teggrogg was angry with himself for now it meant that rather than supervise he had to work so as to keep the quota up and he became particularly surly and vindictive. It meant though that Melvaig and Shuinn were more useful to him so that after a certain point Melvaig fancied that they were beginning to get rather more food although the quantities were so small that it was difficult to tell.

Against all Melvaig's expectations the injured man began to get better. This however meant that he required more food so as soon as he was able to walk he came down the shaft with them and took over the job of dragging the rock-filled cart back to the unloading point. He was still not well; but nevertheless he managed to pull the cart, leaving Melvaig and Shuinn free to spend all their time at the face so that their quota of rock increased.

The first time that the three worked together Melvaig discovered to his delight that the man, Dhiabedd, spoke a similar language to his and that he also spoke in the tongue of Xtlan. So it was that, at last, Melvaig and Shuinn were able to talk to each other, albeit through a third party, but this brought much happiness to them both. Gradually they learned each other's language so that they were soon able to communicate, even if only in a rudimentary way. Melvaig told Shuinn of his life in Ruann, of Jarrah and Morven, and as he told of Bracca the giant's eyes clouded over with a mist of tears. He described the way he had broken with the tradition of the village by allowing himself to love and be loved and to be known to his child and he spoke of the joy they had had together, the laughter and the fun. He told of the village customs, of the way they lived, and Shuinn listened to every word, delighting in the picture that Melvaig's words drew for him.

And Shuinn told Melvaig of his life. Born of one of the Elimsorr he was taken off at birth to be raised by the women of Eggron in one of the warrior nurseries, the Bellkindra. There he proved to be clumsy with weapons and to lack that special streak of savagery, the delight in cruelty and suffering, the joy in killing which marked out a man as being worthy to join Xtlan's warriors. And so he was forced to leave the nursery when he came of age and he joined the wanderers, the Mengoy, those who survived as best they could, living on their wits by pillage, petty theft and occasionally the capture of able-bodied men or women to work as slaves in Xtlan. He had met with and joined Gebb and Nekdog and they had used him for his strength, while he had been grateful to them for their cunning and their guile. He had never felt as one with them though; always the outsider. They never consulted him or asked him his opinions or views; he was simply told what to do. Often he would find them talking together and when he joined them they would go quiet or look at each other in a strange, conspiratorial way so that he felt they were laughing at him.

And yet he stayed with them for he knew no other way of life. Sometimes he would shy away from the excesses of their cruelty, finding some deep hidden part of himself repulsed by their actions despite all his training and conditioning and they would sneer at him and call him weak and goad him, until to spite them and prove himself he would join in and attempt to surpass them in their viciousness. Afterwards, not knowing why, confused and distraught, he would be seized with anguish and a knowledge of his own wrong so that he would leave them for days, wandering through Eggron in a daze of self hate.

Then eventually, always, he would find his way back to them and they would humour him and jolly him along so that he came round and off they would go again into the villages beyond the Hinterland, preying on the weak and the old, the young and the women.

Finding the old Hebbdril, Arkron, had been their greatest stroke of fortune and they had been overjoyed by the value of their find. Quickly they killed the man who was with him, the assistant, though he fought hard and it took all three of them to overpower him. And then, returning to Xtlan through the desert they had looked back and seen the dust cloud left by Melvaig. The rest he knew. For Shuinn, the relationship he had built up with Bracca had been a wonder and a joy. He discovered feelings in himself he did not know existed; gradually his eyes seemed to open so that everything around him seemed different – a new and strange light shone over all that he saw. For the first time in his life he cared about someone other than himself; more than that, he cared more for the boy than for himself. He had of course realized the full extent of this when he had stood up to Gebb at the moment he was about to hit Bracca. It was the first time he had ever gone against Gebb and he had known what it would lead to even then but he had been unable to stop himself and afterwards, instead of regretting his action, he had felt as if a great load had been lifted off his shoulders. A line had been crossed and there was now no going back; he could give himself wholeheartedly to his new self.

But there was still one last vestige of the way he had been: a core of selfishness and cowardice that had to be excised. He had not been aware of it, yet when the black mark was put on him he found himself consumed by a terrible, pitiful and cringing fear. He did not know how long it had taken hold of him but suddenly, as quickly as it had started, it seemed to come to an end and when it did he felt somehow cleansed. Never again would he bow down before anyone, go against his instincts at their command or beg forgiveness and mercy.

And so it had happened that he and Melvaig had come together. And he had been glad, not only because he was the father of Bracca but also because of something he had grown to feel: that in him, Melvaig, was some ultimate purpose or destiny whose nature he was unable to put into words. And it might even be that together they would find Bracca.

While Melvaig was listening to Shuinn's words he felt very deeply affected, for all that he had intuitively felt was now confirmed and the warmth he felt towards him overcame him so that he felt his eyes fill with tears. He stopped the rhythmic hacking at the rock and turning to the giant, clasped him by the shoulders and embraced him.

Now Melvaig was seized with an overwhelming desire to tell Shuinn about the Book, to show it him and share with him the magic of its words and the power of its truths, for this after all was the destiny of which the giant had grown aware. So much then would become clear to him. And yet what of all the warnings given to him by Jarrah and by Arkron; guard the secret closely for none must know, they had said. So he said nothing for the present.

Time wore on, though how many days passed, how many moons waned, was impossible to know. The grinding routine bore them down yet for Melvaig and Shuinn there was a brightness in the cloud of black misery around them. Their friendship and the talks they had while hacking away at the face lightened their hearts and buoyed up their spirits.

Then disease struck. Many of the captives died, mercifully swiftly. All were afflicted with a terrible looseness of the bowels so that the cavern stank even more than normal: a pungent, heavy acrid stench that stuck in the nostrils and caught in the throat. Crippling pains grabbed at the stomach causing men to cry out suddenly and then curl themselves up into a pitiful whimpering ball, their knees forced high up against their chests in an attempt at relief. It became difficult to sleep, whether because of one's own pain or the cries of others and so for a short time no work was done as even the Hurll fell victim to the ravages of the disease.

It passed as quickly and unexpectedly as it had arrived leaving Krill and Gorpenn dead out of Teggrogg's group. Melvaig, Shuinn and Dhiabedd had all survived, as had Beddrang, Schtell and Gebble. It was the weak who went, whether afflicted in body or in spirit. Melvaig and Shuinn, when they had been writhing on the floor clutching their stomachs, had held on to a star of hope which seemed to shine inside their heads and led them on, out and through the pain. The others, well fed, simply staved off the illness with their reserves of strength. Yet Dhiabedd also lived through it. In fact he hardly seemed to become ill at all and busied himself attempting to tend to the others, helping those who were still relatively able to get rid of the bodies of the dead by throwing them into the pit at the opposite side of the cavern. Indeed he now seemed nearly fit again and Melvaig and Shuinn wondered at this; it was almost as if he was being protected, guarded in some way.

Work resumed; the Hurll demanding greater work loads to make up for those who had perished and now Melvaig found himself consumed by one thought: he had to tell Shuinn about the Book. The warnings seemed empty and hollow now, meaningless in the situation he was in. He felt deep within himself that Shuinn was meant to know; this was why they had come together – by design, not by accident. Besides, what if he should die? He felt constantly weak; his shoulder, injured so long ago in another world, gave him terrible pain and his limbs were shaky and riddled with cramp. If he died, what then of the Book, the great destiny which he had foreseen, the great immutable marvels it revealed?

And so, at the beginning of one work session, when Dhiabedd was taking a truckload to the shaft, with the candles in their hats casting flickering tongues of yellow on the rock all around and the specks of gold in the rock face glinting fiercely when the light caught them, Melvaig put his hand into the pouch round his neck and took out the Book. Shuinn stopped working when he saw what Melvaig had put down on the rock floor between them. He looked first at the Book, then at Melvaig, then at the Book again – his eyes wide with wonder.

'I have heard of these,' he said, 'but never seen one before. They are forbidden, though they say that Xtlan has many of them. Where did you get it?'

As he spoke, he slowly and lovingly turned the pages, fingering each one as though it might crumble into dust between his fingers. The patterns of writing on the page seemed to fascinate him, and when he came to a picture he stopped and gazed in awe at the scene before him, shaking his head in disbelief.

'I want to tell you about it. About what it says, what the words tell us.' Melvaig spoke in a hushed whisper, as if the rock had ears. 'But no one else must know, Shuinn. You must never tell what you hear from me, neither must anyone know about the existence of the Book. What it says is of enormous power and importance. I was warned never to talk about it but I feel you should know. I will try and tell you what it says now but we must listen out for Dhiabedd and stop talking when we hear him coming. Do you understand what I'm saying to you?'

'Can you read the words then? Will you read it to me?'

'No,' said Melvaig. 'It was Arkron. You remember, the Hebbdril you captured. He knew of the Book, and of the power of the knowledge it contains. He read it to me, while you were all sleeping and I can remember what it says. I will tell you if you want to know.'

'Yes, yes. Please. Go on,' said Shuinn, anxiously.

And so Melvaig began. At first his words felt clumsy and he spoke haltingly as he struggled to convey the pictures in his head to Shuinn in language he could understand. Silver

Wood, the thick soft layer of white covering the trees and the flakes drifting slowly down to earth. Brock the badger watching out over the fields, seeing two human figures approaching carrying their precious bundle . . .

Shuinn listened intently and then as Melvaig warmed to his task his ideas became more fluid and the words began to flow. The images that had lived in his mind ever since Arkron had put them there now seemed to glow with life, and he stopped thinking about how to convey them; the words tumbled out of his mouth in a torrent, weaving tapestries of magic in Shuinn's spellbound soul. It was as if Ashgaroth had captured Melvaig's tongue and was using it to tell the tale.

Every time Melvaig stopped, and Dhiabedd went to the face to reload the truck, Shuinn's mind refused to return to the present and continued its sojourn in this other world of blue skies, fragrant breezes and unfolding seasons.

The story was not short and Melvaig told it over a number of work sessions. For him also this was a strangely beautiful time as he relived the tale which had never left his mind since Arkron had first related it. And this other world became, through the telling, so real that he wondered at times which world he actually existed in.

After the work sessions, when they had eaten and were asleep, their dreams were coloured with the visions that Melvaig had drawn while they were at the face, so that during the time it took for the story to be told they never left this other world. As they slept, the dreams took the tale deep into their souls so that it became as much a part of them as their blood; it became the very essence of their existence. And when it was over, and Melvaig had come to the end and the final word had been spoken, so an immense anger started to grow within them swelling until it threatened to burst out of them. Tears started to well up in their eyes, tears of sadness and rage at the blindness of their fellow creatures; at the cruelty and the pain and the destruction wrought at their hands. And the triumph of Dréagg tore at their entrails so that they moaned aloud, a pitiful withering moan of anguish at the incredible nature of man's final crime.

Melvaig it was who first recovered from the grip of this terrible fury. He shook his friend by the shoulders, looking deep into his eyes, trying to penetrate the wall of anger that had glazed them over.

'Shuinn, Shuinn,' he called fiercely. 'Stop! It is I, Melvaig – your friend. Come. Talk to me!'

Eventually the giant began to calm down; his breathing grew more regular and his eyes lost their wildness. Finally the moaning grew less frightful and he began to speak, bursts of speech between his heavy breaths, wrestling with himself as his mind struggled to cope with the terrible knowledge of man's history which had been revealed to him. The enormity of that unbelievable crime threatened to crush him beneath its awesome weight so that he felt stifled, unable to see a way out of the gaping chasm that lay before him, dragging him down towards its lost black depths of oblivion. Above all, he felt an overwhelming sense of betrayal and it was perhaps the bitter reality of the anger that this engendered in him that drew him back from the edge. Melvaig's voice sounded, urgent and relevant through the nightmare jumble of jangling cacophonic emotions that blazed inside his head, and he hung on to it as if it were a rope and he a drowning man, pulling himself towards it along this lifeline.

'Listen to me,' the voice was saying. 'All is not lost; it cannot be. Don't you see? It is all meant. You, me, the Book, Arkron: all part of the pattern. That world still exists. It could not perish – it is not possible. Ashgaroth, the Elves, the power of good – all too great, too mighty to have disappeared, vanished. No, it is all here somewhere and we are to find it. This is Ashgaroth's purpose and we are part of it, but we must be strong and worthy even as

Nab and Beth, Brock and Warrigal, Sam and Perryfoot were. This is what I have always somehow felt, Shuinn. Deep down inside, way down so that I was almost unaware of it. And then when I found the Book and Arkron told me of it, I became sure, my feelings all came together and I knew, I was certain. Listen to me, Shuinn! Can you understand what I'm saying?'

And Shuinn heard Melvaig's words and he understood.

'Yes,' he said. 'Yes, I know, I know. It's just – too much. I can't – you've known a long time. For me it's . . .' and he tailed off, shaking his head, lost for words and ways to explain.

Then it was that Melvaig felt a cold chill of panic rush through him as he remembered Dhiabedd and sensed, without looking, that he was in the tunnel. There was no way of knowing how long he had been there nor how much he had heard. And if he had heard, how much had he understood? Should Melvaig tell him also, now that he was aware of the Book's existence. Was he to be trusted? Questions raced through Melvaig's mind as he leaned forward slowly, picked up the Book where it lay so conspicuously on the rock between himself and Shuinn, closed it and, with his back to the tunnel, reached up inside his jerkin and put it back in the pouch round his neck. He could feel Dhiabedd's presence, almost like a force bearing down upon the back of his neck and instinctively felt afraid. Of one thing he suddenly became certain; he must not say anything to him about the incident and above all, must not try to explain.

As if nothing had happened, he took up his pick and began chipping away at the face again, willing Shuinn to do the same, and to Melvaig's relief, the giant followed his example.

'Come on, we shall be lucky to eat tonight,' Dhiabedd's rasping voice came from behind them, almost jauntily, as if for some reason he was trying to hide the fact that he had seen and heard what they were talking about. If he had seen the Book, thought Melvaig, why did he not ask about it? Perhaps, after all, he had only just arrived at the face when the tale had been told and had heard nothing and seen nothing, except perhaps Shuinn acting strangely. Melvaig turned and looked at the thin, worn, grimy face of Dhiabedd.

'Shuinn felt ill; sick and weak. He had to stop.' Then he looked straight into Dhiabedd's eyes. 'Didn't you see as you came out of the tunnel?'

There was a slight pause. Melvaig's heart pounded. He is thinking what to say, he thought. Then came the reply, faltering, with a little quaver in the voice. Too forceful, too positive.

'No,' he said. 'No, I've only just got back. It took me a long time, Melvaig. My gut was hurting. I had a rest.' His eyes dropped and he crawled out of the tunnel pulling the cart and began loading it up with the few bits of rock that lay on the ground.

The rest of the work session passed slowly and awkwardly. Gone was the easy friendship that had grown up between the three of them. The flickering yellow candlelight now seemed to cast dark evil shadows on the rock, whereas before it had been friendly and cosy.

Twice more Dhiabedd went back to the shaft with a loaded cart and during these times Melvaig told Shuinn of his fears and worries. The giant also had felt that Dhiabedd had been listening at the tunnel entrance and agreed with Melvaig that they should say nothing. It came to Melvaig that he ought to hide the Book somewhere in the rock, but when he got it out from its bag and felt it in his hands, the idea of parting with it seemed wrong. Finally the sound of the horn rang through the tunnel. They put their picks down and made their way back, leaving a partly-filled cart at the face. Next session they would fill it up quickly – that always gave them a boost. The others were waiting at the shaft when they arrived. Melvaig looked for some change in them, especially Teggrogg – some indication that Dhiabedd had told him – but there was no sign. The leader's face, fat and greasy, his bald head shining in the candlelight, wore its habitual supercilious smirk.

Suddenly it occurred to Melvaig that he was actually contemplating the possibility that Dhiabedd might betray his friends and he felt ashamed that the idea could have occurred to him. He must banish it before it began to poison him. This was the evil of Xtlan working in him, making friend turn against friend, sowing the seeds of mistrust amongst those who should be allies. He tried to catch Dhiabedd's eye but found that he was unable to. Finally he succeeded and gave him a warm smile, which Dhiabedd returned. Then it was Melvaig's turn to go up the shaft and soon they were all walking along the floor of the cavern to the spot they had come to know so well.

Teggrogg handed out the food ration and they slowly began to chew and savour the small pieces that they broke off, making each mouthful last as long as possible. Normally Melvaig became totally immersed in this process. Now though, for some reason he was unable to analyze, his mind was restless, the cloud of oblivion that had previously enveloped him had dispersed leaving his heart tense and anxious, his muscles taut with nervousness and his head racing with a mass of confused ideas and thoughts, jumbled together into a ball of sickening apprehension that weighed like stone in his stomach.

Was it just because he had come to the end of the story with Shuinn and no longer dwelt in that other world as he had during the telling, reality now once again confronting him with its harsh cold truths? Or was it doubts about Dhiabedd, worries as to how much he had heard and what he might do with the knowledge? Or was it something else, some indefinable instinct of danger that had set his nerves jangling?

He carefully broke off some of the heavy black bread and tore the meat that he had left into two, and put the pieces inside his jerkin for the next work session. Then he lay down on the hard rock floor and closed his eyes. He thought back to the first time he had slept in the cavern and it seemed an age away; so far back that it was as if someone else had then inhabited his body, a stranger to the Melvaig who lay here now and to whom day and night, earth and sky, man and woman were just meaningless memories.

Soon tiredness overwhelmed him and swept over his restless mind but just before he succumbed he somehow knew that this would be the last night he would spend in the mines.

CHAPTER XVIII

He awoke to violent pain and as he fought to rid himself of the clinging threads of sleep he became aware of one of the Hurll savagely shaking him, the man's hands gripped tight on either side of his neck. Standing just a few paces in front he could see the Hurll leader, his face set in a glowering mask of black anger. And then, though his head was being shaken so hard he felt his neck must break, he saw Dhiabedd at the side of the Hurll, and a wave of nausea surged through him. He felt impossibly weak, his limbs shook and his head ached. So his worst fears had been true.

Melvaig's soul writhed in agony beneath the awful pain of betrayal. And now a wave of savage anger exploded within him as he looked at Dhiabedd and he leaped up, breaking free of the Hurll who had hold of his neck, and threw himself with all the strength he could gather upon this vile creature, who fell beneath his furious onslaught. Streams of invective poured from Melvaig's mouth as he grabbed hold of Dhiabedd's hair and smashed his head down on the stone floor, wild with impotent anger, for it was too late now, the damage had been done. Beneath him the fragile broken body of the traitor twisted in a futile attempt to get away and Melvaig, his useless rage spent, stopped his attack and let himself be dragged off by two of the Hurll. He turned to look for Shuinn and saw that he too was being held. The giant looked at Melvaig and smiled. There was a strange calm in his face; the large brown eyes were still, the face quiet, as if nothing now could hurt him. Melvaig knew that he was thinking of Ashgaroth and of the other world and that now, with his faith, nothing could harm him, for what he did was for that world, that majestic golden vision that shone in his mind.

Melvaig saw, and took strength from his friend so that he stopped struggling and put himself at a distance from everything that was happening around him. He saw the Hurll leader pull Dhiabedd to his feet, blood trickling from a gash at the back of his head. How much does he know? he thought. What did he hear and what had he told?

'The Book, where is the Book?' demanded the Hurll leader of Dhiabedd. And now as this cringing creature looked at Melvaig, he felt, not anger any more, but a huge and genuine pity, not for his injuries or the pain in his body but for the barren wasteland of his soul for that must surely be, thought Melvaig, the worst pain of all; how could this wretch now live with himself? Dhiabedd did not look at Melvaig, his eyes cast down, flickering nervously from side to side.

'He has it on him somewhere. It must be on him,' he said in a feeble whining voice.

Melvaig's jerkin was then ripped open and the bag taken from around his neck. The leader opened it and took out the Book, its case glinting in the candlelight. He then found Morven's moccasin and threw it down on the floor while Melvaig struggled to control the anguish that boiled within himself. All the captives were awake, watching – Melvaig could feel their eyes on him, piercing him through like myriads of tiny darts. Morven! Fleeting visions of her flashed before his eyes as he looked at her moccasin. She seemed unreal now, like something he had once dreamed about. Only the presence of her moccasin had proved the reality of her existence and when that was gone, where then would she be?

He watched as the leader opened the Book, his Book, and he felt the bitter taste of revulsion in his throat as he saw the pages being turned, handled, almost fondly by the Hurll. It was a horrible violation of something sacred and as each page opened to reveal itself before the thirsting eyes of the Hurll so Melvaig felt pierced to the depths of his spirit as if his soul was being stripped naked, forced to expose its innermost, precious secrets. Slowly, lasciviously, the man's gaze roamed across each sheet, an absent smile playing across his lips, not knowing what the pages said but feeling the power of their presence. And when he had finished he looked up at Melvaig with a sneer of triumph, his face flushed with happiness, for what rewards would Xtlan not give him for finding this prize? His eyes glittered with a fierce light as he savoured this moment. And not only had he the Book, but also two captives who seemed to be in possession of a great deal of knowledge regarding its contents. Strange things the traitor had told him of what he had overheard: of Ashgaroth and Dréagg, of animals and men, of elves and magic, blue skies and green fields and much else that he could not comprehend. Could it be the Book of which so much was rumoured, the legendary tale of which all who dwelt in Xtlan knew and which all warriors were told to look out for on their raids and battle forays into neighbouring territories? The Book of which it was said that possession would bring such knowledge that truly would Xtlan be ruler over all the lands, yet without which he would never be able to claim absolute dominion. What secrets must it then contain? What keys to absolute eternal power, if even Xtlan was afraid of the knowledge that lay within.

He finished turning the pages and closed the Book, feeling that he was on the crest of a wave, a wave that would carry him, Burgunn, from the relative obscurity of the Gurrtslagg to a pinnacle of power where perhaps only Xtlan himself would be supreme over him. This was what he had worked for all his life, what he had felt himself fitted for from those far away days as a young boy when, in the Bellkindra, he had first begun to cultivate the ruthlessness, cunning and blind cruelty that had taken him to a position of dominance over his peers and got him noticed. The fabrication of elaborate stories of treachery and weakness in those of his equals by whom he felt threatened, allied with the aura of fear he seemed to inspire in others, had helped in his rise. His skills in fighting, fuelled by the sheer sensual satisfaction he felt at the infliction of pain had made even the grown warriors, those who trained Xtlan's fledgling fighters, afraid of him.

When he left, he distinguished himself time and again on raids, helping the growth of Xtlan's power and influence as more and more lands and people were conquered by his marauding bands. The weak they left, to be taken any time, it was the strong, the rival races which they had subjugated first, letting the tales of horror that emanated from these dreadful raids spread before them and so weaken the hearts of any who would stand against them.

Then Xtlan had chosen him for one of his lieutenants – the Hurll – that select band of men whose job it was to lead. These ambassadors of fear and cruelty were feared and reviled, even amongst the other warriors, as they carried the spirit of Xtlan with them. They were the ones who commanded projects, led raids, organized their sport. For a time he, Burgunn, had been in charge of building a section of the wall and then he had been offered this most prestigious of posts, Overseer of the Gurrtslagg, which he had taken not only for the power and position it gave him but also out of prudence, for as fast as Xtlan raised a man, so did he cut him down. Those who grew and rose too fast were apt to find themselves purged, for no reason; consigned to the mines as captives or else used for sport or

217

simply given over to those they had persecuted, their erstwhile victims, who did with them as they pleased. And so Burgunn had taken this position gratefully and with some relief for, as he reasoned to himself, the further away from Xtlan he was, the less chance there was that the moving finger of fortune would suddenly swing over and crush him, like a beetle under a boot. He had stayed, but the initial euphoria of his aggrandisement had not taken long to fade and soon he had chafed to get away, get back to the seat of power and feel himself once more in the centre of everything. Not even the many little satiates to his lusts that he was able to indulge as an inevitable and indeed vitally important consequence and accompaniment to his all-powerful position as Overseer, were able to salve his burning desire to continue his rise in the loose chaotic hierarchy of Xtlan.

Yet he found himself at the same time reluctant to forgo the safety and security he enjoyed in the mines. He grew, to his consternation, afraid of returning to the savage cut and thrust of Xtlan where the constant uncertainty, the need to be relentlessly on guard for others eager to take your place who would stop at no trickery or treachery to achieve it, wore a man down.

Now though, to return with a prize such as this, would surely secure for him huge favour from Xtlan and re-establish him as someone too useful to dispense with. His continued and safe rise would be certain. In any case, the fires of his ambition burned too brightly to allow himself to languish any longer in the mines and there would never be a better opportunity to go back.

All this he thought, as the Book weighed in his hands, and his eyes looked around him warily. Of one thing he was certain; everything must be handled carefully. The other Hurll must not know of the possible significance of the Book, otherwise who could guess what trickery they would indulge in to get hold of it. No. As far as they were concerned it was simply a book; that was important enough by itself to justify taking charge of things himself and returning with it to Eggron. The two captives, the giant and the smaller one who had had the Book, would have to be watched very carefully and killed as soon as their usefulness had run its course and the full extent of their knowledge was known. He had a difficult and delicate task here; he had to tell Xtlan enough for the significance of the Book to be immediately apparent and yet at the same time not so much that Xtlan would feel he might attempt to use that knowledge against him and that he, Burgunn, had become a threat. The wretch who brought him the information, Dhiabedd, would of course have to be got rid of now before he talked any more. He looked at him and Dhiabedd pulled his mouth into an ingratiating smile.

'Come,' Burgunn said. 'Let me give you some of your reward. You have done well. You must eat and drink until you have had your fill.'

Dhiabedd seemed to grow visibly in stature; his chest rounded itself out and he straightened his back. He felt the eyes of the other captives upon him, and gloried in their envy. Burgunn also was aware of them. They must not know of his fate, otherwise others would be discouraged from passing on information about their fellows – so crucial to the maintenance of the atmosphere of mistrust and treachery which sustained their subjugation.

'And after you have eaten,' he went on loudly so that his voice rang around the cavern walls, 'you will come with us to Eggron where you shall indulge in the best of everything, food, drink and women. Women to fulfil the wildest of your dreams.' At this, a ripple of tension ran amongst the captives so that they seemed to shiver with a terrible yearning.

'Hold these two while I take Dhiabedd up the steps. He must have time to eat before we leave.'

Dhiabedd drew himself up to his full height. Gone was

the nervousness of before; now he was cocky, arrogant, his eyes ranging around him with a look of disdain. This was better than he had dared to hope. Confidently he found the eyes of Melvaig and Shuinn. Their looks of contempt could not touch him now. Why should they? Each man to look after himself. He had not asked them to help him, look after him. Why now should he feel anything towards them? He had suffered; now it was his turn for some pleasure.

Burgunn indicated the steps and, limping slowly but with his head held jauntily high, he walked towards them. Burgunn followed and soon they were out of sight in the tunnel.

For some time after, the captives continued to gaze, numb with envy, at the stone archway up which Dhiabedd had walked. They looked, as if by so staring, and wishing hard enough, they could take themselves after him – out, into freedom, and daylight, and morning and evening, and sun and moon. He took their dreams with him and eventually, as the image of his departing figure faded in their minds, they settled back down to sleep once more.

The Hurll who were holding Melvaig and Shuinn, forced them down on to their knees and proceeded to lash their hands together. Time dragged slowly by until suddenly, quietly, Burgunn reappeared alone. His footsteps padded softly over the hard stone floor of the cavern and the yellow candlelight cast his shadow, huge and grotesquely misshapen, on the wall as he moved.

'Bring them. Now!' he said to the Hurll and Melvaig felt the familiar queasy surge of fear in his stomach. He was hauled roughly to his feet and pushed forward towards the stone archway down which they had come so long ago. Shuinn was ahead of him; the guards were trying to man-handle and shove him on quickly but he refused to let them, maintaining his own pace despite them. Now they were climbing the steps, Burgunn leading, Shuinn and two Hurll behind, then Melvaig with two more guards coming last.

The climb seemed to go on for ever. Melvaig's thigh muscles started to ache and his head grew giddy but there was no rest, no respite from the continual upward movement. If he tried to slow down or his legs faltered, then he would feel the hard round end of a club jammed into the small of his back and he would stumble, almost losing his footing on the narrow stone steps. On and on they went; had it been this far down? Melvaig tried to think back but his memory was hazy and confused. Then he grew aware of a change in temperature; it was getting warmer. He had been used to the continual and constant cold of the cavern for so long that it took him a little time to realize exactly what it was that was affecting his body in this way, at first sending a little pleasurable wave of energy through every part of himself, right down to the marrow in his bones, so that it felt as if the substance and fibres of his body were waking up after a long sleep.

But then, as they got higher and the warmth grew into heat, he began to sweat and his body started to prickle all over and very soon he started to wish for the cool again. Suddenly, ahead of them, Melvaig saw the entrance into the shed at the top of the steps. Not much further now and they would be out on top, on the surface, and despite all the uncertainties and the fears, he felt a thrill of anticipation at seeing daylight again, and grass, and the sky. But would they be killed? If so, why bring them up here to do it? What was in Burgunn's mind? What was he going to do with them?

The last step now and they were in the gloom of the shed and already the feeling of heat was oppressive. Sharp arrows of light found their way through the chinks in the walls and sent piercing golden lances into the darkness. Melvaig looked at one but turned away sharply, his eyes filled with pain and his head exploding with little stars. Shuinn let out an involuntary cry as his eyes too found the light and his bound hands flew up to cover his face. Then cautiously Melvaig looked around the shed, taking care to keep his eyes in the dark. Burgunn and the four Hurll were gathered together in a corner around a dark shape on the floor. They were laughing loudly but it was not happy laughter; it was edged with a sharp border of viciousness so that it seemed somehow constricted, not open and free as real laughter is.

He tried to make out what the dark shape was but he could not and then suddenly one of the Hurll turned round and called to them.

'Here,' he shouted above the laughter of the others. 'You, both of you. Come here. We've got a present for you.'

Melvaig looked at Shuinn. They did not move. The Hurll called again, only now the tone of his voice was sharpened with anger at their disobedience.

'Quickly. Move. Over here. We have something to show you.'

Shuinn whispered under his breath, 'Be ready,' and started to edge slowly forward. Melvaig followed cautiously. The Hurll parted to make way for them and then Melvaig realized what it was. He saw the head first, with the mouth still drawn into an inane smile of triumph and then, a little distance away, lay the twisted body. At the look of horror on their faces, the Hurll launched themselves into another round of laughter.

'See,' said Burgunn. 'Your traitor. The one who betrayed you. It is his just end. He deserved worse. We thought you'd be pleased. Revenge! You should be pleased. Thank me. So laugh, curse you, laugh.'

Melvaig's mind was jumbled and confused. Yes, he should be pleased at the sight of this treacherous wretch lying, headless, at his feet – the blood still sticky, staining the stone floor black. Yet he was aghast at the sight; sorrow and pity at the waste of this man's life filled his heart rather than satisfied revenge.

Shuinn too showed no flicker of pleasure at the gory heap before him. But Burgunn was not happy at the lack of appreciation showed by these two ungrateful wretches. Proud, were they? Felt themselves better for being touched with pity? No wonder the giant had ended up in the mines, with that kind of attitude.

'I said laugh. Laugh or as sure as I stand here, I'll make you suffer!' He moved towards Melvaig with a red look of hatred in his eyes. 'I would as soon kill you now as later,' he said, and his mouth was held tight so that the words were forced through his teeth.

The other Hurll had fallen silent, watching with amused fascination. It had become a contest now, a battle of wills between their leader and the two captives. Burgunn knew this and knew also that he dare not back down now if he was not to lose face in their eyes. Yet he could not kill them; they were too important to him alive. A crucial part of his gift to Xtlan. Why had his pride taken him into this stupid situation? He would have to control his pride and his temper when he returned to Eggron. They were for fools and idiots. He had always had control before. His mind had reigned supreme over all his emotions. He had been stuck too long in this accursed backwater; he had lost his edge. Why didn't they laugh? Why? He had never for a moment imagined they would be anything but overjoyed at the man's death.

Melvaig was frightened. Why didn't he laugh? He should after all have been pleased. And yet there was something in the way Burgunn was walking towards him that told him the giant Hurll was reluctant to go further. There was a cloudiness in the eyes, a lack of purpose, of thrust. I must give him a chance to retreat without appearing weak to his fellows, he thought.

'I cannot laugh; it is not my way, nor that of my friend. Yet if what you did was for us, then I am not ungrateful and if I offend you, then I am sorry. It is not meant as an affront.'

Their eyes met and held each other for an instant. Melvaig sensed that he had been right – the Hurll did not want to kill them. And then Burgunn spoke.

'You are lucky today is a good day for me,' he said and Melvaig, if no one else, could hear the relief in his voice. 'I accept your apology. Later you will pay but for now we must go.'

He turned away and said sharply to the others, 'Time for the horses. Eyes! And do theirs as well.'

One of the Hurll went over to a little wooden chest that lay in one corner of the shed and, opening it, took out some strips of skin.

'Here,' he called to Melvaig and Shuinn.

They walked over and he tied the strips round their eyes so that they could see nothing. They stood in the darkness and then they heard a multitude of creaks and groans as the large wooden doors were hauled open. Suddenly a blaze of heat and light rushed in and surrounded them. In front of their eyes, where everything had a moment ago been pitch black, there was now a dazzling brilliance in which myriads of little coloured stars, reds and greens and blues and yellows, exploded, trailed away and disappeared in a never ending succession. Without the eye bands they would have been blinded. As it was, their eyes stung painfully as hundreds of little stabs of light bit into them so that they turned their heads away sharply.

The dry dusty heat chafed against their skin and the air stuck in their throats as they breathed. They could see nothing, but sounds of movement were all around them and then Melvaig heard, with a thrill of joy, the whinnying of a horse. Then another and another, clip-clopping their way over the parched earth and across the wooden floorboards of the shed. He could smell the heavy pungent muskiness of their sweat and his mind swam back to memories of Bendro and riding in the hills round Ruann, so many ages ago.

Now he could sense the presence of the horse near him and he could hear its breathing. A part of himself that he had forgotten about now awoke and a flood of warmth poured through him.

Suddenly he felt himself grabbed by the legs and pushed up and over the back of one of the horses. A rope was lashed around his feet, passed under the horse's stomach and tied to his bound hands so that he lay with his head hanging down one side and his feet down the other. He was able to see a bit now; vague blurred shapes came together in his vision when he concentrated hard enough, and when, with difficulty, he raised his head he could just make out that Shuinn had been similarly tied over the back of another of the horses.

So, thought Melvaig, they were not going to be killed yet. They were to be taken somewhere. Would it be to Eggron? But why? Burgunn had the Book. Was that not enough? No. He was obviously aware of its significance and must have guessed from what Dhiabedd had told him that he and Shuinn had knowledge of its contents. They must be important to him for what they knew. This was why they were being spared, for the moment.

Burgunn's voice broke into Melvaig's thoughts. 'Are they ready? Tied properly?'

A murmur of assent broke from the others.

'I leave you as overseer then, Graalum, until I come back or Xtlan appoints someone else.' With that Burgunn, on the leading horse, began to ride out of the shed and, as the slack on the rope between the horses tightened, first Melvaig and then Shuinn suddenly jerked forward and, with the steady rhythm of the horses beneath their stomachs, rode out of the Gurrtslagg and over the narrow causeway they had crossed so long ago in the driving rain when they first came to the mines.

CHAPTER XIX

It took Melvaig's eyes a long time to get used to the light again. For some distance the brightness penetrated even the eye strips so that he kept his lids tight shut. All he knew was the steady walk of the horse and the feel of fresh air on his face. Hot though it was, he welcomed its touch against his skin and the unfamiliar smells it carried with it so that, beyond the strong scent of the horse, he caught the tang of hot earth, the dry drift of dust stirred up by the hooves, the rocks – exuding the distinctive metallic smell caused by their constant roasting under the sun. Occasionally a whiff of fresh green leaves would come to him as they passed a hawthorn and he would rejoice in its luxuriance, letting his mind wander into visions of dense woodland, until a sudden jolt from the horse or the sharp sound of a hoof striking against stone would break the spell and bring him crashing back into reality.

They began to climb steeply, his horse walking slowly and with some difficulty as it picked its way carefully over what Melvaig guessed was very rough ground. They must have left the main track, probably the route they had come on in the cart, and were now making their way up and over one of the mountains he had seen through the driving rain. He became very uncomfortable as the horse ascended, sliding back against its rear haunches and being tossed about as its back swung from side to side in its awkward manoeuvres up the path.

But to be out of the mines! Out from that damp dark tomb, and to know the sky above and the earth beneath again. That was a feeling of such joy that it overwhelmed him beneath its euphoric blaze. His aching limbs, his worn and battered shoulder, even his worries and fears as to the future and the fate that lay in store – all these, for the moment, were submerged beneath a strange and powerful sensuality that surged through him – the sensation of space and openness, of immense vistas of nothing, emptiness; air that stretched for ever around him.

Eventually, cautiously, he tried opening his eyes. A little at first, with the lids only just apart and ready to shut again should the light prove too painful. But no, to his relief he was able to keep them open and even through the band he could watch the ground drift past beneath his dangling head. He could see the horses' hooves as they found their hold on the stony track, moving steadily and with a delicacy that had always amazed him – that such a large animal should have such a fine deliberation about its movements.

He moved his head and could see Shuinn's horse behind, attached to his by a length of rope. Shuinn's head was bobbing up and down like his, on the same side, with his face horizontal to the ground. Had he opened his eyes? Would he look? How far away was Burgunn? Melvaig turned his head and looked up the other way. Lifting his face he could see Burgunn's broad back astride the horse in front. He seemed relaxed, happy, his back curved, letting his body move from side to side with the movements of the horse.

Melvaig turned his face back to Shuinn and coughed quietly. No response. Again. Still nothing. He coughed more loudly now, timing it so that it coincided with the fall of a hoof. This time Shuinn's head moved sharply in Melvaig's direction and, when he saw his friend, a broad smile spread over his face. Melvaig smiled back, relieved and pleased to have made contact. For a short time they stayed like that, smiling at each other, and then Shuinn mouthed something, a word. Melvaig shook his head, not understanding what he was trying to say. The giant tried again and this time Melvaig knew. Eggron. So it was as he had guessed; they were being taken back to Eggron. Shuinn must have recognized the route. They turned their faces back to the ground again. They could say no more and there was no more yet to say. So, thought Melvaig, Eggron; and one idea crashed back into his mind. Were Morven and Bracca still there? The possibility that he might be near them again sent the blood racing through his veins. Would he and Shuinn get the opportunity to escape? And if they did get free of Burgunn, could they find them? They would have to search Eggron, remain hidden by day and go out at night, for the black brands on their faces would give them away instantly even if their general appearance did not.

Escape! Freedom! Melvaig's spirits lifted and his mind surged with possibilities. Two of them and only Burgunn to guard them. It should be easy. There must be a chance. The opportunity must come some time. Would he feed them? They had not been given food when they were brought in the wagon. What if he pretended to be ill, sick? Would the Hurll stop and get him down and would he then be able to kill him or knock him out? There would be no second chance if the first attempt failed. And yet would there ever be a better time? Once they were in Eggron it would surely be impossible. He envisaged them being incarcerated in a cell, deep within one of those dark forbidding buildings that had struck fear into his heart at his first sight of the place. Entombed again! Memories of it were so painful that at the thought of returning to a life of captive darkness, his stomach retched as a wave of nausea engulfed him. No, better be dead, no matter how terrible the death, than to spend another moment in the

228

living hell of an existence like that again.

And so, as the options became clear to him and the consequences of remaining captive seared across his mind, he was gripped by dread. Melvaig decided that there was no real choice; they had to escape from Burgunn and regain their freedom. Suddenly he found, having made the decision, that the clarity of purpose focused his mind and sharpened his wits so that, for the first time in as long as he could remember, he felt a confidence and an excitement which set his nerve ends tingling and his heart pounding as he fought to control it. 'May Ashgaroth guide me.' The prayer came despite himself; to his surprise the words slipped out under his breath, almost by themselves, and shocked him by the ease with which his mouth formed them. And yet they gave him a strength and a comfort which he was thankful for.

He raised his head with difficulty so that he could look around. Surprisingly they had not come far since the last time he had looked, when he had made contact with Shuinn. Odd that physically they had travelled so little distance for in his head he felt he had, in that short time, come a long, long way. Then his soul had had a bleakness, a fatalistic despairing gloom had weighed down upon it, whereas now, suddenly, that was gone and his spirit was open and buoyant. They were still climbing up the rocky path and around them, shimmering in the heat, the mountains rolled away in gentle undulations, the ground baked and cracked and the few patches of grass and scrub that managed to survive, brown and withered. Occasionally an angular finger of rock would poke its way through the earth but mostly the surface remained unbroken; there was not here the rugged granite majesty of Ruann that he remembered with nostalgic yearning. A long, long way back down the slopes he thought he could make out, as a black speck, the hut by the entrance to the Gurrtslagg but there was no other sign of human occupation. All was still except for a slight breeze which sometimes picked up the dust from the horses' hooves and flung it up into the air, tossing it around until, when it got bored, it suddenly let go and the dust dropped in a little cloud back to the ground.

The sun, pushing its rays through the grey haze of the sky, was on the way down. They were now riding into it and Burgunn's tall shadow, elongated into a bizarre silhouette, was moving over the ground in front of Melvaig, occasionally passing over the lower parts of his horse's legs. There could not be too much time left before Eggron appeared in the distance, perhaps just over the top of the mountain, so that as they reached the summit there it would lie, spread out before their eyes in the valley beneath. He must start to make a move now. He must tell Shuinn, but first he must have clear in his own mind what he planned to do. Instinctively he wriggled his hands and found, to his delight and astonishment, that he could move his wrists inside the ropes with quite a bit of ease. The jogging and jolting up the track must have worked them loose and it should not take too much effort to get them free. The rope under the horse's stomach was attached to that round his wrists so he would then have complete freedom apart from his ankles. He tried to move them. To his disappointment the rope bit tight into the skin. He tried again but it became even tighter. No, there was no way they would work loose. He would have to pretend he was ill. He felt intuitively that he and Shuinn were important to Burgunn alive and in a reasonable state of health so that they could divulge the secrets of the Book. They would have to be clear-minded for that. If any physical pressure was to be used against them then that would be ordered by Xtlan and they would need to be relatively strong and healthy to withstand it and still talk. Burgunn saw his task as delivering them and the Book, of that Melvaig was fairly sure. He should then, hopefully, be concerned if he, Melvaig, showed signs of serious illness. Concerned enough to stop and let him down off the horse? That was a risk, the chance he had to take. And if he did, well, then he would, with his hands free, find some opportunity. The strength would come to him; tired, broken and worn though his body was, his spirit would somehow dredge together the energy he needed. Of that, he was as certain as he had ever been of anything. Now he must tell Shuinn.

It did not take long to convey to the giant, bobbing up and down behind him, by a mixture of signs, gestures and carefully mouthed words, the rough plan that Melvaig had in mind. In fact Shuinn had also been thinking of an attempt at escape and had found, like Melvaig, that the lashings round his wrists had worked loose. When the guards had tied them they had been over-confident or had simply not bothered or cared too much. Two shattered captives. Escape was inconceivable! And Burgunn had not checked. Why should he? And so Shuinn now, like Melvaig, was poised ready for a chance. When they had both worked their wrists free they would signal to each other and then the plan would begin.

It did not take long and very soon Melvaig looked at Shuinn and nodded vigorously, to which the giant responded. The loops that had been tied round their wrists were now hanging loose and to keep on the horses they had to hang on to the rope that went under the stomach. So that Burgunn would not suspect, Melvaig kept the lashings on, making sure that he could easily, when the time came, slip them off.

It was now, then! This was the moment. It would soon be over, whatever happened. They would either be free or, their chance gone, bound up once again beneath the fury and rage of Burgunn. And what would he then do with them? What consequences would follow when they reached Eggron? Melvaig dared not let himself think about it.

Instead he raised his head and looked at Burgunn's huge broad back moving easily with the rolling of the horse. His head was tilted slightly up, as if he was gazing at some far-away star. He seemed jaunty, confident and happy – looking forward to the start of a bright new future.

Melvaig, not giving himself any more time to think, closed his eyes and started groaning. Very low at first, hardly audible above the clumping of the hooves, but gradually growing louder, rising and falling as he imagined waves of pain coursing through him. He did not want Burgunn to become suddenly conscious of him; a gradual awareness that Melvaig was sick was what he wanted to engender in Burgunn's mind, otherwise suspicions might arise. Groaning louder and still louder, he willed his body into a world of pain; the soreness in his stomach, where the horse was rubbing against him, grew until it became a real pain and indeed even Shuinn began to get worried as he wondered whether Melvaig really was putting it on.

Burgunn looked round, a look of annoyance on his face, his forehead puckered into furrows of perplexity. He turned back and Melvaig carried on. They continued on a bit further; Melvaig's heart was pounding furiously beneath the imagined cocoon of pain that he had constructed around himself. Would Burgunn stop? Or would he carry on to Eggron, thinking it best to get there quickly before his captive got any worse? He had to stop! He *had* to stop! Melvaig tried to will the huge broad back of the Hurll to turn round and then out of the corner of his eye he saw Burgunn's horse start to slacken its pace slightly. The groans of pain continued, neither increased nor decreased in intensity; no sign that Melvaig was responding to his captor's actions. Slower went the horse, and still slower until at last, to Melvaig's intense relief, it stopped. Burgunn turned round and stared at him for what seemed an age. Melvaig twisted himself slowly, painfully around, shifting this way and that. He saw Burgunn's mouth move in a curse and then in one swift fluid movement the Hurll swung himself down and began walking slowly back towards him.

'Sick, my prize! Sick, are we? Well, what is it?'

Melvaig mumbled something deliberately inaudible.

'What was that? What did you say? Speak up, curse you! What is it? Can it wait? Not far to go now, you know. Soon be there.'

'My . . . my gut,' said Melvaig. 'Rest. Water . . .' He tailed off. He had to get the Hurll to let him down. Burgunn sidled a bit nearer.

'Your gut.' He went quiet, thinking. Had they time for a rest? A bite to eat and a drink. Maybe it was not a bad idea. There was no real hurry. They had made good time up until now and he would not mind a rest himself. Get off the damned horse. It had been a long time since he had done any riding. He was not used to it. A bit sore. And maybe the captive was really quite bad. If that was the case then he would need a respite. The healthier the condition he arrived in, the better.

'Come on then, filth, let's have you down.'

Melvaig felt almost paralysed with a fearful tension that gripped his limbs. Now, then! Burgunn moved quickly across, took a knife from his belt and cut the rope that passed under the horse's belly, just below his ankles, leaving them bound tightly together. Then he moved round to where Melvaig's head hung. Would he spot the slack in the rope round his wrists? No. He put a hand under each armpit and roughly dragged Melvaig's limp body from the horse, letting him down heavily on to the hard ground. Melvaig let out a sharp cry and, as if from sudden shock, opened his eyes wide so that he could see where Shuinn was. Not many paces back, the giant's horse in fact was standing only just behind where Melvaig was now lying. If only he could get a bit closer to Shuinn. He rolled over as if in agony, clutching his stomach and moaning loudly, and then rolled again until he could see the giant's hands hanging only just above and behind his head.

Burgunn stood still and watched him with a bemused look on his face. Curse his luck! Why couldn't the stupid creature have waited until they had reached Eggron before throwing this fit. How bad was he? Just then, while Burgunn was wondering what to do for the best, Melvaig began to speak.

'Have you – water. Please.' He paused. 'Water,' in a voice that was hoarse and cracked.

Why not, thought the Hurll. He had more than enough for the rest of the journey and it might just do some good. He turned and moved back to his horse to fetch one of the goatskin water bags. Desperately Melvaig swept both arms over the ground feeling with his fingers for a rock or stone until to his joy his questing hand bumped against something hard, sharp and angular. He pulled at it, keeping his eyes fixed on Burgunn's back, as the Hurll delved into his saddle pack for the water. The stone was stuck firmly into the hard ground. It must come free, it must. Frantically he scrabbled with the tips of his fingers, using his nails to scratch away the earth round the base of the stone. Burgunn must turn round soon. Come on! Come loose! He dug his nails as far under it as he could, shut his eyes and putting every fibre of his will into the effort, pulled. It moved slightly. He pulled again, twisting at the same time and it broke free. A wave of glorious relief gushed through him. Slowly now, for fear that Burgunn would turn round at any moment, he moved both arms back until they were stretched out behind his head, the precious stone clutched firmly inside the fist of his right hand. He had just stopped and was fighting to compose himself when Burgunn moved away from his horse and started to walk over to him, the water bag hanging over his arm. He stood beside Melvaig for an instant, deliberating, and then, deciding that the captive would be unable to give himself a drink, and that if he tried, more would probably spill on the ground than go down his throat, he knelt down, untied the thonging round the neck of the bag and, bending over Melvaig's face, placed the neck against his lips and lifted the bag so that water started to trickle into his open mouth.

At that moment Melvaig, with a silver vision of Ashgaroth shining in his mind to fuel his body with vibrant trembling energy, smashed the rock down with all the power he could muster on to Burgunn's skull. There was an awful sickening crunch as it bit into the bone and the huge Hurll let out a cry of rage and pain that rose up into the hot still air and rang out over the mountains. He reeled backwards, clasping his hands to his head as if trying to quench the river of blood that was pumping out of the gash. Melvaig watched, too horrified to move, as Burgunn attempted to get up, tottering crazily on his legs and howling a terrible wailing cry. He lurched first one way then the other, forwards and back.

It was Shuinn who made the first move. He swung himself off the horse, grabbed the bloody stone from Melvaig's grasp and pounded away furiously at the rope that still tied him to the horse. The strands soon frayed and with a final tug the rope snapped. He pulled at the rope round his ankles but it refused to loosen at all. There was no time to get it off; Burgunn was screaming and swaying and had now begun to lash out with his fists at the air, punching at it crazily as if it was responsible for his agony.

Then suddenly he seemed to pull himself together even though the gaping jagged injury on his head was still flowing with red. His eyes fixed on Melvaig and he quietened down as a terrible smile spread slowly over his face. His frantic anger had found its focus. His hand moved automatically to his belt; he drew out his club and then blindly, remorselessly he started to walk the few steps across to where Melvaig was lying numb and paralysed with fear. Shuinn, the fateful stone nestled in his palm, then began to hop over towards the Hurll. Burgunn, his entire being concentrated on Melvaig, did not notice the bizarre apparition dancing over to him until it was too late. The stone found its mark the first time. Shuinn rammed it into the man's chin and Burgunn toppled over but he stretched his hand out as he fell and pulled Shuinn down on top of him. Melvaig was now galvanized into action and he flung himself over the earth, desperately reaching for the hand in which Burgunn was holding the club. The Hurll was trying to wrench his arm free from under Shuinn's weight so that he could bring the club down on him but Melvaig managed to grab the wrist. He twisted it until the grip slackened and then dug his fingers into Burgunn's palm so that he was able to get his hand round the shaft. He yanked at it and it came free.

Now, if he could just stand up and swing it down full on the head of the Hurll. The rope bit deep into his ankles as he levered himself off the ground but as he tried to get upright his legs, cramped and numb from the journey, refused to support him and he fell. Burgunn and Shuinn were now rolling over and over; the terribly injured Hurll, powered by an awful rage, was now kneeling astride Shuinn who, weakened by the deprivation in the mines had found his limbs heavy and his strength gone. Burgunn's hands were locked round Shuinn's throat and the Hurll, with blood dripping into his opponent's eyes, was trying to throttle him. Melvaig now manoeuvred himself into a position where he was kneeling just behind Burgunn who, intent on the struggle with Shuinn, had not noticed him. He raised the club over his head and brought it down on Burgunn's skull. Instantly the Hurll released his grip on Shuinn. His hands clawed at the air as he tried to rise, teetering precipitously on the edge of oblivion, and then he toppled over, landed with a thud on the hard ground and lay still. Melvaig, obsessed by a frantic desire to make sure the man was dead, swung the club down again and again, each blow an act of hatred and revenge. Then, half crazed with sickening horror at the awful sight before him, he flung the club from him and crawled away on his hands and knees, weeping, shivering in the grip of the terrible lusts that had seized him. His stomach retched in sickening revolt at what he had done and at the black passion that had claimed him as he brought the club down into the bloody mess of what had been, mere moments before, a living, breathing, seeing, listening man: Burgunn. All rationality of what he had done escaped him; what he could recall most about those moments, and the thing that struck most deeply into his soul, twisting and turning like a red hot knife, was the feeling of power he had had and, worst of all, the indisputable fact that he had enjoyed it. Visions of the terrible slaughter that they had been greeted with at the mines swam before his eyes; the Hurll purging the captives with their random slaughter, inflicting death and pain for the fun of it. The glazed looks on their faces as their dark souls wallowed in the frenzied lusts which they were indulging. How sickened he had been! Shocked beyond belief by the terrible revelation of what could lie buried in the deepest and most unexplored recesses of the human mind and spirit. How self-righteously he had turned away then! And now – in him! Was he no better? What had happened to him? What awful path had his mind taken?

The questions raged in his brain and he sobbed uncontrollably until the turmoil inside himself boiled up and the churning fire in his guts burst from his mouth. It was as if he was spewing up his very soul as his stomach wrenched against itself and brought up what little it contained. Again and again he seemed to be gripped by the convulsive spasms; his whole body turning in upon itself until at last he grew aware of firm hands shaking him by the shoulders and Shuinn's voice, far away at first but coming closer as Melvaig focused his shattered mind on to it. He felt his feet gripped and turned upwards and he followed them round so that he sat upright facing his friend. Shuinn was busy with two stones, holding one under the thonging and smashing the other down upon it, and he did not look up as he spoke.

'We must be gone: quickly. His shouts. They may have been heard. Are you all right?'

The urgency of their situation and the quiver of tension in Shuinn's voice forced Melvaig to drag his addled wits together.

'Yes. I . . .' he stopped, not knowing what to say, or even how to say it. 'Shuinn, I . . . what I did to his head. I felt . . .' Again he stumbled on the words.

With a last hard knock, the remnants of the rope came apart and Melvaig felt his ankles fall apart from one another on either side of Shuinn's knee where he had been supporting them. The giant looked up at his friend and Melvaig found comfort beyond words, and understanding, in the limpid dark brown oases of his eyes.

'I know,' he said slowly, 'I am the same. Anger takes over and afterwards, I feel as you do. Because it is not your nature. It would be time to worry if you did not feel this way; then would you truly be as they are. But anger for what they have done to you and the others, for the pain they have put upon you; can that be wrong? But now there is no time to talk. Come!'

He helped Melvaig to his feet.

'The body. Where is it?' he said, for there was no sign of it on the track.

'Down there. Under that bush,' Shuinn replied. Melvaig looked and saw a small, low hawthorn a little way down the slope. 'I broke some branches and laid them over him. The ground is too hard to bury him. With luck he will not be found there.'

'When will they find out he is missing and that we are free?' asked Melvaig.

'I don't know. It depends. Nobody in Eggron knew we were coming so it will be the Hurll in the Gurrtslagg who will first raise the alarm, wondering why no new leader has been sent. But they will be in no hurry.'

While they had been talking Shuinn had walked over to the horses and now he got up on to the one that Melvaig had been lashed to on the journey.

'The horse I was on is tied to this one,' said Shuinn. 'Cut Burgunn's free and ride it unattached.'

Melvaig did as he was asked, grateful for the decisiveness of his friend. His mind was still confused, heavy and thick from the emotional trauma of the fight. The tension that had gripped him beforehand had now drained away leaving him empty and vacuous. But a terrible thought flashed into his head.

'The Book!' he shouted. 'Where is the Book?'

'Look in the bags. It is there. I made sure,' Shuinn answered, with a smile.

Melvaig's fingers scrabbled with the fastenings on the bag that Shuinn was pointing to. The top flap opened and there it lay. Melvaig felt a flood of joy and relief spread through him. He took it out, lifted up his jerkin and put it back in the pouch next to his skin. The weight around his neck again reassured him, giving him confidence and strength. The pounding of his heart calmed down and as his breathing grew steady he looked up at Shuinn.

'It is ours again,' he said. 'We have it,' and it was all he needed to say. 'To Eggron then, for Morven and Bracca?'

There was a question in the way he said it, for they had never discussed what they would do if they were free. To search for the world that lived in their dreams, Nab's world, was all that they had held on to with any certainty. And that had seemed an impossible vision: something so remote and intangible that no practicalities had clouded its purity of purpose. But now they were free! With horses and a little food. Now suddenly the pursuit of that vision had become a reality, and always underlying that pursuit had been the unspoken knowledge that without Morven and Bracca the vision was incomplete.

And so, although Melvaig was asking Shuinn whether or not the giant would come back to Eggron with him to find them, he knew that there was really no doubt.

'Yes,' said Shuinn. 'To Eggron. Follow me. I have travelled this way before with Gebb and Nekdog and I think I know the way. We kept to the track then, though. Now we must get off it and keep out of sight. We can take no chance. They may know we are missing but even if they don't our black brands will give us away. Come then, mount up and we will go. First, though, here is one of the knives I took from Burgunn. He had two; I have kept the other.'

Melvaig put the knife under his jerkin, jumped up on to his horse and followed Shuinn as he left the track and cut across the gorse-strewn slope. They had not ridden far when they heard the sound of horses behind them, carried in the hot breeze that fanned their faces. They got off their horses quickly and scrambled down a little slope with them until they were hidden from the road. From behind the trunk of a small bushy hawthorn tree they looked back at the track. Through the shimmering haze they saw a small number of riders making their way slowly up the hill. There was something familiar about them but Melvaig was unable at first to think what it was. Then it came to him.

'It's some of the Hurll,' he whispered to Shuinn. 'From the Gurrtslagg. What are they doing?'

The giant replied softly, 'I don't know for certain but I think they are going after Burgunn. It's too soon yet for them to have missed him in Eggron. No. They must have suspected that Burgunn had not told all he knew – that we were of more value than he made out. They may even have guessed about the Book. I think they are hoping to kill off Burgunn and capture us for themselves.'

They watched as the little group wound its way up the track and waited until the riders were well out of sight behind the rise of the hill.

'Now we must be even more careful,' said Shuinn. 'They will be looking out for us. And if they don't find what they're after they will guess what's happened and raise the alarm, making out that they had missed him and were going after him for his own sake.'

They mounted again and carried on across and up the hill. They rode in silence, Shuinn in the lead with the spare horse and Melvaig behind. It was good to sit astride a horse again and he let his mind and spirit become absorbed in the rhythm of the ride, enjoying the roll of its back and the pattern of its strides as it carried him over the difficult ground. Then as his mind became empty and still and the nightmares started to recede, so the delicious euphoria of freedom flowed in to take its place. For the first time for as long as he could remember he was free: his own master. No one watching him, putting demands upon him, ordering the timetable of his life. And he was going for Morven and Bracca. How he would find them and free them he did not know. That would be faced when the time came. For now, everything was possible. The idea that he might not find them, or that they might be dead, did not occur to him; he did not let it. Hope burned through him, lighting the way ahead like a beacon and he could not risk its extinction, for without it he would have lain down then and there, amidst the scrub and stones of that barren hillside, and simply withered away beneath the scorching sun. He had come from the mines, lived through the Gurrtslagg, and somehow that knowledge filled him with a feeling of strength and certainty. Was this the destiny Ashgaroth was mapping out for him? He looked up into the afternoon sky and saw faint gashes of crimson streaking the hazy yellow murk above their heads. To him, then, it was as if Ashgaroth was showing himself, telling him that beyond all that he had known and all that he was going through, the world of which he dreamed existed.

CHAPTER XX

On they rode, lost in dreams and savouring their freedom. Shuinn led them well away from the track and they saw no other riders. When the sun began to sink in the sky they found a deep cleft, carved out in the old world by a river but now carrying little more than a muddy trickle. It was enough to give the horses a drink, so they dismounted and Melvaig watched with satisfaction as they bent their heads down and slurped up the precious liquid, holding their heads still until they had drunk their fill and then taking their mouths out of the water and letting it spill from their muzzles on to the ground. He went up to the horse he had been riding and put his arm round its neck, using his other hand to stroke its forehead.

'I shall call you Bendro,' he said, and as he spoke the name a picture of his old horse flashed before him, bringing an ache to his throat and a stinging to his eyes. He fought against it but it was no use and, burying his face in the horse's mane, he felt the tears well up and pour from him in a flood. The horse whinnied gently as if he understood and suddenly all the pain, the tension, the sadness and the tragedy seemed to come together and Melvaig lifted his head with the tears streaming down his face and a great cry came from him. It was an involuntary sound that seemed to come from somewhere else, as if the pain of the whole world had found its release through him. The horse remained standing still as Melvaig wailed uncontrollably, letting the man clutch at his hair. Shuinn came across and put his arm round his friend's shoulder. There was little he could do or say to comfort him. For Shuinn, meaning and purpose had just entered his life with the knowledge Melvaig had given him. It was as if everything was just beginning. But for Melvaig, who had been pursuing his vision through so much and for so long, who had suffered and lost those who were part of him and for whom despair had become a constant companion, for him the thought that there was, after all, hope and that finally the dreams he had cherished of seeing Bracca and Morven again were capable of turning into realities, was all too much to bear.

And so Shuinn simply stood by while Melvaig cried away the torment in his soul and when the tears finally stopped and darkness was upon the land, he led him gently away, still dazed from the trauma of his outburst, and helped him down on to a level patch of ground beneath the branches of a hawthorn. No sooner had Melvaig lain down than he was asleep, his body and spirit racked with exhaustion. Shuinn tethered the horses to the tree, so that they could nibble the leaves, before he too lay down and let himself be sucked into the delicious oblivion of sleep.

Melvaig awoke next morning, at that moment when the sky showed itself in crimsons and oranges before turning grey. It was like an omen. He felt refreshed and invigorated, the bitter weeping of last night an eternity away. Its catharsis complete, he was eager for the day to start, to be on his way. There was a life and an energy within him, such as he had not felt since the days in Ruann when he had set out with Morven up into the mountain or down along the old river and they had laughed and played and sung the old songs that Jarrah had taught them. There was a joy in his soul that seemed to fill his whole being with radiance and light. And everywhere he looked, he felt his spirit lifted even more as if the things around him were sharing in his buoyancy; the hawthorn, its dark green leaves waving gently in the breeze that blew up the slope; the horses, whinnying quietly, their ears erect, watching him with interest; Shuinn, his huge body curled up into a ball, vulnerable, innocent and strangely delicate, like a child, as he slept. Even the parched brown earth seemed somehow drawn into patterns that formed themselves into pictures of strange beauty, some like the creatures from Before the War that Jarrah had described to him during their long talks, while others drew in his mind unfamiliar images of remarkable clarity which seemed possessed of a power that he could not explain and that transmitted that power to him. He went over to the packs which Shuinn had taken off the horses. He found a water bag, some goat's meat and some biscuits and then he woke Shuinn so that they could eat and be on their way.

The moment the giant opened his eyes and looked at his friend he could sense the newly born strength and confidence that radiated from him.

'Last night,' said Melvaig. 'I don't know . . . it all just seemed, somehow, too much. I'm sorry . . .'

He paused, searching for words, and Shuinn interrupted him.

'Don't be sorry,' he said. 'Don't be sorry. How did you sleep?'

'Well,' Melvaig replied. 'Very well. I can't remember anything from the moment I lay down. And this morning I feel so different. As if . . . as if the world was ours. As if nothing can stop us.'

Shuinn smiled. 'That's good,' he said. 'Come on then, how about some food?'

They chewed the meat slowly, savouring its flavour and relishing the knowledge that they themselves would decide when to stop eating. They set their own rations now, for the sake of preserving as much as possible of the supplies that Burgunn had brought, and although they ate no more than they had had given to them for a meal in the

Gurrtslagg, it felt as if they had ten times as much. And the biscuits tasted delicious. Melvaig had never had them before but Shuinn remembered them from long ago when he had been in the warrior nursery. There they had been used as rewards for achievement or as special treats, distributed when Xtlan decreed, as a celebration of some victory or conquest. Only the leaders had access to them whenever they pleased for their own consumption, and Burgunn had brought along a supply for the journey. They were dark brown and very hard so that when Melvaig took a bite he tasted nothing at first but then, as he chewed and the biscuit started to soften and crumble in his mouth, he felt a warmth spread throughout his body as the slightly spicy, hot oatmeal flavour was released.

'Are they not the most beautiful thing you have ever eaten?' asked Shuinn, as he watched his friend chew; and in reply Melvaig simply smiled and nodded with his mouth full.

They finished eating, packed the food and water away and, having watered the horses in the old river, mounted and rode on their way. Later, when the sun was at its height, sending its rays streaming through the grey murk of the sky so that the heat seared off the ground in great waves of shimmering haze, they reached the topmost ridge of the slopes up which they had been climbing. Before them, the land fell away in gradually undulating curves broken only by great deep gullys and now, for the first time, they could see little settlements dotted at random along the gully edges.

Shuinn stopped his horse and let Melvaig draw up to him.

'Those are the goat farms,' he said. 'Run by women and children, and the old. Their task is to supply Xtlan with meat and milk, butter and cheese. Some of the farms on the lower slopes grow corn and wheat as well. Each has an overseer, a good position for an old warrior. All the food he wants, the pick of the women that have been lucky enough not to be selected as Elimsorr, and a vestige of power for him to enjoy into his dotage. And for a Mengoy, the height of his ambitions. Gebb and Nekdog will have been hoping for just such a reward for finding Arkron. We must take care not to go too near them.'

He paused and put a hand to his forehead to shade his eyes from the sun. 'Eggron is out of sight yet, in the great valley that falls away behind the lower slopes but look, in the distance you can just see the Black Palace, the Blaggvald, where Xtlan himself dwells.'

Melvaig shaded his eyes like Shuinn and peered into the harsh glaring light. Suddenly he saw it, and the same tremor of fear ran through him as when he had first seen it from outside the walls of the Hinterland. As he looked at its jagged black shape, perched on a small plateau at the summit of a sheer conical hill that towered up into the sky, he was again mesmerized by its aura of pure evil. It seemed to sap the energy and the will from him so that to submit to its dominant power seemed inevitable.

'Do not look too long; it is not good,' said Shuinn.

With an effort Melvaig tore his eyes away. 'How long before we are in Eggron?' he said.

'It is not far,' the giant replied. 'By nightfall, possibly. We will eat just back there, in that hollow behind the ridge, and then ride on.'

So they ate while the horses grazed on the few clumps of grass that managed to claw their way out of the barren earth. Further down, where the goat farms began, the ground grew greener but up here on the summit, the ground was cracked and hard, every drop of moisture licked from it by the hot wind that swept up from the direction of Eggron.

The hollow provided some welcome shade from the blazing midday sun and after they had eaten, they discussed how they would find Morven and Bracca. The reality was now upon them, no more a golden vision of the future with the harsh edges of actuality blurred. Now the mechanics of finding them reared up as an imminent problem.

'We will look for Morven first; she will be most in need of escape,' said Shuinn. 'If she has been an Elimsorr for all the time I have known you, as seems most likely, then she will be coming to the end of her time. If she has lost her looks and her grace she will be banished to Lemgorrst, the Hinterland. We must hope that her strength has been enough to withstand the horrors of life in the Gravenndra for, if not, she will have already been sent away. You must be prepared for her to be very different from the woman you knew, Melvaig. They do not last long.'

For the first time in a long while, Melvaig was forced to confront the awful truth of what Morven had had to suffer and of the effect it might have had on her, mentally and physically. Perhaps she would not wish to come with him or be seen by him but would rather languish in the Lemgorrst till the end of her days. Maybe her mind and spirit would be so broken that she would have lost her reason, turned in upon herself for protection and be unable even to recognize him. He tried to picture her face and her body, to bring an image of her into his head but to his dismay he found it was impossible. The more he struggled to think of her, the more was there just a blank, an empty space before his eyes. And then suddenly he saw her, in a flash, as he had seen her from the cart a long, long time ago on his way to the Gurrtslagg. That fleeting picture of her face, that he had then fought to retain, now came before him with a clarity that took his breath away. And then, as quickly as it had appeared, it was gone and all that was left was an impression – of stature and pride, of an imperious strength and grace that seemed as solid and impenetrable as the rocks beneath his feet. And he was comforted beyond words, his heart flowing warm with hope.

'We will look for her at the Gravenndra where you think you saw her,' Shuinn was saying. 'I know where it is. If she is not there, then we will go on looking until we find her and then we will seek Bracca. He will be, I think, in one of the Bellkindra, the warrior nurseries and will be, for the moment, well cared for.'

He paused and Melvaig interrupted. 'How do we get into the Gravenndra?'

'We will go in openly, passing as warriors,' said Shuinn. 'We will look for her and ask for her by name. Do you think she will have changed it?'

'No – I don't know. Perhaps she wanted to keep some part of herself; perhaps she changed her name to break with her past. I don't know.'

'It will not be easy for you to pass for a warrior. You do not speak the language well, nor do you know their ways. Be careful. Don't talk unless you are addressed and then only very briefly. Watch me, let me do everything and simply follow. The Gravenndra are places of pleasure where every whim is indulged to the utmost. It is where the warriors eat, waited on by the Elimsorr. The Elimsorr wash them and then, when the warriors wish, the women are used for their satisfaction. Warriors have no homes. All their needs are catered for in the Gravenndra.'

Again Melvaig interrupted. 'The black brand. It will be seen.'

'You must get mine off. As I will take yours off. We will use Burgunn's sharpest knife. It will be painful but it is the only way. They will look like wounds but even so, at that place on the cheek, they will be suspicious. Still, we can do no more. Here it is.'

He handed Melvaig a knife. The blade glinted in the sunlight and the gold pattern in the black bone handle shone with a deep glow. Melvaig, horrified, hesitated.

'There is no other way,' said Shuinn. 'You will have to cut the skin and peel it off.'

Melvaig moved round and knelt down at Shuinn's side. He lifted the knife up and started to draw its sharp point all the way round the irregular black splash of the brand on Shuinn's face. The knife was heavy and Melvaig's hand shook; great globules of sweat dripped down his forehead and stung his eyes. The giant never uttered a sound but the clench of his jaw and the sinews standing out from his neck betrayed the pain he was feeling. His eyes, wide and staring, were fixed at a point on the ground. When the knife had almost completed its journey, the weight of the brand slowly pulled away the loose layer of skin to which it was stuck, but it stopped before coming completely off and Melvaig quickly snatched the rest away. The raw skin immediately started to ooze blood from the newly exposed pores, myriads of little pin pricks each shedding a river of red tears for the hurt it was suffering. Shuinn slumped forward, the tension in his body suddenly relaxing as he allowed himself to feel the pain.

'How was it?' Melvaig said anxiously.

'All right,' said Shuinn, under his breath, and then again, as the flood of pain that had made him sick started to recede, 'All right. Come. Let's get it over with,' and he quickly took the knife off Melvaig and before his friend had a chance to think, started to make the cut in Melvaig's cheek.

Shuinn had nearly finished by the time that Melvaig had begun to be afraid but when the rush of pain swept over him and dragged its awful weight through his stomach, he cried out involuntarily.

'Nearly over. Nearly over now,' the words of comfort that Shuinn uttered seemed to come from a long way away, a great distance outside his head, but they reached him and held him fast in their reality as his face throbbed with pain and his vision shattered into a black whirling maelstrom of exploding stars.

The taste of water on his lips brought him back to himself and he sipped the precious liquid delicately, savouring its sensation in his mouth and taking care to avoid moving his cheek which burned with an awful fire.

Shuinn looked at him and nodded his head gently. He did not speak; it would have been too painful, but his mouth was set in a careful smile and Melvaig responded the same way. It was enough. Shuinn took the water bag and had a drink himself and then they both lay back under the shade of the hawthorn and rested.

It was some time later when Melvaig felt Shuinn's hand on his shoulder, shaking him gently. He had fallen asleep. He sat up slowly and saw the haze of the sun a long way up in the sky and felt its heat bouncing off the ground. Gingerly he put a hand up to his cheek and placed a finger on the raw skin. To his relief it was sticky where the blood had started to clot into a scab. He got up and walked over to where Shuinn was already untying the horses. Seeing him, the giant spoke, the words awkwardly coming out of the corner of his mouth.

'We must go,' he said. 'How do you feel?'

'All right,' said Melvaig. 'Better.'

'We must look a strange sight,' Shuinn said, looking at his friend. He paused and then inexplicably his body began to shake and a strange choking noise came from his throat. Melvaig at first thought he was in pain or crying but as he looked into the giant's eyes he realized that Shuinn was laughing; or at least trying not to laugh for fear of moving his cheek. For an instant Melvaig was stunned with amazement, struck by the utter incongruity of the situation, and then he too felt a quiver of amusement pass over him before it took root in his stomach and, despite himself, he found a great tide of laughter growing inside which erupted in an explosive outburst of suppressed giggles; suppressed because he too was afraid of the hurt in his cheek. The more he tried to contain the laughter, the more it grew – swept along by the rush of its own momentum, until he found himself doubled over, clutching his sides and covering his mouth with his hands while tears gushed down his face.

How long this blessed oasis of escape lasted he did not know but it seemed to fade as suddenly as it had started; perhaps when a flash of memory brought into his mind a fleeting vision of the time he had laughed like this in the cart on the way to the Gurrtslagg. Shuinn seemed to stop at the same moment and they were both left standing, feeling a little embarrassed; the magic bond of laughter broken, the smiles on their faces seeming false and slightly crazed, wondering what they had really found so funny in the first place. But the embarrassment soon passed and they mounted the horses, Shuinn leading the way up the short slope from the hollow where they had slept, until once more they were on the ridge looking down the slope at the settlements and feeling their eyes drawn upwards and outwards into the middle distance where the Black Palace seemed to hang in the air, like an obscene malevolent insect, crouching on its pedestal of rock. In the heavy grey haze, the sun's rays reflected off the shiny black walls so that it seemed to give off an eerie, luminescent glow and Melvaig felt an involuntary shudder of fear. He looked away and followed Shuinn as the giant began to descend the slope on the other side of the ridge, following the old dried-up bed of a stream that in the old world had carved a way down through the rock and formed a little valley.

As they got lower down the slope they found themselves going more and more slowly due to the increasing number of riders whose harsh voices would suddenly leap out at them from the still air and cause them to stop. Not until Shuinn knew exactly where they were and had watched them until they were out of sight would he risk continuing on their way. The high banks of the narrow valley along which they were riding kept them hidden but sounds of activity all around them were increasing and soon Shuinn stopped and gestured to Melvaig to dismount. They clambered up the rocky bank and looked out over the slopes. The landscape was dotted with riders travelling in twos or threes along the trails that patterned the ground, little clouds of dust rising up behind them as the horses' hooves scuffed the earth. Their valley track led straight to a goat farm not much further down the hill and Melvaig could now see the goats grazing, white against the dull greens and browns of the slope, while clustered around the farm was a collection of rough huts and enclosures that reminded him of Ruann. On one side of the settlement, a little way away from the other huts, stood a tall, square frame-like structure situated on top of a little mound. Steps had been cut into the side of the mound and walking slowly up these now, he saw the stooped and crooked figure of what was probably a woman. Something large and round hung in the middle of the frame and the woman took down what looked like a long-handled hammer and lifting it over her shoulder brought it down on the round hanging object. As the hammer connected with the gong, a sound echoed out over the mountains that was unlike anything Melvaig had heard before. His spirits seemed to sag beneath the weight of its long and intensely mournful note which seemed to contain within its low ponderous tone the very essence of despair and hopelessness. All his resolve, his personality, his energy, strength and faith seemed to be drawn out by the terrible sound so that a cloud of lethargy slowly descended upon him, enclosing him like a cocoon. It rendered his soul utterly naked, stripped of all self-will.

Then he felt his hands lifted up forcefully and clamped over his ears where they seemed to hang, more by accident than design, while his face was suddenly stung by a series of fierce slaps. Gradually his head cleared and when his hands relaxed their grip on his ears the sound had nearly gone, only a few last lingering echoes vanishing into the distance reminding him of its power. Shuinn was looking at him anxiously.

'The Grayling, the gong of Xtlan,' he said. 'It is struck three times a day to signal the start, the middle and the end but its main purpose is to remind his subjects of his power so that they can never forget his presence. While we were on the other side of the hill we were sheltered from its sound. Always put your hands over your ears; it will not shut out the note but it is some help and it is all we can do. It is rung at various places throughout Eggron so that the whole of the city is flooded with its tone. When they hear it, the warriors shed their arrogance and the slaves sink further into their misery. All stop and listen.' He stopped and while Melvaig was still trying to absorb and understand all that Shuinn had said the giant spoke again, low and urgently, with a hand gripping Melvaig's arm.

'Listen,' he said. 'Two riders, coming up the track. Luck is with us. It would have been hard to pass as warriors in these clothes. Possible, but hard. Now perhaps we can steal some others. Quickly, let's get out of sight.'

They scrambled away from the edge of the little valley and Melvaig tied the horses to a tree that was growing a short way back. Shuinn was lying flat out on top of the slope and Melvaig hurriedly joined him. No sooner had he pressed himself on to the hard ground than, coming round a bend in the valley track further down the hill, he saw the riders Shuinn had heard. They rode carelessly and easily, talking and laughing as they made their way up the little valley. To Melvaig they looked so confident and strong that they seemed invulnerable to attack. In contrast he felt weak, tired and nervous.

'Shuinn,' he said. 'Must we? How important is it that we wear warriors' clothes?' He felt impatient with himself and a little angry with Shuinn. This gentle, amiable giant had now, almost imperceptibly, become a quick decisive leader and Melvaig obeyed him without question. What choice had he? He did not know the land nor the ways of Xtlan. Without Shuinn he would have been lost and floundering. And yet he was not totally happy with this new role of follower. And now, on what seemed to Melvaig a relatively unimportant matter, the giant was risking their lives. What if more warriors were coming up or down the track and caught them in the middle of the attack? Why did they have to pass as warriors anyway in Eggron? Could they not travel at night and break into the Gravenndra? Should he not have some say in whether or not they attacked these riders? Shuinn had not even asked him. It was he, Melvaig, who had the Book, whose destiny was so bound up with it and it was he, Melvaig, who should be deciding how to rescue Morven and Bracca and how to pursue the vision which the Book had given him. He had been entrusted by Ashgaroth with this sacred knowledge and purpose and now he began to feel that he had somehow lost control to this giant of a man whose life had become so inextricably intertwined with his. And then suddenly, like a huge black cloud passing in front of his eyes, a terrible doubt came to him. Was Shuinn an ally of Xtlan, or even of Dréagg? Perhaps Dréagg, the great Lord of Darkness, not content to trust the power to Xtlan, was using Shuinn to gain the knowlege which he so needed. That would indeed be the most cunningly cruel deception, and yet perfectly suited to his purpose. The dreadful fear that Shuinn had shown when he had been marked by the black brand, and then the sudden confident change in him afterwards: was it then that Shuinn had bargained for an alliance with Dréagg in return for protection and power? And neither Xtlan nor his followers would know so that he, Melvaig, would be perfectly deceived.

And as Melvaig's senses were reeling under this ghastly onslaught of doubt, he suddenly felt a frantic shaking and Shuinn's whispered entreaties. 'They come, they come,' he was saying. 'Melvaig, are you ready? They are almost here.'

Melvaig fought to clear his mind and he turned to look at Shuinn. As he met the giant's eyes all his fears vanished in the warmth that enveloped him.

'Shuinn, I . . .'

'Now!' The giant leaped off the top of the slope and Melvaig watched as he fell with all his weight against the second rider, knocking him off his horse so that they both landed in a sprawling heap among the rocks on the valley floor. The first rider quickly turned in his saddle and Melvaig saw him raise his club ready to bring it down on Shuinn's head but the two on the ground were struggling fiercely, rolling over and over so fast that he could not get a good aim. It was then that Melvaig hurled himself forward, pulling his knife out of his jerkin as he did so and jamming it up hard under the ribs of the first rider as their bodies crunched together. They both teetered precariously on the back of the horse for a few seconds before they too fell with a thud on to the hard earth. Both the horses whinnied, raised their forelegs into the air in panic and then raced away up the track. Melvaig had landed on top of his opponent and the man bucked and kicked beneath him, struggling with an awful desperation to get out from underneath and extricate himself from the knife which Melvaig was still forcing into him with all his strength. And then suddenly the man started to swing his head frantically from side to side, letting out a terrible throaty gargle, his mouth opening and shutting in a last desperate attempt to draw some air into his lungs. Melvaig's blood curdled at the sound but he was hugely relieved when he felt the body collapse beneath him and lie still.

Now he looked for Shuinn. At first he could not see him, neither could he hear any sound, but then as he stared down the track he saw the head of his friend slowly emerge from behind a huge rock. There was blood seeping from a jagged gash on his forehead and Melvaig felt a wave of love and sympathy rush over him.

'Melvaig.' Shuinn's voice broke into his thoughts.

'All right?' the giant asked.

'Yes, yes,' said Melvaig, forcing his mind into focus. 'I was just . . . recovering.' And then he saw the pile of garments that Shuinn was clutching under his arms. 'You've got the clothes,' he said. 'I haven't . . . done mine yet. I'm sorry, I . . .'

'Come on, then,' interrupted his friend. 'Let's get them off quickly and get him hidden before any more riders come.'

They went over to the body of the man Melvaig had killed and Shuinn, putting down the garments he was carrying, started to untie the belt around the warrior's jerkin. Melvaig watched, almost in a trance, as the body lolled around, the head rolling on the hard ground, as Shuinn raised his back to get the jerkin off. All that life, he thought, gone. The face looked almost peaceful except for the eyes, which stared out emptily, crazily, at nothing and seemed to be trying to say something. Then Shuinn spoke. 'The boots, get the boots off. And the skirt.'

'Yes,' said Melvaig. 'I'll just . . . close the eyes,' and as he spoke he leaned forward and brushed his hand down over the forehead bringing the eyelids down. Then he started to undo the thonging that lashed the thick hide boots to the dead man's feet and ankles.

Soon they had finished. They left the clothes on the ground while they carried the naked body of the man a little way up the track to where the earth in the bank did not look as hard-packed as the rest. Grabbing a sharp flat stone each, they quickly dug away until they had made a hole big enough. Then they laid him in, Melvaig taking the feet and Shuinn holding him under the shoulders. The white of the body, pitted with scars on the legs, arms and chest, looked like pale gold in the hazy yellow light. They threw the soil back on with their hands, covering it from the feet up, and leaving the head until last. It was Melvaig whose handful of soil landed on the open mouth, filling it up until it spilled out of one corner. It seemed strange to Melvaig that the man did not choke or cough, sitting up to clear his throat; but he did not. It was somehow the most absolute and complete proof of death that Melvaig had ever seen.

Suddenly the man had vanished, gone as if he had never existed, with only the scattering of freshly dug earth as a testament to his life.

'Come on, let's get these things on,' said Shuinn and, taking their old clothes off, they got dressed in the dead men's garments. The thick brown hide tunics and skirts first, and then over the top the outer vests of cloth, brightly patterned with symbols and emblems that struck chords of memory in Melvaig's spirit of the time he had first seen them, in Ruann so long ago, when he had looked over the ridge and watched Xtlan's warriors cutting up his home. Lastly the boots, feeling firm, comfortable and supportive after the looseness of his old, worn moccasins. The helmets, made of toughened leather pulled over a pyramid-shaped wooden frame, felt strange and ungainly when they put them on, as if they were constantly about to fall off. All Shuinn's clothes were too small for him, even though luckily one of the two had been a large man, but Melvaig's fitted almost perfectly. Each of the warriors had carried a money satchel containing a number of gold pieces and Shuinn and Melvaig slung these across one shoulder and down over the chest to rest on the opposite hip, under the outer tunic, as the dead men had worn them.

'Now we can pay for our way into the Gravenndra,' said Shuinn. 'We are fortunate; they do not always carry gold. They must have been recently back from a raid, their reward still unspent.'

'It's a shame the horses ran off,' said Melvaig. 'We have not got much food left.'

'No, and if the horses have been seen by any other warriors then they will be on the lookout. Still, now we have these clothes we should not be noticed.'

They went back up the little embankment, pausing only to pick up the club of the man Melvaig had killed, and went over to their horses which were nibbling the branches of the hawthorn to which they had been tethered. They whinnied quietly as Melvaig and Shuinn approached, not deceived in the slightest by the change of clothes. Melvaig put his mouth against the softness of Bendro's nostrils and felt the horse's warm breath comfort him as it pushed back the memory of killing. Then, when they had attached the captured weapons to the carriers on the horses and packed their old clothes away, they mounted up and began riding across the slope, leaving the little valley behind them.

CHAPTER XXI

They made their way diagonally down across the slope, keeping as much out of sight as possible from the settlement. In the darkening light of the late afternoon, the great square frame of the gong stood silhouetted against the sky and the white shapes of the goats seemed to shine with an eerie silver glow. They joined one of the many tracks that criss-crossed the hill, meeting the occasional rider and waving a greeting as they rode past. Sometimes a group of warriors would clatter over the stony ground, their weapons jangling and the loud brash tone of their voices betraying their presence a long way off. Then Melvaig and Shuinn would take a different route and Shuinn would hail them heartily from afar, waiting until their noise had receded into the distance above and behind them before continuing on their way.

Finally, before too long, they came to quite a steep incline which culminated in a long narrow ridge stretching away into the distance on either side. There was a stillness under the lee of the ridge which Melvaig found immensely comforting and he stopped and they both waited there, lost in the dense silence. There was a slight breeze, sighing over the top of the ridge and sending the clusters of tall coarse grasses into little shivers of movement, but this sound, rather than disturbing the quiet, made it seem more intense. Melvaig became totally absorbed in it. The sighs of the breeze and the whisper of the grasses seemed to float away with him, carrying him up into space on silvery strands of mist and then eventually, after what seemed an eternity, bringing him back down to the ridge. As his mind slowly cleared itself, he felt stronger, calmer and more confident as if Ashgaroth had come to him in that moment in a final sign of strength and love before he descended into Eggron. And suddenly he seemed to see a vision of Silver Wood, of Nab, Beth and the animals; and so real was this vision that, involuntarily, he brought his heels down on Bendro's flanks and called out to them. There, where they had been, was nothing – only the grasses on the ridge as before. They had vanished, gone as if they had never existed. But they had been there; of that he was certain, and instead of disappointment that they were no longer there he felt only a surge of joy at having seen them. Bendro carried him up to the crest of the ridge, past an astonished Shuinn, and he scanned the slope looking for them but there was no sign.

'What is it? What have you seen?' Shuinn's anxious voice broke into his whirling mind.

Melvaig turned to his friend. 'Didn't you see them?' he said. 'Here, on the ridge.' He paused and Shuinn looked at him blankly. 'The animals,' he went on, 'from Silver Wood. In the Book. Nab, Brock and the others. They were here. But they've gone. They were just here; you must have seen them.'

'No. No, I didn't see them.' Shuinn paused, embarrassed. 'Perhaps it was in your mind,' he said. 'You imagined it. Look, there are no tracks.'

'The ground is hard. They wouldn't have left any tracks.'

'No, you're right – they wouldn't.'

There was a difficult silence as Melvaig and Shuinn tried

to work out the implications of what Melvaig had seen. In the end, though, it did not matter. To Melvaig, they had been there – he had seen them; but they were not there now so whether they had existed in reality or his imagination was not important, for that moment had sent Melvaig's senses soaring with confidence and an awareness of that other world which he had never known so completely before. For the first time both his worlds had come together and it had been an experience of such incredible excitement that it would live for ever in his spirit. For Shuinn also, feeling the joy of his friend at this magical occurrence, it had the effect of strengthening his beliefs and of reaffirming his certainty that the strange tale he had heard from Melvaig in the deepest, darkest tunnels of the Gurrtslagg had indeed been the salvation of his questing and discontented soul.

They remained for a little longer, looking along the ridge, without speaking, basking in the golden afterglow of the experience and then reluctantly they brought the horses' heads round until they were facing down the slope once more.

'Eggron,' said Shuinn, almost to himself, as if the word were some kind of magical chant. Melvaig looked down at the city, the core of evil in this land of Xtlan, beyond which towered the tall rocky pinnacle of the Blaggvald. Eggron crouched in the bottom of the valley like some loathsome spreading reptile, smouldering in the evening heat. Above its mass hung a great shimmering haze blurring and smudging the sharp angularity of the ugly buildings. They were of a dark grey stone, some appearing almost black, and they stretched out in a relentless uniformity along seemingly haphazard lines and patterns. The yellow light of evening cast murky shadows amongst the buildings, clothing them with an air of secret evil, the lines of darkness like the innermost folds of hanging skin on this brooding corpulent creature. Occasionally from out of the putrescent shadows a rider would emerge, as a mite will leave the body of its host, and his horse would take him out into the light between the rows of buildings. Slowly and deliberately he would ride, the clatter of hooves ringing out in the still, heavy air and echoing round the hills. Around the outline of its body, tracing the boundary of its bulk, wound the wall, and the sounds of hammering as the slaves worked to build it ever higher and stronger formed a constant accompaniment, almost comforting in its permanence and the accidental rhythmic patterns that emerged, and found their way into the subconscious mind of the listener. But occasionally a new and different sound would interrupt the flow and would jar on those who heard it, the crack of a whip, a scream of pain, and the hammering would dissolve once more into a confused welter of noise.

Melvaig's gaze wandered over the scene and he struggled to fight off the dark feelings of foreboding that drew in around his spirit. He tried to recall the sight of Nab and the others and to summon up the power of Ashgaroth so that his weary oppressed soul could gain some sustenance, but it was not easy under the onslaught of evil that emanated from the dark city that lurked beneath him. And all the time the citadel of the Blaggvald, towering up into the sky, threatened to sap the very identity of those who looked upon it so that, though Melvaig tried hard not to raise his eyes to it, he could not escape its awful presence.

Shuinn spoke and gratefully Melvaig turned to him.

'We will have to go through that gate, there, just below us. See! But I have forgotten – you have no Tang. You will have to change your garments again and deceive the guards into thinking you are my prisoner. Quickly, get changed. Darkness is coming on and we must be at the Gravenndra before the Grayling sounds for nightfall.'

Melvaig dismounted and got his old clothes out of the pack on Bendro's back. As he shook them a cloud of dust fell out and made him sneeze. They smelt terrible and the heavy pungency of his own stale sweat caught in his nostrils. While he had been wearing them he had got used to it but now, after the relative cleanliness of the warriors, he felt disgusted. When had he last washed? In the stream at Ruann, with Morven and Bracca. Long ago. So long ago he could hardly even see it in his mind. Where were they now? Were they really in that terrible place down there and how would they be? He remembered Shuinn's warning last night and the confidence his vision of Morven had given him. Now the certainty that he would find her as she had last been in Ruann had begun to evaporate and he dared not think about her. And Bracca? Would Bracca even remember him or Morven? Would he be so content and settled in his new world and his new home in the Bellkindra with new friends that he would not want to leave? He pushed all these thoughts to the back of his mind, packed the warrior clothes away and mounted up again.

'Come then,' said Shuinn and started to make his way down towards one of the many tracks that converged upon the gate beneath them. As they drew nearer, Melvaig saw the slaves working on the wall, some swarming like ants over the sides and the top carrying boulders and rocks, while others placed them in position, packing them around with stones and earth. And all the time the guards walked to and fro amongst them, their long whips constantly threatening to lash down on anyone whose worn-out limbs were refusing to carry on.

A number of riders, either in groups or couples, were now travelling along the paths towards the gate and Melvaig and Shuinn waited, hanging back to let them get there first. They were at the bottom of the valley now, while behind them rose the slope down which they had come. Melvaig turned round and looked up. He could make out the ridge where he had seen the animals and way up, above and beyond it, the summit. It seemed very high from down here, a different world almost, and already the time spent travelling over the mountains since their escape from the Gurrtslagg had taken on, in Melvaig's mind, a feeling of safety and warmth such as he could not remember since Ruann. Now, once again, the sharp knives of danger were out all around them; fear was churning in his stomach and every breath he drew rasped fiercely in his throat. Everywhere he looked he seemed to see suspicion, from the riders who waved as they passed by in the distance and then turned round in their saddles to look at them again having passed through the gate, to the guards on the wall who would occasionally stop their pacing and stare out into the plain at them.

At last the hard, brown, flatland around them was empty of horsemen and Shuinn quickened his pace towards the gate. The sun was going down fast now, casting a pale golden glow on the upmost reaches of the mountains they had just left, while on the plain the yellow light became harsh and strident and Melvaig felt his eyes start to ache if he looked too long at its reflection on the ground. They approached the gate, two tall, black columns of stone with dark brown wooden gates hung in between. In front of them paced the guards, the light reflecting off the decoration on their tunics, their tall angular hats looking strangely ungainly and top-heavy. Melvaig could see three of them and as Shuinn and he approached, they stopped moving and stood still, their gaze fixed on the two incoming riders. When they were within throwing distance of the gate, one of them walked forward, raising his hand as he did so and Shuinn reined his horse to a halt. Melvaig likewise stopped Bendro and sat with his head sunk on his chest, his shoulders drooping, in the attitude of a captive. The guard walked up to Shuinn who dismounted and began to speak.

'In the name of Xtlan, greetings. May his power ever grow.'

The guard, unsmiling, looked at him hard and then

looked up at Melvaig.

'Greetings,' he said and Melvaig felt the cold hard eyes boring into him. 'Where are you from? Where are you going? What is your name?'

'I am Shemm, a Mengoy. I travel on my own. I have a captive, young and strong – he will work well for our Lord. He had escaped from one of the warrior raids and I found him wandering.'

The guard walked right up to Melvaig and fixed him with an unblinking stare. He knows, he knows, thought Melvaig, and his heart began thumping loudly in his chest.

'I do not know his sort,' said the guard. 'His skin, it is fairer than I have seen. Where did you find him?'

'Many days' ride away. I have not recently had much fortune and was forced to travel far to find something worthy for my Lord Xtlan. Way beyond the Gurrtslagg.'

Again there was silence. The guard reached his hand up and scraped his nails down the wound on Melvaig's cheek, where the brand had been. Melvaig winced as the pain knocked him sick. The guard spoke.

'A bad wound, and recent. You have one the same.'

'He tried to escape, back up in the mountains. He grabbed my knife. We fought and he wounded me on my cheek. When I had beaten him, I taught him a lesson and cut him the way he had cut me.'

The guard laughed and turned round to look at Shuinn, smiling. 'Good,' he said. 'Good.' He paused. 'And the blood on your tunic? From your fight with the captive?' He was looking at the jagged black patch of dried blood from the warrior whom Shuinn had killed.

'Yes,' said Shuinn, feeling the weight of the guard's suspicion lift.

'Show me your Tang.'

Shuinn untied the thonging down the front of the jerkin to reveal the 'X' symbol branded on his chest. The guard looked and then, nodding his head, indicated that Shuinn could get dressed again.

'Yes,' he said, 'you may go on. My name is Kagg, guardian of this entrance, known as the Rowle Gate. We have had warnings, reports of two slaves, one of them a big man, a giant, who escaped from the Gurrtslagg.' Kagg looked at Shuinn. 'You have seen no signs? Nothing unusual?'

Shuinn replied, his voice steady and his gaze firm. 'We saw the horses, two of them, not far back. Fully saddled, they were, at the the top of Rowle Ridge, beyond the goat farms.'

'Nothing else?'

'No.'

'Very well then. Come.'

Shuinn walked forward leading his horse, and the rope between the two horses tightened and pulled Bendro along behind. Though Melvaig kept his head bowed he could see Shuinn talking easily to Kagg. The other guards moved towards the gate as they approached and at a sign from Kagg they began to remove three great boards that were fastened across the two doors of the gate. Then they pushed them open to reveal a clutter of dark foreboding buildings through which ran a wide road. Melvaig looked up to the wall on either side of the gate and could see the slaves toiling amongst the stone, breaking it, carrying it and laying it, their bodies burned black by the sun, their faces devoid of expression – blank, empty and desolate. Kagg and Shuinn walked through and then Kagg stopped.

'On your way then. May you get good payment for your captive. Keep your eye on him though; he has a face full of barely quenched spirit – it will need to be beaten out of him. And keep your eyes open for the two we seek.' He paused and, as Shuinn led Melvaig and the horses down the track and the first buildings appeared on either side of them, he called out 'Hail Xtlan', raised an arm in salute and turning round, walked back through the gates. Melvaig, his heart pumping with relief, heard the creak and scrape of the gates being shut and then Shuinn, without turning round, began talking to him in a low whisper.

'Stay as you are until I say. When we find a safe spot near the Gravenndra, then you can change back. Till then you're my captive.'

Melvaig quickly stilled the ripple of disquiet that ran through him at these words. Strange, he thought, that the last time he had entered Eggron had been as Shuinn's captive.

The road was empty save for the occasional rider who passed them by with a wave before going on his way. At first the houses too seemed empty, their windows like empty, staring eyes and the shadows around the walls holding unknown fears and the ghosts of those who had lived there in the past. Many of them were in need of repair, the roofs either completely gone or else about to cave in and some of the walls cracked or collapsing. Melvaig, as he rode slowly along on Bendro, tried to imagine the place as it had been Before the War: full of people, busy with their lives, talking, laughing and crying. Women and children with the men – families as Jarrah had called them, living together. But although fleeting images rushed in front of his eyes, an overall picture would not come for he did not have enough knowledge to bring it before him.

They rode past these empty houses, the horses' hooves clattering noisily on the hard road, until eventually they started to see the occasional building that was obviously lived in; these were the Gravenndra. Horses would be tied up outside, while from within came the noise of shouts and laughter, disembodied sounds of occupation floating out into the still, breathless heat. These houses had been repaired – new flat roofs had been put on in place of the old and parts of the walls had been rebuilt. Now they came across more riders, mostly Hurll patrolling the roads, for soon the Grayling would sound and then anyone not inside would be taken for a slave or used for sport. Shuinn tried to avoid them as much as he could but sometimes it was not possible and the Hurll would scrutinize them carefully as they rode slowly past. Melvaig kept expecting to be stopped and he kept his head down, frozen with a fearful apprehension. But no – they always rode on, Shuinn's confident wave and greeting dispelling any doubts in the minds of the guards.

Up until now Shuinn had been leading them away from the wall, directly into the middle of Eggron, for it was only from there that he felt confident of getting his sense of direction and finding the way to the Gravenndra where Melvaig thought he had seen Morven. Now, suddenly they came out of a little narrow road, the surface of which was cracked and distorted where the weeds had forced their way through, and found themselves in the great square which Shuinn knew to be the middle of the city. Round the sides of the square the buildings had been fully repaired and here were the Gravenndra used by the administrators, the guards, the warrior leaders and others most favoured by Xtlan. This was the centre of Xtlan's power for here were the men who carried out his wishes, who ran the world that he controlled. Few who came here stayed very long, for betrayal and treachery waited at every corner, yet such is the nature of man that as one went, taken by the guards for some purported indiscretion or wrongdoing, another would eagerly take his place.

These were the finest of the Gravenndra and Shuinn knew well the tales that were told of the Elimsorr in them and the grandeur and beauty of the buildings inside, for to these places came all the plunder and pillage taken by the warriors in their conquests. Here then was all that remained of value or beauty from the old world, Before the

War, brought back from raids or found by the foraging Mengoy. The rumours of the sights to be seen in these Gravenndra and the ecstasy of the physical pleasures and delights to be found there, ran like an ever-flowing river throughout Eggron and the whole of Xtlan, fuelling the desires and ambitions of all who heard them so that their lives became devoted to finding favour and winning acclaim in the eyes of their superiors, and so taking one more step on the road to a position that would carry with it the right to use these most exclusive and coveted of places. Legendary among the inhabitants of Xtlan, even to those dwelling in the Hinterland, were the stories of the luxurious foods and heady wines, the sensuous oils and perfumes used by the Elimsorr, the drinking goblets made of delicately wrought gold or sparkling crystal glass – the ice-cool marble floors and ceilings, carved with unbelievable artistry by some long-dead craftsmen of the old world. And there were marble baths and great hanging tapestried curtains with scenes from Before the War depicted on them. Paintings covered the walls, of the richest hues and most voluptuous of images so that the imagination of those who saw them was fired into an inferno of ravening desire. And then the Elimsorr, chosen for these Gravenndra because of their particular qualities, whether physical or in the nature of their desires (for many of them here were said to enjoy the depravities they indulged in), who would attempt to give release to the fantasied yearnings which the hungers of their bloated lusts craved.

When Melvaig first saw the square he found his sight dazzled by a blaze of bright light and it was only when his eyes had recovered from the initial shock and he was able to look again, that he realized that the square was paved in gold. The last dying rays of the sun were being broken up into myriads of dark yellow rays, reflecting off the paving in piercing shafts of light so that the square seemed filled with a great golden aura. And in the centre, stretching up above the roofs of the surrounding buildings, stood a huge golden cross. As Melvaig gazed, mesmerized by the sight before him, the sun began its descent, turning red as it did so, and the light shining on the symbol seemed to him to become fluid so that it was as if the cross had begun to weep blood. Slowly it came at first, oozing out of the flat surfaces but then, as he watched, the flow increased until great rivers of blood were running down all over it. He blinked his eyes and buried his face in his hands in an attempt to send the dreadful apparition away but when he looked again it was still there; the blood of all those who had suffered in the name of Xtlan and whose lives had been taken so that this golden monument could be created, came cascading down in torrents of thick crimson. As the realization of all this seeped into Melvaig's consciousness, so the obscenity of it struck him and he felt a wave of bile start to rise up in his throat. And then the sudden jolt of Bendro as Shuinn started to ride forward again brought him back to himself. He swallowed the bile and concentrated on the rhythm of the horse as Shuinn took them quickly round the outside of the square to a road that ran off between two rows of buildings on the opposite side to where they had been. Melvaig kept his eyes averted from the cross and only once, when they were riding away, did he look back. It was still bathed in red, standing in the golden square as an omnipresent symbol of the evil of Xtlan.

CHAPTER XXII

They rode quickly now, keeping to the shadows and seeing no one, for the Grayling would sound at any moment and all the warriors and the guards were inside the Gravenndra. Only when the Grayling had rung would the guards come out again to patrol the roads. As they made their way towards the place where Melvaig thought he had last seen Morven the buildings became once again dilapidated and broken down, only the Gravenndra, which became less frequent as they moved out, having roofs. Soon, against the darkening sky, Melvaig could make out the line of the wall ahead of them. There was silence now, the slaves having been herded together in great open-air compounds for the night. Suddenly Shuinn stopped the horses.

'Change back into the other clothes here,' he said quietly. 'Behind that wall. Hurry. We're nearly there and we must be inside before the Grayling sounds.'

Melvaig quickly got down from Bendro and, taking the dead warrior's clothes from the pack, climbed over a pile of rubble that had once been the front wall of a house. As he was getting changed, a feeling of acute apprehension came over him. At last the possibility of seeing Morven again was real. In a few short moments he might be looking at her, talking to her. He pictured her face and her long golden hair, falling in gentle curls down on to her shoulders. How would she react when she saw him? Would she realize that she should not show that she knew him? Would she, in fact, know him? How had the Gurrtslagg, and everything that had happened since he left her on the hill at Ruann, changed him? And the warrior's uniform – would she recognize him behind it? How would she be – dazed, her mind numbed by her subjugation as an Elimsorr, or alert, her wits held intact by her pride? Would she want to go with him or would she have lost the will and the energy to rescue Bracca and pursue a vision so obscure and vague that he did not himself know how to set about reaching it? In the pouch round his neck, the Book hung heavy. For him there was no doubt as to the truth of what he felt; he had experienced the power of Ashgaroth too often for him not to be certain, but how could he convince Morven of its reality. Would she insist on returning to Ruann and salvaging what they could of their old lives?

His mind raced with countless questions, falling over one another like a waterfall, but beneath them all was the one question he could not bear to think about. Would she be there? He could not let that thought enter his head, for the idea that he might have been mistaken or that she had been moved or was dead would, he felt, have stopped his heart beating.

Changed now, he scrambled back over the wall, put his old clothes in the pack and, as a warrior, remounted Bendro, tapped his heels on the horse's flanks and trotted forward to join Shuinn.

'Now,' Shuinn said quietly, 'we are warriors, back from a raid. Our usual Gravenndra is on the far side of Xtlan but we were unable to get there before the Grayling so we would like to stay here for the night. Let me talk; you cannot yet speak the language well enough not to arouse suspicion. And if you see Morven, be careful how you are towards her. I am the one who is looking for her.'

Suddenly the wall was directly in front of them, casting a long straight shadow on the road that ran alongside it. They turned on to this road and very soon Melvaig saw, shining out into the dusk, a dim yellow glow from the windows of a building just ahead of them, while from inside came the sounds of laughter and loud voices, an ugly mash of noise such as he had heard from the other Gravenndra along the way.

'There,' said Shuinn. 'That's the one.'

Melvaig stifled a sudden rush of panic. Was this the road they had travelled along in the cart? And this the place outside which he had seen Morven? He did not recognize any of it. But it had been light and he had had a very limited view through the crack in the wood. The darkness and the shadows would make things look very different.

Now they were outside it, the raucous noise from inside almost deafening them, and the great yellow splash of light from the windows throwing their shadows on to the road. Melvaig's guts rolled with tension.

'Ready?' asked Shuinn.

'Yes.'

'Come on, then,' and Shuinn dismounted.

They tied the horses to a wooden rail outside and then Shuinn pulled up the long latch on the door. As he opened it, the first long low notes of the Grayling began to tear the air apart. At the same time, from inside the Gravenndra, a wave of heat mingled with the acrid stench of bodies swept out and hit them, while a cacophony of angry shouts rose up ordering them to shut the door.

Hurriedly they went in and Shuinn slammed the door, instantly muffling the terrible mesmeric notes of the gong. As they turned to face the room, Melvaig was gripped by a sudden claustrophobia and had to struggle to remain conscious as a wave of nausea swept over him. All he could make out in front of him was a sea of angry faces merging and separating as the dizziness ebbed and flowed. The little room was stifling and most of the men wore only under-trousers. On the walls, which once had been white but had long since started to flake away or go brown with age, the tallow candles threw out flickering smudges of yellow light and a pungent sickly smell. Some of the walls had been decorated, either on the exposed stone or the old white, by patterns and symbols scratched on the stone or drawn in charcoal. On other walls Melvaig saw simple line drawings depicting some past raid or other event. Goatskins hung everywhere and were festooned over the grey stone floor.

Through the confusion in his mind and above the deadened sound of the Grayling outside, Melvaig heard Shuinn at his side talking loudly to the angry men. They were sitting on stone benches around long narrow tables made of stone flags. On the tables there were plates and bowls of rough brown clay with food and broth on them, and each man had a drinking mug at his side. Shuinn's hands were raised in the air, his palms towards the room in a gesture of sorrow and peace and Melvaig marvelled at the confidence in his friend's voice as he tried to calm the men down. Eventually their shouts grew less vitriolic and one by one they fell back to eating. It was then that, relaxing slightly as the tension in the room decreased, Melvaig saw the Elimsorr. They hung back in the shadows against the walls, only venturing out amongst the tables to pile more food on a plate or refill a mug. As they did so the men would call out and jeer, extending grasping hands as they walked past so that many times as they tried to avoid the questing fingers the food or drink that they were carrying almost fell to the floor. They wore only small loincloths made of goatskin, the top halves of their bodies being naked except for the necklaces, armbands and bracelets with which they were adorned. He watched as one of them came to pour drink into the mug of a huge, heavy-jowled warrior who was thumping the table with his fist and beckoning to her. Despite himself he found his eyes drawn to linger on her body, the blood stirring in his veins as he drank in her femininity. As she leaned over to pour the drink the man, leering at her lasciviously, fondled her roughly with his huge thick hands and she forced a desperate smile on to her face. It was a pitiable attempt to show pleasure, frantic in its anxiety not to express the pain and disgust that she felt, and Melvaig felt all desire evaporate beneath the tide of pity for her that overwhelmed him. And now as she walked back Melvaig was torn by the bizarre contrast between the invitation of her body and the tragedy in her face, for although she wore the mask of an alluring smile, her eyes were filled with such sadness that he feared she would break down in a flood of tears at any moment. He ached for her, at the awful open vulnerability which her body presented and felt within himself her struggle to control the raging emotions inside as her lips quivered in their attempt to retain the fixed smile, knowing that she would be banished to the Hinterland the moment she failed to give pleasure. When she reached the safety of the shadows once again, he saw her face crumple into despair and it was then that the realization that Morven might be among these women suddenly burst upon him. His heart pounding, his eyes began to search their faces frantically, while at the same time he saw the huge figure of a woman descending a stone stairway at the back of the room. Great swathes of garishly coloured material were draped around her fat shoulders and enormous bosom, and the vast bulk of her body seemed to slide, rather than walk, down. As he continued looking for Morven, the woman got to the bottom of the stairs and started to make her way through the crowded tables towards them. He had looked at all the Elimsorr in the room now and to his dismay Morven was not among them. But of course they were not all here; there must be others upstairs. She would be there. Yes, she would be there.

His anxiety quietened, he turned his attention to the

woman who was now standing in front of Shuinn. The atmosphere in the room had changed, as if the men were anxiously apprehensive of how she would react to the strangers, and a subdued silence had descended amongst them so that only the sounds of eating and drinking could be heard. In a loud voice, the woman spoke.

'I am the Marll,' she said. 'Welcome to my Gravenndra where all who love and serve our Lord Xtlan well have all their desires met.' She paused and, looking at them both with a smile creasing her fat cheeks, she went on, 'But I do not know you. We have not had the honour of your presence before. Where than are you from?'

Despite her deferential manner, Melvaig felt his blood run cold as her eyes fell on him. The smile had a terrible mocking edge to it and as she looked at him, he felt that her hard black pupils, shrouded in the hanging fleshy folds of their sockets, were driving a hole straight through his mind, seeing everything. Suddenly, to his relief, Shuinn began to speak and she turned away.

'We are sorry that we are late,' he said. 'I was explaining to these good men.' He waved his hand over the room. 'We are of the Company of Kegg, whose Gravenndra is on the far side of the city. Idle for action we ventured out through the gates and have been travelling the mountains searching for the two who have escaped from the Gurrtslagg. Perhaps you have heard?' The Marll nodded her head. 'Well, then,' continued Shuinn, 'you will know the reward that is out for their capture. Greedy for it, we stayed out too long and found ourselves outside your door when the Grayling sounded. We had no choice and would be more than grateful if we could stay the night. We would not like to have to make our explanation to the guards.' He laughed and the men murmured assent, nodding their heads in agreement, for the guards, haughty, arrogant and privileged were not popular among the ordinary warriors. Then the Marll spoke.

'You may stay. We are pleased to have you and all will be done to make you welcome. Find yourself a space at the tables and my Elimsorr will bring you food and drink. After, you will be bathed and oiled and may take your pleasure as you wish. You will find my women eager to satisfy your appetites. I know of the Company of Kegg. Brave and strong men, whose reputation for cruelty is known throughout Xtlan.' She paused. 'Is there anything particular you desire?'

The atmosphere in the room had now relaxed and the men were talking and laughing amongst themselves. Shuinn lowered his voice so that Melvaig was unable to hear what was being said. 'Our Company,' he said, 'some time ago, carried out a raid on a village beyond the Molobb desert, a village called Ruann. Among the women we captured were a number of exceptional beauty. Some are now of course in our own Gravenndra but others were distributed throughout the city. Do you know of any such who are here now for if so we would greatly desire their services?'

The Marll looked at him. 'Ones as beautiful as you say would have gone to The Square. But I do remember, a while back, a few who came to us from this place for they were, as you say, possessed of a rare attraction. But I have forgotten now who they were or even if any are still here for they do not take long to deteriorate. And many are unsuited and we lose them to the Hinterland.'

'May we then look at all the girls before making our choice?'

'Of course, of course. But you must eat and drink first.'

'Thank you,' said Shuinn and then gesturing to Melvaig to join him, he went across to the end of one of the tables, picking up a small bench as he did so, and sat down on it with Melvaig at his side. The warriors next to them shuffled away slightly on their seats, looked up briefly to murmur a curt greeting and then went back to their food and talk. Melvaig saw the Marll signal to two of the Elimsorr and they walked over to a door at the back of the room, disappeared through it and came out a few moments later carrying a plate piled with food and a drinking goblet each. They then made their way round the tables and across to where he and Shuinn were sitting. As before, he felt his gaze drawn to the nakedness of their bodies despite the struggle he felt within himself to resist the temptation and yet when he looked at their faces and tried to meet their eyes a wave of confused embarrassment and shame at the arrogant insensitivity of his maleness swept over him. The Elimsorr who was coming across to serve him was tall with long black hair falling to her shoulders and a small pretty round face. Her full lips were drawn into the awful mask-like pretence of a smile he had seen on the other girl and when he looked into her deep green eyes there was such a desperate sadness and pleading that he had to stop himself, as she bent over to put his food and drink down on the table, her body brushing against his face, from crying out to her that he understood, that he was not like the others, that she did not have to wear that smile or walk that way for him. Yet he knew he could not, that he had to pretend as she did and so, forcing himself against all his instincts, he gave her flesh a hard slap, recoiling at the vulgar laughter which his action aroused in the other men at the table. Shuinn, he saw, was handling the girl serving him and he wondered whether his friend felt as he did or whether, as he supposed, Shuinn was genuinely enjoying himself. For he, as a warrior and a Mengoy, would have lived like this all his life.

When the girls left, Melvaig and Shuinn started to eat. The plates were piled high with steaks of goatsmeat, swimming in a thick greasy gravy, while at the side there were a number of small, flat, round breadcakes, hard but tasty. The drink tasted strange to Melvaig as he had never known its like before. A murky, golden-brown colour, it possessed a fire and a sting which at first took him by surprise but once he had got used to it he found strangely satisfying. He had soon finished his mug and the dark-haired girl, seeing this, came out and poured him some more. As she went back Shuinn turned to him and said quietly, in the language of Xtlan, 'Do not drink too much of the Lerm – it will befuddle your senses if you are not used to it.' He looked furtively up at the men next to them on the benches and then, seeing that they were fully occupied with their companions and were ignoring the strangers completely, he asked Melvaig whether he had seen Morven among the Elimsorr.

'No,' he said. 'She is not down here. She must be upstairs. What were you saying to that woman – the Marll? Did you ask about Morven?'

'Yes,' replied Shuinn. 'She does not know. But there were some women from Ruann brought here. We must look at the women upstairs soon. She will take us to them all. Finish your food quickly!' He paused, worried by the certainty in his friend's voice that they would find her. 'Do not be disappointed if she is not here.'

Melvaig looked up at his friend. 'Don't worry,' he said. 'She is here. I know it.'

Shuinn's heart sank. 'Finish your food,' he repeated. 'And don't drink any more.' He should have warned Melvaig about the Lerm but it did not occur to him that his friend would never have had it before. Even he, Shuinn, brought up on it from when he was old enough to walk, had found his head reeling from the first mouthful. There was no doubt in Shuinn's mind that Melvaig's blind confidence came from the drink. His wits would already have become blurred and his senses dulled and confused. And this at a time when they both needed their cunning and alertness to be at its greatest strength. How would he now react if she was not here? And perhaps even more dangerous, what would he do if he found her? Well, it was too late to worry now. They must search for Morven among the women upstairs as soon as possible. And he himself must fight to keep his senses clear from the desires that he found raging within himself at the sight of the Elimsorr again.

It was then that he sensed he was being watched. He had not looked up from his plate but suddenly a tingle at the back of his neck had given him that familiar sense of unease that comes from the eerie knowledge that someone's eyes are fixed upon you though you do not know whose they are. He tried to dispel the feeling by saying to himself that it was his imagination and he stopped himself from looking up, but instead of going away the feeling grew stronger and more intense. He carried on eating, his self-consciousness making the normally automatic chewing movements seem awkward, clumsy and ungainly. At last he could stand it no more and slowly he raised his head. At first he could see nothing; the men all round him were busily eating and there was no one amongst them who appeared to have the slightest interest in either him or Melvaig. And then a sudden movement from a table across the room caught the corner of his eye. Why that particular movement should have taken his attention he did not know but he was certain that the head that had suddenly turned away held the eyes that had been watching him. Slowly and carefully he looked in that direction. At first, as he looked along the table, all the men seemed as fully occupied as they were around him but then, halfway down, he saw talking to his neighbour a face that sent an awful shiver of recognition down his spine. It was one of the Hurll from the Gurrtslagg; one of those he and Melvaig had seen riding after them just after they had killed Burgunn. Had the man recognized himself or Melvaig? The question burned in Shuinn's brain like a fire. One thing was certain though; he had been watching them closely. The Hurll had noticed them and had been studying them. Was it just idle curiosity about these two strangers or was he trying to compare them to the two captives whom Burgunn had taken with him back to Eggron?

Shuinn carried on eating his last few scraps of food, wiping the rough brown clay of the plate clean with a piece of the black bread. If he had recognized them would he raise the alarm or would he try and take them captive himself? Were there any more of the Hurll in the Gravenndra? Was the man certain? He could not accuse them without first being sure that he was right. What should he and Melvaig do now? He looked at Melvaig's plate. His friend had just finished. Good. They would continue to act perfectly normally, without doing anything unusual that might arouse suspicion. If they did not find Morven, they could not leave before morning; to go before the dawn Grayling would attract instant pursuit that would jeopardize their chances of looking for her at other Gravenndra. If they found her, then they would escape with her in the night when the men were either deep in a drink-heavy sleep or else busily occupied with the Elimsorr. He decided not to tell Melvaig about the Hurll. It was vital that they act as normally as possible and his friend had enough on his mind with thoughts of Morven and trying to act as a warrior of Xtlan. Just then Melvaig spoke to him.

'Shuinn. I'm ready. Let's go now.' His voice was tremulous with barely suppressed excitement. His mind, blurred by the Lerm, was in no doubt that in a few moments Morven would be with him. Everything then was possible. Escape. Finding Bracca, and then ultimately the final solution of finding the world that Ashgaroth had guided him towards. The vision that he had seen on the cliffs above Eggron flashed before his eyes and he saw himself walking side by side with them through the deep hanging green of the woods.

'Yes,' said Shuinn. 'I'll call the Marll. Be careful.'

At a sign from Shuinn the Marll came across to them.

CHAPTER XXIII

'Come,' she said, smiling. 'Let us see if we can find you any of your ladies from Ruann. Though I am sure,' she added, with an expansive gesture towards the Elimsorr posing against the wall, 'we can find you something to your tastes.'

When they got to the foot of the stone stairs Shuinn, looking round for the Hurll, suddenly saw him and thought with a rush of horror that he and the Marll had exchanged quick glances. Shuinn looked at her and she returned his anxious look with a bland smile, her eyes cold and hard – giving away nothing.

They climbed the stairs; the robes around the body of the Marll rustling loudly and exuding a heavy sickly-sweet scent as she moved in front of them. Fortunately Shuinn was immediately behind her but still Melvaig found her so repugnant that his whole body felt disturbed by her proximity. Now, suddenly, they came out on to a long corridor. Through the yellow gloom cast by the flickering candles on the walls, Melvaig saw a row of doors running down either side. The floor was wooden, with goatskins laid out along its length. Morven! The name rang in his head like the clanging of a great bell. He wanted to shout it out, running into all the rooms until he saw her and then when he found her, sweep her into his arms and hold her until all the pain, the suffering, the humiliation had been loved away. Never again would he leave her. He would protect her from all pain, shield her from all hurt. Morven! The urge to cry out was almost too strong to resist. He felt every fibre of his body stretched to breaking point, with a yearning, aching intensity and his intellect, blurred by the Lerm, was barely able to control the physical tension inside himself. The voice of the Marll sounded distant and remote.

'Let me show you what we have to offer,' she said and began to lead them down the corridor.

In the wall of each room, at the side of the door, was a small hole through which the Marll could keep her eye on the behaviour of the Elimsorr and ensure that none of them failed in their duties towards the men. It was through these spyholes now that Shuinn and Melvaig were invited by the Marll to make their choices for the night. Down the corridor they went, peering into each room in turn with Melvaig hardly able to breathe because of the tension he felt before each door. Some of the Elimsorr were on their own, spread out on the low pallets, strewn with skins, that lay along one wall. In the middle of each room was a tub and in a few of the rooms the men were being bathed. In others, Melvaig saw the men taking their pleasure with the women. At the sight of these spectacles, Melvaig's mind reeled and his stomach heaved with repulsion. Horrified by what his eyes were seeing, the strange and vicious instruments being used on the women, the bizarre costumes they were forced to wear, the positions and the combinations they were made to adopt, his mind seemed to glaze over. Unable to accept the catalogue of pain, humiliation and subjugation that was passing before him, his consciousness grew numb so that as he looked for the face of Morven amongst the masks of the Elimsorr, they became blurred into one featureless visage for he could not accept the humanity or the individual personalities behind the faces; that the bodies of these women should belong to people, with emotions and feelings, was too awful a fact to comprehend. And, worse by far than this, would have been to allow into his head the terrible idea that Morven could be among them.

And so, struggle as he might to bring Morven's face into his mind, he could not, though he knew, deep inside, that had he seen her, then he would have known her. Yet as they moved down the row of doors, inexorably, towards the last one, none of the women he saw ignited in him that spark of recognition that would have come from the sight of Morven. As the dreadful realization that she might not be there slowly bore down upon him, so he felt his spirit gradually being crushed and despair gripped him. He saw Shuinn look at him with desperation in his eyes and in answer to the unspoken question, Melvaig slowly shook his head. Was it possible? All this – for nothing: everything he had gone through, the dreams, the visions? This then was the sign; the end of everything he had lived for since that dreadful moment on Mount Ruann when Bracca told him that Morven had been taken. For how could he now go on? No – if Morven was not here, then there could be no Ashgaroth. It had all been an illusion, a fantasy. The Book had simply been a story – the telling of a tale, and his fevered imagination had wrought out of it a reality born of desperation and hope. Jarrah had been fortunate, living his life out in the beliefs that the Book had given him, never knowing the falsity of them or feeling the desolate emptiness of betrayal that was now draining Melvaig's very soul.

Now they were at the last door and Melvaig placed his eye against the cold stone of the wall to cast his gaze around the room. A woman lay alone on the pallet, naked, waiting for whatever the night would bring. Her pretty face, in the supposed privacy of the room, expressed the reality of grief with no attempt to conceal or deny it and it could not be long before she would lose the appeal which kept her in the Gravenndra for her mouth and eyes had already begun to gather wrinkles and lines, the skin of her neck and chin had started to hang and her complexion had lost its youthful glow and become dry, pallid and stark. She was restless, unable to arrange her body in comfort – a body so abused that she had long since lost any sense of pride in it. Melvaig watched her as she tossed around amongst the white goatskins on the pallet. It was not Morven. Of that he was certain. But there was something which stirred in his memory and he fought to clear the blur before his eyes, to concentrate on her features – the delicate nose, her round blue eyes, the shape of her mouth. And then she began to mutter quietly to herself, the words running into one another and the sounds merging, ebbing and flowing like the babbling of a stream. He strained his ears to catch them and then suddenly, the fog in his mind cleared and he knew. She was speaking his language, the language of Ruann. He looked harder at the girl, the doors of his memory slowly widening. Was it one of Morven's friends, Tennga? Again he looked and now as the possibility became implanted in his mind, all doubt evaporated. Tennga! Here. She must know about Morven. He must see her, and speak to her. And as the flowers of hope blossomed again within, he thought back with shame to the moments before he had seen her, for here surely was a sign. All was not lost. His search was not in vain. Now he had the strength to go on. And then, to his surprise and embarrassment, he found himself silently asking Ashgaroth to forgive his disbelief.

Now he became aware of the Marll and Shuinn looking at him – the Marll with a vacuous smile on her face, and his friend with barely concealed anxiety. He turned round and, smiling, said, 'She is from Ruann.'

'Then you may have her,' said the Marll. 'But do not

judge us by her alone. She is coming towards the end of her time and will not be with us much longer. She is for the Lemgorrst.' She paused and then looked at Shuinn. 'You want her also? Together?'

'Yes,' he said. 'If that is all right?'

'Of course. Whatever pleases you. Whatever you wish. Come then. I will take you in.'

Across each door was a length of wood resting in brackets either side to keep the Elimsorr in. The Marll removed it and pushed open the heavy door. As they entered, Tennga pulled some of the skins across herself provocatively and writhed sensually on the pallet in a grotesque parody of anticipated pleasure. The Marll looked at her disdainfully.

'Two guests – from the Company of Kegg. They have chosen you; give them your best. And let me hear no complaints.'

Tennga smiled at Shuinn and Melvaig in a pathetic attempt to be coquettish. The Marll turned to them.

'Take your pleasure as you will. If you wish for anything let me know. Goodbye.' She retreated backwards through the door, smiling at them blandly. It slammed shut and for a few moments there was silence. No one moved. Then Tennga, spreadeagled on the bed, extended both her arms upwards in an expansive gesture of invitation.

'No,' said Melvaig, moving quickly towards her. 'No, Tennga. Do you remember me? It is Melvaig. From Ruann.' He waited as her face froze in an expression of bewilderment. He quickly glanced back at Shuinn who was standing by the door, looking confused. 'This is not Morven. I am certain she is not here. It is a girl from Ruann – Tennga. She will know where Morven is.'

Shuinn came forward to join him.

'I am sorry about Morven. Still, as you say, this girl may know something. We will stay here all night, Melvaig, so there is no hurry to find out. In the morning we will leave and continue our search. Things must look normal, though. We must get undressed and get under the skins with her. The Marll will be keeping an eye on her through the spy hole. First though, a bath.'

Shuinn turned to Tennga and gave her a brief word of command. She got up from the pallet and, as Melvaig and Shuinn took their clothes off, she walked over to two large earthenware tubs against the opposite wall and began to fill them with water from some big jugs at the side. Shuinn climbed into one of them and then Melvaig, feeling intensely vulnerable and vaguely foolish, followed Shuinn's example and got into the other. As he did so, he looked across at their pile of clothes to make sure that he knew exactly where he had put the goatskin bag containing the Book. The water was warm, brought up from the kitchens below at a word from the Marll just before the men began to go upstairs. As Melvaig's body slowly became immersed, he was for a few short moments transported into sensual luxury, the water enclosing and caressing his limbs, expelling all thought from his mind and all feeling from his body. He closed his eyes and allowed himself to drift away on a blissful cloud of oblivion. After a little while he grew dimly aware of a gentle pressure over his body, hands moving sensuously over his neck, his shoulders and his back, across his chest and then, under the water, along his tired thighs, his legs and finally his feet. He felt a tide of guilt cast a dark shadow through his mind but he was unable to resist the power of the sensations that Tennga's delicate caressing hands sent flooding through his body and so he surrendered. And then he heard the sound of his name, repeated over and over, and Morven's name, and 'Ruann' spoken quietly and insistently as if they formed some strange magical chant. He opened his eyes and saw her vacant faraway look and the yearning in her face. Hearing his name, and the others, again, had turned the key in her mind with which she had locked her past away and now, slowly, she was delving back into those precious, forgotten memories. Melvaig could almost see the village in her eyes, the peak of Mount Ruann, the pony slopes, the vegetable plot and the huts, she and Morven walking happily together chattering and laughing. And suddenly he had to get out of the tub – to talk to her. He looked across at Shuinn. The giant's eyes were shut and a contented smile lay on his face. Well fed, bathed and, he guessed, relieved, his friend had abandoned himself. He felt a wave of happiness at Shuinn's well-being and, as the thought of all they had gone through together flashed through his mind, a sudden rush of affection for him. He turned back to the girl and spoke quietly to her in their language.

'Tennga. Look at me. Listen.' He grasped her face gently in his hands and bent it towards his so that she was forced to look into his eyes. 'It is, truly, Melvaig, from Ruann. And a friend, Shuinn. We will not hurt you.' Her glazed eyes seemed to float around his face. 'Do you understand?' he said. 'I am Melvaig. I want to talk to you, to ask you about Morven.'

She looked at him. Slowly the mists in her eyes seemed to clear, to draw apart like a veil, and Melvaig sensed the struggle within herself to pull together the threads of reality from the welter of fantasy in which her consciousness had taken refuge.

'Melvaig?' she said, and for the first time Melvaig felt she knew him.

'Yes. You remember me? You know me?'

She nodded her head gravely.

'I want to get out of the tub. And then we will talk. Just talk.'

She nodded again, her face expressionless. He stood up and let her dry him down but when she automatically started to fondle him he grasped her wrists.

'No,' he said. 'I do not want that.'

When she had finished drying him he took her by the

hand and led her over to the pallet. She seemed content now to allow him to lead her, secure in the knowledge that he neither wanted nor expected anything from her. He pulled back the goathair blankets and the skins and climbed between them, their coarseness tickling and irritating his skin. He beckoned to her to follow and she did so and as he felt the warmth of her body and the softness of her skin, he pulled her close to him, drawing her into his embrace and cradling her head against his shoulder. Yet despite the intense sensuality of the feel of her body next to his, he was surprised, and indeed relieved, to find that there was no stirring in his loins for her – partly, he guessed, because of the thoughts of what she had endured at the hands of men since that dread day in Ruann and partly because of Morven and her unmistakable presence with them now. And so he simply held her against him and eventually her resistance lessened, the stiffness in her body disappeared, the hardness of her spirit crumbled and she melted into him, clinging as if to lose herself in him, immensely grateful for his consideration and concern and familiarity. Desperately now she wrapped herself around him, grasping him as if she would never let go, as if the closer his body was to hers, the more alive became her memories of Ruann. And then as she snuggled against him and he folded his arms around her tightly, as if to shield her from any more hurt and pain, so her tears began to flow, running down her face in great rivers of release, all the miseries she had endured pouring out of her in terrible soul-wrenching sobs which made Melvaig's heart ache with a huge pity for her.

She wept until there were no more tears; until her tortured soul had exhausted its capacity to express what it felt, and then she grew quiet – basking in the twilit afterglow from the release of the raging fires in her spirit. And now Melvaig judged it the best time to ask about Morven. She answered his gentle but urgent questioning with a frustrating obtuseness, her words obscure and vague, ignoring the sequence of time and jumping from one part of her tale to another as her confused and shattered mind attempted to piece together her life since the raid on Ruann. At times Melvaig had to question her further, make her go over some part again or prompt her by inserting some piece of information which he already knew or guessed at.

He began by asking her about the ride in the covered wagon.

'Morven was not with us,' she began haltingly. 'They found her later. She had been with Melvaig, always with Melvaig. Everyone knew that. And Bracca, her Bracca. She fought but they stopped her. Oh, they stopped her all right! We used to milk the goats together. Me and Morven. And fetch the ponies . . .' She began to ramble on about the past, in Ruann, her voice growing stronger and more confident as her mind took her back to those halcyon days. For a little while Melvaig let her continue and then he interrupted.

'What happened when you got to Eggron?' he said. 'Do you remember – when you arrived in Eggron?'

She did not answer him at first, going back instead over the time in the cart, her fragile voice cracking with emotion as she described fragments of the horror of that terrible journey: the hunger and thirst, the brutality of the warriors, the floggings, the public humiliations, the foul squalor inside the wagon. Many had died, some through disease, others at the hands of the guards and some had killed themselves, unable to take any more.

'And Morven,' prompted Melvaig, his pulse racing. 'Did she die?'

Tennga gave a little chuckle.

'Morven? No. Not Morven. She was strong. She had a strength . . . She thought Melvaig would come for her. She fought; she would not give in. They made her pay; but she held on. "Melvaig will come" she kept saying. "With Bracca: I know it".'

Then Tennga paused, a sudden flash of realization penetrated the clouds in her mind. She lifted her head and looked at Melvaig's face.

'You?' she said, questioningly.

Melvaig nodded. 'Yes,' he said. 'I have come to find her. Where is she? Do you know?'

A dark shadow seemed to pass across Tennga's face and she turned her head away. At the same time Melvaig felt her body freeze and go stiff in his arms. A wave of panic turned his stomach over and he blurted out again:

'Where is she?'

'She is not here, not at the Gravenndra.'

'Where then?'

Tennga did not speak.

Struggling to control the raging frustration inside himself, he took her face in his hands and gently lifted it so that she was forced to look into his eyes.

'Tennga,' he said. 'You must tell me. Where is Morven now?'

At first she hesitated and then, very slowly, she began to answer.

'She was here, but they took her, took her away. To . . .' and the word seemed to stick in her throat, 'to the Blaggvald. To the Lord Xtlan.'

Melvaig let go of her face, his mind reeling. The name echoed through his brain: 'Blaggvald'. He felt as if he had been struck by a terrible blow. Dazed, he tried to gather his thoughts together. The Blaggvald! What hope was there then for her? And could they even attempt to find her and get her away from there? Dark thoughts rolled through his mind like black clouds as he tried to picture her fate there, at the very core of Xtlan's evil, at the mercy of Xtlan himself and the few he had chosen to reside there with him at the very pinnacle of the hierarchy of evil he had so painstakingly constructed, and who stayed but a brief spell before being ensnared by the web of treachery and deceit that had its roots in the Blaggvald. He felt sick to the very depths of his spirit. And then eventually, after what seemed an age, his mind cleared and he grew aware again of Tennga, her face on his chest and her body still clinging to him.

'Are you sure?' he said, the question faint and hopeless and she replied as he knew she would.

'Yes. The Blaggvald. They took Morven to the Blaggvald.'

'What does that mean for her, for her life? Could we find her?' Again he took her face in his hands and held it up to his, to seek for the answers with his eyes, but the brief clarity of her mind had left her, shattered by what she had had to tell Melvaig, and all she could do was keep repeating, in a hideous little rhythmic chant,

'The Blaggvald, the Blaggvald: she's dancing at the Blaggvald.'

Melvaig gently prised her away from him and then, laying her face down on the pallet, he got up and walked slowly over to where Shuinn was still lying in the tub, a peaceful smile lighting up his face. He bent down and grasped him by the shoulders.

'Shuinn! Wake up!' he whispered urgently in his ear. Instantly the giant's eyes opened and he sat forward, water splashing on to the skins on the floor.

'What! What is it?'

'Shuinn. I've been talking to Tennga. She told me that Morven was taken to the Blaggvald.'

A dark frown passed across Shuinn's face and he stared down into the water, his shoulders hunched, muttering quietly to himself. Melvaig, anxious and impatient, could only wait for his friend's response. At last he looked up.

'It is not good,' he said. 'I don't know whether we shall be able to get into the Blaggvald; it would seem impossible.

And . . .' he paused, 'I know very little of what happens to those Elimsorr who get taken there. It is, I know, the thing most feared by women yet they could not say why for they did not know. It was a nameless dread and the rumours of what would happen to them there were so terrible as to be almost unbelievable. And yet none ever leave. There is no fear of the Hinterland for them for, once in the Blaggvald, they stay until they die.' He looked up into the stricken face of Melvaig. 'My friend,' he said, 'we must not give up hope. We have life, and our freedom and we know where she is. Ashgaroth is with us.'

As Shuinn said this, Melvaig realized with a jolt of surprise that the faith in Ashgaroth and in the existence of the world which Melvaig had described to him from the Book, when they were in depths of the Gurrtslagg, had never left him. And the strength of this faith, which Melvaig perceived in his friend, was like a great rock for him to cling on to in that most desolate of moments, so that he felt it pulling him back from the abyss of despair into which he would otherwise have fallen. He felt a wet hand on his shoulder and heard Shuinn speaking.

'Pass me a cloth. I'll get dry and then we must both lie down with Tennga. In the morning we will leave.'

Shuinn dried himself and then he and Melvaig got on the pallet with Tennga in between them. She lay still, lost now in a world of her own, the memories which Melvaig had awakened now swarming all around her so that she was back again in Ruann or else reliving the horrors of capture and the journey to Eggron.

Now that Melvaig knew where Morven was, he found, lying down on the soft skins, that exhaustion suddenly overcame him. His limbs felt heavy with tiredness and his mind weary and it was not long before sleep swept over his body. Shuinn too was soon asleep, the stirrings in his body caused by Tennga's nearness soon giving way to the irresistible pull of oblivion.

CHAPTER XXIV

It was with a heartstopping lurch of fear that Melvaig felt the grip on his shoulder and the sudden fierce kick that sent him sprawling on to the floor. For a few moments the warm cocoon of sleep still clung stubbornly to him and he did not know where he was. Then with a ghastly rush of panic he remembered. He looked round quickly. Shuinn was being held by two huge warriors at the far side of the room. Another two were now pulling him to his feet whilst just inside the door stood the Marll, a triumphant leer of pleasure on her bloated face, and next to her, a warrior whom Melvaig now recognized, as Shuinn had done earlier, as one of the Hurll from the Gurrtslagg. In between them, to Melvaig's horror, stood the fragile, naked figure of Tennga, her face streaming with tears. She was looking imploringly at Melvaig, beseeching him for forgiveness for what she had done. When the Marll had come into her room in the middle of the night and called her and she had quietly slipped out from between the sleeping bodies of the two men, she had had no idea what the reason could be. She did not think, nor ask questions – she simply did as she was told. That was a lesson she had long ago learned. In any case her mind was still full of Ruann and Melvaig and she was in that strange unreal world of dreams and visions into which she so often lapsed. She had assumed she was wanted for the pleasure of some other warriors. But when she had been led into the private room of the Marll and seen the figure of the warrior she knew as Loomogg at the Marll's side, she had feared something else. They had questioned her about the two men she had been with that night, the one she now knew as Melvaig and the other. Did they both have Tangs? How had they behaved with her? What had they revealed about themselves?

Something deep inside her told her that she should not say anything other than that they were normal warriors and so that is what she had said. Then they had started to molest her, to hurt her in her tender places and she had had too much pain in the past to bear any more. She knew what was coming and could not stand the thought of it. And they had stopped, and promised her all sorts of privileges if she would tell what she knew. They would not send her to the Lemgorrst. A place in the goat farms, they had said, or in the warrior nurseries. It was too much for her. She was not strong like Morven had been. She had no faith; her will was shattered and so she had told them everything she knew. Her mind had grown confused but they had prompted her where she had drifted off, with information which they themselves seemed to have from somewhere. And when they asked her about a Book she had not known what they meant but she remembered Melvaig taking a large pouch from around his neck. Perhaps it was in there? They had smiled and seemed pleased with her and then they had all gone out to pick up some other warriors and now here they were. And seeing Melvaig, seeing the confusion, bewilderment and anger in his eyes she had felt such remorse and guilt that she would have suffered anything to be free of it. How could she have been so weak? And yet she knew that were it to happen all over again, she could be no stronger and so now she cried out to him for forgiveness as the two warriors dragged him out of the pallet and across the floor, his white nakedness making him appear ungainly and awkward.

When Melvaig had first seen her standing with the Marll and the Hurll, he had been seized with terrible anger at her for her betrayal and he had spurned her eyes, turning away from her towards the wall where he had left his clothes. He looked for Shuinn and saw the giant quietly getting dressed, flanked by his guards. The Book! He started to put on his clothes, trying not to show the panic with which he picked each garment up from the floor, desperately hoping to see the familiar shape of the pouch. Then as if reading his mind, the Hurll called out to him, addressing him by name.

'You will not find it, Melvaig of Ruann,' he said in a harsh thick voice, quivering with pleasure. 'I have it here.'

Melvaig looked and saw his fears confirmed. The Hurll had the bag in one hand and was holding the Book in the other. Melvaig said nothing. So they knew everything! Tennga must have told them about the pouch, and they, knowing what they were looking for, were then certain that their search was over. Again a surge of bitterness rose in him against the girl and he looked at her, hoping to show her his rage but when he saw the pain in her eyes, he remembered their closeness and could feel again the smoothness of her body and the warmth of her breath. And then he saw the marks on her and he tried to make himself compassionate, to understand why she had done what she had. He looked at her face, and all that she had told him of her life since Ruann came into his mind, all the suffering, the degradation, and he found himself unable to blame her for grasping at any ray of hope of a release from it. She lifted her face and met his eyes and he felt all trace of anger evaporate before her desperate yearning for forgiveness. She was begging him, with every fibre of her being, to release her from the prison of shame in which she had incarcerated herself. How could he then be so cruel as to refuse her? Was he as vicious as those who served Xtlan? Was it such a man whom Ashgaroth had chosen to know the secret of the Book, to seek and find the world where he still reigned?

So Melvaig smiled at her and she, hardly daring to believe what she saw, broke free of the Marll and ran the few paces towards him, throwing herself down on her knees at his feet, crying his name out loud, as if in worship. So unexpected was her outburst that the guards merely stared open-mouthed as Melvaig, moved almost to tears, pulled his arms free and reached down to lift her up. Then he held her to him, trying to calm her sobs, and whispered in her ear, in the language of Ruann:

'It's all right. I understand. I forgive you. Please, don't cry for me. You need feel no shame or guilt. I will give your love to Morven and Bracca when we are together again.'

And then the Marll came forward and, gripping her by the hair, wrenched Tennga away from his grasp and, spinning her round, slapped her hard across the face. The guards, recovering from their confusion at this strange display, shouted to him to get dressed.

'Swine,' spat the Marll venomously. 'You thought you could fool me, play me for an idiot. From the Company of Kegg? Never for a moment did I believe you. Ha! You will sing a different song in the Blaggvald before my Lord Xtlan, while we shall reap the rewards for your capture.' Fear fuelled the poison in her words for she had been taken in. If it had not been for Loomogg, the Hurll from the Gurrtslagg, she would have let them go on their way. What would Loomogg say about her to the officials? Turn her in as not being vigilant enough in her duties? No. He could not prove she did not know from the beginning. And the acclaim she would receive for having taken such a part in capturing this man would, if what the Hurll had said was true, be great indeed. Perhaps she would be taken away from this stinking place, serving these wretched lowly scum, and be moved to be Marll of one of the Gravenndra in the Square. Yes, that would be it. That was her true place. Not here, in this foul pit.

For a few moments after she had finished her diatribe Melvaig's confused mind had failed to grasp the significance of her last words though, as he finished putting on his clothes, they echoed round his head. They were being taken to the Blaggvald. And then with a sudden rush of joy he realized: Morven! No need now to worry about how they were going to get in; they were being taken. At last he would be near her; and then he would find a way. So what had seemed this cruellest trick, their recapture, was in fact going to prove his salvation. He looked across at Shuinn, standing quietly between his two guards, and they exchanged glances.

Melvaig's hands were bound tightly together and the guards led him past Loomogg, Tennga, and the Marll out of the door, along the passage and then down the stairs into the room below. Shuinn, the other guards and Loomogg followed, leaving Tennga upstairs with the Marll. As they reached the bottom of the stairs there was a loud crack followed by a terrible scream. So the Marll was having her fun, crushing all the poor girl's hopes and dreams with a single crack of a whip. Melvaig's heart ached as he imagined Tennga's confused and bitter grief: to have betrayed her friends for promises that were then shattered. And yet, Melvaig thought, if she had not believed those promises, they would not now be going to the Blaggvald and Morven. The sound of the Marll's laughter now drifted down, a vicious, high-pitched cackle mixing with Tennga's shrieks of pain in a hideous cacophony of noise – the Marll's enjoyment deriving added piquancy from the crushed expectations of her victim.

Loomogg led them through the room, empty now save for the few who lay sprawled on the floor or the tables, too drunk to know or care about anything, and as they walked out of the door, the awful sound from upstairs seemed to grow more intense so that Melvaig felt his head start to ache as he tried to block it out. When the door slammed shut behind them, muffling it so that it could hardly be heard, he felt guiltily grateful. In the distance the sun was just starting to blaze orange and red for those few moments before it became lost behind the yellow-grey of the sky. Already it was hot, the ground beneath their feet throwing up a wall of heat into their faces. Beyond the far buildings rose the great black citadel of rock upon which stood the Blaggvald, like some dark crown of evil. The sun rose behind it, silhouetting it against the sky, and Melvaig felt again the icy fingers of fear which had encircled him the first time he had seen it. And inside it, somewhere, was Morven.

'Quickly, find your horses.' It was Loomogg.

Melvaig soon found Bendro and the horse whinnied a greeting. With his hands tied, the guards had to help him up on to Bendro's back and as he sat once more on his horse he felt a little thrill of joy and comfort. The guards lashed his hands to the saddle and then attached a rope from Bendro to one of their horses. Then Loomogg, in the lead, started to ride away slowly down the road, leaving the Gravenndra behind them, and soon Tennga's screams grew so faint that Melvaig could hardly hear them. He found himself straining his ears for their sound, fearful that he would forget her as soon as they faded and feeling in some strange and illogical way that as long as he could hear her, they were close enough for her to feel some comfort from the knowledge of his nearness. Eventually though, as they rode further and further away, he realized that the screams were in his imagination and as he did so, they suddenly disappeared, leaving an empty space where Tennga had been.

As the sun began to rise, the dawn Grayling's piercing notes pealed out into the dry heat of the air. Melvaig saw

Loomogg and the guards scrabble about in their saddle pouches for ear plugs and then felt himself being dragged into a nauseous haze where he had to focus all his attention on hanging on to Bendro to stop himself falling. It seemed to go on and on, sapping his will and energy as it had before on the ridge above Eggron and then, as suddenly as it had started, the notes began to ebb and he felt the darkness in his head start to clear. He opened his eyes and saw the guards looking at him and Shuinn with amusement. Melvaig had not realized it but they had stopped riding and he and the giant had collapsed on to their horses. He lifted himself up and glanced across at Shuinn who smiled back at him. Loomogg barked an order and the strange little procession once again set off: Loomogg in the lead, Melvaig after him with two guards on either side and one behind him, and then Shuinn with one guard behind him to bring up the rear. They seemed to take all the little-used tracks – many that Shuinn did not know existed – so that they met few riders. He guessed that the Hurll was wary of being seen; there were many, far more direct routes to the Blaggvald. It could well be, he thought, that the party of Hurll from the Gurrtslagg had split up to find them, arranging somehow to meet again if any of them were successful and so share the rewards. Loomogg was greedy. But he had to be careful. News of their capture might have leaked out and his colleagues could be out looking for him.

On they rode, winding round the narrow paths and alleys, past old ruined buildings filled with rubble, the horses picking their way over the stones, while all the time, ahead of them, the Blaggvald grew slowly nearer. The guards rode happily at the side of their charges, chatting and laughing with one another. They had been the first group that Loomogg had come across last night as he came out of the Gravenndra to find a troop who would help him take his quarry to Xtlan He had stopped them and told them all he knew and they had been delighted at the prospect, for news of these two fugitives had been circulating among all the guards for some time and they had been looking out especially for them. Now the prize had fallen to them quite unexpectedly and they could expect a great increase in their privileges. Tshonn, their leader, looked across at the man at his side, Melvaig, dressed in the murdered warrior's clothes and wondered at the truth of the rumours that had been running like fire around Eggron, about the enormity of the knowledge that was contained in the Book which Loomogg had been so keen to get his hands on. Did the man Melvaig know what was in it? How had he got hold of it? Had he truly, with his companion, the giant whose face had betrayed no emotion since his capture, escaped from the dreaded Gurrtslagg? He looked ahead to the arrogant posture of Loomogg, riding cockily along on his horse as if he owned the world. There was something about him he did not like, something both in his manner, furtive, sly and wheedling, and his appearance – the shifty eyes set in that pointed face, whose skin after so much time in the mines was pallid and almost translucent. Was it really true that he had accompanied Burgunn on his own, with the two captives, on their journey from the Gurrtslagg to Eggron and that, as he had told them, the captives had overpowered them both – killing Burgunn and leaving him, Loomogg, for dead? No! Tshonn would have staked his life on the falsity of that story. Someone, somewhere had been betrayed. Of that he was certain. Well, there would be more; there was no way he was going to let this swine of a Hurll from the Gurrtslagg take any credit for finding these two.

Melvaig looked up as a sudden movement from the guard on his right, Tshonn, caught his attention. It seemed to be a signal, for the other three guards suddenly seemed to increase their pace so that they were just behind Loomogg. Then Tshonn on the one side of Melvaig and the guard on his other side pulled forward so that they flanked Loomogg. They all turned a corner and as they did so, the Hurll, sensing that something was wrong, suddenly broke free of his dreams and, looking up, was just in time to see two clubs smashing down through the air towards him. He gave a terrified squeal and instinctively raised his arms over his head in a desperate attempt to protect himself. Melvaig watched, grimly fascinated, as the blows knocked Loomogg off his horse, blood pouring from a great gash on top of his head. Immediately Tshonn and the other guard jumped down and stabbed him savagely in his chest until he lay still on the road in a pool of blood. Loomogg's horse, attached by rope to Bendro, was whinnying and stamping with fear and Melvaig had to cling on tightly with his legs to avoid being thrown. Tshonn left the body of the Hurll and walked over to the dead man's horse. Gripping it by the reins he soon calmed it down and then he delved in the saddle bags until he found what he was after: the Book. He took it out, still in Melvaig's goatskin pouch and then he removed it from that, holding the Book gently and delicately, as if it might break. Melvaig watched his face as he looked at it, the furrowed lines of concentration as he tried, carefully, to open it, the intense fascination in his eyes as he gazed in wonder at the delicate etchings inside. But then Tshonn noticed with a start of fear that some of Loomogg's blood smeared on his hands had stained one of the pages. Quickly and clumsily he slammed the Book shut and then, as he was putting it back in the pouch he noticed Melvaig looking at him. Confused and slightly in awe of his strange captive, Tshonn was surprised to find himself leering in an attempted smile at Melvaig. Then, hoping none of the other guards had seen, he turned away and opening one of his saddle bags, put the Book inside. Then he untied Loomogg's horse, tethered his own to Melvaig's and told one of the other guards to look after the spare horse. Finally, when Loomogg's body had been dragged inside one of the old buildings at the side of the road and buried under a pile of rubble and stone, Tshonn remounted and, leading Melvaig behind him, they all set off once more down the track.

The heat soon became intense and Melvaig felt the sweat running inside his clothes. His mind had become vacant; a blank emptiness had descended upon him and the steady rhythmic clopping of Bendro's hooves and the distant sound of the slaves working on the wall lulled him into a daze. The killing of Loomogg had left him completely unmoved, even pleased; and the fact that they were now heading towards Morven and that captivity was working to their advantage meant that, for the time being, he could give himself a rest and let himself be carried along by events. At times he remembered Tennga and felt guilty about forgetting her, while at other times he would find images coming into his mind of scenes from the past, before and since his departure from Ruann.

Melvaig let the images roam freely through his mind, exorcising his fears and worries and building up the strength and the resolve he would need to face the Blaggvald. What would happen there? How he would find Morven and escape with her, he did not know. They would face that when they came to it. They! It gave him a shock to realize that he was thinking of himself and Shuinn almost as one. His friend, the Mengoy scavenger who had become so close to him it was almost as if they were of the same blood. He could picture now the warmth in the friendship between Shuinn and Bracca and the hope this had given him. Those hopes had not been realized in the way Melvaig had expected but in a far greater way, for what he had seen in that relationship was the awakening of the spirit of Ashgaroth in a man who, until that moment, had floundered uselessly in a world of evil. It frightened Melvaig to speculate about where he would be had it not been for Shuinn. If chance had not put them together, how long could he have survived in Xtlan? And now, the comfort, and the feeling of security it gave him to feel the presence of the giant at his back and the strength of Shuinn's faith in Ashgaroth and the world of the Book! He remembered again the vision he had had on the ridge above Eggron – and then, as the picture hung before his eyes, he heard the voice of Tshonn call out the order to stop and dismount.

The guards helped Melvaig and Shuinn down and then, after the horses had been secured, they were led off the road into the shade of one of the ruins. Melvaig was grateful for the rest and the relative coolness as they sat down on a pile of stones with their backs against an old broken-down wall. They were given pieces of dried goats-meat and a skin of water was passed round; Tshonn was going to make sure these most precious of captives were delivered in good condition. As they ate, the guards chatting among themselves, Melvaig met Shuinn's eyes for a moment and they gave each other a brief reassuring smile. The stones on which they were sitting had been shaped into a square or rectangle, the corners sharp and accurate where they had not broken when they fell. Some had even been decorated with patterns, etched into the facings, and Melvaig marvelled at the effort and the time such work must have taken. To have such a vista of time and peace, he thought, must have been very wonderful. He looked around at the ugly ruins of Eggron and as the whole desolate shambles of the world he knew seemed to concentrate itself into his mind in a single image he felt again the surge of anger, bitterness and betrayal that he had first experienced after Arkron's recital of the Book had revealed to him the world Before the War. He looked up and saw the black pinnacle of the Blaggvald, not far away now, casting its shadow of evil over all that he knew.

CHAPTER XXV

When they had finished eating, they remounted and continued on their way, Melvaig losing himself once again in the rhythm of the hooves on the track and the movement of Bendro's back beneath him. Occasionally they crossed one of the main arteries of the city, crowded with warriors and officials, but for the most part, like Loomogg before him, Tshonn kept to the back ways where they saw few other riders. All the time, through the meander of his daydreams, Melvaig was conscious of the growing nearness of the Blaggvald. It touched him physically in strange ways; his scalp would suddenly start to tingle or he would feel a prickle at the back of his neck. At other times he would feel an uncontrollable fluttering in his stomach so intense that he would feel his whole body start to shiver. As they rode nearer and the afternoon sun began its decline in the grey murk of the sky these feelings grew stronger, until he had to fight to keep from losing control of his body. They came now into an area where the ruins had been flattened and Melvaig could see nothing but piles of rubble for a great distance on either side, while in front of them, immediately around the pinnacle of the Blaggvald, the land was completely flat and empty. It was a place of utter desolation, stretching right around the base of the rock, the ground brown and scorched, shimmering in the heat, not a blade of grass to be seen. Cracks ran like black veins across the surface and occasionally Melvaig could see a great gaping fissure where the ground had opened up.

Tshonn stopped and the rest of the guards reined in their horses. An intense stillness hung over everything like a cloud, only the panting of the horses breaking the eerie quiet. Nothing moved: not an insect, an animal or a man. Shuinn gazed in awe at this moat of land around the Blaggvald. He had heard of it but never before seen it, this great protective circle of desert round the Blaggvald, across which nothing could move without being seen from the pinnacle. He peered through the shimmering haze at the rock that rose straight up from the flat earth around it and he could just make out, halfway up the rock, the circle of lookout posts, hewn out of stone, through which every handspan of the ground was kept constantly in view. And then he saw, starting at the base and winding its way around the pinnacle, the flight of steps which provided the only way up to the Blaggvald. He followed its steep, tortuous route until finally, at the top, he found his eyes resting on the sheer black walls of the Black Palace itself, growing out of the stone. He shivered and looked away, back to the ears of his horse, to the figure of Melvaig in front and to the guards all around, themselves rooted to the spot with terrified fascination.

Tshonn had never before been to this place but he had spoken to those who had. None, he knew, were allowed to cross the wasteland, only the Aylinn, Xtlan's private guards, were allowed access to and from the Blaggvald. They would have to ride out a short way and wait. When they were spotted from the rock, riders of the Aylinn would come to them. And so kicking his heels gently on his horse's flanks he urged her slowly out into the baking heat. Soon they were well clear of the ruins and should be easily seen. He dismounted, telling the others to do the same and then, having got the horses to lie down so as to provide shelter, they settled down to wait.

The water was passed round and Melvaig, wondering why they had stopped, gripped the container with his tied hands, poured the liquid gratefully down his dry aching throat and settled his back against the stomach of his horse. Thoughts of Morven drifted through his mind again. But they remained vague, the intensity of the emotions they would normally arouse being somehow dissipated by the overpowering presence of the Blaggvald. It dragged at his will, its great black jagged shape dancing in the heat, so that the outlines were blurred and for an instant Melvaig imagined he was dreaming.

Then, as he looked, he saw a sprinkling of black dots at the base of the rock. For a time he found it hard to focus on them through the haze and he thought his eyes were playing tricks, but suddenly they grew larger and he could make out a group of riders. On they came, for a long time seeming to stand still, their shapes bouncing monotonously up and down, eerily silent, no sound betraying their presence. Then suddenly the riders seemed to burst out of the desert, the drumming of the hooves on the hard earth and the heavy breathing of their horses shaking off the lethargy of Tshonn and the other guards so that they stood up in a flurry of activity and, drawing out clubs and swords got their horses up from the ground, and mounting them, formed themselves into a circle around their two captives, with Tshonn at their head. Melvaig and Shuinn, having been hurriedly helped up on to their horses, watched as the Aylinn slowed down so that by the time the two groups were in speaking range their horses were walking. Tshonn rode forward to meet their leader and the Aylinn pulled their horses to a halt.

Melvaig felt a sickness in his stomach as he looked at them. They had about them the same air of evil that emanated from the Blaggvald; in their deep-set eyes, no flicker of emotion – simply a cold glazed look that now, as it ranged across the group before them, froze with fear those upon whom they gazed. Each rode a huge black horse, adorned with fine saddlery decorated in gold. Their costumes were also black – loose leather leggings tucked into knee-length boots, long black goats-hair cloaks over their shoulders and, on their heads, round basin-shaped helmets festooned with plumes of hair.

'All praise to Xtlan,' called out Tshonn with his arm raised in salute. 'I am Tshonn, a leader of the guard, and I would have words with you – we have important captives.'

One of the Aylinn, a huge man with a long dark beard, rode slowly forward, his black horse panting in the heat.

'Hail the Lord Xtlan,' he said. 'I am Bringdagg – a leader of the Aylinn. Come – we will talk.'

He motioned to Tshonn to follow him and they rode a little way off to one side. Their conversation was low and mumbled and Melvaig could not hear it, though he saw Tshonn take out the Book and pass it over. Soon their talk became animated, Tshonn turning round frequently and pointing excitedly at Melvaig and Shuinn, until eventually, as Bringdagg accepted his story, he relaxed and smiled. Now, Melvaig guessed, they began talking about the reward and it was not long before Bringdagg turned round and picked out from one of his saddlebags a pouch from which he proceeded to extract a number of large golden coins and count them out into Tshonn's eager hands, finally giving him two large square tablets. Tshonn was well pleased, for one of these gave him entry to the Gravenndra in the Square while the other was a Stygg – a symbol of merit. If he gained two more of these he would be eligible to become one of the Aylinn himself. He bowed his head in acknowledgement of Bringdagg's generosity and decided he would somehow have to dispose of the Marll in the Gravenndra. He had not told of her part in the finding of the captives as he did not want to share his reward, neither had he mentioned Loomogg, and if she waited too long for her share she might well go to one of the officials in the Square with her story. She could easily damage him with some invented tale of his disrespect for Xtlan. He put her out of his mind for the present as he rode, smiling, back to his troop.

The guards around Melvaig and Shuinn now broke up and rode to meet their leader to collect their share of the coins before riding back together to Eggron. None of them would be sorry to leave this place where the proximity of the Blaggvald, the presence of which, at a distance, they had got used to, had filled them all with a fear and dread they would never forget. Yet they also knew that their part in the capture of these two would hasten their ascent in the hierarchy of Eggron and would give them a greatly privileged status among their fellows.

Melvaig, left alone with Shuinn and their two horses and the Aylinn, watched Tshonn and the other guards ride away over the short stretch of desert before finally vanishing among the buildings of Eggron. He turned back when he felt Bendro's head move as Bringdagg tethered the horse to his mount. He glanced round at Shuinn, whose horse was being tied in turn to Bendro and again he found comfort in his friend's smile. Then, at a signal from Bringdagg, the little group started to ride back over the desert towards the Blaggvald. They rode fast with Bringdagg in front and the other Aylinn in a huddle around the captives. Melvaig clung on with his legs while his tied hands frantically gripped the saddle. He had the feeling that if he had fallen, the Aylinn behind would have ridden right over him in their headlong dash across this barren wasteland. And Melvaig felt the reason for their haste, because every moment spent under this searing heat with nothing but the arid earth all around, seemed like an age, weighing down upon his spirit and his heart with a relentless force that sapped his energy and the marrow of his bones so that he became lifeless, like a rock. If it had not been for their furious, unthinking speed he felt he would simply have crumpled beneath the crushing weight of the heat, fallen off the saddle and withered like a dead leaf on the ground that passed by in a blur beneath Bendro's racing hooves.

On and on they sped, and all the time, though Melvaig did not look up, he could feel the darkness of the Blaggvald drawing nearer.

The plumes on the helmets of the Aylinn in front bobbed up and down with the rhythm of the riders and the drumming of the hooves pummelled his ears with their rolling thunder. Then suddenly a great shadow fell all about them and as he looked up, he felt his blood run cold as if his heart had turned to ice. There, just in front of them stood the pinnacle of rock and as Melvaig raised his head he could see, towering way above them, the sheer walls of the Blaggvald growing out of the stone. The hazy light from the late afternoon sun was behind it so that it cast a silhouette around the rock, accentuating its outline with a strange white light and throwing shadows over its face.

The riders slowed down now as they came up to the base and turned their horses towards a huge gateway beyond which the steps began their climb up the rock. They halted before a pair of great black iron gates, hanging on pillars of stone, and two Aylinn emerged from a shelter that had been hewn out of the rock. They looked at Bringdagg, shouted a greeting and moved across to open the gates. When the group had ridden through slowly, the gates were slammed shut again. Bringdagg dismounted and the others similarly got off their panting horses before leading them up a few steps and turning along a short track cut into the rock parallel to the ground at the end of which was a small trough filled with water. There was only space for one horse at a time so each rider and horse took it in turn to drink before going back along the track and waiting on the steps. Melvaig followed Bringdagg and watched Bendro delicately place his lips in the water and suck up the precious liquid before he himself knelt down on the stone surround and, cupping his hands and closing his eyes, he poured the water down his parched throat, feeling it flood to every part of his body with a sensual ecstasy. All too soon he heard Bringdagg's sharp voice say 'Enough,' and he moved away, following Bendro, who was still tethered to Bringdagg's horse. When they got back to the steps they moved a little way up to give the others room behind them and waited.

Bringdagg sat down on a step and Melvaig felt the man's gaze on him. He looked up to catch it and for an instant their eyes met. Involuntarily Melvaig smiled at him and the blank expressionless look in Bringdagg's eyes changed momentarily as a flicker of response swept across his face. Then as quickly as it had come it passed and he turned his head sharply away as if embarrassed. Melvaig felt the urge to speak raging inside his head, to say anything, to establish some thread of communication with him; but he could not think what words to use, they stuck in his throat, and soon the chance was lost when Shuinn and a second Aylinn joined them on the steps.

When the horses had been watered, Bringdagg started walking up the steps, leading his horse carefully up the awkward twisting stairway. Melvaig followed, holding Bendro by the thongings round his head and urging him on gently. The steps were barely wide enough and it was a difficult climb. Melvaig stayed on the inside with his back against the rock wall and through the frame of Bendro's legs he could see the ground getting further and further away, receding into the distance beneath them. He talked constantly to Bendro, comforting him when his hooves slipped on the smooth hard surface of the stone, encouraging him and stroking him when, coming round from the dark side of the rock, they were met by the glare of the evening sky. Bendro would falter then, stubbornly refusing to go on until finally, under Melvaig's gentle cosseting and chiding, he would relent and continue forward slowly.

Higher and higher they climbed, their circuits round the rock getting smaller as they came nearer the top. Melvaig could see the whole of Eggron now, spreading out before his gaze in all its ravaged ugliness, while beyond it lay the slopes down which he and Shuinn had come. He could make out the goat farms and even, he thought, the ridge where he had had his vision of the animals. And there was the valley where they had killed the two warriors whose clothing they now wore. Further round lay the Lemgorrst huddled against the gate through which the Mengoy, Gebb, Nekdog and Shuinn, had taken himself and Bracca. It lay there, bathed in the red glow of the dying evening sun, like a festering open wound, and Melvaig shuddered at the ghastly memories of the things he had seen there. Beyond the mountains which bordered the Lemgorrst he could see nothing. Hidden from view was the desert of Molob and still further away the mountains wherein lay Ruann.

They came now to a wide track which led off the steps and away to either side. Along it Melvaig could see some of the lookout posts; large dome-shaped shelters hewn out of the stone with a wide slit in the front facing the desert. Bringdagg stopped and, turning round, watched dispassionately as all the other Aylinn filed-off down these tracks. As each one turned off the steps he raised his hand in salute and Bringdagg responded similarly and then, when they had all gone, he turned round and continued upwards.

Further and higher they went, Bringdagg, Melvaig and Shuinn, until Melvaig's weary limbs ached and throbbed with the effort of climbing and, at each step, screamed with pain. Mercifully the heat had lost its intensity and a slight breeze fanned refreshingly against their faces but Melvaig was now too exhausted to notice. Head down, he plodded doggedly on, thinking of nothing but the need to mount the next step and the prayer that Bendro would come easily. And then they stopped. For a moment, Melvaig, dazed and numb with weariness, did not realize and then, as he slowly lifted his head, he understood that, at last, they had arrived.

They were standing on a great plateau, the edge of which dropped sheer away down the rock to the ground far below. In the centre, its black stone walls growing out of the rock and soaring way above them, stood the Blaggvald, whose presence had dominated Melvaig's consciousness ever since that first moment he had seen it from outside the gates to the Lemgorrst. Inside lay Xtlan. And Morven? Huge square towers rose up from three of the corners while at the fourth, a tall round turret pointed, like a finger, to the sky. In between the corners, the top of the wall was serrated in little squares and as he looked, Melvaig could see the figures of the Aylinn looking out between them over the desert towards Eggron. His gaze lingered on the round tower in the far corner. The part facing him lay in shadow while the glow of the evening sun poured gold over the rest of its smooth blackness. It tapered up gently to a sharply pointed minaret. The walls were unbroken save for a few small slits spaced at intervals in a band around the top.

As Melvaig looked at them, a prickle of fear ran from the base of his spine up to his neck as from somewhere deep within himself came the certainty that Xtlan was looking through them at him. He strained his eyes to see further inside but there was only a deep, deep blackness. It seemed to Melvaig to be the darkness of eternity and then, as he peered desperately up at the window slits, the darkness he perceived through them seemed to undergo a change and he started seeing flashes of light in the black, like stars, whirling around faster and faster in dizzying spirals that seemed to suck him towards the spinning vortex of their madly careering paths. He lifted his bound hands to his head and, slamming his wrists against his forehead, raked his nails down his scalp in an attempt to banish the terrible feeling that he was flying through the air towards the round tower. He shut his eyes but still Xtlan drew him onwards and upwards into the dark void beyond the tower. He felt himself collapse on to the hard rock and heard his voice shouting and screaming and then, through the darkness, in the midst of the maelstrom, he saw in the distance a calm, quiet, silver glow. Slowly it came towards him, growing larger all the time, and as it came so the seething madness quietened and fell away until at last the light seemed to come within his grasp. He held out his arms and made a leap towards it and as he touched it, it seemed to envelop him in its silver serenity so that his terror vanished. He opened his eyes to see Shuinn's anxious face looking down upon him and Bringdagg standing behind, uncertain and ill at ease at the behaviour of the captive.

'What happened?' murmured Shuinn. 'Are you all right now?'

Melvaig spoke and his voice at first sounded remote and distant as if he was speaking from a long way off.

'Yes,' he said. 'Yes. The round tower. The slits. I . . . I saw darkness. It . . .' but the words would not come. Yet he knew that Ashgaroth had saved him. The silver light. And now as he looked up and saw the window slits again, he felt the rage of Xtlan burning through the air towards him. The silver light had gone, yet Melvaig still felt its glow in his spirit and the warmth of its protection, and he smiled. Shuinn, seeing the smile and sensing something of what Melvaig was unable to express, felt the strength of his friend's confidence.

'Up. Hurry.'

It was the harsh voice of Bringdagg, worried that some harm had befallen the precious captive.

Melvaig, still dazed, held on to Shuinn's hands while the giant pulled him to his feet and then, when he had got hold of Bendro again, Bringdagg led them off across the centre of the plateau towards two wooden gates set in a huge archway in the great square front wall of the Blaggvald. As they approached, Bringdagg produced a horn from his belt and blew two short blasts on it; they lingered on the air until the breeze carried them away over the edge of the rock and across the desert. At this signal the gates were opened from the inside to reveal a large square courtyard. Melvaig felt a breath of cold stale air sweep out and pass over him and he shivered at its touch.

They walked on until they were just outside the gates when, without warning, Bendro suddenly tossed his head and stopped. Melvaig pulled him but the horse refused to go forward. Melvaig urged the horse on, panic making him desperate so that he found himself losing his temper; he shouted and yanked fiercely at the thongings round Bendro's head but still he would not move. Suddenly Bendro reared up on his back legs and began to whinny. The reins were torn from Melvaig's grasp as the horse pounded at the air with his front hooves, as if fighting some invisible enemy, all the time letting out an awful sound that rang out over the heavy stillness of the plateau. Melvaig watched Bringdagg cut the tethering rope and then, to his horror, the horse swung round, its eyes wide and staring, foam dripping from its mouth, and galloped away in a frenzy of fear towards the edge of the plateau. It did not even try to stop. Melvaig turned his head away as the whinnying slowly receded until, once again, silence fell. Into his mind there came a terrible image of Bendro tumbling slowly through space, turning as he fell, his mouth agape and his lips drawn back and then he imagined the terrible sound as the horse fell on to the hard earth below. The image lingered in his mind, repeating itself over and over again as he saw Bringdagg approach him. He felt the end of the tethering rope, frayed where it had been cut, passed between his wrists and tied around the cords that bound them. Bringdagg said something, smiling with a smug self-satisfied look on his face as if to say that Melvaig was not going to be so lucky as to escape that way, and then, when he had got back to his horse, Melvaig felt his wrists lifted and pulled forward as Bringdagg started to lead him on through the open doors of the Blaggvald.

It was as they passed under the great stone archway that Melvaig understood Bendro's terror. The evening sun was just going down, throwing narrow shafts of golden light through the gloom upon the flags of the huge square courtyard which now lay before them. High up on the walls, tapers burned, their flickering light sending the shadows dancing. A chill air seeped out of the walls smothering him in a shroud of fear that turned his blood to ice. Slowly they walked across the courtyard, the sound of the hooves echoing against the walls in the unearthly silence. Melvaig looked up to the top of the walls. It was almost dark now and he could only dimly see the Aylinn guards patrolling, constantly alert for any unusual sounds – sounds that would cause them to ring the alarm bells and call out the rest of the Aylinn. Only once, a long time ago when Xtlan was young, had this happened; a man named Pakkon had felt himself powerful enough to lead a small army of men across the desert to try to storm the pinnacle. Their revoltingly mutilated bodies had hung in the Square in Eggron for many days afterwards as a warning for others while the stories of the terrible sufferings they had endured before they had died were known by all. Since then none had dared to try; the network of deceit and treachery in Xtlan trapped any who even dreamed of any thoughts of rebellion long before they could begin. And now the web of Xtlan was too strong to break; yet still the Aylinn guards patrolled and still the lookout posts were manned.

They walked on through the gloom, broken now only by

the tapers in the courtyard and the dim orange chinks of light that escaped through the slit-like windows in the walls. They were walking in a curve now away from the round tower, the top of which was lost in the dark, towards one of the square towers. Bringdagg stopped in front of a small wooden door and pulled at a rope which hung outside. Melvaig heard Shuinn and his horse stop just behind him and then the door opened and a man came out. He was short and stocky and was dressed differently from the others; loose flowing robes hung from his shoulders and even in the dim light from the doorway Melvaig could make out their bright colours. The light glittered and twinkled where it fell on them so that they sparkled with gold and silver. As Bringdagg spoke to him and handed him the Book, his round face glistened with sweat and his thick lips broke into a smile. They talked excitedly while Melvaig and Shuinn waited and Melvaig felt the man's eyes feasting themselves upon him. Then, abruptly Bringdagg turned away and with a last blank, expressionless look at Melvaig took the reins of Shuinn's horse and, leading his own horse with the other hand, walked away, back across the courtyard.

'Come with me,' said the man, whom Melvaig had heard Bringdagg call Gakk, and he led them through the doorway into the square tower. Melvaig saw a small room just inside the door, which he presumed was where Gakk had been sitting on guard, while two long narrow passageways stretched away on either side. From one of them, a little way down, there came a splash of light and Melvaig heard the sounds of talk and laughter drifting out into the silence. As he looked, two women came out of the light carrying trays and turned away from him down the passage. Morven? He peered into the gloom but they were soon lost in the murky darkness. His heart was pounding furiously, the blood racing in his head. Now they were here – how were they to find her and escape?

He felt a gentle push on his shoulder from behind and turning round quickly saw Shuinn pointing in front. Gakk was standing a little way up a winding stone stairway leading up into the tower, waiting for them, a strangely benign smile on his face. Melvaig walked forward and began following Gakk up the stairs. He was surprised at the attitude towards them that had been shown by both Bringdagg and now, particularly, this man Gakk. It was almost as if he and Shuinn were guests. There was little sense of hostility towards them, no obvious signs of restraint since the Aylinn saw not the remotest chance of escape. Further than this there was an interest, even a feeling of awe, which Melvaig felt in the way the Aylinn looked at them. Perhaps also, remote in this pinnacle of power, those who had reached this place had expunged their appetites for cruelty and suffering and had no further need for it, existing on a different plane from the rest of Xtlan – content with power alone, using their evil skills not for enjoyment but in the maintenance and pursuit of that power. It was enough for them that mention of the Blaggvald should turn the stomach of the strongest man to jelly. No need for them to wallow in the pain of others, fear and total subservience were enough. Besides, their minds had to be clear, clear to plan the campaigns that would eventually spread the rule of Xtlan over all, till the whole world lay in his shadow, until the will of Dréagg was complete. And they had to keep their minds uncluttered to watch for the trickery of their fellows; to retain their place in the hierarchy against those beneath them and to seek the overthrow of those above by deceit or treachery or whatever means they could.

Higher they climbed, round and round the narrow twisting stairway, sometimes stumbling in the gloom or slipping on the smooth stone of the steps, worn down by centuries of use. Then Gakk would wait for them, even help them up, until finally the stairs led to a small door set in a stone wall. Gakk pulled up a wooden latch and the door opened. He turned and spoke.

'Now, inside! You will find food and drink on the floor.'

Melvaig gingerly walked in and when Shuinn had joined him the door quietly scraped shut and they heard the sounds of a wooden bar being placed against it. Then Gakk's footsteps padded away till they could be heard no more. For a time neither Melvaig nor Shuinn spoke. The room was pitch black. They could see nothing, neither the width nor the height and Melvaig felt as if he were hanging in mid-air.

'Shuinn,' he said. 'Shuinn. Are you all right? Where are you?'

'Here.'

'Where?'

'Here.'

'I'll come to you,' said Melvaig, getting up again and moving slowly in the direction of Shuinn's voice. As he did so he heard a giggle of suppressed laughter.

'Where are you?' he said again.

'Here,' came the reply.

'Where?'

'Here,' and they both burst into uncontrollable gales of laughter. As the tears ran down his face Melvaig tried to stop. He felt pangs of guilt: Morven suffering somewhere else in the Blaggvald; Bracca, Tennga, Bendro lying crushed and broken at the base of the rock, yet still he could not stop laughing. Wasted time, they should be planning how to get out, how to rescue Morven, and all they could do was laugh.

Eventually, when Melvaig, waving his hands in front of him finally touched Shuinn's arm, they calmed down and sat on the wooden floor next to each other. He felt refreshed, his mind happy and alert. Morven was here, of that there could be no doubt. They would find a way to get out and find her and then break away from the Blaggvald, take some horses, cross the desert to Eggron and then find Bracca. Ashgaroth would show them a way. It would not be easy, but then could it be more difficult than what they had come through? He clutched Shuinn's wrist.

'Let's find the food,' he said, his voice still full of laughter at the thought of groping their way, on hands and knees, over the floor till they found it.

'Yes,' Shuinn replied. 'Yes. You go on.' There was a pause. 'I'll stay here.'

Melvaig heard a quietness, a melancholy plaint in his friend's voice and he found himself being irritated by it, by Shuinn not sharing the joyful optimism that he was feeling. All this time the faith of Shuinn had buoyed him up, carried him along with its unbroken strength and now, now that they were on the threshold of success, he had become moody and doubting.

'What's wrong?' he said, with more crossness in his voice than he had intended.

There was a pause. The darkness hung between them frustratingly like a barrier and Melvaig longed to brush it away with a wave of his arm. What expression was on his friend's face? What was in his eyes?

'What's wrong?' he repeated angrily. 'We're here. We have made it. The Blaggvald! Where Morven is! We have nearly succeeded.'

Shuinn began to speak and his voice was heavy and tired. The laughter had somehow drained him of his last resources of energy.

'You have felt his power. From the Round Tower. You have seen the pinnacle, the desert – observed the Aylinn. If Morven is here . . . then how . . .'

His voice trailed off and Melvaig realized. Since the Gurrtslagg he had relied on Shuinn almost as a cripple leans on a stick. Shuinn knew Xtlan: its people, its ways and its geography. It was Shuinn who had led them to Eggron, Shuinn who had got them through the gates, Shuinn who had got them into the Gravenndra. And now again, without knowing it, Melvaig was trusting his friend to find a way. He, Melvaig, had the visions, the dreams, the knowledge of the Book, but it had been Shuinn who had had to make the pursuit of those dreams possible. Even here, in the Blaggvald, Melvaig expected Shuinn to have a scheme. His faith in his friend had been unquestioning, implicit. And now there was no plan; no way that Shuinn could see. He had crossed the desert, climbed the rock, looked at the Blaggvald and had seen no chance, no hope. And to have to admit this, not only to himself but to Melvaig, had crushed him. As they had followed Gakk up the steps, he had wrestled for an answer but there was nothing.

Melvaig saw all this in a flash of understanding and guilt. He felt as if he had been like a child. Now he must help Shuinn. He must not let the giant feel as if he had failed. They must have faith. They would talk.

And so, quietly, Melvaig crawled off in the darkness and found the plates and bowls in a corner. He brought them back, gave Shuinn a mug of water and then, breaking off a chunk of hard, dry goatsmeat, put it into his friend's hand.

'Try and eat,' he said. 'You'll feel better.'

Then, as they chewed the meat and sipped the precious water, Melvaig began to speak, weaving again the pictures from the Book, the images that hung like golden shadows in his head until, in the cold, clammy darkness of their stone cell they both once again walked in that other world, the world that could not have perished, the world that they must one day find. At last, lost among the woods and the flowers, the trees, the mountains and the seas, they fell asleep.

CHAPTER XXVI

Melvaig woke to the feel of Shuinn's hand shaking his shoulder.

'Someone's coming,' said the giant, and Melvaig heard the sound of footsteps coming up the stairs towards their room. They stopped outside and Melvaig shook his head free of sleep while the wooden boards against the door were drawn back. He felt his body tense and his heart ache with tension and then the door opened to reveal Gakk accompanied by a number of Aylinn guards.

'You slept well?' said Gakk with a cruelly cynical tone in his voice. He looked down at the empty plates on the floor. 'Good. You enjoyed your food. You will need all your strength. Follow me.' He nodded to the guards and they moved quickly to either side of Melvaig and Shuinn, holding them firmly by the arms, and marched them towards the door.

There was no room on the stairs for more than one at a time so they walked down in single file, the guards both behind and in front of them. Through the window slits in the outside wall, Melvaig could see that it was early morning; he snatched brief glimpses of Eggron beyond the brown expanse of desert, already shimmering in the scorching heat of a new day. As they passed, they felt the hot air from outside brush over them, driving the chill from their bodies. When they reached the bottom of the stairs they saw Gakk's room again and turned along the corridor where Melvaig had seen the women last night. The guards again moved to either side, marching them swiftly down the passage. There were doors at frequent intervals, set in the wall. Some were open and through these he saw parts of a huge room, its vaulted ceiling reaching up higher than he could see, great carved pillars of stone supporting huge arches and balustrades. At the far end was an enormous rectangular recess where the smouldering remains of a fire glowed red while, above the fireplace, the wall was adorned with magnificent paintings. To his surprise and shock he saw that many of these paintings were of animals. Most of them he did not know but he recognized a few from the drawings and descriptions in the Book. Set on the floor of the room were long tables and benches, not the rough tables of the Gravenndra but smooth and finely carved with ornate legs. From the ceiling hung long chains holding great round chandeliers while the floor was scattered with brightly coloured rugs and mats.

Melvaig looked at all this in amazement, bewildered by the magnificence of what he saw – his head swimming in the colour and grandeur of all that passed before his eyes. Then suddenly they were at the end of the passage and at the head of a flight of steps which descended away beneath them. At the bottom Melvaig could see a tiny glow of orange light whilst the tunnel itself was dimly lit by occasional tapers set on the walls. Melvaig felt a terrible chill of apprehension spread through his body. Gakk turned and smiled coldly at him.

'Nearly there now,' he said in mocking amusement. 'Just down the steps.'

He began to make his way carefully down the narrow tunnel and Melvaig, Shuinn and the guards followed him. As they got deeper and the entrance receded behind them, visions of the Gurrtslagg passed before Melvaig's eyes and for an instant he imagined he was back there. The smell of damp, the feeling of incarceration, the descent into the earth; they all came together to rekindle in him the awful terror of the mines and then, suddenly, they were at the bottom, standing in front of a small black wooden door. Gakk lifted the latch and pushing it slowly open motioned Melvaig to go through first into the room. Melvaig walked forward with two guards just behind him. The room was very low and wide and at first, in the slow dance of the orange light from the brackets on the walls, he could see nothing. He took a step forward, his body numb with tension, and then, in the far corner of the room he saw something, two raised wooden pallets with a wheel at one end, the spokes throwing grotesque shadows on the wall. A terrible sense of foreboding clamped itself around his mind. He felt a push from one of the guards behind, urging him on. He saw a man with his back to them, standing at the head of one of the pallets. He had a black hood over his head, dropping in creased folds on to his shoulders, yet there was something in the way he stood, the set of his body, that struck distant chords of memory in Melvaig's mind. Another man, an Aylinn, was standing with two hands on the wheel, as if about to turn it. Gradually, painfully, Melvaig forced his eyes down to the pallets, dreading what every fibre of his being told him he would see, trying with every last vestige of his strength and will to prepare himself. And yet, when finally he looked upon the pallet, and saw Morven lying on her back naked, her wrists and ankles lashed to the corner posts, her golden hair falling over the side and spilling on to the floor, there was nothing that could have lessened the terrible flood of anguish, the piercing thrust of pain that seared through him.

'Morven!' he cried, and his voice resounded between the walls. 'Morven! I'm here.'

He lunged wildly forward towards her, but the guards were ready and they held him back. Desperately he struggled, kicking and lashing furiously, tears pouring down his face and blinding his eyes, flailing madly until his strength was all gone, his will crushed beneath the impotence of his body and he collapsed on the floor. The guards dragged him to his feet and pulled him forward, closer to where Morven lay, and he could see her mouthing his name as she wept. And then through the red blaze of his vision he saw her lips form another word and he fought to concentrate. Bracca. Was it? Bracca? He looked up and away from her to the other pallet. The little boy lay there lashed to the corners like his mother. He had grown, his hair was shorter, he was dressed in different clothes but it was he. His face was turned towards Melvaig and he was sobbing uncontrollably, his face contorted into a mask of terrible, uncomprehending pain.

'No!' Melvaig heard himself screaming, and then over and over, 'No! No!' until the voice of the man in the hood shouted, 'Enough. Leave us.'

Gakk moved forward to speak to him. 'You will be all right with them? Alone?'

'As I have said, it is the only way.' Again, through the blazing in Melvaig's mind, something about the man's voice sent a tingle of familiarity juddering in his head. The man went on, 'Go then. He will soon tell me. Do not doubt my powers.'

'Very well,' replied Gakk. 'If you are sure.' He turned to the Aylinn who were standing by the pallets and those holding Melvaig and Shuinn. 'Leave them. Follow me.'

Gradually the room emptied, the Aylinn shuffling out slowly, sullen and reluctant to leave the sport they had been looking forward to. The hooded man stood still. Melvaig, the hold on him released as the guards left, stood shakily on his feet, struggling to clear the pain and confusion from his head. The Book lay open on the pallet, next to Morven's leg. He would tell them everything. Everything. And if then they were all put to death, well then, so be it. But there was nothing he would not do or say if it might prevent their suffering.

He looked into her eyes. They met his and he felt the thrill of their contact but then the blaze of joy in her eyes ebbed and in its place was fear and pain and a swirling mist of bewilderment.

'Why?' she said, and her voice was quiet and soft, heavy with grief and the anguished yearning of her question. 'Why?'

And then the door slammed shut behind them. For a moment or two there was silence and then the hooded man turned round.

'Melvaig,' he said. 'Do not be alarmed.'

Melvaig looked on in disbelief as the man slowly pulled off the black hood and then, 'Arkron!' he said. 'Is it Arkron? It cannot be. You! But you . . .'

'Yes, Melvaig, my friend. It is Arkron you see before you. But do not ask too much. We do not have time. Quickly, untie Morven and Bracca. I have waited long and worked hard for these few moments. We must not waste them.' He turned to Shuinn who was standing, rooted to the spot, staring open-mouthed at the old man.

'Come, Shuinn,' said Arkron. 'You have done well. It is as I had hoped.'

There was silence as Melvaig and Shuinn worked at freeing Morven and Bracca from the pallets. Then Melvaig picked up the crumpled pile of clothing that had been thrown on the floor and gently dressed her. There was, about all of them, a dazed joy. So much to be said, yet for now all they could do was rejoice in the singing of their souls and let the buzzing of the questions that hummed in their heads remain unanswered for the moment; for nothing mattered save that Melvaig was with Morven and

Bracca and that here, in this most desolate of places and times, they had found Arkron. And now Arkron, the Hebbdril, began to speak and his words were urgent and glistening with clarity, for there was much to say in so little time. They sat on the floor, Morven and Bracca nestling in Melvaig's arms again while Shuinn, a stranger yet to Morven, sat with his hand on Bracca's shoulder.

'Melvaig,' said Arkron. 'Here is the Book. Take it and place it once again round your neck. They have, as you will have guessed, brought you here to make you reveal all you know of it. I have been in the Blaggvald for some time, earning myself a position of some power and trust. I have told Xtlan more than I would wish and sometimes done for him what I would rather not. Yet I have had to weigh my actions against the consequences of your failure and if I had not acted thus, this moment would not have been possible. It had to be that you would come for Morven. I guessed who she was when she was first brought here from the Gravenndra. Your description, and the fact that her home was Ruann. She did not know who I was. A strange inquisitive old man.' He paused and looked at Morven who was staring at him in astonishment. 'I asked her carefully about you, to find out if she had known you. I have tried to guard her from the worst excesses of the Aylinn without arousing their suspicions. But . . . take care. It will be long before she can forget, if ever. Yet she is very strong. She has had a faith – in you.

'As for Bracca? When news of your escape from the Gurrtslagg came to me I told them that Morven was your woman and that you would come here for her but if, as happened, you were captured, orders must be given that you should be brought here. But I believed that you would not reveal the secrets of the Book to save your own pain, nor even perhaps that of your woman. Torturing your little boy Bracca would though, I was sure, make you tell all you knew. And so orders were given that Bracca was to be found. I went round the warrior nurseries, the Bellkindra, until I saw him; though I did not dare let him see me. He arrived but a few nights ago. Last night, when Ashgaroth answered my prayers and you were here, I went to see Xtlan and managed to convince him that I should be left alone with you; that this was the best way to get you to talk. Xtlan wanted to see the Book last night. I took it to him and read parts of it through yet he thinks there is more than is written. He believes you to have the knowledge to find the remnants of the other world and he believes you to have been chosen by Ashgaroth to oppose his rule. Now you are in his power he means to destroy you but first he must learn everything that you know, so that he can find that world and crush it for ever. When you have told me I am to go to him but if you are stubborn and refuse then he will come himself. I am the touch of soft goatshair, to wheedle the truth from you by using my knowledge of the Book. He is the iron glove, to bludgeon what you know out of you by force if I fail. Yet, and this is why he gave me this chance, because he does not know the Book and cannot read, he would not know when you were lying. He does not trust me, as he trusts no one, but he has no choice.'

Arkron paused. There was silence outside the door and in the room a hushed air of anticipation. The orange light glowed on the old man's face and beard and he smiled.

'I have spent many hours among the books which Xtlan has salvaged from his conquests. Nights spent poring over the words of the most learned of men, learning of the world Before the War. And always, hovering like a shadow over all my learnings, has been the Book. Could it be that anything of the world you seek still exists and if so, where would it be? I studied maps and writings until my mind grew weary of the search and I felt my task was futile. And then slowly my vision cleared. Painstakingly I put together all my knowledge and, guided I am sure by the spirit of Ashgaroth, eventually I found what I believe to be the answer. I have put it down on parchment. Here, in this scroll.'

He drew a small tube-like container from the inside of his robes and handed it to Melvaig. It was made of wood, a deep dark ochre-brown, and the patterns of the grain ran in delicate swirls around it. On it were carved some patterns, intricate and beautiful so that Melvaig felt his eyes lingering on them with an awed fascination, his spirit stirred. He looked up at Arkron and the old man smiled.

'It is my gift to you,' he said, 'that in the times that follow you may remember Arkron whenever you look at it. The wood I found here, in the Blaggvald. I carved it while I sat thinking, pondering on my readings and letting the pattern of ideas fall into place. Inside you will find the scroll. One of the ends of the container has a small knob. Pull it and the end will come out. The scroll will then drop down.'

Melvaig did as Arkron said, tipped it up and the tightly bound scroll fell out into his hand. A length of thonging was tied around it and Arkron gestured to him to undo it. Melvaig pulled the ends of the bow and the parchment sprang open of its own accord.

'It is a map,' said Arkron as Melvaig looked at it in bewilderment. Melvaig felt Bracca's head heavy against his side and looking at him saw that he had fallen asleep. He turned back to the parchment on his knees as Arkron went on.

'On it is the way you must go to find what you seek. It is many days' journey, beyond Xtlan, and to get there you must cross the sea for it is an island. Your task will not be easy, for Xtlan will pursue you with all the power he has. He may try to recapture you again, to bring you back here and force you to reveal what you know. If he does that, you must not let him take the scroll; destroy it, bury it, but above all do not let it be taken. Or he may simply follow, let you lead him to the place and then get rid of you. Every particle of his energy will be directed at you for his fear of the existence of such a world as you seek is immense. While such a place exists, his power, his rule, can never be complete. His evil vision will be constantly threatened, the final victory of Dréagg unfulfilled, for do not forget that Xtlan is merely the pawn of Dréagg, his earthly presence. Yet do not feel alone, for the hand of Ashgaroth is with you. He has brought you safely here and he will continue to guide you, for the world you seek is his world, all that is left of the paradise he created. And, I believe, it is indeed as Xtlan fears, that the spirit of Ashgaroth is in you. Look at the map.'

Melvaig, his head swimming, tried to absorb all that Arkron was saying.

'It is as simply drawn as I could make it,' said Arkron, sitting down in front of them and gesturing to Shuinn and Morven to look at it as well. Morven, delirious with happiness, her mind still reeling with relief at all that had happened, tried to follow Arkron's words but found her attention wandering, able to comprehend little of the present save that she, Melvaig and Bracca were together and that her trust and her faith, which she had had to fight so hard to keep alive, had been rewarded. She watched as Arkron pointed to the drawings on the scroll.

'Here,' he said, 'is the Blaggvald. Your path takes you from here, beyond the wall of Eggron, across these mountains and thence to a mighty plain, which is now called the Dammfenn. This is indeed a barren place, for the most part bare rock and earth. Blasted by the War, you will find no living thing existing there. Eventually, the Dammfenn sweeps down to the sea. Leave shore in the early morning and head towards the sun. You should not then be long before you reach your destination.'

Melvaig and Shuinn felt a shiver of intense excitement at the mention of their arrival in the world they had dreamed about for so long and through so much. That it existed and that they now knew how to get there, filled them with a warm glow that set their bodies tingling with a sense of yearning anticipation.

'I have drawn in any landmarks as best I can,' Arkron continued. 'The oddities of the landscape I have tried to guess from the old maps. Some may be there no longer, blown away by the War; while some, I hope, flat-topped mountains, rocks in the shape of a man's face, deep ravines, will have remained to mark your way. Do not ask me what you will eat and drink. Do not ask me how you will cross the sea; and do not ask if you will succeed. These things I do not know. It is in your hands; with Ashgaroth to watch over and guide you.'

Melvaig looked at the old man.

'You are wondering,' Arkron went on, 'how you will escape the Blaggvald. This place is old, built many, many years ago Before the War. Always it has been a place of evil, a fortress of cruelty and oppression, and those who have dwelt in it have been those through whom the power of Dréagg has worked through the ages. In my readings I came across a number of books telling of its history, of who lived here and of how they met their end. Fear of revolt, or rebellion or of defeat in war made those men look for ways of escape should the Blaggvald be overthrown. One such man, a vile and vicious leader known as Helltor, had a secret tunnel built down through the rock and away under the surrounding land for a good distance. I am not sure whether it was ever used, nor even that it was completed, but I have made sure that it exists. As you may know, the great wall of Eggron at one point passes close to the Blaggvald and, if the diagram of its construction which I saw is correct, then it should take you under the wall and ...'

At that moment Arkron's words were suddenly drowned by a great knocking on the door behind him and a voice which turned Melvaig's blood to ice, harsh and strident, heavy with the resonance of evil, called, 'Arkron. Arkron the Hebbdril. We are impatient to know what you have so far learned from our guests. Would you have me yet enter?'

The ugly, guttural tones reverberated around the wall of the room. Melvaig felt paralysed by terror. Unable to move, he sat riveted to the spot, his mind blank. Then he felt Arkron's hands gripping his wrists tightly, pulling him up from the floor, and heard the old man shout out his reply.

'I have learnt much, my Lord Xtlan, yet there is more to learn, as much more again. Still I am progressing well. Our friends are being most co-operative. It will not be long now before we know everything. I beg you for more time. I fear your entry now would only hinder our eventual success.'

There was a pause outside and Melvaig heard a low mumbling from the other side of the door. He and Arkron had now got the others up on to their feet. Bracca, who had been woken up by the voice, was sobbing quietly, Shuinn, his face ashen, was yet resolute and clear-eyed and Morven, her eyes wide and staring with terror, clutched his arm and buried her face against his chest. Quietly but fiercely Arkron was whispering to him.

'Put the scroll back. You must go now. The tunnel leads from here. Come, follow me.'

Melvaig, putting the scroll back in the container and placing it next to the Book in the pouch round his neck, felt his heart jump with relief; he had not thought that their escape could start here. In the others too, the flame of hope thawed out the frozen numbness in their souls and they felt the blood coursing through their veins.

As the mumbling outside continued, Arkron led them quickly to the corner of the room, furthest from the door. Then, bending down he pulled up from the floor a small piece of stone next to a large square flag. Stepping over the flag he pulled up another similar piece of stone from the other side and then motioned to Melvaig to put his hand in one of the spaces left by the stone. Arkron placed his hand in the other.

'Now, lift,' he said.

Melvaig closed his hand around the edge of the large, square flag and pulled. To his surprise it came up easily, swinging on two large hinges that he guessed Arkron had recently covered in fat. He could see steps leading down into the darkness.

'Morven, quickly, take Bracca,' said Arkron, and picking up the sobbing boy she descended carefully into the darkness.

'Now you, Shuinn.' Lowering his head the giant followed, and then from the door came the sound of that terrible voice again.

'Arkron. My impatience gets the better of me. I would learn now what you have found; yet I will not spoil your work. Come outside and reveal to me your findings so far.'

Arkron looked at Melvaig and his old eyes were misty with tears. Yet he was smiling and the smile was true, filled with a deep contentment and a happiness that radiated his face with light.

'Go then, Melvaig, my friend. And by all that was ever sacred may you succeed.'

Only then did Melvaig realize that Arkron was not coming with them.

'Why?' he said quivering with anxiety. 'Why are you not coming?'

'There is no place for me on your journey. I am too old. I would hold you back.'

'But when they find we have gone. They will kill you.'

Arkron smiled. 'I have no fear of death, nor of anything that Xtlan can do to me. My only fear is that you will not succeed. Go . . . Go now.'

A surge of love for the old man swept through Melvaig and quickly he moved towards him and embraced him, holding the frail old body as if to give him strength and to will him to come with them. Gently Arkron pushed him away.

'I beg you; come with us,' said Melvaig.

'No. I cannot. Now, quickly and without thinking, take this stone and hit me on the head with it, just enough to raise blood. I shall tell Xtlan you attacked me and escaped through the door.'

He handed Melvaig one of the small stones he had taken from the sides of the large flag and blindly Melvaig dashed its sharp corner across his forehead. Blood immediately began to seep from the cut.

'Good,' said Arkron. 'Now go.'

Reluctantly, his heart breaking with sadness and guilt at leaving the old man, Melvaig began to climb down the narrow stone steps to join the others. Above him he heard Arkron's urgent whisper.

'A little way along you will come to a small chamber. I have left some things there you will need. Farewell.'

Melvaig looked up in time to see Arkron's head framed in the square orange light from the room above him. Blood was now running down one of his cheeks yet the look on the old man's face and in his eyes was of such a deep and ultimate satisfaction at the fulfilment of his destiny that Melvaig felt its power run through him, giving him confidence and strength for whatever lay ahead. He remembered that look from the last time he had seen Arkron, in the enclosure when the old man was taken away, before he and Shuinn had been transported to the Gurrtslagg. Then, he had never thought he would see the old man again nor could he have imagined in what circumstances they would once more meet and separate.

Melvaig stood on the steps watching and waiting while the slab of light grew smaller as Arkron lowered the flag. Finally there was only a thin orange sliver and then that disappeared and there was only deep blackness; his last link with Arkron had gone. At that moment, heavily muffled but still loud enough to send a shock of terror through him, Melvaig and Xtlan's roar of anger. Beneath him, on the steps, he heard the others shuffling and the sound of their breathing, harsh and uneven with fear, came to him through the darkness. Then he heard Shuinn's urgent whisper in his ear.

'We should not move yet,' he said. 'It is too dark to see anything and if anyone falls the noise may be heard above.'

'Yes,' whispered Melvaig. 'We'll stay here until the room is empty. Could you tell Morven? I must stay and listen.'

The giant carefully went down the few steps to where Morven was sitting, trying to comfort Bracca. Above them Melvaig could hear Xtlan's cries of rage and frustration, his voice quivering with a terrible fury.

'Scum! Scum of a Hebbdril! How? How could they escape? I was here. Outside the door. You said you had made good progress, that you were finding out the truth. How then, you wretch! Tell me how!'

And then, straining to hear Arkron's reply, Melvaig heard him say, in a voice that was calm and devoid of emotion, 'They escaped before you came, my Lord Xtlan. I was attacked soon after Gakk left, but I was afraid to tell you when you first came. I beg forgiveness. I was wrong to question them on my own. It was unwise. Yet, I did not think . . .'

'No, you filth. You did not think. Nor will you have a chance to think again. Gakk, take him. Tomorrow will his foul innards adorn our golden cross in the square and his ugly head be marched through Eggron on a pole as a lesson to all.'

Melvaig, listening in the darkness, buried his head in his hands and felt hot tears flow through his fingers as he fought to banish from his head the terrible images that lashed his mind. To go back up into the room and try to save Arkron would be to sacrifice everything and gain nothing, yet the fires of anger in him burned so fiercely and with such all-consuming passion that his body shook with the effort of holding it back. Then, of their own accord, words started to come from his mouth and, almost surprised, he heard himself saying, 'I will avenge you, Arkron. This I swear. You, and Jarrah, and Tennga and the people of Ruann, all those who have suffered because of his evil. I swear revenge.'

From above him came the sound of heavy footfalls and muffled thumping and into Melvaig's vision came a picture of the limp and broken body of the old man being dragged away through the door. Then from a little further, as if coming from the stairs beyond, he heard the voice of Xtlan once more, strained and shaking with anger.

'Get me Bringdagg and Senn. The Blaggvald must be torn apart for them. I want the desert surrounded and I want word given to the guards in Eggron. None shall rest until they are caught and brought before me. Gakk. Let word go out. For those who find them the rewards shall indeed be high. Yet any who are deemed to have failed in their vigilance, or in their duty will suffer the same fate as that accursed Hebbdril. I want the warriors to search all the land; there shall be no campaigns or forays till they are found. Tell the commanders so to organize their search that not one part of the land is left unwatched. And when Eggron has been combed, so shall they go into the surrounding country. They shall be found! The fury of Lord Xtlan is raging as never before. Let it be known.'

The voice receded into the distance yet its echoes seemed to hang in the darkness on the stairs, filling the air with evil and the cold chill of fear. The door slammed shut yet still no one moved. Xtlan's presence seemed to be there with them, surrounding them, sapping all their energy and their will as his words reverberated through their heads and the awful reality of their situation slammed into them. It was Bracca who finally broke the silence and shattered the awful cloud of lethargy which hung over them.

'Melvaig,' he called. 'Melvaig. Where are you?'

'Here,' replied Melvaig. 'I'm only here. It's all right. I'm coming down to see you now.'

Gingerly in the pitch black, Melvaig groped his way backwards down the stairs.

'That was me,' said Shuinn, as Melvaig's foot caught him on the head. 'Here, little man,' he said to Bracca, 'let me pass you to Melvaig.'

Shuinn's hands found the small body and lifting him, he handed him up to where Melvaig was waiting with open arms. In the darkness he took hold of his little boy and clasped his body tightly against him, and the power of the love he felt sent his head spinning.

'Oh, Bracca, my little Bracca,' he said and as he cradled the small head against his chest he felt the hot sting of tears in his eyes. 'What have they done to you? How did they treat you?' The questions burned in his mind and he voiced them quietly, under his breath, without expecting an answer, yet Bracca heard him.

'They made me fight,' he said, 'with the other boys. And the ones who were no good . . . who wouldn't – they set us on to them with stones.' He paused and Melvaig hardly dared listen. 'I didn't like that,' he went on. 'But we had nice things to eat. I was quite good at fighting. But I didn't like them; I didn't like it – the ladies. Horrible ladies. And they – they said you were dead. You and Morven. That you were against Lord Xtlan and they'd killed you.'

He pushed himself back from Melvaig's chest so that he could see him.

'Why is it dark? Why can't I see you? I want to see you . . .'

He began whimpering and then, as all the pain and fear and confusion of his life in the warrior nursery came together, and for the first time his mind relaxed the protective wall it had built up around his fragile soul, so the tears began to flow in a great rush – a torrent of anguish and misery pouring out in a huge flood of release. And Melvaig held him tight, feeling the little boy's suffering as a knife in his brain, desperately trying to infuse in Bracca some part of the faith that had kept his own spirit from sinking in the mire that had so often threatened to submerge it. If only the little boy could see some glimpse of the golden vision that burned so brightly in his mind – the world of trees and fields, of animals, flowers, rivers and streams, woods and mountains and magic – the world of the Book that even now he could feel in the pouch against his chest. And along with his faith he tried, through the strength of his will, to impart to the boy the enormity of the love that poured out from him as if to build, by the weight of that alone, a cocoon of protection which nothing could violate. And slowly, as if Bracca understood what Melvaig was trying to tell him, he quietened down, the sobbing stopped and he became calm and still – only the occasional shudder revealing the furore that had raged in his heart. And all the while Melvaig spoke to him – of Brock and Sam and Warrigal, of Perryfoot, Nab and Beth, of Silver Wood and the enchanted forest of Ellmondrill, of the dancing silver bodies of the Elves and of the three Elflords – Wychnor of the Woods and the green growing things, Saurélon of the Seas and Malcoff of the Mountains and the high places.

As Melvaig talked, his words were touched with the magic he wished to express – they flowed and rippled and cascaded in time with the rhythms of the story so that they formed pictures in the darkness before the eyes of Morven, Bracca and Shuinn, who were transported to that other world. To Melvaig, as the words tumbled from him, it was as if someone else were speaking; as if they came from Ashgaroth himself to create a faith and a vision as strong in Morven and Bracca as that which shone so fiercely in the souls of Melvaig and Shuinn. In his words was the silver of a mountain stream in moonlight and the sparkle of a dew-sprinkled cobweb in the sunshine of an autumn morning; in them was the majesty of the mighty elm and the power of the sea as it crashes in a storm-driven frenzy against the mighty cliffs that defy its onward march. They possessed the beauty of a snowcapped mountain as it glistens in spring sunshine and the clarity of the first cry of a curlew after the winter, and when finally the story ended and the words came no more, so they understood completely – Morven with a rejoicing in her soul and a blossoming in her spirit as the buds of hope, which she had cherished and nurtured since that terrible day when she had been carried off from Ruann, began to open. She had held on grimly, stubbornly, through all the horrors, to the dream that, one day she, Bracca and Melvaig would be together once again. Now suddenly, within a space of time so short that she still did not totally believe all that had happened, that dream had become reality. And along with Bracca and Melvaig had come this new, strange knowledge – this vision that gave a meaning and a purpose to everything. There was so much she wanted to ask, questions that raged within her, but for now they should be left. It was enough to let the magic of Melvaig's words drift in her mind, so that they should become as much a part of her as they were of him.

And for Bracca, although there was much that he could not understand, still the power of Melvaig's vision came across to him and the images that had danced before his eyes filled his heart with a joy and happiness to lighten the awful darkness in his soul that had threatened to engulf him.

Shuinn it was, who eventually broke the silence.

'We should go,' he said quietly. 'Before someone comes back into the room. They may force Arkron to talk.'

'Morven,' said Melvaig. 'That is Shuinn, my friend. Without Shuinn I would not be here with you. I owe him everything. He is as dear to me as my eyes. I will tell you all later, when we have time.'

'You embarrass me,' said the giant in a voice that

quivered with repressed pleasure and gratitude at Melvaig's words. 'You do me too much kindness.'

'No, my friend. That would be impossible.'

'Then I thank you,' said Shuinn. 'Though still I say I do not deserve such praise.' He paused. 'And you, Morven,' he went on. 'Melvaig has spoken of you so much that I feel I have known you for a long time already. A day would not pass when you were not on his mind and he would talk of you to me, of your times together in Ruann. So often has he described you to me that I would have known you in a crowd: your face, your hair – everything about you.' He stopped himself from going on to tell her of the way Melvaig had, at those times when the desperate yearning for his woman had overcome his reticence, described her to him in the way one man will talk to another, the beauties and hidden mysteries of her body, the feel of her skin and the depth of her passion. In those moments, fuelled by dreams of her, Melvaig had used words to transport them both into the intimacies of her embrace, to know the hunger of her desires and the warmth of her love. And so, giving vent to the cravings of his body and his spirit, he had fed their imaginations with such a vivid picture of her that Shuinn felt that he knew her the way a man knows a woman in love.

Now, faced with her reality, he felt almost ashamed of this knowledge as if, in some way, it was a violation of her. As the memories of these talks with Melvaig came back to him, so the image of her as he had seen her on the rack in the torture room upstairs came suddenly crashing into his mind: her smooth white nakedness, the mounds and curves, clefts and valleys of her body held fully exposed to his questing gaze. Frantically, as he realized the way his mind was taking him, he crushed the image and banished it from his head. Shocked and angry with himself at these treacherous and disloyal thoughts, he shuddered with revulsion at the weakness of his own nature and determined never to let them come into his mind again. Morven, the woman of Melvaig, his friend, whom he loved as he had loved no one before, with whom he had seen, suffered and endured so much. Morven, the woman whose pursuit and rescue had been their aim, their purpose, for so long now that Shuinn could hardly believe they had achieved it. Such thoughts of her were a blasphemy, a gross and evil betrayal of all that he had lived for since he had come to know Melvaig and the vision and the faith that his friend had given him.

'We should go,' he said abruptly. Then Melvaig spoke.

'Shuinn, you go first. Bracca can follow you. Then Morven, and I'll stay at the back.'

Gingerly the giant worked his way down past Morven on the narrow stairs, trying hard not to let his body come into contact with hers. When he had taken his place at the front of the little procession, Morven felt for Bracca and, finding him, lifted him round so that he was in between Shuinn and herself. Then, at last, they began the difficult descent down into the black depths beneath them.

CHAPTER XXVII

Progress was slow. The stone steps were narrow and uneven, and there were no supports or rails for them to hold on to. So they walked down sideways, facing the wall, with their hands touching the rough stone of the tunnel side. Often they missed their footing, stumbled and bruised a knee or a shin and it was not long before Bracca started to cry. Confused, shaken and frightened, he was unable to judge where to put his feet and once or twice, as he fell forward, he banged his head against the wall, scraping it against the jagged stone. It was not a complaining cry that he made but the sound of utter dejection, a pitiful expression of misery and no sooner had it begun than Shuinn stopped, picked him up and cradling him in one arm, continued the descent with only his free arm for support.

They had not gone far when the steps brought them to level ground.

'What's happened?' said Morven. 'Are we at the bottom of the Blaggvald?'

'No,' Melvaig replied. 'No. I don't think so. This must be the chamber that Arkron mentioned. We must find what he left for us. Come on. If we hold hands and walk slowly, we should feel it with our feet.'

Shuinn put Bracca down and they all took each other's hands, Melvaig gently sliding his fingers in between Morven's in a gesture of intimacy and thrilling with excitement as she responded by squeezing his hand. Then, together, the four of them gradually edged their way over the hard stone floor. When they bumped against the rock face at the far end they turned round, moved a little to the side and made their way back across the floor. They had only gone a few paces when Morven's foot stumbled against something.

'Here! It's here,' she said and the others stopped as she bent down and fumbled around for whatever it was that she had walked into.

'It . . . it feels strange. I don't know – what it is,' she said, as her fingers felt against little pieces of something smooth, hard and flat. 'I thought it would be soft: a goatskin bag . . .' and then as she ran her hands down and around the shape on the ground, the awful truth slowly dawned on her. 'Bones!' she gasped under her breath. 'They're human bones,' for there was no mistaking the pattern she had traced nor the instinct which told her with unerring certainty what it was. 'Melvaig. They're human bones!'

'Come on,' he replied. 'Get up quickly. Walk over them. They can't hurt us now.' As she hesitated he bent down, felt for her shoulder and pulled her forward sharply. She half-fell over the skeleton on the floor and as she stumbled he gathered her to him in his arms to comfort her. He had expected her to melt against him but was shocked to feel her body stiffen in his embrace and to sense displeasure in her response. It was as if a wall had suddenly sprung up between them and Melvaig felt shocked by her rejection. As she held her body rigid in his arms Morven, too, was surprised and confused at the way she had reacted to his touch. Frantically she fought against the surge of bitterness and revulsion that had swept through her as his arms had drawn her against his body and she had felt his masculinity. This was Melvaig! Yet try as she might she was unable to divorce the maleness of his body from that of all the others, the others who, in the Gravenndra and the Blaggvald, had ravished and humiliated her so often that in the end she had almost got used to it, drawing in upon herself and forcing her mind to think of the good things – Bracca and Melvaig and Ruann – so that she forgot what they were doing to her body. And through all this, the nightmare of those days and nights in hell, one thought had sustained her, kept her soul and spirit alive and untouched no matter how lascivious their degradation of her – the belief that one day she would be reunited with them. And now that faith had been rewarded; Melvaig and Bracca were here with her and they were travelling in search of a magical vision that would make all their suffering worthwhile. How many times had she dreamed of this moment in his arms again, feeling the hardness of his body against hers – their lips pouring out love from one to the other.

And yet now, now when that dream was a reality, she found that the legacy of her violation was too great to overcome. She felt the keenness of Melvaig's hurt, but so frightened and confused was she that she could say nothing and Melvaig, disappointed and angry, not thinking and not understanding, pushed her from him roughly.

'Come on,' he said brusquely, 'let's get away from it quickly.'

Morven felt in the darkness for Bracca's hand and then, when she found it, she forced herself to go forward. A few more steps on and it was Shuinn's turn to call out.

'Another! I've found another!' he said and walked over it, crunching down in the darkness on the thin and brittle bones of the skeleton on the stone floor of the cave. As they went on towards the far wall, they found more and more of these grisly reminders of some past time and past event, till they imagined the floor to be littered with them.

In the light it would not have been too terrible, the white human frames meaning nothing beside the grand purpose of their journey and the sufferings they had seen, but in this dense black darkness their minds began playing tricks. They dreaded the awful crunching noise underfoot and the feel of the bones through the soles of their boots; they walked in terrible anticipation of the clatter the bones made as they knocked against them and the skeletons toppled over on to the floor. In their imaginations, already strained and weary and ready to play tricks with them at the least provocation, there loomed bizarre images of the skeletons rising up and cavorting around them in eerie sepulchral dances, joining hands to encircle them, mocking and teasing them as they tried to break through the circle. But Melvaig and Shuinn continued to pull Morven and Bracca along, fighting the visions in their minds until they reached the end wall of the cavern. Then, turning around, they went back again only this time Melvaig kept his shoulder to the side wall so that they were walking along the edge. Suddenly Morven's foot thudded into something soft and yielding and she stopped, pulling the others up short.

'Melvaig,' she said. 'At my feet. I can't . . . Could you?' The memory of the feel of the skeleton sent a shiver through her and she was unable to force herself to touch whatever it was that lay at her feet this time.

Melvaig let go of her hand and felt around on the floor. He soon found it.

'I think this is it,' he said, feeling the soft fuzz of goat hair beneath his fingers. He pulled open the drawstring at the neck of the bag and placing his hand inside, felt the long, round thickness of a 'brand. He lifted it out, the rancid smell of the grease-soaked bolt of cloth gnawing at his nostrils. Saying nothing while the others waited in silent apprehension, he put his hand in again and brought out a tinderbox.

'Yes,' he said, and the relief of the others flowed over him like a breath. 'This is what Arkron left for us. Soon we should be able to see where we are; he left a taper and flint.'

He felt the tension in the others as he fumbled around with the flint, trying to make a spark that would ignite the tinder which he could then use to light the brand. Once, twice, three times he tried and then on the fourth he succeeded and soon the brand was sputtering into life. Gradually it took, and its flickering orange glow chased away the darkness and the spectral images of the skeletons as they looked at each other in wonder, almost as if for the first time, blessed again with the magic of sight.

'Ah!' said Shuinn. 'It is good to see again.'

When their eyes had drunk their fill of each other's faces and they had drawn enough comfort and reassurance from the visible proof of each other's presence, then they turned and looked out into the cave. It was much smaller than they had imagined and whereas in the panicky blackness of a few moments earlier the floor had seemed littered with skeletons, now as they looked they could see only a few – lying together in a fallen heap in the very middle of the cave, the whiteness of their bones dancing with the orange light from the taper. No one said anything as their eyes settled on this bizarre little group. How they had died, how long they had been there and who they were they could only guess and their guesses they kept to themselves. Melvaig had the feeling they had been there since Before the War, victims of some treachery at the hands, perhaps, of their own companions, while escaping from a force invading the Blaggvald. As he looked at them, their jaws fallen into the curious half-laughing, half-screaming attitude that skulls adopt, a cold chill of mortal vulnerability swept through him as the realization struck him that under all his flesh and his power of thinking, he and the others were indistinguishable from the little group in the middle of the cave. Melvaig turned away and looked at Morven while her gaze was riveted on the skeletons and he luxuriated in the study of her features.

He was seized by the desire to put his arm round her, to hold her and comfort her and protect her with his love, but the thought froze in his head and he felt sick to the stomach as he remembered the rejection of a short while back. Bitterly and angrily he fought against the almost overwhelming impulse to embrace her and she, sensing his eyes on her and the inner turmoil inside him, resisted, for reasons she did not understand, the desire to turn to him and try to explain the confusion raging within her and then, in a catharsis of release, bury herself against him. In her mind's eye she went over the scene, imagining how it would be, but instead of succumbing to its lure, she sat with her eyes fixed straight ahead, feigning total absorption in the sight before her. And then, to her relief, she felt Melvaig's gaze leave her and she heard him say, roughly and abruptly, 'We'll eat here. Now. Can you hold this?'

He passed the taper over to Morven and she held it above the goatskin bag while Melvaig brought out slabs of dried meat, some hard black biscuits and a container full of drink which exuded, as Melvaig opened the neck, a delicate scented aroma unlike anything he had known before. He handed it to Morven, taking the brand off her and wedging it into a narrow crack in the floor. As she drank, the golden liquid seemed to send a fire coursing through her veins, reviving her flagging spirits and giving her renewed energy. Then she gave some to Bracca, holding the container up for him so that he would not take too much and choke. At first, as the heat bit into his throat the little boy coughed and spluttered, but as he got used to it, so he too felt invigorated and refreshed. When Morven judged he had had enough she took it away from his lips and passed it on to Shuinn but Bracca wanted some more.

'Please,' he said. 'Please can I have another drink? I'm still thirsty.'

'No,' said Morven, feeling embarrassed. 'It's Shuinn's turn now.'

'Let him have more,' said the giant. 'There's enough for us all,' and he ruffled Bracca's tousled hair with his hand.

'Thank you, Shuinn,' said Bracca, and the giant smiled at him.

When the boy had had another mouthful Shuinn took a drink and then finally it was Melvaig's turn.

Arkron had judged their needs well. The drink seemed to lift them all from the trough of despondency into which they had sunk and to drive out the shadows of terror which lingered on in their minds from the awful echoing memory of Xtlan's words. The old Hebbdril had made the drink himself, secretly, painstakingly gathering the herbs and spices which he remembered from the recipe given him by his mentor, Derrionn. Now as they ate, chewing on the meat and biscuits and washing it down with the drink, their spirits grew high and they began talking excitedly to each other. Now suddenly, everything seemed possible and, full of enthusiasm, Melvaig put his hand inside his tunic and brought out from the pouch the Book and the tube-like container in which lay the parchment map Arkron had given him.

There, under the flickering orange glow of the light from the brand, their shadows dancing on the walls, he showed Morven the Book. As she opened it, feeling the smooth white pages fall open to her touch, she felt inexorably drawn to the world within it. Though the writing meant nothing to her, nevertheless the images that Melvaig had described so magically, now came alive again for her, and the power of the story and the revelations in it fuelled her spirit with love and hope and dreams. And as she grew more and more excited so Melvaig, caught up in the infectious vitality of her enthusiasm, moved closer to her so that almost without knowing it, their legs touched and their shoulders rubbed together. Leaning across her, he drew her attention to the drawings and as they went through the Book, turning the pages in wonder, their imaginations led them through the deep green splendour of the woods and fields, the jewelled majesty of the flowers and the awesome splendour of the mountains. Finally when the last picture had been marvelled at and the covers of the Book shut, so Melvaig drew out the map Arkron had given him from its container and spread it out on the rock floor of the cavern, holding it down so that it did not roll back up into itself. Once or twice his hand slipped and it did spring back and then Morven found herself laughing as she had not done since their days in Ruann. And Melvaig, hearing the music of her laughter, joined in and the great walls that had grown up between them, the invisible barriers of tension, started to crumble and collapse so that, without thinking, Morven put her arm around his waist where they sat and leaned her head on his shoulder.

Shuinn, sensing their coming together and their joy in the rediscovery of each other, turned to Bracca and asked him if he would like to learn how to make fire. Eagerly the little boy answered yes and so, picking up the tinderbox, Shuinn and Bracca moved away a little and the giant started showing him how to use the tinder and flint. As he did so he began talking gently to Bracca about his time in the warrior nursery, prompting the little boy's recollections by relating his own experiences, drawing his attention away from his mother and father so that they could fly undisturbed in their private world. Brimming over with excitement, Melvaig and Morven pored carefully over the map, talking, discussing and debating about the symbols and the route, their earnest deliberations punctuated frequently with laughter as the container full of drink grew gradually more empty. And then suddenly, as if waking up to the reality of the moment, the rosy euphoria of the drink fading as quickly as it had come, they stopped the frivolity of their laughter and became aware of each other's physical presence – her arm around his waist, his lips against her hair. And with the coming of that moment they turned to each other and their eyes met and such a world of love was in each for the other that they seemed to swim together in an ocean of eternity, a sparkling crystal world of deep blue where nothing mattered save the blessed intertwining of their souls. It was but a moment yet it seemed for ever and when at last it faded Morven found that the shackles which the bitterness and revulsion of her degradation had locked around her, had faded away. Gently then, aware of Melvaig's reticence, she put her hands around his head and pulling his face down towards her, delicately placed her lips against his mouth. Melvaig felt the sweet softness of her lips against his as if he were being anointed by their sacred touch. And the yearning in each was strong for the other, a hunger barely restrained, fuelled by their time apart and the delicious unexpectedness of what they now found happening to them. At last, suddenly aware of the presence of Shuinn and Bracca, Melvaig carefully took his lips away and, stroking her cheeks with his fingers, eased her face away from him so that he could look at her and he spoke, very quietly, his voice shaking with emotion.

'Oh Morven, Morven. I have lived for this. Just for this. I love you,' he said, and the words were awkward and clumsy, ridiculously inadequate and paltry besides the enormity of what he felt and was trying to express. Silently Morven took a hand from behind his neck and with a fingertip traced a line across his cheekbone, down his nose and along his lips. His words were, for her, the final ingredient in the salve with which the ugly memories of her life since Ruann had been cleansed away. The realization that, despite the terrible depravities of her time in the Gravenndra and the Blaggvald, she was still able to respond to and love this man was for her a discovery of such relief and joy that she felt as if she might burst with happiness. Gone now was the freezing of her spirit at his touch which she had felt only a short while ago. Instead her body sang at his nearness, shivered with excitement at his touch, her mind reeling with a joyous dizziness that set every nerve end tingling. Nothing else mattered, neither Xtlan nor Dréagg nor Ashgaroth, this was all – this moment, this world. Hungrily she reached up for him again and their lips met this time, not in the delicate apprehensiveness of before but in a confident thrust of passion, each burning with greed for the other, holding each other in an embrace so tight that, even with the heavy layers of garments between them, their bodies felt as one.

Eventually Bracca, growing restless with the talk of Shuinn, looked across at Morven and Melvaig and felt uncomfortable at their closeness. Then despite Shuinn's attempt to distract him, he got up and after walking across to them, put his arms around Morven's back. Reluctantly then, their bodies brimming with unspent passion, Melvaig and Morven broke apart and turned towards the little boy, feeling guilty at their selfishness and slightly embarrassed by their display in front of Shuinn. While Morven put her arms round Bracca, Melvaig called across to Shuinn, who was sitting in the gloom of the cavern in the corner where the little boy had left him.

'Shuinn,' he said. 'Come over here. Come on. Have some more drink. See here – there's plenty left.' Melvaig tried to focus his mind and his judgment on now his friend would be feeling. He would have to be very careful not to let the giant feel any resentment or jealousy. Yet as his body still basked in the afterglow of his embrace, he knew it would not be easy.

Melvaig had been right in his forebodings. Despite himself and in spite of struggling against it with every fragment of self-will that he had, Shuinn did indeed feel jealous of his friend. Jealous of Morven for, as he felt it, coming between himself and his friend, driving a wedge between their closeness and for filling a role that he could never fill – that of a lover, with all the special intimacies and confidences that lovers share. He had watched them looking at Arkron's map together, talking, discussing and analysing. Before, it would have been he, Shuinn, who would have been there with him. He felt pushed to the back, rejected. Even with Bracca he could never be as Melvaig or Morven were to him. He could be friends with the little boy but never more than that. No matter how close they grew, it would always be Melvaig the little boy would choose. And the other way round. Not only was he having to share Melvaig with Morven, but also with Bracca. It was all right now, the boy was small. But in the future? In the world they were seeking, the world of the Book? When Bracca had grown, it would be Bracca who would be first in Melvaig's affections, Bracca who would be closer to him than he, Shuinn.

And so, as Melvaig and Morven had been locked together, bathed in the gentle orange glow from the taper, these thoughts had run around Shuinn's spirit and, try as he might, he had been unable to quench the insidious poison they left in their wake. Yet over and above all these tangled and twisted feelings, one emotion had burned high and bright and with an intensity that outshone all the others. For, with a terrible sparkling clarity the realization had come to him, awesome and undeniable in the enormity of its passion, that above all other things, he desired Morven. As he had watched her being kissed and held by Melvaig, his senses had raged with the fires of jealousy; he had imagined her responding to him the way she was with Melvaig. He saw her again naked as he had first seen her on the rack and imagined her passion as Melvaig had so lovingly described it to him on so many occasions. As he had tried to talk to Bracca, his eyes had feasted on her face, lingering over her eyes, her cheeks and the fullness of her lips as they drank so hungrily on Melvaig's mouth. The fall of her hair, the tilt of her head, the wandering of her hands as she held her man to her, all aroused and inflamed his senses so that he was consumed with longing for her. The feelings of treachery and disloyalty he had felt when these images of her had first entered his consciousness, had now been rendered impotent by the force of this omnipotent obsession and he was powerless to resist.

And so when Melvaig called him over, he got up and walked across to them in a daze, his mind whirling in emotion. Struggling to contain himself he came unsteadily over the floor, not knowing where to look or how to act. He was aware of them both smiling at him, Melvaig happy and confident and Morven, her face flushed with excitement, giving him a look of genuine warmth so that he felt even more resentful that she should be so unaware of the turmoil inside him. Embarrassed and sullen in his confusion he did not dare let himself look at her and instead spoke directly to Melvaig, his voice shaking with repressed emotion.

'We ought to go,' he blurted out curtly. There was a pause as Melvaig and Morven sat and stared at him in surprise. Without lifting his head Shuinn said it again, his feeling of awkwardness compounded by the silence. 'We ought to go. Now!'

Feeling uncomfortable and disconcerted by his friend's manner Melvaig replied, 'Yes. Yes, all right. You're right; we should make a move,' and taking Morven by the hand he helped her to her feet. 'Do you want to carry this or shall I?' he said addressing Shuinn and pointing to the container that Arkron had left. Still in it was some food, the remainder of the drink and one more taper.

'I'll take it,' said the giant, and bending down, he quickly picked up the bag and slung the long strap handle over his shoulder.

Melvaig walked over to his friend and putting a hand on his wrist, steered him a little way away from Morven and Bracca, stopping against one of the walls of the cavern.

'Hey,' he said, his voice urgent and clipped with worry. 'What's wrong? Shuinn, my friend. What is it? What's the matter? Look at me! What's wrong? Tell me!'

Shuinn shuffled uncomfortably about, head down, shifting from foot to foot. What could he say? Tell Melvaig the truth! No. That was impossible. Besides, perhaps it would go away – this awful thing that had happened to him, to them. Fade and die as quickly as it had arisen, to be a vague discomforting memory in his past. Perhaps some day he would be able to look at her face calmly, and dispassionately, without his heart palpitating wildly and the blood racing so furiously through his veins. Perhaps then the lascivious image of her nakedness would lose its shimmering clarity and fade so that it would no longer torment him. Would that that day would come soon! For now though, he was totally enslaved in this mesh of desire and so, enraged with himself and demented with confusion and grief he lashed out with his tongue.

'I'm all right!' he shouted. 'There's nothing wrong with me. It's time we went, that's all. If you two have finished, then we'll go. The longer we stay in here, the more time Xtlan has to organize his search.'

'It's us, isn't it?' Melvaig persisted. 'Morven and me. You don't like it, do you? You don't like seeing us together.'

Shuinn turned his face full towards Melvaig and his eyes blazed with a terrible light.

'Listen. I wouldn't have your woman if she lay on the ground and begged for it.' The words spewed out venomously, smashing their friendship with a terrible relentlessness as Shuinn poured all the bitter vitriol of his pain into them, and the awful significance of them lay heavy and thick like a great black shroud about them.

'No,' he went on remorselessly, spitting the words out in a voice that was so strangled and ugly that Melvaig could not recognize it. 'Not if she spread herself out and begged.

After all that she's had! The best sort she is. You can tell by looking at her. Some of them, a few, enjoy it. All of it – the pain, the degradation. They love it. She loved it! She'll never enjoy it with you again. You'll see!'

And so the words poured forth, growing more and more foul as they fed on their own putrescence, and each word slammed into Melvaig with the force of a body blow, leaving him stunned and aghast with horror. Through the daze of his own disbelief he became aware of the sound of Morven crying and felt her clinging to him. And then Bracca started, the clamour of his wails reverberating eerily around the walls of the little cavern.

And far away, above and beyond the farthest reaches of the world, echoes of the bitterness and anger in Shuinn's voice and words penetrated the darkest corners of the Universe where Dréagg lurked, and he was well pleased with what he heard for this was the beginning of the growth of the seed that he had planted in the giant. Now, it had truly started, the beginning of the end. No matter now if the forces of Xtlan did not find and take them: better even perhaps if they remained free. For now that Shuinn had succumbed to the lure of his bait the end was finally in sight – the discovery and destruction of the last enclave of Ashgaroth, the one place where the powers of light still reigned and his darkness could not penetrate. To watch the seed grow would now be his delight; to nurture it and cosset it where it lurked in Shuinn's breast until at last it blossomed forth to wreak its terrible consequences and exact the final toll of revenge for his defeat at the hands of Nab and the Elflords and the escape of the animals and the Eldron so many aeons ago, the escape which had been as a thorn in his side ever since, and without which Ashgaroth would have been utterly vanquished. Let the giant then do the work of Xtlan for him.

'No more! No more or I'll kill you.' Melvaig uttered the words quietly but with a piercing edge of resolve that penetrated Shuinn's cloud of hatred. Suddenly he stopped and as he did so it was as if scales had been removed from his eyes for the spirit of Dréagg left him for the moment; the seed stopped growing temporarily to bide its time, for to grow too strongly and too quickly would be to alert Melvaig too soon and force the hand of Ashgaroth too early.

'Melvaig,' he said, and the terrible anguish of remorse was heavy in him and painful to bear. 'Melvaig. Forgive me. I did not know what I was saying. Something happened. I'm sorry. So sorry. Morven . . .' He turned to her. 'Morven, I cannot face you. Those things . . . I . . . beg you . . . There is nothing I can say . . .'

He stopped, staring down at the floor, his face eerily illuminated by the light from the spitting, crackling brand. On the wall behind, his shadow loomed large like some grotesque caricature, the shoulders slumped, the head sunken. Melvaig was terribly, icily silent, the fury and the shock and the sickness still raging inside his spirit in a mad, frenzied turmoil. The only sounds, apart from the noise of the taper, were the sobs of Morven and Bracca. Now that the terrible tirade had stopped, Melvaig was hardly able to believe that it had happened. It had all been a nightmare, sent from Xtlan to confuse and damage them. It could not have been real. He looked at Shuinn, the giant, at the familiar friendly features, as much a part of himself as his own hands and, when he saw the terrible mask of pain etched on his friend's face, he grew numb with the awful realization that it had in fact been true. What could he say? What could he do? For moments that seemed like an age his mind whirled incoherently and then, from somewhere deep within, came a great thrust of will and with a conscious effort he brought his frantically careering emotions under control and savagely banished them. He would forgive Shuinn and then behave as though nothing had happened.

'It's all right, Shuinn,' he said, the words sounding strange and false and his lips finding it hard to form the words. 'It's all right,' he repeated. 'I know you didn't mean the things you were saying. Morven knows it. We are all tired. The darkness of Xtlan is heavy upon us – there is nothing to forgive. Let us forget it ever happened.' And as he spoke the words and saw the look of gratitude come to Shuinn's eyes, forgiveness did in fact seem to come. Suddenly the giant crossed the few paces between them and embraced Melvaig silently, wordlessly, and it was as if a gentle soothing balm had been poured over them, the balm of relief from the horrors of only a few moments earlier. There was suddenly, amongst all of them, Melvaig, Shuinn, Morven and Bracca, a determination and a will to forget and a new atmosphere of hope reborn.

'Come on, then,' said Melvaig. 'It's time we went. I'll go first, then you, Morven, then Bracca and lastly you, Shuinn. I'll light the other taper with this old one, it's nearly finished anyway.'

When the new taper was lit, he put the remainder of the old one into the bag which hung from Shuinn's shoulder and then, leading the way, he walked out of the cavern, the scene of so much joy and so much despair, and back to the narrow passageway to continue their descent through the dark rock pinnacle of the Blaggvald.

CHAPTER XXVIII

The light from the taper which Arkron had left made the walk down the narrow twisting steps much easier than it had been before in the darkness. As they got further and further down, the atmosphere grew stale and foul yet from time to time they would become aware of a new feel in the air, a freshness as if in some way air from outside had managed to seep in through the rock. Perhaps, thought Melvaig, those who had dug this escape route in that remote age long ago had put in air shafts. At times the tunnel grew very narrow and, apart from Bracca, they were hard put to squeeze their way through. At other times they would find themselves in large natural caverns and luxuriate for a short time in the feeling of space about them.

They were making their way through one of these caverns when Melvaig slowly grew aware of the fact that they had been walking on the level for rather longer than they had ever done before. They came to the end of the cavern yet still the little tunnel along which they continued was flat. They must, he thought, have reached the base of the Blaggvald and be making their way now under the wasteland. Indeed, the chill that the rock walls had given out during their descent had given way to a heavy heat which grew more and more overbearing and claustrophobic the further they went. He felt beads of sweat start to break out all over him, making his body itch uncomfortably.

They walked slowly, in silence, each of them buried in the wanderings of their own minds and trying to sort out the emotions which Shuinn's outburst in the cavern had engendered in them.

They were exhausted both physically and spiritually and the second and last taper had nearly burnt out. Melvaig wanted to keep the remains of the first to use in case of an emergency and this meant that soon they would have to exist in darkness again. Bracca had become too tired to walk soon after they had left the cavern and Shuinn had carried him ever since. He was asleep now, in the cradle the giant had formed with his arms, his head lolling gently against Shuinn's chest with the rhythm of the walk. Should they continue to move so fast? Could they have a rest now? If they delayed would this give Xtlan's commanders more time to organize the massive and all-encompassing search for them, the promise of which still echoed in their heads?

Suddenly Melvaig made his mind up. They were probably safer in here, at least for the moment, than they would be when they were out on the surface again. They would rest for a while here. The thought crossed his mind that he hoped Shuinn would not take offence that he, Melvaig, was making the suggestion. In the past it would not have occurred to him to think this way but now . . . He must bring his friend into the decision.

'Shuinn,' he called. 'When do you think we should have a rest?'

There was a short pause and the sounds of their feet shuffling and scraping along the rough stone of the tunnel seemed to increase in intensity as Melvaig waited apprehensively for the reply. At last it came and as he had hoped, it contained no trace of anything other than agreement with his unspoken wishes.

'Why not stop now?' said Shuinn. 'Better now than later, on top, where the whole of Xtlan will be looking for us.'

So they stopped and sat down next to each other. Bracca had opened his eyes as Shuinn had laid him down and they had a mouthful of the precious drink each and a piece of meat to chew on. But it was sleep they all needed more than anything else; their limbs had grown heavy and almost numb with tiredness and several times Morven had involuntarily closed her eyes and, stumbling over her own feet, come to with a shock. So, feeling pleasantly replete after their food and drink, they lay down on the hard floor after Melvaig had extinguished the taper and, stretching out luxuriously, closed their eyes.

For Bracca and Morven, oblivion was blessedly instantaneous but the soothing caress of sleep did not come easily to Melvaig and Shuinn. The giant, tired though he was, seemed afraid to abandon himself to his subconscious as if he were somehow unwilling or reluctant to let himself go. For a long time his mind seemed to be fighting away the weariness of his body but in the end he succumbed. However, sleep when it finally did come, was punctuated with a series of images of startling, unnerving clarity, each of them portraying himself and Morven in some delicious and wanton act of love, and he tossed around restlessly as these lurid visions assailed him. At one time he became so confused between the dream and reality that he woke up suddenly in a blind panic, convinced that he had just played out one of the scenes in real life. He shook his head frantically and pressed his palms against his eyes as if to try and erase the picture from his mind and only then did he carefully light the taper and dare to look at Morven – lying peacefully in between Melvaig and Bracca, her beautiful features languid and sultry as she wallowed in the indulgence of a deep and blissful sleep. Hugely relieved that his fears had turned out to be a fiction, Shuinn carefully

359

lay back down again but no sooner had he closed his eyes than the picture of Morven's naked body once again invaded his tortured senses.

Melvaig's thoughts were also centred around Morven and were of the most disconcerting nature. The poison which Shuinn's words had planted in his mind, though unequivocally rejected at the time, now began to spread insidiously as his subconscious took control from consciousness. Had Morven enjoyed the sport of the guards? Had she, in truth, been so 'good at it' that they had brought her here, to the Blaggvald where, it was known, only those of the Elimsorr with special qualities came? Why else had she been here? Was that why she had rejected him at first, back in the tunnel, before they had reached the cavern, when she had shrunk from his touch? His guts churned over in a terrible sickening lurch as he pictured her with them. He watched in anguish as she disported herself in lascivious abandon, revelling in their depravities and thriving on the grossest obscenities which their debauched minds could conceive. Again and again he pushed the pictures away yet still they returned to torment him and, as one will probe at a wound, he forced himself to look at her face for it was the look of blissful lusting rapture which he saw there that so struck at his heart.

And then a notion came into his head that he embraced and clung to as a drowning man will hang on to a piece of wood. Perhaps she had just pretended to enjoy it! Yes, that was it. This was her means of survival. The more satisfaction she gave them, the better would be her chances, the more hope she would have of living to see Melvaig and Bracca again. And her faith in that was so strong, so implacable, that no price was too high to pay.

And then he would examine the face in the vision minutely, the full, moist lips; the look of wild exhilaration in her beautiful blue eyes. Could she really put all that on?

His head swam, the thoughts ebbing and flowing like

some evil tide, and he was aware of turning from side to side and a pain, a dull ache, starting to throb between his eyes.

How long they all slept, Melvaig, when he finally woke from his fitful tossing and turning, was unable to tell. When he first came to, he welcomed wakefulness as an escape from the nightmare going on in his head and groping around for the taper and the tinder box he lit the brand. He looked across at Shuinn and saw that the giant was already awake. The smiles they exchanged in the light were tentative and tinged with embarrassment. Then Melvaig gestured to Shuinn to wake the others and as the giant bent over Bracca and began to shake him gently by the shoulder, Melvaig stroked Morven's cheek delicately with the tips of his fingers. She sat up instantly, a look of alarm on her face and for a few crazed moments stared wildly about her until her gaze settled on Melvaig and, as recollection came to her, the fear melted into relief and then pleasure at seeing him.

'Oh, Melvaig, Melvaig,' she sighed. 'I had forgotten . . . I did not know . . .' Her sentences remained unfinished as she leaned towards him and embraced him fiercely. For a few precious moments they clung to each other and then the sound of Bracca's voice, bleary and slurred with sleep, caused them to break their embrace and turn to him.

'Can I have a drink?' he said plaintively. 'Please. Like we had last night.'

Hesitantly Melvaig opened the bag and brought out the container. It felt light and when he opened the top he could see there was not much left. They would have to try and make it last as long as possible.

'Are you really thirsty?' he said. 'Do you think you could wait a bit? See,' and he showed Bracca the container, 'there isn't a lot left. We don't know when we'll be able to get anything else to drink.'

The little boy studiously looked through the open neck

of the pouch for a few moments and then raising his head he said that yes, he could wait.

'Good boy. That's good. Thank you,' said Melvaig, pleased with the understanding and responsibility Bracca had shown. He had changed a lot, grown up a lot during the time they had been apart. In some ways it was good but Melvaig, thinking back to how the boy had been during their ride down from the desolation of Ruann to the plains of Molobb, missed the air of carefree childish abandon, the innate sense of fun and mischief which had tinged their relationship. He was serious now, grown old ahead of his years; his life in the warrior nursery had crushed all the childhood gaiety from him, had exorcised the laughter and the precious purity of naïve innocence. Careworn before his time, his young face wore a mask of gravity which disturbed Melvaig. Perhaps one day, he thought with a savage and heart-rending rush of yearning, they would laugh again and Bracca's lovely face would once more radiate the light and joy which used to fill his heart with such warmth and happiness. At least they were all together again. That was all that mattered.

'Can everyone else wait for a drink?' he asked. Morven and Shuinn nodded.

'Come on, then. It should not be much further until we're out.'

So saying he picked up Arkron's bag, hung it over his shoulder and led the way down the tunnel.

The heat now became stifling and they took off all their top clothes and carried them, but still the sweat soaked through their undershirts and ran in little trickles down their backs. Suddenly the tunnel narrowed drastically, shrinking both in width and height so that they were forced to get on their hands and knees and crawl, with the roof only a handspan above their heads. The familiar twinges of pain in Melvaig's knees as they scraped over the unyielding stone floor brought back awful memories of the

Gurrtslagg and a sudden spasm of sickness gripped him as images of that terrible place flashed before his eyes.

On and on they crawled, twisting and turning and squeezing their way round the tight corners and bends, their knees by now almost numb with pain and their legs and arms scraped and scratched so that the skin felt aflame. No one uttered a word; each grimly determined not to let the others down by asking for a rest, and absorbed in their own private struggles with themselves as well as thoughts of their recent past. Morven's mind kept letting in flashes of her times in the Gravenndra and the Blaggvald, the horrors of her ride in the cart from Ruann. The faces of the warriors and the guards who had possessed her seemed to merge together into a continuous blur and float past her eyes, almost comic in the ludicrous intensity of their lecherous passion. Yet she shivered with repulsion and she felt her skin crawl with disgust as the memory of their carnal lusts flooded in upon her. Resolutely she fought against these images, determined not to let them get through to her and so with all the strength she could muster she focused her attention on those few precious moments in the cavern when her closeness to Melvaig had made her feel alive and at peace again and the shimmering silver star of hope had rekindled within her.

At last, when they felt they could take their aching bodies no further, they found to their relief that the tunnel widened again and became high enough for them to stand. Also it began to slope upwards quite steeply so that they were climbing. The atmosphere, too, felt different – less stale, with an occasional puff of fresh air that caused the flame on the brand to dance with such a crazy motion that Melvaig was certain it would go out. Up they went, and as they did so there arose in each of them a nervous flutter of anticipation as they realized they would soon be out. Where would the tunnel bring them up? What would they find on the surface, and what lay in store for them on the journey ahead? Unconsciously, as if for reassurance, Melvaig put his free hand up and placed it on his jerkin so that he could feel the pouch that lay on his chest. He ran his finger over the large square shape of the Book and the round wooden cylinder containing Arkron's map and for the first time felt truly that they were on the threshold of achieving his vision. And he became aware again of the awesome responsibility which he carried. Without the knowledge that lay within the Book's covers, Xtlan could never truly be supreme over all the land and Dréagg would never achieve that total and complete domination for which he thirsted so avidly; final victory over Ashgaroth would forever elude him. Yet with the Book in Xtlan's grasp, so would the last lingering traces of the world of Ashgaroth finally be crushed. And he, Melvaig, was the guardian of this knowledge. Fail in his mission, and the land would forever languish in the darkness of Dréagg, crushed beneath the heel of Xtlan to dwell in his shadow and dance in agony to the tunes he played.

Suddenly, ahead of him, Melvaig sensed rather than saw a dead end. He said nothing, his heart pounding furiously with excitement, and continued the steep upward climb until the orange light from the last remaining length of brand, no longer than a finger, reflected back from the rock that lay in front. Morven's voice, tremulous with anticipation, asked the question that was in their minds.

'Is this the end? Melvaig, have we come to the end?'

'I don't know. I think so. Here, could you hold this?' and he handed her the brand while Shuinn moved up and stood alongside him.

'What do you think?' Melvaig asked.

'It looks like a large boulder, doesn't it? Look, it's wedged in tight but I can just feel the edge of it. I can just get my hand in the gap.'

'It's not a rock fall is it?' replied Melvaig. 'It's too deliberate. It's been put there from the other side. Either the tunnel's been blocked up or we are at the end. Shall we try and move it?'

'I'll help you,' said Morven and she passed the brand to Bracca and, putting her shoulder to the rock in between Melvaig and Shuinn she started to push.

Time and again they heaved against the rock in response to Melvaig's shout of 'Now' and time and again their hopes were dashed as the rock remained utterly immobile; it was as if they were trying to push against the wall of the tunnel itself. Yet on and on they pushed, each time trying to summon up the energy and the enthusiasm they had had for the first few attempts. To make things even more maddeningly frustrating, they had begun to feel small gusts of fresh air seeping in through little undiscoverable gaps so that they felt certain now that freedom from the Blaggvald was in truth just the other side of the boulder.

It was Bracca who drew their attention to the other, smaller, boulder in the wall of the tunnel, just to the side of the large one. Waving the brand gently around in the air to amuse himself, he had taken to examining the walls and noticed the shadow of this other rock.

'Look,' he said suddenly, excitedly. 'There's another one here.'

'Where?' said Melvaig.

Bracca moved the brand closer to the wall and pointed to the dark outline.

'Yes. You're right. Well done, little man. Good boy. Now, let's have a look.'

Just then the light began flickering fiercely with a juddering staccato pattern and, looking up, Melvaig saw that the taper was at its end.

'Quick,' he shouted to Shuinn. 'Pass me the other one – what's left – from the bag.'

Shuinn rummaged around and brought out the remains of the first brand. He handed it to Melvaig just in time, for no sooner had Melvaig lit it than the old one expired, flaring up wildly in a last sudden blaze of glory before it finally died.

'When this goes, there's no more,' said Melvaig, voicing all their thoughts. 'I hope it lasts until we're out.'

Melvaig and Shuinn bent down and began feeling around the edge of the small round stone while Morven and Bracca watched.

'Let's give it a push,' said Shuinn and together they placed their backs against it and braced their feet against the opposite wall.

'Now,' he said, and they pushed with all their strength. With a skip of joy, Melvaig thought he felt a movement in the boulder.

'Again!' said Shuinn, and this time there was no doubt; the rock definitely moved. Their hearts pounding with happiness and relief, they heaved again and it rolled away from them so easily that they fell forwards into the small tunnel that now lay revealed before them. Almost drunk with exultation, they all burst out into a fit of spontaneous laughter and Morven and Bracca jumped forward, exhibiting huge mock effort as they made a great show of lifting Melvaig and Shuinn up from where the two men lay sprawled on their backs.

'We've done it! We're out,' laughed Morven, and Melvaig did not have the heart to quell her joy by sewing seeds of doubt in her mind.

'Come on, then,' he said. 'Let's see where it goes,' and, taking the light from Bracca, he began to lead the way into the darkness ahead.

The tunnel grew wider after the entrance so that they were able to squeeze past the boulder which had previously blocked its mouth, but it was still so low and narrow that they were forced, once more, to crawl on hands and knees. Yet the pain they felt was nothing to them now as the glorious prospect of freedom shone like a beacon in their minds. For a while the tunnel wound tortuously down and then, as they rounded a corner, Melvaig's heart leaped with joy as he saw, directly ahead of him, an unmistakable sprinkle of daylight and perceived on his face the feel of the air from outside, playing against his cheeks and his forehead.

So on they crawled, their pace quickening with excitement until at last they reached the narrow mouth of the tunnel. Directly in front of the tunnel mouth there was a large hawthorn tree which served to conceal the entrance, and now all four of them pushed their way out of the tunnel and settled down behind the sweeping branches, well hidden from any outside view. It was midday; the sun directly overhead poured its intense heat down upon them, making the arid brown slope that led gently away from where they were shimer and dance in a haze. Melvaig looked around and tried to take stock of their position. They had emerged a little way up one of the hills that, along with the others that formed the range, formed a kind of large semi-circular amphitheatre around the city of Xtlan. The city itself lay in the heat, naked and exposed in the glare, dominated by the huge black crag of the Blaggvald which rose up from the centre of the plain just beneath them. Melvaig shivered in fear as he felt his gaze drawn up, despite himself, to the round tower that pointed like a vengeful finger towards the sky, as if gesturing to Dréagg in a constant assertion of its link with the Lord of Darkness. A cold chill gripped him as he looked at the window in the top, its impenetrable blackness once again drawing him into the vortex of its hypnotic void, but he struggled against its lure and tore his eyes away to look at the wall winding snakelike around the perimeter of the plain. He felt amazed and jubilant at the knowledge that they had made their way under both the plain and the wall to where they sat now, nestling in this old dried-up river valley behind the protective boughs of the tree. Free again, he thought, as he had been the last time he, with

Shuinn, had stared down at Eggron in this way, from the cliffs across on the other side of the amphitheatre. Now, though, his freedom was complete, with Morven and Bracca beside him, and they were truly making their escape in pursuit of the vision that had impelled him with such burning intensity for what seemed to be the whole of his life.

CHAPTER XXIX

How long they stayed like that, wallowing in the luxury of feeling space about them and in the relief they felt at having made their escape, Melvaig could not say, but suddenly he became aware of movement at his side and turning languidly he saw Shuinn sitting down next to him. Morven and Bracca were lying together just a few paces away in the shade of one of the gnarled old branches of the tree and they appeared to have fallen asleep, exhausted. All the terrors of the Blaggvald and, before that, Bracca's time in the warrior nursery and Morven's in the Gravenndra, seemed now, for the first time, to be truly over and Morven felt able to relax in a way she could not remember since Ruann.

'We'd better not move until the sun starts to go down,' said Shuinn quietly. He paused. 'Can you see the activity in the city? Look. Normally at this time the roads are almost empty but now they are swarming. It won't be long before they realize that we're not there and then they'll start to come out after us. But if we risk a move now we might be spotted.'

'Let's look at Arkron's map,' said Melvaig and putting his hand under his jerkin he delved inside the bag round his neck and brought out the carved wooden cylinder. Despite the resolution he had made to bury the terrible echoes of the incident between himself and Shuinn he still felt uneasy with his friend. Conversation seemed forced, and they avoided looking each other in the eyes. Now vague prickles of apprehension fluttered at the back of his neck as he pulled out the map and, spreading it out on his knees, started to examine it with the giant.

'We're here,' he said, pointing to a spot that Arkron had marked on the parchment. 'There's the Blaggvald. He's drawn our route with that red line. It seems to lead up this hill we're on now and then across to that strangely shaped crag there. From the way he's drawn it, it appears to look like a face. Hopefully we shall be able to spot it once we're on top.'

'Then we go through that deep cleft and past what seems to be a rocking stone.' Shuinn was now running his finger excitedly along the red line. 'I wonder what that is?' he said, pointing to a tall thin representation with straight sides and a sharp pointed top which appeared to grow out of a little mound. 'It should be easy enough to recognize once we see it.'

From there they traced along Arkron's line where it appeared to drop down from the mountains and meander out through the Dammfenn. There were no landmarks drawn here and finally the line stopped on what Melvaig guessed was the shore, beyond which stretched the sea. Once there, Melvaig knew, they were in the hands of Ashgaroth and they would see then what the final outcome of their search would be.

For some time they both studied Arkron's painstaking drawings trying to imagine the layout of the terrain they would have to cover, to calculate how long it would take them, to get into the mind of the old man as he pieced together all the knowledge and information which he had, drawing on the Book and the other material he had managed to find in the archives of the Blaggvald. They pictured him working away in some little room on his dangerous occupation, praying to Ashgaroth for inspiration and for the meeting with Melvaig. Constantly under the watchful gaze of Xtlan and uncertain of the success of his enterprise, they marvelled at the old man's spirit. Was he correct in his assumptions and his findings? What would they find when they reached the end of that wavering red line, drawn, it seemed, in blood? Faith was all that would drive them on, as it had done until now; until finally the point was reached where that faith would either blossom into the full bloom of achievement and success or crumble into dust.

'It is a long way,' said Melvaig. 'There isn't much food left from what Arkron gave us.'

'There are some goat farms on these slopes. Not many, the land is poor – but there are a few. Do you want to risk breaking in and taking one?'

Shuinn was deferential, almost humble, in the way he spoke to Melvaig – asking his advice in a way he would not have done before.

'I don't know,' he replied. 'Should we not, perhaps, wait a bit until we're further away from Eggron?' As he spoke the words, the sounds of work on the wall drifted up on the still air, as if to emphasize the closeness of the city.

'You're right. We'll wait,' said Shuinn firmly, and there was something in his tone which showed the resentment of one who feels he is not in a position to argue even if he wished to do so. 'I didn't mean we would try now.'

They stayed where they were, silently musing or passing occasional remarks, until evening started to fall and the light began to fade in the sky. Then Melvaig woke Morven and Bracca and they all started to make their way up the old river valley, Melvaig in front and Shuinn in the rear. They all felt refreshed after the rest and they made good progress in the relative cool of this time of the day but they were hungry and thirsty and as time went on Melvaig was more and more tempted to finish off the drink and use the last of the food that Arkron had given them. But he decided to postpone it for as long as possible. They were all used to hunger and thirst and he knew that their cravings were much more bearable with the knowledge that food and drink were, as a last resort, available than if there was none to be had at all. For Bracca, though, it was different. He had been well fed at the warrior nursery and his growing body required sustenance as his lungs needed air so Melvaig tried to judge how much the boy needed, rather than how much he wanted and gave him, at intervals, just that much while the others, looking on, fought with the churning in their stomachs and the rasping in their throats.

By the time the brief magic moments of dusk came to light up the horizon, Eggron was a long way beneath them, dim and shadowy and sprinkled with yellow spots of light from the Gravenndra. Only once during their climb had they seen riders, a small troop of them coming diagonally across the hillside, and they had crouched fearfully in the shelter of some large boulders while they had gone past. From their conversation Shuinn had gathered that they had been called back to Eggron to help in the search. It could not be long now, thought Melvaig, when Shuinn later repeated what he had heard, before Xtlan would realize they were not in Eggron and would send warriors out beyond the wall. They must put as much distance between them and Eggron as they could before that time came.

Night descended but luck was with them for there was a full moon, bravely trying to shine through the murk of the sky and succeeding in diffusing the landscape with a dim white glow so that they were able to continue their journey, picking their way over the stones and rocks in the narrow winding valley. There was a strange security and contentment in the rhythm of the walk as they moved quietly up the mountain. For Shuinn, though, those feelings were marred by the clouds of jealousy and desire that, for ever lurking in the upper reaches of his mind, would suddenly loom down and dominate his very soul until, inexplicably, they would depart, leaving him relieved yet weak from the effort of fighting them back. He had once again taken to carrying Bracca, sometimes on his shoulders, other times on his back, and he found that the presence of the little boy helped him to drive away the darkness but still, as he walked a few paces behind Morven he found his eyes lingering over her body, the gentle grace of her movements as she climbed the slope, the swing of her hips.

He became obsessed with her, and his mind envisaged her nakedness, and he imagined her with him, beneath him, responding hungrily to his passion. The fire built up inside him again, raging with an almost unquenchable fury and then he would force himself to talk to Bracca about something, anything, and the flames would slowly subside.

They had walked a good way, far enough for the lights of Eggron to appear only as tiny dots in the far distance, when gradually they became aware of a settlement ahead of them. Faint sounds came through the silent night, a shout, muffled conversation, and the bleating of goats as they grazed on the hillside's sparse vegetation. Then, suddenly they heard a sound immediately in front and, emerging from behind a large boulder, they saw two goats. Melvaig froze in his tracks and the others stopped behind him while the goats, rooted to the spot in curiosity, stared at them in amazement. Then, regaining their confidence, they bent their heads again and resumed their grazing. Very gently, so as not to disturb them, Shuinn lowered Bracca down off his shoulders and walked up to Melvaig.

'We will keep one for milk and kill the other for meat,' he said and gone from his voice, in the tension of the moment, was the deference with which he had recently addressed Melvaig. Once again he seemed to be his old self; taking swift command in situations where he felt himself to be more experienced, for he had taken stray goats many times in the past with the two Mengoy, Gebb and Nekdog. 'I'll get that one,' pointing behind, 'and you grab hold of the other.'

Very carefully, moving gradually and slowly so as not to alarm the animals, they moved towards them, talking quietly to them in the way that Melvaig remembered from Ruann. Once or twice the animals stopped their grazing and, looking up, eyed the two humans with nothing more than idle interest. The thought of one of them being killed disturbed Melvaig in a way he had not felt before. In Ruann he had killed goats frequently, never liking the task but accepting it as something which had to be done. Now though, after the knowledge he had gained from the Book about the place of animals in the world and their relationship with man, he felt uneasy as if this was a betrayal of everything he was aiming for and everything he had learned. But what choice was there? Soon he and Shuinn were close enough and at a signal from the giant, both men put their hands out gently and took hold of the collars round the goats' necks.

'Got them,' said Shuinn. 'Ashgaroth has indeed smiled on us.'

The two goats appeared not in the least disturbed by the event and at once started to try and chew the bottoms of the jerkins that Melvaig and Shuinn wore, to the amusement of Morven and Bracca. They both had belts under these outer jerkins and, taking them off, they slipped them through the collars to form leads. Bracca came up and started to fuss them, stroking their soft muzzles and patting them on their heads.

'They're a nice pair,' said Morven. 'It's a shame we have to kill one. They seem very friendly and easy to handle.' She had always loved the goats in Ruann and had enjoyed working with them and being with them. Looking at these two now her mind went back to those days, milking in the mornings and evenings, looking after the little kids, the special relationships that had built up between her and certain of the nannies – a unique bond of friendship and understanding so that she knew instinctively when one was unhappy or not well. Even the unmistakable sickly-sweet pungency of the billy-goat smell, drifting across on the air now from the settlement, filled her with a yearning sense of nostalgia for the peace and happiness of those times. How ignorant and blessedly innocent she had been then of the terrors and horrors of the world outside. Looking back on those days, filled as they seemed now in retrospect, with laughter and love and security, she marvelled at how young she seemed to have been then and how immensely old she had become during the age she had been away. And yet it could not have been, in all, more than a year since Melvaig had left her on the slopes of Ruann to go and see what the raiders were doing in their village. She pushed the thoughts from her head and, like Bracca, began stroking and talking to the goats. As with Melvaig, the idea of killing one of them filled her with acute distaste and a sharp stabbing sense of guilt.

'Come,' said Shuinn abruptly. 'It's time we were going, before they are missed.'

At the sound of the giant's voice Morven felt once again the twisting coil of ambivalence in her towards this man, this friend of Melvaig's. She knew how much he meant to Melvaig, and to Bracca, all he had done, how without him they could never have become reunited. At times she too felt his goodness, his sincerity, and his honesty and she was grateful for his strength, but at other times a terrible flash of doubt would sear across her vision of him and she felt witheringly afraid. She could not so easily forgive the things he had said about her in the cavern when they were in the tunnel and there was no mistaking the way he looked at her, imagining her unclothed as he had first seen her on the rack in the Blaggvald.

They started to walk forward, Melvaig and Shuinn in front now, as the two goats would not be separated, and Morven and Bracca behind. Soon the smell of the billy goats faded and the sounds of activity receded into the distance. On they trudged, up and up, tiring now and stumbling more and more against the rocks that lay along the bed of the old river. Melvaig found himself venting his irritability on his goat, jerking at it savagely if it tried to go a different way from the path he was taking. He became angry with it if it pulled him along, yanking it back and even, momentarily, threatening it with death for its recalictrance and stubbornness. 'We'll see how you pull with a knife across your throat,' he would utter under his breath and then, as soon as the thought had been voiced, he would be overcome with compassion and regret and repugnance against himself.

Bracca, walking now that Shuinn had the goat, soon got so tired that, without saying a word, he began whimpering pitifully and both Melvaig and Morven snapped at him to stop it and felt pangs of remorse as soon as they had done so.

'I'm sorry, little man, I'm sorry,' Morven said. 'We'll soon be stopping for a rest, I promise you. Look, I'll try and carry you for a while,' and she hoisted him up on to her back.

Eventually the first strands of dawn appeared on the horizon and gradually, imperceptibly, the darkness was driven back, so that the ground once again became clearly arrayed before them in all its barrenness, the bleached white rocks and stones reflecting the sun's dazzling light until their heads began to ache as they furrowed their brows and narrowed their lids in an attempt to keep out the glare. They could hardly see Eggron below them now and they had long since lost sight of the settlement from which the goats had strayed. They were not so frisky now, these two white creatures, as they had been in the relative cool of the night and they kept lagging behind so that Melvaig and Shuinn frequently had to stop and almost drag them up the little valley.

At last Melvaig suggested a stop and after tethering the goats they all gratefully sank down on the hard earth, finding what shade they could and letting their bodies relax completely as they stretched out. Melvaig's blissful spell of oblivion was interrupted by the voice of Shuinn whispering urgently and quietly into his ear.

'Which one shall we kill?' he said, and a black cloud of depression and anxiety floated in and settled itself in his consciousness.

'I don't know,' he replied. 'I don't care. Whichever you think?'

'That's not really fair,' said the giant. 'I don't want to do it any more than you do but it's got to be done. If we do it now the meat will have some time to dry out in the sun before it's time to move on. But why should I have to choose which one? Let's decide together.'

And so, while Morven and Bracca slept, they walked over to where the two animals sat peacefully chewing on their cud. As the humans approached they looked up at them with a benign sense of interest, mildly quizzical in their attitude, and regarded them almost patronizingly. How could the choice possibly be made?

Melvaig bent down and stroked them both on the side of their face and they responded by nestling against him, pushing their noses up under his armpits. Suddenly, as if in a flash, everything became clear to him. Here and now, in their situation as it was, they had no right to kill either of them. They were all alive and could survive solely on the milk from the goats for a long time yet. There was no need to make the choice, no need to kill, for there was no need for the meat. A desire maybe, but no need and until that need arose unequivocally they could not kill. A wave of relief washed over him as the dark cloud lifted and he felt himself tingling with a sense of overwhelming joy. He looked them in the eye, turning from one to the other happily and then, giving them each a vigorous pat on the head he got up and turned to face Shuinn.

'We will not kill either of them,' he said. 'Their milk will be sufficient for us for the time being.'

The giant looked stunned, shocked.

'But,' he protested in a voice aghast with disbelief, 'we will die. Is that what you want, that we should die? Without meat we shall die!'

'No, we will not, at least not for the moment. If the need eventually arises, then we shall have to make the decision but that time is not with us yet. It would be wrong, Shuinn – there is no necessity. Can't you see that?'

The note in the giant's voice became supplicatory and he began to speak in a tone that was almost pleading.

'I don't agree, Melvaig,' he said. 'I don't agree. We've got to have meat. It will make us feel so much better, stronger. I really don't feel the same way as you do about it.'

As he spoke his manner changed from the almost sulky petulance of his opening words to a tone that had an air of threat about it, an underlying menace such as Melvaig had never heard Shuinn use to him before.

'We may feel better with it,' Melvaig replied, 'but that is not worth taking life for if we can get by without.'

They were looking each other straight in the eyes now bristling with hostility, the tension connecting them as if there were a wall around them, locking them together into their own private battle of wills. Melvaig surprised himself by the strength he found to meet the giant's piercing look of barely suppressed anger with a feeling of such over-whelming determination that he felt his friend quavering in the face of it.

'I shall,' began the giant in a voice that shivered with

barely perceptible uncertainty, 'I shall have to kill on my own then.'

Melvaig's retort came swiftly and surely and though he knew it was he who formed the words, it was as if he was hearing someone else speak them.

'Before you've laid a hand on either of those two goats, you'll be dead.' There was no anger in his voice, nor any other emotion to clutter up its purity of expression. It was simply a statement of fact and for a moment or two Shuinn regarded him in stunned amazement until he turned and walked slowly away, feeling the core of bitterness and resentment which now lurked within him grow until it threatened to overwhelm him. Melvaig watched him go and felt himself swept up in a wave of terrible sadness. Once again a barrier had driven itself between them like a wedge and another part of the great love he bore for his friend had withered and died before the icy blast of their altercation.

And Dréagg was well pleased. For Shuinn's heart had been turned another degree away from Melvaig. And all the while the giant's spirit grew restive and increasingly receptive to the notions Dréagg planted there.

Morven and Bracca had slept throughout the fierce confrontation and when Morven awoke some time later, oblivious to the dreadful significance of her words, she called out to Melvaig, 'When are you going to have to kill one of the goats?'

Shuinn remained where he was, immobile and impassive, sitting in the lee of a large rock and looking away, down the slope in the direction of the settlement. Melvaig turned round to face her from where he still sat stroking the two animals and said in a voice that trembled with a casualness he did not feel:

'Not yet. There's no need to for the time being. We can live on their milk. Here, look, I've filled the container.'

He got up and walked over to her with the precious milk

which he had got from the goats since the quarrel. He had enjoyed the feel of milking again, the steady rhythm of the squirt, the soft feel of the teat in his hand.

'Have a drink,' he said, and passed the container to her. It felt reassuringly heavy and after putting the neck in her mouth she lifted it up and drank. It tasted delicious, the smooth silky texture of the liquid quenching her thirst and satisfying the emptiness in her stomach; the richness of the flavour filled her with sumptuous delight.

She lowered the container and took it away from her lips, a trickle of white liquid escaping from the corner of her mouth and dribbling down over her chin. As she looked up at Melvaig where he stood watching her, he saw the deep pleasure in her eyes and a sudden warm burst of yearning for her flooded through him, almost painful in its intensity. He was possessed by a fierce desire to embrace her, to wrap her safely within the shelter of his love and yet he held back, aware of Shuinn's anguished presence on the rocks and, despite the anger he felt towards him, unwilling to do anything which might alienate him still further.

Morven, seeing the stiffness in Melvaig's body and the distance in his eyes, sensed that something was wrong again between them and her heart sank. Then, on an impulse, she called gaily to Melvaig's friend:

'Shuinn, come and have some milk. It's lovely. Come on. You'll feel much better.'

If Melvaig had called him he would probably not have responded but when he heard her voice, addressed to him, calling him by name, he was unable to ignore her. It was as music to him, lifting the darkness from his spirit. Slowly he turned round and gradually, with an obvious reluctance displayed for Melvaig's sake, he got up and walked over to her. He took the pouch from her hands and lifting his head began to drink the milk. As he drank and the cravings of hunger and thirst were assuaged by the satisfying liquid, so the rancour and bitterness seemed to evaporate, so that when he stopped and gave the pouch back to Morven he was able to look at Melvaig and say he was sorry and that Melvaig had been right and that the milk would, despite what he had thought before, be enough for them. And Melvaig, overjoyed by the change in his friend, embraced him and they smiled warmly at each other. Yet despite this outward display of affection there was a coldness in their hearts for each other which would not thaw out so easily, a barrier of reserve which each man tried to break down within himself but found to his grief that he could not.

Now it was Melvaig's turn to drink and he took the pouch back from Morven and did so with relish before taking Bracca gently by the shoulder and shaking him until the little boy's eyes opened and he slowly came to.

'Here, drink this. It'll do you good,' he said, passing him the milk. Dreamily Bracca took it and drank his fill, feeling his body revive as the richness of the drink spread throughout all his limbs.

The container was still half full when Melvaig took it back from him; there was enough to last until the goats could be milked again. The fierce heat of the midday sun had gone now and they were well into the short afternoon, a good time for them to continue their journey. So they left their shelter and carried on up the ravine, walking slowly in the heat but feeling better now that they were no longer hungry and thirsty. The narrow creek which they were following began to widen out and as it did so they were able to see the terrain through which they were walking. They were high now and the earth seemed less scorched; the thick wiry tufts of grass were plentiful and they were grateful for the warm breeze that played against their faces.

Suddenly their little valley came to an end, the slope levelled out and they found themselves at the summit. Ahead of them there stretched a wide plateau, the ground uneven, pitted and rock-strewn, and then beyond it in the near distance, the land rose up again in a series of sharp jagged peaks which stood in a row like a line of sentries, their bluffs and outcrops stretching up and out like limbs. The sun was just going down behind them washing the sky with colour, great livid splashes of golds and crimsons and reds and deep dark purples, and the craggy jutting pinnacles of rock were silhouetted in front of them, cloaked in darkness, throwing great elongated shadows on to the plateau. It was a magical sight and the travellers stood rooted to the spot in wonder. Somewhere beyond it, Melvaig knew, lay the answer to their questions: where they would find either salvation in the world of their dreams or damnation in the futility of their search. But as he looked at this glorious sky, he felt his spirits lift with hope, and he searched the range until he found the landmark he sought, the one with the outline of a face that Arkron had drawn on the map. There was no mistaking it; the old man had drawn his outline well from whatever picture he had copied.

'There!' said Melvaig turning to the others standing alongside him. 'That's the one we head for. Come on.'

Then a sudden impulse made him turn round and he looked back down the mountain to the dark and shadowy outlines of Eggron where it lurked far beneath him. Immediately something different about it struck him. At first he could not tell what it was, but then slowly he realized. It was evening. The Grayling would have tolled the curfew. The city should have been deserted save for the occasional group of guards riding slowly along the roads. But now there was about Eggron an atmosphere of vibrant activity, like an ant-hill that has just been disturbed. He could not see individual riders or men in the gloom yet he sensed their movement, their hectic bustle, and a shiver of fear ran down his spine when the realization came to him that the purpose of it all was the search for the four of them. He glanced sideways fleetingly at his companions:

Morven beautiful and poised yet delicate and fragile, her enormous courage and spirit surely near the end, taxed to breaking point. How much longer could she continue without a rest, a convalescence of calm and peace to obliterate the nightmare of her life since Ruann? Bracca, standing at her side, grown old beyond his years; brave, stubborn, and courageous yet so very, very young. He stood now exhausted, his tiny body wilting yet his face aglow with marvel at the glory of the wondrous sky, his mouth open, his eyes rapt. And beside Bracca, the figure of his giant friend standing awkward and aloof. What to make of Shuinn now; his outburst, the change in him – were these the result of a mind so utterly worn out that it no longer even knew itself? How long could such a consciousness continue before it finally collapsed?

He turned back to Eggron and saw now to his horror that a band of warriors was leaving the walled confines of the city and making its way towards the mountain they had just climbed. How long would it be before they were making the ascent towards them? Before the mountains around them were swarming with warriors? The city must by now have been combed for them and realization come that the fugitives had escaped. They must move as quickly as possible, to try to get at least through the mountains before Xtlan's warriors reached the summit.

He turned back to the others, deciding to tell only Shuinn what he had seen. For Morven and Bracca, there was no reason to burden them with the added anxiety and stress that such knowledge would lay upon them. Better to make steady constant progress without panic. With the goat pulling him gently forward he walked past them and started the long trek towards the crag with a face, calling to them to follow. As before, Morven came after him, then Bracca and finally Shuinn with the other goat. He would have to pick his time to tell Shuinn of the pursuit, when the other two were asleep perhaps.

CHAPTER XXX

After the long hard climb, it was almost luxurious to be walking on level ground again and for a time they almost bounded over the humps and tussocks and rocks, enjoying the feeling of height, the breeze, and the colours of the evening sky. Then suddenly the sun sank down behind the mountains and the milky white light of the moon lit the way ahead. There was something exhilarating about that moonlight trek across the plateau with the line of peaks in front of them throwing eerie shadows on the silvery ground. There seemed a clarity of air and a purity of vision up here that reminded Melvaig of the mountains of Ruann, and as he walked he felt an inexplicable lightness of spirit and a flutter of wild anticipation and hope in his heart. It was as if the presence of Ashgaroth was somehow all around them, urging them on.

And so they journeyed on through the night, stopping briefly just once for a rest and another drink of milk, tethering the goats to two large boulders to graze on the relatively luxurious vegetation up here. Morven was particularly conscious of the need to draw Shuinn in on their conversation and she made a special effort to be interested and warm towards him, smiling and encouraging him as he spoke. The giant, flattered and pleased, found his confidence with the unattainable, tantalizingly beautiful Morven growing and as he talked he found his imagination burgeoning with fancies that she was being provocative and enticing instead of merely friendly. All this time Melvaig was silent. He had one ear on the conversation and the other anxiously alert for sounds on the air, any noise that would betray the presence of Xtlan's warriors behind them. But there was nothing and when they decided to move on again and he and Shuinn went over to untie the goats, he took the opportunity to tell the giant quietly what he had seen down the mountain, with an admonition not to tell the others.

'It is to be expected,' replied Shuinn. 'But it is sooner than I had thought. Still, we are going well.' He was full to bursting with the excitement that Morven's attitude towards him had engendered and suddenly everything seemed possible; nothing seemed to matter as long as she was near.

After this small but, for Shuinn, momentous rest they continued on towards the range of peaks ahead of them. Dawn came suddenly, daylight appearing and the heat returning almost simultaneously, and it found them just under the lee of the chin on the crag with a face. They walked through the narrow pass in between it and an adjacent peak and then stopped to look at Arkron's map. They were to turn to the left and head towards the rocking stone. The old man had again done his work well and there was no mistaking the sight of it in the middle distance ahead of them, like a huge egg balancing on the apex of a narrow pyramid-shaped rock that rose sheer out of the earth.

With their spirits high they set off towards it, pausing only once for a short rest when it was decided that Bracca, who was worn out but stoical in his lack of complaint, would be carried on Shuinn's shoulders again while Morven took the goat. By the time they reached the stone, Melvaig judged it to be around the middle of the day, and even with the breeze it had become extremely hot. They slunk gratefully into the shade and lay down with their backs against the cool smoothness of the rock. But Melvaig stayed standing.

'The goats need some grazing and water,' he said. 'I'll take them with me to look for some. You stay here.'

Shuinn immediately offered to go in his place but Melvaig turned him down. He was pleased at the way the giant and Morven had begun to get on better and felt that this might be a good chance for them to learn more about each other, to help break down the barriers between them. Shuinn for his part was thrilled at the prospect of being alone with her but also apprehensive. Morven, sensing what Melvaig was trying to do, was nevertheless filled with foreboding.

Melvaig went and the others settled down to doze in the dry heat. The little boy was soon fast asleep where he lay curled up against the rock but oblivion did not come so easily to Shuinn and Morven. She was aware of his attention focused on her with such intensity that it was almost tangible. Yet when she looked at him he seemed to be asleep. Her imagination, she said, and felt herself falling back down towards the delicious emptiness that beckoned her, but just before she finally succumbed to its lure the thought struck her with a sudden awful jolt that maybe Melvaig was testing her, Shuinn's poisonous words back in the tunnel had got through to him and he was trying her out alone with a man. The idea left her almost as soon as it came, her subconscious mind banishing it immediately as too horrible to contemplate and she fell fast asleep.

It was then that the turmoil began again in Shuinn; lewd images of himself and Morven swirled around in his mind, tormenting him with the passion they aroused. He opened his eyes and saw her lying there next to him, her beautiful face deliciously calm and serene in sleep, her eyelids fluttering delicately, her lips slightly parted. Truly, he thought he had never seen anyone, anything so desirable. It was wrong, unfair, that one man should have the kind of claim on her that Melvaig seemed to exercise. Beauty such as hers should belong to everyone, to be shared and enjoyed by all who were able. Indeed she must have been used by enough men in the Gravenndra and the Blaggvald. She must be used to it. She may even, as he had said with so much venom in the tunnel, have enjoyed it. Well then! What harm could it do? Besides, he wasn't just anyone. He was Melvaig's friend, who had been through so much with him and without whom Melvaig would in all probability not be here now with her and Bracca. Bracca! Damn the boy! Would he wake up? What would he do if he did -- he wouldn't know what was going on. Anyway the little boy liked him; they were friends.

And all the time these questions raged through his head his eyes wandered over her face and her prostrate body, elegant and graceful even in sleep; something about the lie of her limbs expressed a sensuality which inflamed his lust until he felt he would burst. He had to have her!

Morven felt his hand on her cheek and slowly, fearfully, opened her eyes. His face was very close to hers; her awful apprehension was confirmed when she forced herself to look in his eyes. She had seen that crazed light before so many times, that barely suppressed fire that burned so intensely in the soul of a man in the throes of passion that he seemed to quiver with the power of it. As she met his eyes, she saw in them bewilderment, a desperate yearning, immense sadness and above all the raging of a desire which would not be suppressed. What was the point in resistance? She would regard it as she had all the others who had had their way with her. It would not affect her as much as a fly settling on her arm. But if it was to be done it must be done quickly, before Melvaig came back, and quietly so as not to wake Bracca. As she thought of Melvaig a strange notion came into her mind again; far from 'testing' her with his friend had he perhaps intended this to happen, wanted it to happen? No! Surely not. She pushed the thought away from her and looking up at his hungry eager face, mouthed quietly to him, 'Now, then, before Melvaig gets back. And quietly . . .'

At once she felt the fleshy grizzled impact of Shuinn's face and beard as he pressed his lips against hers. As she fought to get her breath he lay down on top of her and began to fumble around clumsily with the thonging on her jerkin, at the same time using his knees to hitch her skirt up. Irritably she decided that she had to help him so as to get the whole thing over as soon as possible and so she undid her jerkin exposing herself to his gaze and making herself accessible to the squeeze and prod of his fingers as they probed her and explored her roughly. Then suddenly he forced her thighs apart and rammed himself into her. She winced with pain but he did not notice, intent as he was on nothing save the appeasement of his rampant surging lust. She lay there, looking up at the sunlight throwing its rays off the rocks above her head and feeling the stones beneath her body cut and scrape and dig into her. Absently, as if in idle play, her hands reached for and found some little stones and she turned them around in her palms, feeling them, running her fingers over them to gauge their shape and size. She was aware of her body being buffeted and tossed, jerked around in the wild thrashing of his passion as he pulled her first this way and then that while he pumped himself to oblivion inside her. The odour of his sex drifted up and stung her nostrils with its sharp, acrid pungency. Oh hurry, hurry! And then suddenly, as if in answer to her prayer, it was all over. She felt a warm gush inside her and heard the stifled moan that escaped his lips before he collapsed upon her, crushing her beneath the weight of his limp, spent body. Now she must extricate herself from under him. Feeling slightly winded, very sore and pummelled and bruised all over, she pushed his shoulders away from her and tried to slide out. As she did so, something in his consciousness stirred and he raised himself, looking down at her with a gaze that was heavy with remorse and despair. He knew how it had been for her, had felt the sullen unresponsive woodenness of her body but had been unable to stop himself. Now that his desire was assuaged and the single-mindedness that had gripped him in the pursuit of its release had evaporated, he was left with a terrible empty feeling of loneliness and guilt: guilt at his betrayal of Melvaig and guilt at his debasement of Morven. Morven, who now seemed even more distant and remote from him than before, despite the bleak, wan smile that she threw up at him. With his eyes he tried to implore her forgiveness, to receive some sacrament of understanding from her, some flicker of emotion, but her expression was blank, like a mask. Morven, who had received his crude, brutal and ugly ministrations with such a dogged stoicism. He opened his mouth and tried to speak, to explain, to apologize, to tell her he could not comprehend what had come over him.

'I . . .' he blurted, but she frowned and putting a finger over her lips glanced at Bracca who, mercifully, was still asleep. Then she continued sliding out from under him until she was free of his body at which point she busied herself with fastening up the thonging on her jerkin again and smoothing out her torn and crumpled skirt. As he watched her, a feeling of almost unbearable clumsiness spread over him. She seemed so fragile and delicate, so achingly beautiful, that a dull pain enclosed his heart at the thought of what he had done to her. And again she smiled at him, that same empty meaningless smile that was worse for him than a scowl of hatred, before lying back down on the ground and closing her eyes. Then he too, after straightening out his garments, lay down and tried to sleep, his mind and spirit beset by a whirling maelstrom of turbulent raging emotion that would not let him rest.

Melvaig came back some time later, towards the end of the afternoon. He had been lucky, finding water not too far away, albeit little more than a trickle. Still the goats had drunk long and thirstily, slurping back the brackish liquid with obvious pleasure. The grass had been reasonably plentiful there also so he had tethered them to some protruding fingers of rock and let them graze in peace whilst he had lain back against a boulder and dozed. His dreams though, had been unsettling. Swathes of golden thoughts, he and Morven and Bracca running and laughing and playing in deep green caverns of trees, had been bordered with ominous dark clouds for ever hanging malevolently at the edge of their happiness. When he awoke it was to a feeling of relief, for the dreams had made his sleep restless and disturbing.

When he arrived back with the others, Morven and Bracca were still asleep, curled up contentedly under the rock, but Shuinn was awake, sitting a little way from them on a large flat ledge of stone. His shoulders were hunched over and he had about him a brooding melancholic air. He appeared not to see or hear Melvaig and the goats, not turning his head in the slightest, and the lightness of Melvaig's mood was shattered by a piercing and poignant stab of anxiety for his friend. He had hoped that, in his absence, Morven and Shuinn would have got to know each other better and perhaps grown closer so that the giant would not feel quite so much an outsider. It was incomprehensible to him, and fiercely painful, that two of the only three people he loved should not love each other as he loved them.

And yet the obvious truth was that far from becoming closer, Shuinn had got into one of his terrible moods again. Was it because of Morven? Had they had a row? Well, there was no time to find out now. Xtlan's riders could not, surely, be far behind and they had to continue their journey at once. If Arkron's map was correct it should not be long before they reached the Dammfenn. And then, beyond that, the sea and the answer to their dreams.

Gently he woke the others up and called over to Shuinn. The giant turned round slowly and reluctantly and came over. He said nothing, his face sullen and fixed on the ground in front of his feet as if he was unable to look any of them in the face.

They passed round the last of the goat's milk in the containers, milked the goats again and then set off in the direction of the next of the landmarks on the map, a flat-topped hillock next to a jagged needle of rock. Melvaig had tried to talk to Shuinn but had got nothing by way of reply save a meaningless grunt. The giant now resumed his place at the rear of the little procession following on behind Morven, Bracca and, in the lead, Melvaig.

They kept on the move all through the night, stopping only twice for a rest and a drink. They had begun to descend now, each landmark being a little lower than the one before.

Shortly before dawn, when the sky above them seemed to be at its darkest but, as if to compensate, slivers of silver began to appear on the horizon, they became aware of a pungency in the air. It caught their nostrils and stuck in their throats making them feel like retching, and then suddenly the ground on which they were walking came to an abrupt and jagged end. Melvaig stopped to let the others catch up and they all stood in line, looking over the edge of what in the gloom appeared to be a steep incline. The land looked as if it had been torn apart, ripped open by some strange force, leaving this great gaping void in front of them. In the darkness they could see nothing beyond the first few outcrops of rock on the way down the almost sheer cliff. After that the pale light from the moon seemed to be absorbed into the dense blackness beneath them, which appeared to swirl with strange wraith-like shapes as they stared down into it.

Its all-enveloping atmosphere of horror touched them with a cold shudder of fear. And then Melvaig realized where they were.

'The Dammfenn,' he said, partly to himself and partly to the others. 'At last, the Dammfenn.' Ever since Arkron had told him of this place, the knowledge of its existence had lurked like a dark shadow at the back of all his thoughts, tempering all his little bursts of optimism and faith with a sense of gloom. Arkron's neat map, the detailed way he had drawn their path past the rocks and landmarks, seemed here to have suddenly debased itself as the Dammfenn was represented by crude black squiggles, drawn in thick heavy lines across the route. No way was marked through it. The dotted red line of their track simply ended where the black lines began and then beyond it, pictured in blue, lay the sea.

'We must wait until daylight,' he said, turning towards the others. 'Wait here and rest till we can see more clearly: can see something, anything!'

And so they moved back from the edge and sat down, but rest did not come to them. Bracca was silent, snuggled up with his arms around Morven while she cradled his head against her breasts, rocking him gently to and fro in an effort to soothe the frantic pounding of his heart and the nervous shivering of his body. Shuinn sat, still and remote, looking out into the empty darkness over the Dammfenn, his wide and staring eyes fixed in the distance as if he were mesmerized by whatever his mind saw out there.

Eventually the silver chinks of light on the horizon grew into full daylight and as the sun shone around them, so they stood up and went back again to stand on the edge of the Dammfenn and look down into its great gaping expanse. And there they saw a vision of such terrible ugliness that it rooted them to the spot, paralyzing them with horror. At first they fancied that their eyes were playing tricks on them, making them unable to focus as the floor of the Dammfenn seemed to move, almost to shimmer, in the pale light. It would not stay still; rather, it ebbed and flowed in a chaotic rhythm, pulsing and vibrating, it seemed, in time to the beating of their hearts. And then their vision grew used to the light and began to sort out and separate the dense mass that lay stretched out before them into myriads of shapes, writhing, twisting and squirming over the sickly yellow floor of earth. The light shone on the deathly white pallor of their bodies, rendering them almost transparent and giving them a luminescent sheen; for a terrible moment Melvaig imagined he could see darker shapes through the skin, inside the bodies – the organs of these creatures, functioning to invest them with a futile pretence at life. But the ultimate soul-wrenching revelation came when, on closer examination still, they became aware of the exact shapes of the bodies and with a sickening jolt recognized them as human. True, the arms and legs had shrunk so that they resembled flippers as they thrashed around uselessly on the ground; the heads and bodies were completely hairless and the eyes had a thin, filmy mucous membrane across them, but they were human – there could be no doubt about that. The set of the small round heads on the thin necks, the backbones, the ribs, the trunks – elongated so as to be almost wormlike – the rudimentary hands on the ends of the flippers with which they seemed to be scooping out something from the earth; all these betrayed the presence of humanity in these awful creatures. Sometimes a cluster would appear to form and Melvaig would watch in terrible fascination as one of the creatures disappeared bit by bit as a group of its fellows devoured it, first an arm, then a leg vanishing in the throng.

And all the while, assailing their ears with such unfathomable despair that the hearts of the four travellers ached with pain, the creatures wailed their torment. They could do nothing but watch; stare out at the terrible sight before them and let the agony of these tortured souls wash over them.

Eventually, Melvaig dragged his gaze away, up towards the great cloud that hovered above the canyon. It hung malevolently in the air, like an enormous shroud, its dull brown giving way in parts to streaks of red and yellow and purple and maroon. It was from this that the acrid stench appeared to come, although at times wafts of a different smell drifted up from the creatures below, a foul aroma of rancid and putrescent flesh.

Then Melvaig took his eyes back to earth again, to a spot beyond this barrier of mutants beneath the cliff edge. There, in the near distance, the ground was free of them. They appeared to have stopped their colonization along a line, the line of a deep ravine over which, he guessed, they could not cross. He could see the nature of the terrain clearly there, the same sickly yellow pallor to the earth as the mutants crawled on but the land there seemed almost to be alive itself, bubbling and gurgling constantly from fissures, cracks and gashes that would occasionally spew forth great fountains of brackish brown steam. As Melvaig watched he saw parts of the earth break open and puffs of flaming gas erupt to drift up and join the cloud above. A terrible, pock-marked landscape, covered in sores and scabs from which the poison beneath the skin constantly oozed, it gripped him with almost as much horror as the sight of the creatures. He brought his eyes nearer now to look at them again. He saw that the earth upon which they crawled appeared shiny and wet, reflecting glints of light. Rivulets of foul brown water seeped out from the ground as a festering wound leaks pus and ran slowly over the yellow earth turning it into a quagmire of slimy mud. It was this which the mutants seemed to revel in, sliding over it and in it with an almost voluptuous abandon – burying their mouths in it and slapping it over themselves.

Just then, at Melvaig's side, Morven spoke.

'Will they attack us?' she said. 'If we try to cross over – do you think they'll attack?'

'I don't know,' he replied, half to himself and half to her, trying to answer this same question that had been nagging at his mind also. He looked up from the scene below and across to Shuinn.

'Shuinn. What do you think?' In a gesture of infuriating apathy the giant simply shrugged his shoulders. 'Damn you,' Melvaig cursed him under his breath.

It was then that, above the noise from the creatures, Melvaig thought he heard another sound in the distance. It was the drumming of horses' hooves, a steady rumbling drone travelling through the earth so that he believed he could feel its vibrations under his feet. Well, he thought, whether it was in his imagination or not, there was no time left to muse over the dilemma any longer. They would have to take the chance. He looked again at the giant to see whether or not he had heard the hoofbeats as well. Shuinn, though, was still staring at the mutants, his eyes wide with repulsion. He called to him again.

'Shuinn. We'll have to take the risk. Do you agree?'

This time the giant looked up and returned his gaze with a wan and watery smile.

'If you say so,' he replied weakly.

Depressed and frustrated by this new posture Melvaig nevertheless determined to stir them all out of the trance-like state of shock which the sight of the creatures had induced. He pulled Bracca towards him and giving Morven the goat, lifted him up.

'Are you all right, little man? Not too frightened?'

The little boy's eyes were glazed with fear but he spoke bravely.

'No,' he said with a tremor in his voice. 'But . . . what are they? Are they fierce? I've never seen anything like them before.'

'Don't worry. I'll carry you through them.'

Morven was looking at him and even Shuinn was looking in his direction though not directly at his face.

'We must be as quiet as possible. Their eyes look strange; they might not be able to see us but they've got ears. Shuinn, if you follow Morven you could watch out behind us and I'll keep an eye in front. We may have to fight our way through but if we can just get as far as the ravine we should be all right. They don't seem to go across that.' He paused, waiting for someone to say something but there was silence except for the moaning that drifted up from beneath them. 'Right,' he said. 'We'll go. Bracca, you walk down here and I'll pick you up and carry you at the bottom.'

CHAPTER XXXI

Melvaig led the way down the cliff, taking them zigzagging down along little outcrops and buttresses, turning round often and lifting Bracca down the more difficult parts. He and Shuinn had let go of the goats which were making their way easily down ahead of them. They would have to take the risk of not being able to catch them at the bottom but it would have been impossible to hold on to them. Sometimes, having helped Bracca down, he waited to give Morven a hand. Shuinn seemed to be deliberately going slowly, hanging back so as not to be involved in a situation where he had to help her. What had happened back there, when he had gone to find water for the goats? No point thinking about it now, anyway.

The descent was not as difficult as it had appeared from the top because there were plenty of handholds, footholds and ledges to hang on to. In places the rock was crumbly but it was always possible to test it first. A number of times though, warily trying it to see if it would take his weight, Melvaig dislodged a piece of rock and heard it bounce and tumble down the cliff to land with a loud thump on the earth below. There would then be a flurry of frightened shrieks from the creatures and looking down he would see them scuttling around, crawling over one another in their efforts to get away.

Soon they were standing on a long ledge just one step away from the bottom. Melvaig had, with some difficulty, managed to guide them to this spot where there were fewer creatures than elsewhere. Indeed, there was even a path through them leading away from the base of the cliff, which would enable them to get to the ravine without going too close to any of the mutants. The goats were already down, standing on the area of clear space up against the cliff from which the path began. They had helped Melvaig find the best route down, always taking the easiest and safest way and coming down instinctively on this least populated of areas; Melvaig merely had to follow them as best he could. Now, though, the sight of the creatures so close had turned them rigid with fright. They stood stiffly, ears erect and noses twitching, with their hackles raised and their backs arched. For one dreadful moment Melvaig was afraid they might try to butt them, and so they might have had he not jumped down gently just at that moment and quickly caught their leads. Still they did not turn to him or even appear to notice his presence, preferring instead to continue their consumingly attentive vigil of these strange animals.

The stench down here on the ground was overpowering, its rancid flesh-based pungency driving out the dryer, sharper tang of the fumes from the cloud. Yet the cloud still cast its sickly yellow glow over everything, bathing them in its eerie light.

Melvaig turned and, holding both the goats in one hand, crooked his free arm round Bracca's waist and lifted him down on to the ground next to him. Then he helped Morven before waiting for Shuinn to complete his descent. The giant eventually clambered down beside them, disdainfully ignoring Melvaig's proffered hand.

Around them now the moaning tide of despair was

intense, pummelling at their senses and threatening to submerge their will. The creatures however gave no sign of being aware of the strangers' presence among them, continuing either to grovel in the mud or raise themselves up on their front flippers and, moving their necks back howl their demented arias to the sky. And so, handing one goat to Morven and the other to Shuinn, Melvaig hoisted Bracca up on to his shoulders. Then, his sword firmly gripped in his hand, he started to walk carefully along the path.

It was a long and agonizing journey, constantly fighting back the instinct to run and forever having to stop and redirect his route, threading his way around those of the creatures which suddenly slithered in front of him. From up on the cliff edge, Melvaig had felt only repulsion and a yawning sickness in his stomach. Now, seeing them close to, never less than one or two paces on either side of him, that revulsion was tinged with both fear and pity.

On his shoulders he could feel Bracca shivering with fear and with his free hand he patted the little boy's leg gently in an attempt to comfort him. The heavy weight of the Book moved constantly on his chest as if to remind of its presence, of the dreams it contained, and the prayers.

On they went, and their feet grew accustomed to the slippery feel of the mud they walked on; their eyes got used to the yellow gloom and their ears learned even to cope with the sounds let forth by the creatures. And then, at last, the dark gash of the ravine became visible ahead of them and Melvaig's heart pounded with the prospect of success. Suddenly, without warning, one of the goats pulled itself free of Shuinn's grip, raised itself up on its hind legs, and brought its head crashing down on the skull of one of the creatures. The sound of the goat's hooves drummed through the earth, sending shock waves out into the ground and immediately, as if at a word of command, the mutants froze grotesquely in whatever attitude they were holding at the time. The second goat had now pulled free and had joined the first in pummelling at the ground. The heads of the mutants slowly began to turn; their blank eyes were fixed in the direction of the travellers. There was a pause, a terrible stillness during which time the goats continued unabated and the only thought that came into Melvaig's mind was whether Shuinn had let them go deliberately to prove that he had been right after all and they should have been killed as he had said.

And then, with a swift ferocity that numbed Melvaig with shock, the creatures suddenly swarmed towards them, slithering and squirming over the ground in a headlong scrambling dash, the purpose of which was horrifyingly apparent. Their doleful mourning turned into an awful juddering cacophony of staccato shrieks of excitement and then suddenly the mutants had fallen upon them. He heard Morven's hysterical screams from behind him, and felt his legs clutched at by the cold clammy firmness of their flippers while, looking down with horror, he saw them open their mouths and clamp them upon him with awesome pressure. For an instant repulsion paralysed him as his legs tingled with a burning wet fire. But then, steadying Bracca on his shoulders and fighting back the urge to be sick, he hacked down blindly with his sword. He felt the blade connect and slice into something soft. One of the creatures cried out and released its hold on him, and as it fell back white froth erupted from the jagged gash in its neck. As it did so, Melvaig was nearly overwhelmed by the foul smell that poured from the wound. Again his sword crashed down, and again and again, until he had managed to free himself and fight his way back to Morven who was lashing out with her fists and kicking furiously with her feet to dislodge them. But they were stubborn and would not let go no matter how savagely she shook them, and their hideous white faces with their cloaked unseeing eyes remained attached to her calves and thighs. She felt as if they were drawing out the very marrow from her bones and her strength and spirit began to fade. But just as she found herself becoming submerged, she felt the pressure start to recede and was aware of Melvaig at her side and a whirling glimmer of light around him as he wielded his sword in great arcs wreaking destruction among the creatures. And now on her other side she saw the giant, and around him also were golden parabolas of power and she saw the mutants fall back in row upon row of flapping white suffering.

But even as one fell, more took its place, so that Melvaig and Shuinn had to redouble their efforts, swinging and cutting and hacking and thrusting in the terrible struggle to drive them back. The goats had already gone, charging and butting until the weight of the mutants who had fastened on to their backs and their legs became too much and they collapsed kicking out vainly until the darkness claimed them.

Eventually Melvaig felt his sword-arm grow weary and his back start to throb with pain as Bracca's weight pressed down upon his shoulders. His vision became blurred and his head swam so that he no longer saw where his sword fell. He fought now purely from instinct and if it had not been for Morven at his side and Bracca at his head he would have succumbed to the temptation to cease his futile struggle and surrender himself to oblivion.

Finally though, with an icy chill of despair, he found his body unable to respond to his commands. Surely, he cried soundlessly, surely it could not all have been in vain. To end like this? Surely not! And a great wave of anger and bitterness surged through him at what he saw as his betrayal. His sword flopped uselessly at his side, in a hand that could scarcely hold it. His legs tottered beneath the weight of his son and, turning his head to Morven, he saw her slowly sinking to the ground. Beyond her, Shuinn was also struggling to stay on his feet. He felt the wet, firm, clamp of jaws spread up the warm flesh of his legs and waited for the end.

And it was then that, through the dark mists that swirled around inside his head, he became aware of a change in the attitude of the throng. They had given up their relentless onward thrust, and as they ceased their chattering and squeaking a stillness descended. The coldness dropped away from Melvaig's legs and he no longer felt the awful pressure upon him. He raised his head slowly, disbelieving, wondering if this was death, and then he saw, as if in a dream, a man standing in front of him, bathed in the strange golden light of the cloud. Looking closer, struggling to focus his vision, he perceived that it was, after all, not quite a man, for where his arms should be, there protruded instead two thin white flippers. His back was bent almost double and his legs were thin slivers of bone wrapped in a layer of skin. Under one of his flippers, where it joined the shoulder, there rested the end of a long, dark polished wooden stick, shimmering and glinting in the light, and it was with this that he supported himself. From his enormous round head with its high curving forehead two huge eyes stared out piercingly. They were of the deepest blue, limpid pools of irridescence which mesmerized Melvaig as he gazed back into them. Lidless and hairless, the whole of the rest of his face seemed to have been arranged around them, the small thin nose and flabby toothless mouth. But it was the eyes that riveted Melvaig with their power and beauty; they belied the grotesque ugliness and fragility of the rest of his body. He felt a steady quiet strength flow out from them, a caress of gentle warmth and kindness that brought the sting of tears to his eyes, so poignant and yearning were the feelings they aroused in him. And yet in those eyes also was a depth of suffering that was beyond Melvaig's comprehension, as if all the pain of the world were encapsulated in those searing blue flames.

At either side of the man, the creatures drew back, not,

Melvaig sensed, because of fear but from deference, respect and awe. He hobbled painfully forward to within a pace of Morven and then he stopped and inclined his crippled body slightly forward, as if bowing to her. He looked long and hard at her as she lay on the ground still in the position she had assumed under attack from the mutants and then he raised his head and inspected the others. The creatures had now resumed their moaning and the sound of it in the background emphasized the silence among this bizarre little group. Melvaig felt as if he and the others were being examined, read, as if they were a book – the piercing blue eyes seeing inside them to the innermost depths of their souls. No one moved.

And then at last the stranger spoke, very slowly, in a voice that croaked and rasped with age. Melvaig felt his whole body tremble with a shiver of anticipation as if he were in the presence of something truly awesome. The words hung in the hot putrid air, but they were meaningless to Melvaig, in a language he did not know. He shook his head and said, in a tone that shook with nervous excitement, 'We do not understand.'

At this the stranger's mouth contorted into what Melvaig guessed was a smile and he spoke again in the same voice: heavy, ponderous and grating with the effort of drawing breath.

'It has been a long time,' he said, in their own tongue, 'since I heard the speech of those from Ruann. I trust I can still make myself understood. I am Snaarquoll and these are my people, the Drenngg. I am sorry you were treated so badly by them. Do not fear now; they will bother you no more. The warmth of your flesh, your blood. It was more than they could stand.' He paused and they heard the breath rattle in his chest. Then he drew himself up and again his face seemed to smile.

'It is indeed good to see the like of you again. We do not get many who pass our way. Who can blame them! We are not, I imagine, pleasant. We must present a frightening visage to your sort. And for those who do venture among us . . . look what happened to you. You will pay us no return visits! What are your names? Tell me your names. Let me hear you.'

Melvaig told the old man who they were, while the voice of Snaarquoll resounded through his head as a bizarre accompaniment to his own thoughts and words. The old man looked at each of them and then finally at Bracca and when he spoke again there was a crack in his voice, as if he were fighting to hold back his emotions. Looking at him, Melvaig was shocked to see a large crystal tear ooze out of the corner of his eye, reflecting blue as it did so, before it trickled down the ashen pallor of his cheek. He inclined his body forward gazing in rapture at Bracca.

'Your little boy,' he said, intoning the words slowly and deliberately to himself as if they were some kind of magic spell. And then he repeated them over and over again in an incantation of wonder as Bracca looked back at him, an uncertain half-smile on his face at first but soon gaining in confidence until he was grinning broadly at the old man and, turning to Melvaig and clutching his hand said, 'What a funny-looking old man.' He stopped then and looked at Snaarquoll. 'But you're kind. I like you.'

The old man looked up and spoke again, half to himself and half to the others. 'Perfect,' he said in a tone of reverence and awe. 'He is immaculate, every limb – every part of him.' And then he turned to Melvaig. 'You cannot know what this means to me. The sight of him – I had long ago given up all prayers of setting eyes on such a child.' He paused. 'As you see we are not, now, as you. But it was not always so. Before the War we were normal, like you. We lived by the sea; we fished for our existence. We were not all killed. Some survived and they tried to carry on. But there was something in the air, the fish we ate, the water we drank – I don't know what, but something – and gradually, slowly, we became like this, as we are now, grovelling in the dirt for our subsistence, unable to see, our hearts so sick with pain that we can only relieve our torment by uttering the lament you hear. Speechless, devoid of all emotion save bitterness, unable to survive except on this small patch of earth which for some reason affords a little relief to the constant hurt of our bodies. Immobile, except to slither around here like worms.'

He looked at Melvaig and the blue of his eyes was clouded.

'But you . . .'

It was Morven who had spoken, hesitating even as she started, unable to find the words to voice the questions that whirled around in her head. He turned to her.

'Why am I able to speak, to see, to stand? Why am I not like them? I do not know. The others, the ones who survived, all died soon after. Their children were born, only slightly disfigured at first and then, as each generation succeeded the one before, they got worse. And they died. But I, who survived the War, I did not die. I watched as the generations came and went, as their humanity gradually disappeared, and still I lived. Perhaps it is something in me from Before the War. I have always been like this – as you see me now – younger, but my limbs have always been like this. Yet surely now I am near the end. May I at least be granted release from all this. And from the burden of my knowledge. It is more than I can bear.'

His voice trailed off into a low mumble of half-spoken mutterings and the travellers stared at him in disbelief. From Before the War; he knew the world Before the War! It was beyond their comprehension, more than their minds could grasp. This old man, this frail, gaunt, bizarre creature before them had lived in the world of the Book; he had known blue sky, the green of the trees and the fields full of animals, the power and majesty of the sea.

Melvaig burned with curiosity for all this man's knowledge and yet he felt numb, unable to ask him anything, afraid that what he would learn would be too much for him. The story of that world and its destruction, how could he ever live with that? No, better that he find what remained of it, as he believed. And as he was thinking all this, the ancient voice of Snaarquoll broke in upon his thoughts.

'But you,' he said. 'Why are you here? What can your purpose be that you would come among us? We do not see many strangers.'

The clear blue eyes were fixed upon Melvaig and without a thought he started to tell the story. It was muddled at first and he was hesitant in the telling but Snaarquoll listened gravely and silently, nodding his head at strategic moments to indicate understanding or concern or sympathy. Soon Melvaig warmed to his tale and his language began to flow as he became caught up in it, reliving and describing vividly all those moments since the days of Ruann. Not once, however, did he mention the Book. The omission was not deliberate, rather that its presence was so taken for granted by him as to render mention of it superfluous. Only at the end did he realize that he had not explained the purpose of their journey to the Dammfenn. It was then that he related how he had found the Book and how, when Arkron had read it to him, he knew he had discovered his destiny. He also described his faith in what the Book set out and his determination to rediscover its world. Now, he continued, he knew that it was the hand of Ashgaroth that led him along his way. He paused then, aware that he might have been saying too much; carried away by the intoxication of his beliefs, he had begun to ramble.

He looked then at Snaarquoll and the old man's eyes were still a calm and liquid blue but his face seemed somehow transformed as if some inner light had arisen in his spirit and was shining out from him.

'There were rumours,' he said, 'of such a Book. I remember the older ones talking about it After the War. I had been too young to read it Before the War and after . . . there were no books around that I can remember. They had all been destroyed. And no one cared; it was the last thing on our minds. But I can hear some of them now talking about this Book. It passed; the old ones died, and we forgot such matters but the way they spoke of it – they had this faith too, that you have – and they were determined to keep it alive within them. And I never forgot the story even though, with time, it faded. Parts of it kept coming back to me. You have this Book?' he said. 'And you are searching for its world?'

'We are,' replied Melvaig. 'The map that Arkron gave us led us here, to you, and thence across the sea. He believed that this was the way.' He fumbled under his jerkin and brought the Book out. 'Here, this is it.' And he walked across to Snaarquoll's side and began turning the pages before his eyes, reminding him of the story, watching his face light up as he recognized the images in his mind in the pictures that Melvaig held in front of him.

Finally it was over; the story was ended. Time had passed without knowing and looking round, Melvaig saw to his surprise that they were all sitting down on the muddy earth. The sky above them had grown heavy with the gold of late afternoon and to his astonishment he saw, as if in a dream, an amphitheatre of the pallid heavy-lidded faces of the creatures surrounding them. Their moaning had stopped and they were still, gazing in the direction of Melvaig as if lulled by his voice and the magic of the story into some strange mystical trance. Maybe it was just that they were so attuned to Snaarquoll that they felt and responded to the old man's feelings, his delight and his rekindled yearnings, his joy and aching sadness at hearing the tale again and seeing the Book with its poignant reminders of the world as it had been and of the dark evil presence in man that had destroyed it.

A breathless silence, delicate as crystal, hung over them all, the creatures, the travellers and Snaarquoll as the last echoes of the story shimmered in their minds.

It was the old man who stirred first and broke the spell. Lifting his head up to look into Melvaig's face and leaning forward slightly, he said very slowly and in a voice so intense that it pained Melvaig to hear it, 'You will find it. You must find it. For all of us. All who suffer as we do, all who have ever suffered. For them.' He paused before continuing, his tone now flushed and tremulous with urgency and excitement.

'You believe that what you seek lies beyond the seas. Our village, what is now left of it, is just beyond the Dammfenn. There you will find boats, in the old harbour. You will need them to cross the ocean. What they are like now I could not think. You will have to use your judgment and ask Ashgaroth for a wind to take you in the right direction, more I . . .'

He broke off abruptly as, through the air, came the whinnying of horses and the cries of voices raised in triumph. Melvaig looked up, his heart pounding in dreadful anticipation of what he knew he would see. On the brow of the ridge above them, in exactly the same spot from which he and the others had looked down such a short time before, was a row of mounted riders. The dull metal of their helmets reflected gold in the yellow sulphurous light from the cloud, and the reds and greens and blacks and purples of their costumes took on a rich, verdant glow. They were gesticulating wildly and pointing downwards in the direction of the travellers, leaving Melvaig in no doubt but that they had been seen. They seemed to be shouting and arguing among themselves. Now that their quarry had finally been spotted and was within their grasp, the thought of the limitless rewards that capture would bring had already nurtured the seeds of greed and selfishness in each one of them, bringing in their wake division and rancour.

'The warriors of Xtlan,' Snaarquoll said. He paused and then went on. 'I am sorry; we spoke for too long. You should have gone. You did not tell me they were so close. Go now! Our presence will frighten them off until their greed overcomes their revulsion. When they come through us we will try and hold them back, delay them for a while, though I do not know how successful we can be. We will do all we can; of that you may be certain. More, I cannot say. Now go!'

Melvaig put the Book away and started to walk quickly away from Snaarquoll with the others following close behind. Suddenly he stopped and, turning back, took a last look at the strange old man. He was gazing after them, his head held awkwardly on his shoulders as if he were in pain. Still though, even from this distance, the brilliant blue of his eyes seemed to draw Melvaig in towards them to take cover in the protection of their deep, all-seeing wisdom and lose himself in their omniscience. He called out softly,

'Is there anything you . . . we can do . . . ?'

He faltered over the words, but Snaarquoll replied, his voice strong and clear,

'Nothing . . . except succeed,' and then he turned away and began addressing his people in their own language. In front of Melvaig, the circle of creatures shuffled back and separated to make a path through which he led the others. As he passed close to them, Melvaig half-expected to feel that awful cold pressure on his leg again, as when they had been attacked by them before. But this time there was nothing; they simply turned their heads slightly as the travellers walked through, almost as if they were bowing, and then finally when Shuinn, who was last, had gone past they closed their ranks and began shuffling up towards Snaarquoll, twittering excitedly in their peculiar high-pitched squeaks.

CHAPTER XXXII

Soon they were at the ravine. Melvaig led the way down, helping Bracca and Morven, while Shuinn followed after, a little way behind, his face still bereft of emotion – a mask of indifference. As they climbed down the steep incline, the sounds of the creatures behind them were blocked out and they descended into an eerie, unreal stillness. At the bottom they clambered over the rocks, scratching themselves often against sharp splinters of stone. To add to their difficulties it was so dark down here that they frequently stumbled and fell. Nothing grew, the stone was dry and abrasive. The air was foul and there was a cold chill that seeped through their clothes and wrapped itself around them.

They reached the far side and began climbing up the slope. The bank here was full of loose shingle and they kept sliding back down, unleashing clouds of heavy clinging dust which got in their eyes and throats and made them sting. Melvaig had to push Bracca up ahead of him and then, when the little boy was at the top he went back down and helped Morven, hauling himself up on the few boulders that were embedded firmly enough and pulling her after him. Shuinn followed and soon they were standing facing this last part of the Dammfenn. They could hear the sound of it all around them, hissing and retching and groaning as if it was tearing itself apart in agony. It was night now; the sun had gone down and all should have been darkness, and yet everywhere was bathed in a dull crimson glow from the tongues of flame that licked their way out of the earth on jets of escaping gas. The fires flickered all about them, spitting and crackling and throwing out huge red shadows which leaped and danced on the earth like manic beasts cavorting in some grotesque orgiastic ritual. As they stood, mesmerized, the ground suddenly broke open near them and unleashed a spume of gas and flame. Melvaig heard Bracca's little scream of fear and felt the boy clutch him tightly round the waist, burying his face against his leg. He put his arm down and ran his fingers through the boy's hair.

'It's all right,' he murmured. 'All right. Don't worry. It'll soon be over. Here, get on my shoulders.'

He bent down and hoisted Bracca on to his shoulders. Then, turning to Morven and Shuinn, he set off across the slimy surface of the earth towards the distant horizon. Behind them, receding into the distance as they walked further away, they heard the sound of the mutants. Melvaig looked round but could see very little in the red-tinged gloom. Had Xtlan's riders descended amongst them yet? He guessed not; if they had, he was sure there would have been a commotion. Perhaps they were waiting until morning, afraid to venture amongst the creatures in the darkness. But when they did, how long could Snaarquoll and his people hold them back? They must get as far as they could before daylight.

They trudged on, weary now and hungry. Often Melvaig had to hang on to Bracca to stop him falling as he fell asleep. The earth was difficult to walk on and they kept sliding on the yellow ooze that trickled out all around them. Once Morven fell and, putting her hand out to save herself, found it covered in the stuff. It stung terribly. She wiped the slime off on her clothes and the pain grew less but she became so wary, afraid of slipping again, that Melvaig had to keep stopping and waiting for her. Shuinn still hung back, slowing down when she slowed down.

Melvaig picked his way carefully, keeping close enough to the columns of flame to see where they were walking in the darkness and yet not too near for fear of being sprayed with the burning gas. The heat was intense and the sweat ran in rivers down their faces. When Melvaig turned round occasionally to see where the others were, he caught glimpses of Morven's face, drained and worn with exhaustion, splashed in the red reflection of the flames so that it looked as if she herself was on fire. When she realized he was looking at her she quickly composed herself, smiled, and assumed a mask of dogged, stoical, cheerfulness again. But it was too late; the damage had been done and Melvaig's heart ached with sorrow at her pain.

The land was now littered with small hollows. Melvaig led the others up and down the sides of them, trying to avoid the worst of the ooze but found nevertheless that it clung to their feet and ankles as if unwilling to let them go. Sometimes they would come across the stump of what had once been a tree and in his fatigue Melvaig imagined that it was a person or a creature of some sort and he would stop and wait until a nearby spurt of flame illuminated it and revealed its true identity. Then, as he passed it, he would try and imagine it as it had once been, tall and majestic. Had this, then, been a forest, bursting with life and abundance? The thought was so poignant it was almost unbearable.

And then it began to rain, huge fat droplets which stung their faces and their hands. Melvaig could see the skin on his hands turn purple where the drops had landed. They all stopped and he put Bracca down.

'Cover your hands and face,' he called to Morven and then, tearing strips of skin from the bottom of his jerkin, he bound both Bracca's hands and tied lengths loosely round his head, leaving only a space for the eyes. The little boy was whimpering in fright.

'It hurts,' he cried. 'It hurts,' as the milky drops fell on him.

Soon they were on their way again, heads down to protect their eyes, scrambling up and down the pits and hollows made even more slippery by the rain. He could hear hisses and crackles all round him as the water met the geysers of flame, and the red reflection of the fires ran like blood in the streams of water on the ground, eddying and swirling around his feet.

On and on they walked and the only thought in any of their minds was 'How far? How far?' When would they get to the end of this accursed place? Melvaig felt the cold chill of despair encircle his heart; his legs were numb; he could not feel his neck and his back throbbed and ached as if it was about to break. If only Shuinn would offer to carry Bracca for a while. He stopped and looked around. There was the familiar figure of the giant, his friend, striding doggedly along after Morven. Why could he not ask Shuinn after all they had come through together? And yet he could not; not the way he was now, with that awful cold aloofness, the distance that now lay between them.

He turned back and made his way, lurching and staggering, up the side of another hollow. And then, when he got to the top he saw just over the rise of the next slope, a black expanse of nothingness, stretching away into the distance as far as he could see. Out of it, on the very edge of the horizon, there rose a great flaming arc of fire which filled the sky with livid gashes of orange and crimson, red and yellow and green and purple.

At last they had reached the sea! Just over that next rise and there surely would be Snaarquoll's village. But Melvaig was filled with disquiet, and a sense of foreboding made his spine tingle, for it was not how he had imagined it from the

Book. He hurried forward until he reached the next ridge with Morven and Shuinn at his side and then he stopped and looked down. Below them, dropping gently away to the edge of the sea, lay a wide expanse of black ooze which eventually met a scattering of walls that had once been Snaarquoll's village. The sea itself lay like a stone, still and unyielding, without a flicker of movement or life in its great stagnant depths. The first glimmers of daylight were now appearing in the sky and they showed up huge oily blue streaks on the stillness of its flat surface. Some way from the shore, the blazing arc rose up in its great parabola of flame and drew a curtain of fire across the blackness while, in between, hundreds of little fires flickered and licked their way across the surface. And drifting up from the shoreline came a most terrible stench, dripping with the sickly sweet pungency of dead and rotting flesh, so that a flood of nausea swept through them and Morven retched violently.

Must they cross this? How could it be possible that the world of Nab, Beth and the others lay beyond that? Melvaig felt the iron strength of his faith wither beneath the onslaught to his senses from the picture below, for stupidly he had imagined that the sea would be as he had held it in his mind's eye, from the words that Arkron had read to him in the desert of Molobb. Now, as he peered through the sheets of rain in the silvery morning light, his heart sank in despair. A spot of rain fell on to the top of his cheekbone and ran down between his skin and the strip from his jerkin leaving a trail of inflammation as it went. How long he stood there with the others, lost in a trance of misery, Melvaig did not know. What finally brought him back was the voice of Bracca, coming to him through a claustrophobic veil of despair.

'Come on, it's not far now. We'll soon be there,' he said and his voice was bright and cheerful and danced with hope. As the little boy spoke Melvaig saw a bright silver light appear high in the sky, above and beyond the fiery arc. As it hung there, its glow began to unfreeze the icy prison of hopelessness around his soul as the voice of Ashgaroth seemed to talk to him, echoing Bracca's words, 'Not far now; you'll soon be there.'

He looked down at his son. Bracca's head was raised and he was staring up at the sky with a sparkle deep in his eyes. When he realized that Melvaig was looking at him he turned and their eyes met and between them there passed a wave of understanding that left Melvaig breathless with excitement. It was as if, by some miracle, Bracca knew everything: about the Book and Nab and Brock, Ashgaroth and Dréagg and the War. He knew about their search for the last enclave of Ashgaroth in the hope of finding some part of the old world that remained. He knew all this without being told, because of the part that he was to play in the unfolding of destiny. The story of the Book was engrained in him, as much a part of him as his blood, for the spirit of Ashgaroth was within him.

Melvaig's head reeled as he tried to absorb all of this and to comprehend its significance. He bent down and, very gently, put both his arms round the little boy, holding him as if for the last time and then, quietly, with tears stinging his eyes, he spoke.

'Yes, little man,' he said. 'You're right. It's not far now.'

Then he stood up and turning to Morven and Shuinn he called out to them.

'Come on,' he said, and his voice was strong and powerful.

It was then that they all heard the uproar behind them from the direction of the Dammfenn. Melvaig knew what it was; Xtlan's warriors had waited until the first light of morning and were now attempting to cut their way through Snaarquoll's people. A great chorus of wailing and shouting drifted through the rain and Melvaig's heart bled for the creatures as Snaarquoll's words came into his head.

'You must find it,' he had said. 'For all who have suffered.'

He lifted Bracca back on to his shoulders and, glancing round to make sure that Morven was at his side, he set off down the slope as fast as he could, his head bowed against the rain and his feet slapping on the mud.

They had not gone far when the rain stopped, only to be replaced by a great bank of fine drizzly mist that swept in off the sea. It enveloped them in a damp embrace that seemed to penetrate through to their bones. Without a thought in his head except reaching the sea Melvaig hurried forward, hanging on to Bracca's legs to keep him steady. On and on he went with the flaming arc ahead turning the mist before his eyes into shifting patterns of colour.

Suddenly a chill of disquiet rippled through him. At first he refused to let it break into his concentration, refused to let it interrupt the rhythm of his run and so he did not allow himself to think of the reason for it. But it persisted until it broke through the barrier of his defences and he realized what it was. Morven! Where was she? He stopped and turned. The mist swirled and billowed in a dense impenetrable wall. He could see nothing. 'Morven,' he called, again and again, and each time the only answer was the rushing hiss of the mist. A ball of panic formed in his bowels and his legs became weak and started to tremble. He put Bracca down. 'Stay here,' he said, 'and don't move.'

'Why? Where's Morven?'

'I don't know. She must be back there somewhere. I'm just going to find her.'

'Don't leave me.'

'You'll be all right.'

'I'm frightened. Please . . .' and he began to whimper.

'All right, all right! Here, get on my shoulders again'; and he lifted him up.

'Where's Shuinn?' said Bracca. 'He isn't here either.'

'No, no, you're right. I hadn't realized. She'll be safe then. He'll be looking after her. She must have fallen,

416

slipped and fallen and hurt her ankle or something. Come on; we'll soon find her. You call as well.'

And so they turned back and began wandering through the mist, calling her name in turn. They were confident at first; it could not be long before they found her and anyway Shuinn was with her. But as time went on and the search proved fruitless, the feeling of panic returned and a note of desperation entered Melvaig's voice as he shouted her name. They were almost back now to the top of the slope; they would have to start going from side to side. Why was she not answering? Perhaps Xtlan's men had fought their way through Snaarquoll's people already and had captured both Shuinn and her. He stopped and listened. No, he could still hear the sounds of battle from the Dammfenn. He found himself calling on Ashgaroth to help him; to keep her safe, and he began to shout louder and louder, heedless of whether they might be heard by Xtlan's warriors or not, uncontrolled now, stumbling blindly through the mist with tears of frustration and anguish boiling behind his eyes. Bracca was crying loudly, whimpering and juddering on his shoulders.

Then Melvaig stopped. He had heard a sound, not too far away. A cry, short and stifled but a definite cry. He called and again, as if in answer, he heard the sound. His heart leaped with relief and joy and he lurched forward in the direction from which it had come.

'Morven. Where are you? I'm coming.'

And then, through the swirling mist, he saw them; Morven and Shuinn locked together on the ground. His heart shrank in horror and disbelief; what were they doing? Frantically he looked for other explanations but as his eyes took in the picture before him, the methodical pumping rhythm of Shuinn's body, Morven's torn skirt lying about her like a ragged fan and the position of her legs, held apart by the giant's huge hands, the ghastly truth came down upon him and he went dizzy with the force of the rage that

417

welled up inside himself. Hatred and pain surrounded him like a wall, locking him in so that he was temporarily paralysed. Shuinn was lying on top, facing away from him and was too near the apex of his passion to be aware of Melvaig's presence. Morven, though, had seen him. She threshed around wildly under the giant but was unable to disengage herself from his enormous bulk. Her eyes spoke worlds to him, beseeching him to believe her unwillingness and pleading with him to stop Shuinn. In fact, when the giant had first leaped upon her she had thought, like before, that it would be better to succumb easily and quietly and pray that it would be over quickly before Melvaig realized. He had found her too soon. Would he believe her now, trust and forgive her, and agree with the reasons for her submission?

And now Melvaig began to wonder about Morven. How often before? Was she enjoying it? How hard had she tried to resist? He saw her with the Hurll, with all the guards at the Blaggvald, in the Gravenndra, visions of frenzied copulation pulsed through his mind and he felt sick with anguish and jealousy and doubt.

But then the answer came from within himself. It was clear and pure and strong and he was ashamed of himself for losing his faith in her.

'What's Shuinn doing to Morven?' Bracca cried out, and the terrified howl of the boy's words pierced through the giant's lust-befuddled consciousness. Melvaig saw him stop still and then, before he could move, Shuinn had rolled off Morven, drawn his knife and was holding it against her neck, pinioning her with his other arm. He lay there, still flushed and panting with excitement and glared at Melvaig. In his eyes there burned a strange light and his pupils were dilated as if there was nothing behind them, no soul, no spirit and no mind. Melvaig looked and could not see his friend.

'Come any nearer and I'll kill her,' he rasped in a voice so cold and harsh Melvaig did not recognize it. Morven lay still, the whiteness of her body bejewelled in the droplets of mist which glistened in the pale light from the sky.

'Not the first time I've had her,' he said and his voice was vile with rancour. 'She loves it. See the way she squirms beneath my fingers. Look at her! You like what you see? Well, you aren't the only one. You should have been more generous with your woman, shared her. You can't keep her all to yourself. Makes no difference anyway; think how many times she's been enjoyed; one more won't matter.'

He stopped and his face was contorted into a triumphant leer.

'Well,' he went on. 'What have you got to say for yourself, my fine friend. Melvaig, the marvellous Melvaig – who found a Book and thinks he's a king. Everyone thinks he's wonderful, Arkron and Snaarquoll; he's going to save the world! Ha! Without old Shuinn you'd be nothing, nowhere. You'd never have survived Molobb, let alone the Gurrtslagg. You'd be long dead and forgotten. But oh, no! Old faithful Shuinn pulled you through. Always been the same; it was the same with Gebb and Nekdog. "A little bit slow," they all think. "Not all that quick-witted, but he'll do." Well, you'll see! You'll all see! It was all right, wasn't it, until we found your precious Morven again and your darling little son. All right until then. Oh yes. I'd do fine to help you along. But once you had them . . . No time for me then. It was Morven this and Morven that. What do you think, Morven? Is Morven all right? Well, it doesn't matter now. It'll soon . . .'

'Stop!' Melvaig fought to control the fury that seethed through his body. 'It's not . . . You know that's not right. None of it. You and I, we were so close. I love you; you must know that. But I never felt better than you – that never came into it. If you think I thought that then I'm sorry. I know that if it were not for you, I'd never have survived, never have found Morven and Bracca. But surely it's not thanks you want; we came this far for ourselves as well as each other. To find the world of Ashgaroth. You believed in it! And if I shut you out when I found Morven and Bracca then I'm sorry, I tried not to. I thought you would understand. But I could not share Morven unless she gave herself to you of her own free will. Only then. How could I make her love you as she loves me? It is to get away from ideas such as that that we have fought.'

He stopped; his words seemed futile. How could he explain; what could he say? He could see from Shuinn's eyes, hard and blank, that he was having no effect. And all the while, as if to torture Melvaig further, to taunt and goad him, he fondled Morven, pulling and squeezing with his free hand as she winced in pain.

'Fine words, my clever Melvaig. You try and sweet-talk me? It will do no good. Your world, your dream, may exist. Out there somewhere beyond that stinking sea, through that wall of flame. But it may not. It probably doesn't. What then? But I've got you now, and the Book. Think of the rewards Xtlan will grant me for such a prize. I shall be higher than any man, granted positions of honour and power, festooned with the finest of clothes, offered the choicest food and drink and have the pick of the finest girls in the best Gravenndra. Surely you understand the reasons for my action?'

Melvaig was stunned with horror.

'You mean to keep us . . . to hand us over?' he said, and his tongue felt thick in his mouth as he formed the words.

'Certainly I do. We shall wait here until his warriors arrive.'

'They will kill you. Do you think they will share their rewards with you?'

Shuinn laughed.

'You see,' he said. 'You take me for a fool. It is as I said. No, they will not, for I shall bury the Book here somewhere, where only I shall know its location. I also know its story which you, my honourable friend, will not divulge. I shall tell Xtlan and no one else. He will respect that. He may then kill me but I doubt it; I am too valuable alive – the knowledge I have is too useful to be wasted by destroying me and I shall take great care not to let it all go at once. Anyway . . .' and his manner changed from one of patronizing arrogance to a curt and businesslike briskness, 'it is a risk I would rather take than remain with you, where I am not wanted, searching for your stupid dream.'

Melvaig could not believe what was happening. Shuinn, his friend, who had been through so much with him, who had believed even as he, Melvaig, believed; who had helped him and looked after him and guided him; who meant more to him than anyone except Morven and Bracca. He must be dreaming! And then, as his mind raged in turmoil, the truth gradually came to him. This was not Shuinn who was speaking. His friend had been taken over by Dréagg. The words, the voice, the eyes – all were different. Only the body remained the same; the rest of him had gone. And Melvaig wept bitterly inside for the death of his friend but rejoiced that the figure of evil in front of him was not Shuinn and that the memory of the giant could remain untarnished.

Suddenly a piercing wail shattered the mist. It was Bracca, standing forgotten, a little to one side of them, shocked and confused until now, but who had just been struck with an intuitive flash of understanding and with it a seizure of blind terror.

'No,' he shrieked, and for an instant Shuinn's attention was caught by the boy. Morven felt his grip relax slightly and with all the energy she could muster she tore herself away from him and found herself rolling in the mud a few paces away. At the same moment Melvaig pulled his sword from its sheath and leaped forward so that his foot landed on Shuinn's knife wrist and the point of his sword was pressing against the giant's heart.

'Stay Shuinn, stay,' he said, his voice thick and cracked with emotion. 'I do not want to kill you.'

But the giant seized Melvaig's ankle with his free hand and jerking it savagely sideways pulled Melvaig over. As he fell he let go of the sword which splattered tantalizingly out of reach a few paces away. Frantically he pushed his hand under his jerkin and drew out his knife and then the giant fell upon him, crushing Melvaig beneath his enormous bulk so that he felt the breath go out of him and a dizzying claustrophobic blackness engulf him. Desperately he pulled himself out from under Shuinn's bulk and put his free hand up to grab the giant's knife hand at the same time as his friend pinioned his own knife wrist against the ground.

And so they fought, these two friends, rolling over and over in the foul mud; the strength and weight of the giant pitted against the speed, skill and agility of Melvaig. And the hatred of each for the other was so much greater because of their past love that it boiled and festered in their throats and their eyes and their mouths. The silver light of Ashgaroth burned with a pure silver flame in Melvaig's spirit and many times he would have succumbed without it. And in Shuinn was the black spirit of Dréagg so that he fought with evil cunning.

And so it was that, because there is compassion in goodness, whenever Melvaig felt himself on the ascendant with his knife tip poised to plunge into his adversary's body, then he would hold back, unable to pursue his advantage and Shuinn would seize the opportunity to escape from his perilous position and take the upper hand once more. Time and again Shuinn's knife plunged down and only by desperate strength and the hand of Ashgaroth did Melvaig avoid death by a hair's breadth. He would feel the whisper of the wind as the blade grazed his face or hear the rending of leather as his garment was cut. Then the warmth of the blood as it oozed from a gash on his cheek or pulsed from a wound in his arm.

As the terrible fight wore on he grew weaker and his resolve started to ebb as his mind played tricks on him. He imagined the whole thing as a dream; saw Shuinn's face contort into grotesque caricatures of his friend's features – eyes that danced and leaped with fire; huge blubbery lips pulled into a sneering smile and a great hooked nose that wavered before his gaze like a sword. And so it was that finally, through the hazy clouds of confusion that swept through his mind and the waves of pain that raked over his body the realization came to him that he was losing the fight. He had come to the end; he could do no more. His limbs would not respond to the commands he sent them and a great leaden weariness descended upon him. Now Shuinn was on top of him, pinning him down, sitting on his chest with his knees trapping Melvaig's arms against the ground. Then he saw the giant's knife raised high in the air and felt a welcome rush of peace as he resigned himself to his fate. In front of his eyes there raced a series of images, scenes from the past. Ruann, Jarrah, Arkron, Bendro who had carried him over the plains of Molobb, Shennsah – the old woman he had left behind in what had once been his home. Pictures of the Gurrtslagg flashed before him – Teggrogg, Dhiabedd the traitor and Burgunn the leader of the Hurll: in the Gravenndra – the gentle Tennga, the loathsome figure of the Marll. And then the chill blackness of the Blaggvald and the terrible sound of the voice of Xtlan.

He prayed to Ashgaroth that the giant had changed his mind; that he would kill him rather than take him captive, and in his weariness he forgot about Morven and Bracca. But then he saw her, standing above him. Was it his imagination – a last picture of her that he would carry with him into oblivion? He saw the sword in her hands lifted high into the air, heard the crack as the flat of the blade fell on Shuinn's skull and felt the pressure on his knees and arms relax as the giant crumpled over and fell on to the earth, a low groan coming from him. Then, as if to confirm her reality, he heard her voice through the dazed turmoil in his head.

'I had to wait. I couldn't risk hitting you. Are you all right? Oh Melvaig, I thought . . .' Her voice, faint and blurred as if from a great distance away, tailed off as her face swam into his vision. 'Come,' she went on. 'Let me help you up.'

He felt her arm round his waist and Bracca pulling him by his wrist as he struggled to stand up, fighting against the faintness and nausea that threatened to engulf him.

'I . . .' he said, his voice faltering and strange. 'I'm all right. Could you just, hold me up . . . for a while.'

As he stood there, propped up by Morven and Bracca, the mists in his head slowly began to clear. Again, the great arc of fire in the sky seemed to beckon him on, to draw him towards it, and he heard himself saying, 'Not far now; soon be there,' over and over, repeating the phrases again and again like some magical chant until at last his vision cleared, the pains in his body receded into a dull, throbbing ache and he felt able to walk by himself.

'Come on then, let's go quickly, before Xtlan's men get here.'

Morven gave him his sword back and he replaced it in its sheath. The wound in his side was still bleeding but looking down at it he saw that Morven had tied a strip from her dress round it and the flow of blood had begun to slow down. He put his hand up to the cut in his cheek and the blood there seemed to be thickening already. Good. They must go now. And then, as if he had been kicked suddenly in the stomach, he remembered Shuinn. Was he dead? Had Morven killed him?

He walked the few paces to where the giant lay, crumpled in a heap. Bending down slowly so as not to make himself dizzy, he examined his friend's skull. There was no blood, no cut – only an enormous lump which protruded through his long, lank reddish hair. He put his head against the giant's chest. He was alive; still breathing. And Melvaig felt a curious mixture of elation and apprehension go through him. What was he going to do? He heard Morven, standing next to him, say urgently, 'Come on, hurry!'

And then he knew that he could not leave his friend. Lying there, silent, unconscious, his face still and peaceful, Melvaig could only remember the old Shuinn, Shuinn as he had been. And already he found it impossible to see him as he had been in these recent days.

'We must take Shuinn with us,' he said, and Morven's face froze in astonishment.

'He was going to hand you over to Xtlan,' she said, her voice strained and tense. 'We cannot carry him; he is too heavy. What will happen when he recovers? No, Melvaig, surely not. Leave him, please.'

But her pleading was in vain.

'No,' he said. 'I'm sorry. Some day, I'll try to explain. You take one arm; I'll take the other. We can drag him. Bracca, you walk in front – where we can see you.'

Reluctantly Morven did as Melvaig asked her and together they began to pull the limp body of the giant down through the slimy ooze towards the sea. They made slow progress; Shuinn was heavy and his huge frame seemed to pull against them as the mud clung to it. His head lolled from side to side and his heels left two lines in the centre of the shallow ditch left by his body. Pull, stop – pull, stop. The rhythm repeated itself over and over until Morven's arms grew numb and Melvaig, dizzy and weak before he started, was hardly able to stand. The dank, heavy mist covered their garments with a fine layer of moisture in which the tiny droplets shimmered and sparkled as the light from the great arc of fire caught it. Ahead of them walked Bracca, his head held high, proud to be leading his mother and father down towards the sea.

Every so often he would stop and turn round, making sure they were still there and waiting for them to catch up with him. When they were together again, off he would go, striding purposefully over the mud. Melvaig watched him and sensed with satisfaction the feelings that were going through his son, smiling inwardly at the recollection of them in himself at Bracca's age. The first awareness of responsibility, when he had been allowed to look after one of the goats in Ruann . . . once again images of the past came before his mind's eye. He saw the face of Jarrah; looked once again into the kindly eyes that sparkled with the secret knowledge, that he was his, Melvaig's, father. He heard Jarrah's voice, warm and reassuring, painting a picture of the world Before the War even as the descriptions had been handed down to him: stories of the animals and the birds, the rivers and the forests and the oceans. And he felt again the thrill that had coursed through his veins as the old man had revealed to him the existence of the Book that even now hung around his neck. And, lastly, he remembered the old man's final request to him, as he had lain dying in Melvaig's arms, and the note of desperate urgency came across to him still, after all this time. 'You must look after the Book,' he had said. 'Follow it. It's yours now. Promise me.'

Well, he had done as his father had asked. He could have done no more, and soon they would know whether all the hopes and the prayers and the dreams would be answered. For an instant then, Melvaig had the feeling that Jarrah was at his side, walking next to him down the muddy bank towards the oily black vision in front. And then in his confused brain, the presence at his side altered, the detail blurred, and instead of Jarrah there was Arkron, reciting to him again the words from the Book as the old man had first done as they crossed the desert of Molobb. The words came to him clearly and he felt himself being transported again into that magical other world, inhabited by Nab and

Beth and their animal friends; a world of changing seasons, from the icy grip of winter and the silver sparkle of the snow, through the delicate greens of spring and summer to the golden-browns of autumn. He saw himself wandering through the woods or over the fields, sitting down by the river or lying on his back watching the blue sky through a latticed roof of leaves.

He heard a voice calling him as if from a long way off. At first he ignored it, supposing it to be a part of his visions, but it persisted until, with a jolt, he realized it was Morven. Reluctantly, grudgingly, he tore himself away from the security of his imaginings and forced himself to concentrate on her, on what she was saying, and on the present. He looked around him. They had stopped in the middle of Snaarquoll's village. He could not even remember coming into it! There were buildings all around, old, crumbling and falling down and yet there was an atmosphere about the place which warmed the spirits of the travellers. It was almost as if the houses were still occupied – the people inside loving, caring and warm. The sound of their laughter and the joyful mosaic of their voices seemed to ring out in the air and hang in the spaces between the buildings, echoing down the narrow winding street that meandered along in front of them until it reached the old harbour. And then, before Melvaig's eyes, there flashed an image of Snaarquoll's people as he had left them, their white bodies floundering in the mud and their terrible wailing cries leaking from the space that served for a mouth. And as the enormity of man's crime against himself and the world was once again brought before him, Melvaig was gripped by a surge of anger so intense that it shook him free of his reverie and shattered the fetters of weakness and pain that had bound his body. It was at that moment also that he heard from behind them a great chorus of triumphant shouts. He could not see back through the mist but he knew what it was; the men of Xtlan had broken through.

From the nearness of their cries he guessed they were even now at the top of the long slope down to the sea. They would soon be sweeping down towards the village. It would not take them long on horseback.

He looked at Morven.

'You hear them?' he said. 'They are almost upon us.'

'Yes,' she replied, her eyes reflecting the relief she felt at his return to awareness. 'You did not answer me. I was worried. Are you all right?'

'I was tired, just tired. I'm sorry. And I was thinking. But I'm all right now. We must hurry. Look – the boats – just as Snaarquoll described them.'

CHAPTER XXXIII

They went as fast as they could down the narrow winding alleyway; Bracca in front while Melvaig and Morven dragged the weight of Shuinn behind them, his body heavier with every step they took.

The mist grew less dense as they neared the water's edge and the sea had taken on a strange black sheen. Out on the surface of the water, the little fires flickered and the crackling of their flames echoed out in the stillness while, further away in the distance, the great flaming arc suffused everything around them, the sky, the water and the moisture in the air, with its reflections; oranges and reds and purples and crimsons all dancing together in a kaleidoscope of colour.

They walked along a high stone embankment at the edge of the water until they came to some steps that led down to the sea. Carefully, for the steps were worn and crumbling, they made their way down on to the narrow expanse of black mud between the quay wall and the sea. The boats, for such Melvaig assumed they were, lay haphazardly along this stretch of mud on their sides. Old iron rings, orange with rust, protruded out of the wall and frayed lengths of rope ran from them to the boats. They made their way over to the first of these and leaned over the side. The wooden sides glistened in the damp and there was a constant dripping as the moisture gathered and then fell in drops from the mast on to the bottom of the boat. Little patches of red occasionally showed through the layers of green slime and dirt that lay so thickly over it and Melvaig guessed that this must once have been its colour. For an instant he saw it as it must once have been, bobbing eagerly up and down on the waves, the shiny red of its body showing up proudly against the sparkling crystal blue of the sea.

Then the image was gone, shattered beneath the urgent reality of the moment. Would this fragile old hulk be able, to carry them over the forbidding black expanse that now stretched out endlessly before them to the distant horizon? Snaarquoll had said he would have to trust his instincts and his judgment. What was he supposed to look for?

'What do you think?' he said to Morven.

'I don't know. I can't see any holes. I don't see why not.'

A number of other boats lay nearby and they moved over to look at them, but there were obvious gashes in the sides and the bottoms of most of these, and for some reason he could not explain, Melvaig felt uneasy about a black boat, the only one that had no such faults.

And so they went back to the boat they had first seen. Melvaig and Morven then lifted Shuinn's limp body up and over the side where it dropped with a dull thud and rolled down until it lay sprawled along the bottom. Melvaig then used his knife to cut the rope attaching it to its mooring ring in the wall and, with Morven and Bracca pushing from behind he began trying to pull the vessel across the mud to the sea. At first it would not budge. Try as he might to move the thing it seemed stuck fast in the unyielding ooze. He heaved and strained until the blood pounded in his temples and his vision blurred but still he could not move it.

It was Morven who suggested that they break some

wood off one of the nearby boats and try and prise it free. They tore three lengths from the nearest boat and were soon using them to lever the front end up, forcing the broken planks down between the side of the boat and the mud and then sliding them along to try to make a space. They repeated the process at the stern and then, gently so as not to break the planks, Melvaig and Morven began pressing on the ends with all their weight. At first there was nothing, not a movement, and Melvaig started to feel the flutter of panic and the sickness of desperation rise into his stomach.

'Move, damn you, move,' he implored under his breath. 'Don't let us down now.' But in his panic he pushed down so hard that the length of wood snapped and he found himself falling on to the mud. Quickly, Morven broke another length off the neighbouring boat, shoving it down into the space where the old one had been. Fighting against the awful temptation to admit defeat and give up he forced himself to go on, to push down again on the new plank. And then, with a delicious rush of joy, he thought he felt a movement. Hardly daring to believe it he looked across at Morven who was leaning with all her weight on a plank round the other side. He caught her eye.

'Together,' he said. 'When I say.' He waited for a moment and then 'Now!' he called. There was no mistaking it this time; with a glutinous sucking noise the boat moved up a full hand's breadth out of the mud before they let it down again gently.

'We've done it,' said Melvaig and felt relief and exhilaration flow through him.

He moved back to the front of the vessel and began pulling once again on the rope while the other two pushed from behind. This time it moved, slowly but surely, out of its cradle of ooze and then down along the beach towards the sea. It was not easy; the boat was heavy and the mud reluctant to let it go but none of that mattered to Melvaig.

They were on their way; and the pains in his back and legs, the wound in his side, were forgotten in his excitement.

Now, at last, they were at the water's edge. Melvaig had gone round to join Morven and Bracca who were pushing from the stern. When the whinnying of horses and the harsh cries of men first shattered the quiet, he ignored it; frightened and unwilling to accept what it meant. But Morven stopped and, grabbing his arm, swung him round to face the way they had come. For a few moments he saw nothing, only heard the pounding of hoofbeats over the cobbled alleyway down which they had walked. But then they appeared out of the mist. Xtlan's warriors, the horses wide-eyed and panting, mouths flecked with foam while their riders roared in exultation at the sight of their quarry. As they saw the leading horse Melvaig and Morven felt their blood freeze, for it was the great white horse, the horse they had seen for the first and last time on that terrible day in Ruann so long ago. The horse that symbolized for Melvaig both the destruction of his old life and the dawn of his new one. Then Melvaig recognized the rider, sitting arrogant and proud now as he had then, his brutal face leering in satisfaction at the delicious irony of recapturing the one whose village he had destroyed and whose woman he had taken all that time ago; the one who had escaped him then, of whose existence and importance he had only later learned and who would not elude him again. Now he, Sienogg, would have all three of them together; the woman, of whose body he had dreamed since the moment he had first had her, the man and the boy. Great indeed would be his rewards; how elevated his name – above all others save only Xtlan himself.

Desperately, their bodies shivering with fear, Melvaig and Morven pushed against the boat. Where before, with no panic or rush, it had seemed easy, now it seemed stubborn, every movement forward agonizingly slow. But, at last, it was more than halfway into the water; they could feel the sea lift it so that it became lighter, seeming to help them by drawing it in towards itself. Suddenly there were but a few paces of beach left for the boat to cross and Melvaig shouted to the others to get in. They did so, Morven lifting Bracca up and over the side before she herself clambered in. He pushed it the last short stretch by himself and then, with the shouting of the warriors clamouring in his head, he pulled himself over the side and found himself falling down on top of Shuinn's body. Grabbing the edge of the boat he hauled himself upright and looked back warily at the beach.

It was evident that there was some confusion amongst the warriors. They had not seen the high sea wall and the drop down to the beach until they were upon it and had assumed they would be able to ride straight down to the sea. Now their momentum had been upset and they were muddled; Melvaig heard angry shouts as the rider of the white horse attempted to instil some order into them.

From the boat which was now floating gently on the water and whose rhythmic movement was making him feel strange, Melvaig watched as the warriors, with some apparent reluctance, left their horses on the quayside and swarmed down the narrow stairway. Once on the beach they ran towards the water's edge, yelling and brandishing their swords, but the boat was too far out by now for them to wade in after it and they dashed to and fro on the mud, enraged and frustrated.

Then, on Sienogg's orders, they ran back to the other boats and Melvaig could see them carefully examining each one. They finally settled for the black boat that had made him so uneasy with its atmosphere of despair and gloom and evil and soon they were dragging it out of the mud and down to the sea.

And all the time, as Melvaig watched the activity on the shore, he was aware of the land slipping further and further back, the figures of the warriors growing smaller. Their boat seemed to be gliding through the water as if propelled by some unseen hand; some force beneath the dark surface seemed to push them inexorably out into the vastness that stretched before them towards the great wall of red and gold and yellow flame. There was no wind, not even a breeze to disturb the steady flickering of the little fires all around them, sputtering in the heavy mist that lay over the water like a great grey shroud. Only the feel of the air against his face and the feel of the boat beneath his feet told him that they were moving, these, and the increasing distance between them and the shore. Now, as he watched, the rider of the white horse urged the other warriors into the boat which had by this time been pushed into the water. As soon as they were aboard, the dark craft started to move out across the surface of its own accord, following in the wake of the boat it was pursuing. Melvaig wondered at the forces that were propelling the two vessels. Was it just the currents, the slight breeze that had now begun to ripple the otherwise calm water? Some natural pull of the ocean? Or were there, as he had begun to think, greater forces now guiding the pattern of events? Were Ashgaroth and Dréagg making here their final play for him, for Morven and Bracca, and for the Book?

And so the desperate race continued. At first Melvaig's vessel lost the length of its lead as the dark craft sped towards them and the three fugitives heard the crescendo of triumphant voices as the warriors sensed their gain on the craft in front. Melvaig, powerless, held Morven and Bracca tightly to him as he watched the vessel's approach in horror. But then, just as he had begun to anticipate the two boats coming together and had drawn his sword in readiness, though unable to foresee the course that a struggle on the water would take, their own boat started to pick up speed and to Melvaig's delight the dark craft fell behind again. So the pattern of the chase ebbed and flowed. The sky above their heads grew lighter through the yellow haze of mist and cloud as midday approached and the shoreline grew further and further away until it vanished in the distance. Melvaig, Morven and Bracca became accustomed to the feel of the boat beneath their feet, the rolling rhythm as it ploughed through the water, and the creak and groan of the old wooden planking as it strained against the waves.

The euphoria they had felt when they had first got their boat on to the water had now become lost beneath the tension of the chase and they had lapsed into a state where their minds had become numb. Melvaig existed in a state of semi-consciousness; the pain from the wounds Shuinn had given him had returned and he did not dare let his thoughts turn to what lay ahead of them. They could go on no further; of that he was, at least, certain. Whatever waited for them at the end of this journey would be the conclusion of his search; whether capture by the warriors behind and a return to Xtlan or the fulfilment of the promise in the Book and the culmination of his dreams. Or, and this perhaps was what he dreaded more than anything, the discovery of yet more dead and barren land beyond the water. If such was the case then he knew that they would simply have to stay where they landed for there was not enough strength or will to carry them on. Then he would have to live with his failure and the loss of all his faith. How could he bear that!

Midday came and went and still the two craft scudded across the water. Bracca had succumbed to his weariness and lay asleep in the bottom of the boat next to the body of the giant. Morven and Melvaig stood at the back, holding each other while they watched the progress of their pursuers. She rested her head on his shoulder and he caressed the back of her neck with his hand. They drew strength and comfort from each other, enjoying, despite everything, the intimacy of the moment. And then Melvaig gently turned her face up towards his and, bringing his head down, kissed her on the lips. Tentative and wary at first, their mouths soon softened under the warm intensity of their passion and their kiss developed into the creation of a world, a world in which nothing mattered save this moment and nothing existed except their love.

And so it was that, locked in their embrace, they entered the mighty wall of flame. Suddenly they were surrounded by colour; leaping dancing colour, rich and dark and deep, whirling in a kaleidoscope of flame and fire. The withering ferocity of the heat suddenly struck them and they broke away from each other with a jolt of shock and terror. Melvaig's mind raced in confusion. It had not occurred to him that they would go through this barrier of fire. How could they now avoid it? The boat seemed to be speeding ever faster, purposefully, deliberately into it. Was this then the hand of Dréagg sending them to their final end? Or was it Ashgaroth pushing them deeper into nightmare? Perhaps destruction, death was the only possible conclusion. Their death and the loss of the Book, forever cheating Dreagg of his quarry, robbing him of what Xtlan, his ambassador on earth, most wanted. Was this the way Ashgaroth had chosen to protect his lost world, to keep it forever secret?

He flung his arm around Morven and pulled her down into the bottom of the boat, his spirit seething with anger at what he saw as a vicious betrayal. Frantically he looked for Bracca but already great tongues of flame were leaping around and across the boat. The little boy was at the far end and Melvaig called out to him but there was no reply. Bracca was huddled against the side of the boat in a ball, his arms wrapped instinctively over his head to protect himself from the heat. His shoulders were quivering, whether from fear or crying Melvaig could not tell. There was no way even of knowing if Bracca had heard the shout above the roar of the flames. Melvaig looked in horror at the barrier of fire that separated him from his boy.

Finally the fumes and the heat began to drag him down

into unconsciousness. The last thing that fought its way through into his mind was a sudden searing chorus of screams, wild cries of unbearable agony that sounded high and shrill even above the noise of the fire. Xtlan's warriors, he thought, and along with a vague sensation of relief at the ending of the pursuit, he felt a pang of sympathy and sorrow at their pain. But above and beyond their terrible squealing he heard another sound, indescribable, enormous. It was a cry of such rage that the waters seemed to boil and seethe beneath its power. Melvaig knew instinctively that this was Dréagg, venting the fury of his frustration over all the world. In it was a promise of such revenge and terror that all men's hearts froze at the sound of it. It flared up fiercely in the dying embers of his soul before the bright star of his consciousness succumbed to the tide of darkness that rolled over him.

CHAPTER XXXIV

Melvaig's eyes opened slowly, but a flash of pain shot through them as they met the light and he shut them again, trapping behind his lids an image of such intensity that it seemed to reverberate throughout the whole of his body. Slowly he became aware of himself and his surroundings. Memory started to seep through the darkness and reawaken his shattered spirit. He felt the wooden planks beneath his fingers; he reached out and touched Morven, Morven's arm. Bracca! Where was Bracca? He had been at the other end of the boat. The boat! Flames, those awful flames. The screams of the warriors. The roar and crackle of the flames. The wrath of Dréagg, ringing still in his head.

He had to open his eyes! He placed his hands over them and opened his eyelids a little at a time so that he got used to the light. Now he also became aware of a throbbing pain in his head and a terrible dryness in his mouth and throat, the taste and smell of the fumes from the fire still lingering on his tongue.

He took his hands away from his eyes and saw the planks of the boat beneath his head. There was something strange about the light; apart from its brightness it had a new clarity and purity. He put his hands on the bottom of the boat and raised himself so that he could sit upright, his heart beating wildly with a terrible apprehension at the thoughts and fears of what he would see. He forced himself to raise his eyes from the boat, which he been staring at as he sat up, and to look out over the side. As he did so and saw the sparkling blue sea shimmering under the deep blue sky, smelt the fragrant tang on the air and felt the gentle breeze caress his aching head, he found himself shaking in wonder and overcome by an intense humility. His heart seemed about to burst with joy as, through the tears that had begun to pour from his eyes, he looked further out and saw the cliffs not far away, great majestic walls of rock crowned with a thick carpet of green. Further along, the land swept all the way down to the water's edge, land that dazzled him with its patchwork of browns and greens and yellows and purples. It was the world of his dreams, the world of the Book; the trees and bushes and grasses and plants all tumbling together in great cascades of foliage as the ground fell away into the sea. The fresh clear air all around, the sky, soaring up into the infinite blue above his head. In the distance, from the woods on the cliffs, he could hear the singing of the birds while all around him the seagulls wheeled and cried and cormorants sped low over the water. The sea lapped gently against the boat as it drifted slowly on towards the paradise ahead. He had been here so often in his imaginings that he felt as if he had finally come home. He put his hands up to the Book that had travelled with him so far and sustained him through so much and clasped it in what was almost a gesture of thanksgiving as the truth of its pages revealed themselves before him. But was this just another vision? The thought suddenly struck him with a rush of anxiety, but it was quickly dispelled for nothing he had envisaged before, not even the pictures that Arkron's reading from the Book had created in his mind, could have prepared him for the unbelievable splendour of the world that now lay all about him. His eyes swept all around, feasting on the magnificence before him, the brilliance of the colours, the majesty of the sea, the vibrant power of the birds, the overpowering luxuriousness of the woods and pastures on the land in front.

Euphoria such as he had never known seized him, singing through his whole being; each fragment of his body burst into life as if for the first time and soared away into the sweet air to explore for itself the excitement and magic of this paradise. And then, to his surprise, he found himself shouting out as if to release the explosion of feelings inside himself.

'Ashgaroth,' he cried, again and again. 'Thank you. Thank you.' His eyes were raised to the sky and he held his hands out in supplication.

And then a soft low murmur at his side reminded him of Morven. Feeling suddenly guilty that in his wild joy he had forgotten her and Bracca he quickly turned to her and, seeing that she was stirring, put his hands under her arms and gently pulled her upright so that she was sitting looking out to sea with her back resting against him. Like him, she found the light too bright at first and was forced to cover her eyes with her hands, head between her raised knees. They said nothing for a few moments, Melvaig simply holding her and comforting her. He was worried about Bracca now; he could see the boy's legs protruding from under the body of the giant as they both lay together, unmoving, at the other end of the boat.

He had to go and see to Bracca now; Morven would be all right. The daze of confusion and darkness, from which he guessed she was struggling to free herself, would pass soon. Time enough then to share with her the blessed joy of their arrival; the fulfilment of their dreams.

'I will be back in a moment,' he said quietly. 'I must go and see to Bracca.' He paused and then added, 'Don't worry. We're quite safe now.' Slowly she nodded her head and, shakily, he got to his feet. When he stood up, he felt a wave of nausea pass through him and he clung to the side of the boat to stop himself falling, but it soon passed and he found his gaze wandering once again to the beautiful panorama of sea, sky and land that stretched away before him. Turning back briefly he thought he saw, on the distant horizon, the great wall of fire through which they had passed, but he could not be sure and the more he tried to focus on it the more blurred and indistinct it became.

When he turned back to the front of the boat and Bracca, he was surprised to see that they were still moving quite quickly through the water and that the land was quite a bit nearer now than it had been when he first saw it. He could make out the individual shapes and colours of the trees and bushes and could see ahead of them a tiny bay surrounded by huge cliffs, where a sandy beach lay gleaming in the sun. There, a number of birds could be seen rushing along the water's edge, their heads nodding at frequent intervals as they speared the sand with their beaks for food.

He made his way carefully to where Bracca and Shuinn were lying and started to pull the giant slowly off the boy. It was with some shock that he saw that, while the flames had left himself and Morven relatively untouched, Shuinn's jerkin had been burnt off his back and the exposed skin was scorched raw and tender. Gently he moved Shuinn's heavy, inert body. Their heads were close together and he had some difficulty separating them until he saw that the little boy's hands were clasped around the giant's neck. Bursting with emotion, he took hold of them and slowly prised the fingers apart until he could lift the giant away completely, for he had not yet seen Bracca's face, buried as it was under Shuinn's chest. The movement seemed to affect them at the same moment, for they let out a moan almost simultaneously. Quickly, his heart pounding with excitement and relief at this proof that Bracca was still alive, he moved Shuinn off the little boy and laid his friend face down on the bottom of the boat as carefully as he could. The giant was groaning in pain and Melvaig felt every cry as if it were a knife turning in his own body. For now, though, he must turn all his attention to Bracca. He knelt by the boy's side and lifted his head up.

'Bracca,' he whispered, cradling the body against his chest. 'Can you hear me? It's Melvaig. We're safe now. It's all right. Can you hear me?'

Melvaig felt as if the tension of waiting for the boy to react had stopped his heart. But when Bracca's eyelids fluttered and he heard his son try to say something, his head seemed to swim with joy. With tears of relief he clasped the little boy to him, rocking him gently to and fro as he did so, repeating his name over and over. Then he felt the presence of Morven behind him and turned to see her standing at his shoulder looking down at the face of her son.

'He's all right,' she kept muttering, more as a statement of fact than a question, but still Melvaig felt the need and the desire to answer her.

'Yes,' he said. 'Yes, he'll be back with us soon.' His voice was strained and quivering with excitement.

'Have you seen?' he said. 'Seen where we are? What's happened? Where we've come to? It is as I have always seen it in my head, only more wonderful than I could ever have thought. The world of Ashgaroth, the last enclave. As I had dreamed and prayed all this time. And we are here!'

'Yes,' she said. 'I've seen,' and her smile and her face were suffused with such happiness and peace that Melvaig knew she felt even as he did and the sight of her joy filled his spirit to overflowing.

But then Bracca spoke and, though at first they could not tell what he was saying, he said it again and again and as the words became clear to Melvaig, he felt a cloud of sadness descend upon him for, slowly and falteringly, he was asking about Shuinn. And the realization came to

Melvaig then that the giant had covered the boy's body with his own to protect him from the flames and the heat. The fire must have roused him from his unconscious state and, seeing the danger, his love for the boy had compelled him to use himself as a shield to save Bracca's life. It might also have been at the price of losing his own for, Melvaig thought, without the awful burns he had suffered, it might have been that he would have survived the injuries from the fight.

He gestured to Morven to look after Bracca and as she did so he moved the few paces across to where Shuinn was lying on the hard wooden planking of the boat. He bent down closely to look at the giant's face and then he saw, with a start, that his friend's eyes were open.

'Shuinn,' he said quietly. 'It's me, Melvaig. How do you feel? Does your back hurt . . . the burns?'

The giant did not move but he tried to speak. His voice was no more than a whisper and Melvaig had to strain to hear it.

'Bracca,' he said. 'How is he?'

'You saved him. He'll be all right. Morven is with him.'

'Good. That's good.' Shuinn then worked his mouth soundlessly. Melvaig dipped a hand over the side of the boat into the cool green sea and brought out a palmful of sparkling water which he held against the giant's lips. The taste of salt was strange to him but the cold liquid was wonderfully refreshing.

'Back there,' he went on. 'With Morven . . . everything. I don't know . . . can't remember much. All seems blurred. I'm sorry . . . I . . . don't know why. Do you think . . . Dréagg . . . ?' Melvaig interrupted him quickly. The giant was torturing himself; he must stop thinking about it. Melvaig had got his friend back; the evil that had possessed him had gone, vanquished now that they were here in the realm of Ashgaroth. As Melvaig looked into Shuinn's gentle eyes and recognized once more the man he had known and loved through all these terrible times, he felt as if a part of himself had become alive again.

'Hush. Don't talk,' he said. 'It doesn't matter. It's all over, finished with. We've found it, Shuinn, the world we've dreamed about all this time. The Book told us the truth. Arkron was right. We're here now. The sea, the sky, the trees. All as we thought.' Melvaig saw Shuinn's mouth, crushed though it was against the bottom of the boat, slowly pull itself into a smile.

'Then it has all been worth it,' he said. 'Ashgaroth has blessed me with the time to see it before I go. Lift me, Melvaig. Quickly, while I can see. Never mind my back, I will not feel it.'

Gently, his heart bursting with emotion, Melvaig gradually began to lift him up from the bottom of the boat. Shuinn's face twisted with pain but he did not make a sound and Melvaig, steeling himself against his friend's hurt, continued lifting as carefully as he could. Only when Melvaig let the giant's back rest against his chest so as to prop him up did Shuinn cry out, an involuntary shriek that tore an ugly incongruous gash in the still, fragrant air. It took a little while for the gush of pain to subside from Shuinn's body. Melvaig watched as his friend's face slowly regained its composure and then slowly, as if wishing to relish every moment to its fullest, he opened his eyes, letting them roam over the miracle that lay spread out before him. Despite the dark shadows that flitted across his vision the sight before him was still one of such bright sparkling beauty that he felt his spirit start to soar away into the beckoning blue corridor between the sea and the sky, up, up towards the little white puffs of cloud that floated so high above his head. And as he felt himself going, he grew aware for a last brief moment of unnerving clarity of the three people clustered around him. Morven, her delicate, sweet face looking into his with a love so pure and intense it humbled him even at the moment of his departure. Bracca, his little friend, the tiny head laid against his chest; Bracca whose purity, innocence and laughter had first made him aware of the meaning of love and who, at the last, had been the one he had been blessed with the chance to protect and cherish against hurt.

And lastly, Melvaig, his only friend, more precious and vital to him even than the air he breathed, without whom life would have been as empty as the deserts and plains they had crossed together: who had revealed to him the possibility of another life and who, in the end, had led him there so that ultimately all their suffering had been as nothing compared to the joy and peace that filled him now. And the tragedies and successes of their search together had rendered his life so rich and purposeful that he felt himself to be the most fortunate of men. Melvaig, away from whom the dark forces of evil had torn him towards the end but with whom, at the last, he was reunited. Melvaig, holding his hand and stroking his face, surrounding him with the tenderness and warmth of his love. And he heard himself say, in this last lucid moment, in a voice so resonant with majesty and strength that he did not recognize it as his own:

'No, do not mourn me. For I have known your love and I have seen this place and I am called by Ashgaroth.' And then the silver light in the sky called to him and he followed it, feeling as he did so such a sense of peace that he knew that he would never be able to go back.

Through the misty veil of tears that blurred his vision, Melvaig saw his friend's head slump forward on to his chest. Then, tearing his eyes away he saw that the boat was taking them into a tiny bay. He looked up to the top of the cliffs and then he saw the badger, sitting watching them from underneath the low sweeping branches of an old oak tree.

The badger, every muscle shivering with tension as he saw the boat move towards the beach, waited until it fetched up against the sand and then, his black nose-tip twitching with excitement, shuffled off quickly through the undergrowth down to the hollow to tell the others.